Ryan Stark, real name Austen  and former IT professional.

Austen was born in Reddit Birmingham. Throughout his successful career as an IT Consultant, he produced many technical documents and non-fiction works. However, Austen's true passion for storytelling drove him to move to fiction writing and become an author.

Writing as Ryan Stark, *An Invisible Murder* is the fourth book in the Daley and Whetstone series, with two in the Aidan Beckett Amber Rock series. Austen's understanding of human nature and his ability to construct intricate plots and multi-dimensional characters have garnered him a dedicated following.

Beyond writing, Austen also shares his expertise and experiences with aspiring writers and enthusiasts. He has spoken at many events about taking an idea from concept to polished, finished work. His advice has inspired many to chase their writing dreams.

Now fully dedicated to his writing, Austen remains grounded and values his family life. Austen is married with two adult daughters.. He enjoys writing stories and spending time with his grandchildren.

Austen is represented by Fuldean Press.

Twitter:	@RyanStarkAuthor
Facebook:	RyanStarkAuthor
Web:	www.ryanstarkauthor.co.uk

Also by Ryan Stark

The Daley and Whetstone Crime Stories
Killing by the Book
The Farm
Unnatural Selection

The Aidan Beckett Thriller Series
Proof of Life – Amber Rock Book 1
Proof of Death – Amber Rock Book 2

For Arthur, whose love of books
is already shining through.

A Daley and Whetstone Crime Story

AN INVISIBLE MURDER

Ryan Stark

www.fuldeanpress.co.uk

Copyright © 2024, Ryan Stark
All rights reserved.

The right of Ryan Stark to be identified as the author of this work has been asserted in accordance with sections 77 and 78 of the Copyright Designs and Patents Act 1998.

This is a work of fiction. Names, characters, corporations, institutions, organisations, events or locales in this novel are either the product of the author's imagination or, if real, used fictitiously. Any resemblance to actual persons (living or dead) is entirely coincidental.

No part of this book may be reproduced or transmitted in any form or by any means, electronic or mechanical, including photocopying, recording, or by any information storage and retrieval system without the written permission of the author, except where permitted by law.

ISBN 9798321329153

Acknowledgements

In many ways, *An Invisible Murder* can be considered a COVID baby, started pre-COVID and then the world got in the way. The project got delayed, life intervened, and Daley and Whetstone sat twiddling their thumbs for a while. I stopped working for the man (person?) and sank into the hinterland of retirement before the State recognises me as retired. I became a professional writer.

As always, many thanks go to my wife and family for their unending support and forbearance. A special mention has to go to Amelia and Arthur, two of the most wonderful, and challenging, people on the planet. They kept me sane when the world had lost the plot. Now they keep me insane as the world becomes normal again.

Special thanks also to Jenie Grogan and John Dean for their help and support leading up to and during Kirkcudbright Book Week, where I was able to present my ideas, demonstrate my passion and be spurred on to achieve greater things. Then there are the people at Fuldean Press, specifically Emma Shaw, who helped me develop the idea into the final product.

But my most profound thanks goes to you, the reader. Many thousands of you have read my books, provided reviews and spurred me on to greater things.

Part One

The Lean Man

Chapter 1

At that moment, Andy Mason knew he was in trouble. What was he thinking? Was he so desperate he had to pay? What had Jake said? *You have one life, so live it.* But where was Jake now?

She leaned against the door and closed it with her backside. Mason turned, his heart pounding, and made to kiss her, but she raised a hand to his lips.

'Easy, tiger. I need to freshen up first, and, er…' She flipped her fingers.

Mason fumbled inside his jacket for his wallet. He took in the small tired sitting room and the forlorn shoebox kitchen beyond. Tired wallpaper, aging furniture past its best, a cup, plate, and a single saucepan on the drainer. Nothing personal.

'You wait here.' She nodded at a bottle of whisky and two glasses on the grimy melamine surface of an ancient table.

As he sat in the creaking chair, his nose prickled at the fug of cheap scent and a disturbing undertone of musk and sweat. A tart, for God's sake. How many men had sat in this chair, drunk her whisky, and pawed at her body? As before, he was letting his dick rule his head, diving in feet first with no thought of the consequences, and where had it got him so far? He nearly lost his job last time, and what would Hannah say if she found he was up to his old tricks again?

'I think I better be going. This is a mistake, sorry.' He opened his wallet and cast a pile of notes on the table. 'That should more than cover it.'

'First time, eh? It's just nerves, dear. Have a drink. It'll be fine.'

She breezed behind him, her hand across his neck, sending a quiver down his spine. The whisky bottle was open, two feet away. The bedroom was five yards away. She filled his glass and handed it across, and he felt his resolve weaken. He sunk the contents, the vapour barely burning the back of his throat. He was here now, and if he walked back through the door, who'd know whether he'd slept with her? Schrödinger's tart. He chuckled wryly, past the point of no return. With his track record, they'd prefer to believe he had screwed her. Thirty minutes, an hour tops, and he could be out the door, his collar pulled up and around the corner into Sefton Street. Who would know?

The first scotch was already going to his head. If he dallied any longer, the alcohol would make the job impossible.

Or he could leave now. Cut and run. She wasn't interested in the sex, just the money, right? He reached for the bottle and poured another glass. After all, he'd paid for that too. He tipped his head back and took a large draught, stifling a gag. The liquid numbed his tongue. In the ceiling, the unshaded lightbulb pirouetted.

'Bloody hell, Sonia. This is good stuff.' He tilted the glass between his fingers, and the facets sparkled under the light. Her glass was still empty on the table. 'You not having one?'

'Maybe, afterwards, Andy. Now finish up. Time's money and you've got a job to do.'

'Come on, Sonia, take a drink. A little *stiffener*.'

She suppressed a girlish giggle, and he felt himself harden. She was gorgeous. Comfortable and familiar, as if he'd known her forever. Maybe that was how she got her punters?

Punters, plural. He pushed the thought from his mind and sunk the rest of his Dutch courage, but though his brain commanded, his arm was frozen. The distance of a few inches seemed like miles. Confused, he checked the bottle, still full above the label. Had he only drunk one glass, or had he already had a second and simply forgotten, lost in the moment? No, he was sure - just the one.

Mason had never been a great drinker, pissed at the sniff of a

An Invisible Murder

barmaid's apron. Hannah always warned him to slow down before he embarrassed them both. He flexed his fingers, but again, nothing happened. His arm just lay on the table like the dismembered limb of a mannequin. Beneath the table, a numbness was climbing up his legs. He couldn't feel his feet. Everything was suddenly jet-lagged. The room shimmied in and out like an old AM radio. Something was very wrong.

'What the hell is going on, Sonia?' At least, that's what his brain said. It told his lips to move, but their sound was slurred, unintelligible. He was not even sure the words had left his lips.

She was standing opposite, across the table, another blur of light and dark as his eyes failed to focus. Somewhere, the tick of a clock hammered against the wall. A tap was dripping. Feet shuffled on the linoleum but he could not move, as if his whole body had gone. The shape drifted across the light bulb and whispers warmed his cheek; the scent filled his nostrils.

'I thought this was what you wanted, Andy. It's certainly what I want. Exactly this.'

The glass slid away, clinked against the bottle, which slid away too. With enormous effort, he tried to sit upright, but without a body, it was too difficult. Below him, the chair creaked.

'Do you feel it? The helplessness. Just like I did? Frozen, unable to move or cry out. What's it feel like, Andy?' The voice was a ship on a distant horizon, almost an echo in his mind, floating in and out, like the roar of his breath as a storm approached.

'And all the time, you're asking what's going to happen to me? Where will it all end? When will it all end? Anyway, not long to wait now. This is very real, Andy, just like it was for me.'

His eyes saw the surface of the table as his head dropped. Saliva warmed on his cheek and stuck to the melamine and suddenly he was comfortable. But only for a second, as the woman's face filled his vision.

'Hey, Sleepyhead, don't nod off now. You'll miss the best bit.'

His muscles, his limbs, his whole body had melted away. His

entire world once more collapsed down to the pale blue melamine. A tear formed in the corner of his eye and ran cold down his cheek. It was the last thing he felt as an overwhelming desire to sleep swept him away.

Chapter 2

Oliver Mansell's eyes widened as he peered into the plastic carrier. He found packets of ham and cheese, some apples, oranges, and bananas. Again, the warmth and gratitude overwhelmed him.

'I only came in for a paper, Mr Mohammed. I must give you some money.'

At least once a week, Ashad spoiled him. The shopkeeper flashed his brown eyes and waved it away. 'You don't look after yourself, Oliver, and anyway, it's all short-dated. Better you today than the bin tomorrow. And don't give it all to that dog of yours.'

He nodded his gratitude, knowing it was all that was necessary, but he had his pride. He pulled out Cheryl's old purse, his hand lingering on the creased leather, as, in his heart, he felt the loss.

The shopkeeper feigned irritation. 'Okay. Fifty pence - for the paper. After all, it is technically yesterday's.'

Ashad was a nice man, the salt of the earth. There were so few of them about these days. He pulled out a coin and pressed it into his fingerless gloves.

'I don't know how you manage, Mr Mohammed, this time of year.' Plumes of vapour left Oliver's mouth as he spoke. These days he felt the cold. Late September and already it was like the depths of winter, particularly in the early morning when Moxy insisted on his constitutional. The air chilled his legs through his thin trousers. It seemed to permeate his flesh and gnaw at his bones.

'Some things you just have to get used to, but at least it gets cold here. Back home, it was never less than thirty-five degrees, and believe me, it was just as bad.'

Oliver waved as he left the shop, and sunk back into himself. Did Mr Mohammed realise he was the only person Mansell spoke to most days - apart from the podiatrist on the last Thursday of the month? And those bloody people on the phone trying to sell him stuff. Perhaps if they had a proper conversation, he might want to buy. As it was, sod 'em. He looked up and sighed. Cheryl would scold him for his foul language.

'C'mon, boy. It's getting late.' He untied the leash from the bollard. The small wire-haired terrier bounced up and down, tail flicking back and forth, in that pure, unremitting joy only dogs can show. Or perhaps he had smelled the ham?

'Steady on, fella. You will have me over.'

Moxy was eager for his bed and, at ten years old, he knew the way home. After all, they walked the route every day, sometimes three times, even if it was a little slower these days on account of both their dodgy hips. Oliver envied his dog, granted a simplicity in all things. To go to sleep and wake up, taking each day, each walk, each meal, as it came. Someone even cleared up his mess. What a flaming life! And all that was required was unconditional love. And Oliver Mansell willingly gave it with all his heart. After all, he had plenty now to give.

At this time of night, there was no one about. Even the constant hum of the city seemed more subdued. A few pigeons cooed from the eaves. A smug cat sat out of Moxy's reach. He yanked the dog away from another interesting smell and looked ahead at his entire world; four hundred yards of empty pavement, battalions of parked cars, and the sound of his shoes on the slabs. He turned the corner onto Green Street and sighed at another four hundred yards. A couple walked past, pulling up hoods behind plumes of white, and disappeared into the empty blackness of St Dunstan's churchyard without so much as a nod. The woman's scent lingered in the air, floral and thick, intoxicating. Cheryl used to wear one like that, though, on anyone else it lost its appeal. She had been his world for fifty years, and then one day, she was gone. He bit his lip and felt the chill of a tear. Since Cheryl died, he had not set foot in church. His faith in God had deserted him, but he would visit her grave - soon. Life was all they had. Now he had to face it alone. If not for Mr Mohammed and Moxy.

As if on cue, the clock on the church tower chimed. A single, mournful bell, heard only by insomniacs, shopkeepers and widowers. 1:00 am. Tomorrow already. Another day. He pulled Moxy close. At this time of night, you couldn't trust anyone. All sorts about, especially in this street. Everyone knew what they got up to in these houses. Brazen about it. Not that the scrap of a hound was much protection, but he was better than nothing. He could bark for England when he had a mind.

Setting off, Mansell felt his hip catch. His home was calling. The freezing sheet where he would shiver until his body made a small tunnel of warmth and only his nose was cold. Where he could imagine the radiated heat of Cheryl. She was always the warm one, except for her feet.

A tremendous thump pummelled his back, and a blast of hot dust sucked the air from his lungs. The dog yelped as its leash tightened. For a moment, he was weightless, swirling in a maelstrom of dust, debris, and roaring flame. The entire street tumbled and spun. With an enormous smack, he landed and bright lights filled his brain. Then everything stopped, and he was a child again, emerging from the shelter to an alien landscape of rubble and smoke and death. His ears chimed to a thousand striking clocks. Above him, ranks of street lamps flickered down, freckled through the London planes, mottled by thick swirling clouds of debris. Something dug into his back. Had he passed out? He could not remember. His head hurt, and his hip. Ge rolled onto his side and looked across to the church. Someone was there, under the lychgate, ethereal in the smoke and dust. Mansell reached out an arm, nauseous from the pain.

'Can you help me? I think I've taken a tumble.'

But the shadow stood, then faded back into the murk.

Mansell felt helpless. He laid his head back on the tarmac and coughed away the acrid stench. He thought of Cheryl. Of the kids, of the grandkids he never saw, of the years that passed in the beat of a heart. Was this the end? Would Cheryl reach out and fold him in her arms, or would he fade into oblivion, to nothing, never to think of her again?

He turned his head to the other side and saw the hill of chaotic rubble where the house had been. In his hand, the leash was limp.

'Moxy? Moxy! Here, boy.'

***

The thud was a memory in Detective Chief Inspector Scott Daley's mind as his eyes blinked open; a book falling from the bedside table, the cat knocking over an ornament downstairs. Except he never read in bed, they didn't have a cat, and neither he nor Terri liked ornaments. Beside him, she rolled onto her back, her baby bump lifting the covers.

'What was that?'

'Who knows? I'm sure I'll find out if it's important.' He nestled against her, hearing her heart, feeling the gentle rise and fall as she drifted back to sleep. With the baby imminent, she slept fitfully, pacing the floor, cursing cramps or sciatica, or blaming him for putting her in that situation. He reached over and turned over his work phone, dazzled by the screen, relieved there were no texts or missed calls, but the spell was broken. He eased himself out of bed, crossed to the window and gazed out at the orange umbra of West London. Around four miles away, a smudge of smoke rose into the sky. Then the echoing wail of the sirens began. A fire appliance, maybe two, an ambulance and a police car. Someone's day had turned to crap even before it started. All he could hope was it wasn't *his*. That they would not require him to turn out on a Saturday morning. He grabbed some clean underwear, a tracksuit, and his work phone. With sleep such a rarity for Terri in her third trimester, he left her to it and trotted downstairs to wait for the inevitable.

***

The thud had also jolted Father Joseph O'Donnell awake, but

An Invisible Murder

for him, it was significantly nearer. The windows in the sacristy had clattered in their old frames, sending a pepper of ancient dust from the ceiling. An empty glass rolled a wine-red semi-circle across the table and smashed into fragments on the floor. He checked his watch, slapping his dry tongue against the roof of his mouth. 1:03 am. He must have fallen asleep. First Friday of every month, Latin Mass, then the parish meeting. A gaggle of senior parishioners with nothing better to discuss than the laurel hedging and the state of the varnish on the church pews. What was it they said about empty vessels? At least it was over for another month - may God forgive him for his annoyance. Maybe patience and perseverance were sufficient virtues.

For a moment, blinking away the sleep, he stared in awe at the flickering lights through the stained glass, convinced he was still dreaming before the realisation hit.

'Holy Mother of God.'

Scraping out of the chair, shaking away the remnants of sleep and communion wine, he made the sign of the cross and raced to the rear door, fumbling with the handle, cursing and reaching for the ancient key hanging on the wall. He pulled open the door and his jaw dropped. Through the trees, beyond the pall of smoke, it seemed like half the street was ablaze. Memories of Belfast made him nauseous, and a terror buried for so long gripped his chest. Pulling on an overcoat, he ran across the churchyard, stopping as a wall of flame scorched his face. Across the street, a valley had opened up in the row of terraces, filled with a cracking, popping mound of rubble and wrecked furniture, crushing cars, and toppling street lamps. On either side, floors sagged and curtains fluttered. Spurts of flame flashed in the pall of smoke and dust.

Now, as then, his first thought was to search for the living, expecting the dead. He prayed for divine intervention that came so rarely these days. Please let him find someone alive. O'Donnell caught his breath as his prayers were answered.

'Mr Mansell?' The old man was blinking skywards. His leg lay twisted at an unnatural angle. 'Rest easy now, Oliver. Someone's on their way, I'm sure.' But up and down the street, Father Joseph saw no one but bewildered householders open-mouthed, tugging dressing gowns tight.

'I don't know where my dog is.' Mansell's jaw trembled, as shock starved him of warmth.

'He'll be in the churchyard, away from all - this. We'll take care of him until you're better.' O'Donnell removed his overcoat and laid it over the old man, who slumped back unconscious.

Some neighbours were venturing onto the ruins, doing what they could, thwarted by the unstable rubble, beaten back by the heat. A lump stuck in O'Donnell's throat as he remembered the Old Country, the Troubles which left him questioning so cruel as a God. He crossed to the kerbside, sat down and buried his head in his hands. All he had left was prayer.

In the distance, the two-tone wail of sirens funnelled along the street and flashes of electric blue strobed the walls. Soon, vehicles crowded the street. O'Donnell felt the hand on his shoulder and he looked up into the eyes of an anxious young woman in a luminous police overcoat.

'Are you okay, Father?'

'Yes, oh, yes. Mr Mansell. He is not good.' He pointed toward the old man.

'We'll see to him. Right now, we have to clear the area. The gas is still on. There might be another explosion.'

'But I can help?' He gestured across towards the old man, to the pile of rubble.

'Leave it to us now. Please. The firefighters are looking for the stop valve. Until then, we can't risk anyone else.'

O'Donnell wanted to argue, to convince her this was his moment, the reason for his calling, but her expression told him it was futile. She was in shock too, somehow driven by an automatic process, so he smiled and stood, letting her lead him away to the blue and white tape marking the perimeter.

'I will open the church.' He flung a hand behind him. 'Make

An Invisible Murder

some tea, find blankets. Please, could you spread the word?'

'Thank you, Father. We will need a base until we set up the Incident Room.'

He knew she was only appeasing him. 'God bless all of you.'

Back in the churchyard, away from the flames, he fell back into the monastic silence of the church. What else could he do? His part in the tragedy was over. Once the focus of every community, the church was an anachronism. A relic. A sign of the times. Congregations were dwindling, faith was disappearing from peoples' lives, and they used the word *God* as a curse rather than in praise. Still, he said a silent prayer for the rescue crews, for anyone trapped in the ruins, but also for himself, alone on an island of dark in a sea of chaotic electric blue.

The sacristy door had closed on its spring. He remembered the keys were in his overcoat, draped over Mr Mansell, so he used a key from the coded key safe and entered via the small kitchen. He busied himself with the meagre task the Lord had left him, filling the ancient water boiler, organising clean cups on the sideboard, and fetching out the catering tin of coffee and the mammoth bag of tea. They were short on milk. The women from the parish group had seen to that. He would send someone to the corner shop. Mr Mohammed always had a bottle or two spare.

The blankets were in the study room across the choir, away from the dust and the moths. He found the keys to the huge oak doors at the front of the church. He needed to show a lamp of welcome, an open door in these lawless times, even if no one came. Maybe he could show the warmth of the church. Restore a little of its place in the community.

Honestly? Did he believe that?

'It's going to be a busy night, Holy Mother.' He glanced up at the alabaster Virgin over the altar. Her welcoming arms, her tender face, a caring smile for everyone, despite their sins. But as his eyes fell to the altar, he caught his breath, as if a second explosion had knocked the life out of him. Daubed in red across the pristine cloth, the letters and numbers danced.

JO - Dt 8:5

He fumbled for a pew and fell into the seat, drawing out his beads, reciting the Rosary under his breath, over and over, hoping for absolution. Hoping for protection.

But he knew the sins of his past were catching up with him.

Chapter 3

Half an hour later, Daley's work phone began buzzing like a wasp in a jar. The inevitable three-nines call would despatch first responders and divert the nearest patrol car. Together, they would deal with any immediate threats to life, set up a perimeter, and make a preliminary assessment. Then they would decide whether it warranted dragging the Homicide Assessment Team leader out of his bed at *stupid* o'clock. It did. A gas explosion in Green Street, Harrow, at least one fatality.

'Send the details to my phone. I'll be there in ten minutes.'

Daley and his team were the HAT for September. Forty-eight hours later, Hillingdon would have taken over. He could have enjoyed a weekend lie-in and a fry-up. It turned out to be only five miles. Annoyingly, the Hillingdon offices were closer to the bang; they probably felt the ground shake and had a chuckle at his expense.

In the early hours, the streets were almost dead. The rumble of London dulled to a subdued, if disturbed, doze. Daley loved the city in the early hours. There was a serenity about it. Yet he also hated the early hours in equal measure. Awake at 2:08 pm meant one of two things: either he couldn't sleep or something had cropped up to keep him awake. In Daley's view, there should be a curfew on crime. Say, around 6:30 pm until 8:30 am, after breakfast. That would keep everyone happy. More civilised.

Rounding the corner, the strobing blue of Fire Service units and ambulances briefly blinded him. He showed his warrant card and an officer on the outer cordon pointed out the Incident Control Unit. The scene was oddly calm. Emergency teams were kicking their heels, waiting for someone to stem the reek of gas hanging in the air. A fractious collection of neighbours murmured and stamped their feet in the cold, pulling dressing gowns and coats tight. A similar fractious collection of reporters from the local rags were already milling about, conscious the deadline to meet the stop press was fast approaching. Fifty yards further on, the blue and white tape marked the inner cordon. Inside it, Number 5, and a significant proportion of the neighbouring properties, had been lifted into the air and fly-tipped over the tarmac. Nothing moved except wisps of smoke fading into the black sky.

Daley pulled a heavy hi-vis overcoat from the boot of his car. Autumn had left the door open for a draughty, wet winter, and the air was almost brittle as he drew it into his nostrils, and puffed it out in clouds. Detective Sergeant Deborah Whetstone was already there, but then these days, she rarely slept. She was leaning against a van, warming her hands on a styrofoam cup, deep in conversation with a uniformed officer. Momentarily, Daley remembered Keith *The Uniform* Parrish, whose death had cast a shadow over Whetstone for the past six months.

'What do we know, Deb?'

'Not a lot, Scott.' She stifled a yawn. 'Until the gas is off…One fatality so far and four seriously injured in the neighbouring houses. Mike Corby's interviewing the rest. They have evacuated neighbouring properties and are opening the church for waifs and strays. God knows where Jane Morris is.'

Daley sighed. 'She'll turn up.' It was too early in the morning for team politics. He'd hoped the simmering feud between Whetstone and DC Morris would burn itself out. He could do without another explosion in his own team. They would have enough to contend with in Green Street.

A gas leak. Accidents happen. Hopefully, they could wrap up the whole thing in time for a late lunch and a trip to the football. Yet somehow, he doubted it. In his experience, domestic gas explosions were rarely serious enough to take out the house. Usually, the occupier smelled the gas and dealt with it. Even then they happened early doors, when the occupants woke up, or upon their return from a time away. Number 5, known to be a brothel, was in constant occupation according to the uniform who attended. The rule book said to treat every reported death as suspicious until circumstances, or evidence, said otherwise.

With everyone, except paramedics, at a loose end, Daley and Whetstone sought the Fire Services Command Unit, which would always have a brew on, so it made more sense to hang around there. Inside, two fire officers in red and white chequered tabards were talking into radios.

'Hi, DCI Scott Daley, North West London MIT. How long before they turn off the gas, mate?'

'About fifteen minutes, sir. The Gas Board is on it now. They're having to isolate the entire street.'

'Time for a brew, then.' He nodded at a chrome urn. They each pulled on a white paper baby-grow, trying not to tear the material, and carried their coffees to the perimeter. It was as if a monstrous beast had swooped down and taken a giant bite out of the street, then soared into the air and crapped it back into the gaping wound. Number 5 was a scree slope of treacherous rubble. Here and there, recognisable items - a lavatory bowl, a door, half a wardrobe. Numbers 3 and 7 were also beyond salvation, their upper floors precariously suspended above the void, roofs canted at an impossible angle, flapping curtains, and torn carpets. Daley couldn't believe that a single microsecond of devastating energy could cause so much damage. How could such an immense quantity of gas have collected in a residential street yet no one, least of all the occupants, had noticed?

The blackened body lay on the rubble, smoke billowing away by the breeze. In the surreal silence, he thought of his own house, fifteen minutes away, solid, usually when he tried to drive Rawlplugs into the walls. He imagined Terri asleep and shuddered.

A shout from the Command Unit informed them they had isolated the gas. Taking a deep breath, Daley joined a small army of people searching for casualties. Scenes like this were too common, all heartbreaking, yet each one subtly different. So he concentrated on the routine elements. Preservation of the scene, observation, evidence gathering, and interviews. He was responsible for uncovering the truth, bringing closure to the victim's families, and locating those responsible.

If indeed anyone was.

Fifteen minutes later, the body count had risen to two; the one that lay on top of the rubble, and another, more badly damaged one, scattered over a wider area behind the house. The Chief Fire Officer insisted on removing the corpses to enable a more thorough search for victims beneath the rubble. An hour later, Daley and Whetstone entered a forensic tent where two plastic sacks lay side by side.

'Len?'

'Chief Inspector. Sergeant.'

Len Ganlow, the Home Office Pathologist, was a small matter-of-fact man with the air of a Trade Union Convenor. Day or night, he arrived wearing a pullover under his jacket and a tie with a well-set knot below his bobbing Adam's apple. Khaki corduroys and a pair of brown brogues. A product of industrial South Yorkshire, he was succinct, punctilious and cautious. Now, dressed in the regulation white baby-grow, wheezing behind the uncomfortable mask, he eased himself up, knees cracking with the effort.

'Female, twenties or early thirties. Other than that, you'll have to wait for the PM.'

The body was a blackened mannequin, a shining layer of scorched skin and fat beneath tattered rags. Singed remnants of hair lay about a round face, the mouth partly open, caught taking a last breath. The smell of burnt meat would taint Daley's nostrils for weeks to come.

'Give me something, Len. Was it an accident?'

Ganlow turned, dramatically surveyed the mountain of rubble, and shrugged. 'Maybe, but I'll wager she didn't die in it. There are the remains of a tourniquet on her arm and the syringe is still in the vein. Don't quote me until after the PM, but my guess is she died of an overdose before the main event. Main event? Gas main? Get it?'

Ganlow's shoulders bobbed, and Daley huffed. His sense of humour was still dozing in Terri's radiant warmth under a duvet. 'What? She left the gas on when she shot up, passed out and it went bang?'

Ganlow peered over his glasses. 'You'll have to wait for the PM. As regards the explosion, talk to the guys in white helmets.'

'Any ID?' asked Whetstone.

'They have hi-vis jackets and badges.' Again Ganlow's shoulders bobbed.

'No, the deceased. Any ID.'

'Not much of anything, poor girl.'

They crossed to the next victim, recoiling as Ganlow removed the covering - a charred torso, glistening black and cherry red, almost unrecognisable as a human, except for the remnants of a leather jacket. No legs or arms and most of the head was gone. Assorted lumps of carrion lay beside it.

'Based on the proportions of the pelvis and chest, male. It looks as if he was close to the point of ignition with his back to it. His leather jacket remained broadly intact throughout the half-second of intense heat, protecting his upper torso. His wallet was in the inside breast pocket. Driver's licence in the name of Andrew Philip Mason. I'll carry out PMs early on Monday.'

By 6:30 am, with no more casualties being uncovered, and everyone resident in the street accounted for, they scaled down the search while they waited for a specialist crew to arrive and begin a more thorough search as soon as it got light. Daley leant a hand on the shoulder of a police constable as he pulled off his overalls and dropped them into a plastic bin.

'Found out any more about the victims?'

Whetstone opened her notebook. 'According to neighbours, the female is Sonia Judd, a sex worker who lived in the top-floor flat. The male, Andrew Philip Mason, lives in Ruislip.'

'So what was he doing here?'

'Man and a woman, a flat on Green Street. What do you think he was doing?'

The street had a reputation, and Daley was an advocate of Occam's Razor. The simplest explanation usually being the right one. A prostitute and her John, who got a much larger bang than he expected. Simple.

'Go round to his house. Speak to his wife. Get the lie of the land. We need to know why he was visiting prostitutes. What else was going on in his life?'

Hopefully, things would be clearer by the end of the day. Daley wondered if he could make the match at Craven Cottage. Fulham were playing Cardiff City. He took another look at the mound of rubble, now haloed by the grey of dawn. Today, *The Whites* would need to lose without his support.

***

Father Joseph O'Donnell held tight to the spindly bannister halfway up the tower staircase, relieved the old, uneven glass in the window was intact. It gave the scene across the road an unearthly, surreal appearance, like seeing the world through the bottom of a whisky glass, which was how he usually saw it these days. He wondered, did the world also see him that way? They had all found new gods or turned their back on religion entirely. He saw the same faces each week and watched them grow older and die. Even he was a relic of the past.

The past. It was all he had now, and it left him damned.

As dawn broke, the hubbub outside had died down, and the church thronged with the displaced. They were all only too willing to drink his tea and eat his bloody biscuits, and to hide under his blankets when the world outside became too hostile. But tomorrow, Sunday, would they be here to offer their thanks to the Almighty? Would they, hell? Right now, he needed them all to pack up their things and go. He had hidden the desecrated cloth, leaving the altar unadorned, but at least the church could remain unlocked. At least it could welcome the ungrateful wretches in their time of need. At least he could uphold a modicum of decorum.

His first thought was for the victims. The police had already asked if he knew the deceased. They told him the man's name, and it was all he could do to hold himself from retching as images from so long ago swam through his mind. The blood, the panic, the deceit. He lied. *Andrew Mason? No, the name means nothing*, when it meant everything. Twenty years trying to atone for a moment of indecision for a few ill-thought-out actions.

Then there was the inscription. JO - Dt 8:5. The words of the verse, remembered from years of sermonising, had always seemed vacuous and absurd, but now they were aimed at him - JO - Joseph O'Donnell.

> "Thou shalt also consider in thine heart,
> that, as a man chasteneth his son,
> so the Lord thy God chasteneth thee."
> (Deuteronomy 8:5)

Chapter 4

Saunters Green, Ruislip, was an aspirational place to live. A class above the surrounding streets, it smacked of houses whose owners spent more than was sensible to impress, or infuriate, their neighbours, at least on the outside. Still rubbing sleep from her eyes, Detective Sergeant Deborah Whetstone pulled up in front of Number 53 Bennetts Lane, where Andrew Mason had lived, and wondered if she had accidentally driven through the back of a wardrobe. Sun-dappled and verdant, it was set back behind generous pavements and well-kept gardens. Even in context, it was breathtaking. With high walls and an ocean of biscuit gravel, the imposing mock Elizabethan house sat on its own. A double plot, double frontage, double garage, and double electric gates to keep out the unwanted. It smacked of money on a different level, even from a car salesman.

'This is posh, ma'am. How do people even afford them?' Detective Constable Jane Morris lowered her head to peer through the windscreen, nodding in naïve appreciation. Much to Whetstone's irritation, the young DC seemed unfazed by the early start.

'They don't, Jane. Their parents die and they buy out their siblings, or they win the lottery, or they run a dodgy business.'

As the gates lazily swung open, Whetstone waved to Judith Marner, the appointed Family Liaison Officer, and the single point of contact with the family. She was the invisible type, nondescript and businesslike, yet friendly and caring. In another life, she could have been a geriatric nurse or a funeral director. They followed her down a dim parqueted hall and into the stark brightness of a garden room overlooking a tennis court-sized expanse of lawn. Hannah

Mason sat at one end of a brown sofa, shrew-like, beneath an ivory-coloured satin dressing gown, her feet tight together inside fur-trimmed slippers. She gripped a cup and saucer as if letting go would send her spiralling off to another galaxy.

'Morning, Mrs Mason. I'm Detective Sergeant Deborah Whetstone and this is Detective Constable Jane Morris. North West London Homicide Unit. I'm so sorry for your loss.'

'Hannah Mason, Andy's, er…' She rose and offered a hand, the china clanking on the saucer as the other hand quivered. For a moment, Whetstone recognised the pain. Her mind saw Keith Parrish lying in his own blood. She drew in a deep breath and took hold of the hand. Hannah was tall and slim, with dark shoulder-length hair pulled back into a tight ponytail, giving her a rather plain look. Tears had brought a taut salt blush to her cheeks. She gestured towards a second sofa, brushed the dressing gown behind her knees, and sat down.

'Homicide? You're saying murder, not suicide?' Hannah looked across to Judith Marner. Having hardened herself to suicide and the cruelest form of desertion, now there was another possibility. One that reflected badly, not on her, but on someone else.

'No, Hannah,' The FLO cradled her hand. 'Until we know for certain, we treat every death as suspicious. It's just routine.'

'May I call you Hannah?' Whetstone paused for the faintest of nods. 'At the moment, the circumstances of your husband's death are unexplained. We should know more by the end of the day.' She paused momentarily, allowing the statement to permeate through the shock. 'I know it's a difficult time, but it would help if you could answer a few questions.'

Hannah Mason shrugged. Now was as bad a time as any.

'What time did Andrew leave yesterday morning?'

'8:00 am. He needed to set up a promotion at the showroom before it opened. He grabbed toast, made some remark about ships in the night, kissed the girls and left.' She looked across to a photo of two children, briefly screwed up her eyes and caught her breath.

'And what were your movements on Friday, Hannah?' Before she could show her annoyance, Whetstone added, 'It's just routine.'

'After Andy left, I ran the kids to school, then I did the weekly shop at the Waitrose by the station. I was back here by around eleven-thirty for the cleaner. She left at 3:00 pm and I went to pick the girls up from school.'

'And during the day, did Andy call home?'

'No. He never does.' Hannah Mason almost spat the words.

'And yesterday evening?'

'He goes - went - out most Fridays with his mates into town. Jacob Foster and Will Hughes. Jake is a Project Development Director at Stanford Clarke-Mitchell. He and Andy go way back. Will and Jake work together. I've never met Will.'

'So, what time did Andrew leave for his night out?'

Hannah shrugged. 'No idea. I wasn't here. I took the girls to dance class at five. By the time I got back, perhaps a quarter to seven, Andy had been and gone. It's the same every Friday.'

'And when he didn't arrive home?'

She shook her head. 'He lost his licence a few years ago, so rather than drive home drunk, he would stay over at Jake's. He often did that.'

'And he didn't call to say he'd be stopping over?'

'No. He must have left his phone in his car, or maybe the battery was flat.'

Whetstone glanced across at Jane Morris, who was scrawling in her notebook, avoiding Whetstone's gaze, probably thinking the same as her. Long ago, when Whetstone met Keith Parrish, he and Morris were already an item, until a night out drinking turned an infatuation into an affair, and Parrish discarded Morris like yesterday's underwear. Had Mason fallen for someone new? Had he used the regular drinks night as a cover?

Hannah looked out to the garden, at the roses needing dead-heading, the autumn leaves mottling the lawn, anywhere but at

Whetstone and Morris. There was a familiar pattern emerging. *He kissed the girls, but he didn't kiss me. Never rings home during the day. Ships in the night.* Maybe that summed up their relationship. Tired. Seeking a little excitement in the wrong place.

'How did Andrew seem to you yesterday? Did he have any worries, anything on his mind?'

'Andy - everyone calls him Andy.' She was growing tired of the questions. 'Okay, he seemed okay. I've already said. It all seemed normal. He was a little stressed about work. Sales were down. It was always the same after the new autumn registration rush, but Andy is - was - the eternal optimist. Things would pick up.'

'And how are things financially?'

Hannah nodded behind her. 'Everything is in the bureau in his office. I didn't get involved in that side of things.'

'Do you know a woman called Sonia Judd?' asked Whetstone. Hannah Mason jumped as a penny dropped and hit a nerve.

'Our cleaner. She comes in on Mondays and Fridays.' Her voice had cracked, hinting at the obvious implication. She reached across to the side table and handed over a card she had found earlier.

It was a turn-up for the books, mused Whetstone. The Masons in Pinner employed a prostitute from Harrow to be their cleaner - or was it the other way around? The Masons' cleaner moonlighting as a prostitute? Either way, it jarred with what they knew of Judd to date. With Andy working, and the kids at school, what did Hannah do to fill her time, apart from tidying up before the cleaner arrived and agonising about what her husband was getting up to?

'Why do you think Andy was in Harrow last night with Ms Judd?' Morris asked, rather too bluntly. Judith Marner tightened her grip as Hannah turned and stared.

'I do not know,' she said defiantly, 'but it's not what you think. Andy was a good man, and people took advantage. Maybe he was helping this *woman* with a problem, or she was buying a car and there was paperwork to sign, something like that. I'm sure it was perfectly innocent. It had to be.' Hannah's eyes flicked about the room, a hint of desperation, as she clung to the wreckage as the ship disintegrated around her.

Whetstone felt they had laid enough crap at Hannah's doorstep for now. She looked across at Jane Morris, who closed her notebook. They would speak again.

'We'll need to take away his laptop and phone if that's okay?'

Hannah shrugged, tired of the interrogation already. Whetstone thanked her for her time, apologised for the distress and expressed once more her sorrow for her grief. Hannah gave a dismissive nod as they rose to follow Judith Marner back along the parquet, relieved to be away from the charged atmosphere of the Mason household.

Chapter 5

Four months ago, Superintendent *Bilko* Bob Allenby suffered a heart attack in the golf club car park. He survived but decided enough was enough, so he and his wife Philippa moved to a charming cottage on the banks of the River Tay, where Allenby, having gone off golf, now indulged his passion for fly-fishing from dawn to dusk, whilst his wife made herself indispensable to the great and good of the local community. It augured change for the North West London Homicide Unit.

Nature, and the Metropolitan Police Service, abhor a vacuum, so teams of Machiavellian management tosspots set about turning the problem to their advantage. Assistant Chief Constable Diane Browning stepped down to fill Bilko Bob's shoes with grand schemes to replace the old order with an altogether different one. Unfortunately, Scott Daley and his team were on her list. Fortunately, she was implicated in a gangland extortion racket and her chickens came home to roost before she could do any actual harm, and with her went most of the Hillingdon Drugs Squad. Daley, basking in the afterglow of his promotion to Detective Chief Inspector, had relaxed for a while. The new ACC, Vic Fraser, even stepping him up in *Bilko Bob's* place. Yet the respite had been brief and the axe continued its slow descent on his team.

Fraser's first appointment was Leslie Hacker, catapulting her from Chief Inspector in a hick Derbyshire town to superintendent in a Borough Operational Command Unit of the Met. At thirty-six, she was already a force to be reckoned with. Slim, blonde, tall, and somewhat severe, a graduate entrant, who had ripped through the ranks, climbing the greasy pole to greatness with the tacit goal of running the show. She brought new ideas around natural staff wastage and brave new worlds, yet no one could identify a single achievement she'd made along the way. Now she was involved in reducing Operational Command Units from thirty-two to just twelve. Soon, they would throw together a hotchpotch of units, including Daley's Murder Investigation Team, and expected to play nicely, as part of an über-team, the WLCHDU, or West London Combined Homicide and Drugs Unit. It tripped off the tongue like a drunk down pub steps. Still, another Machiavellian tosspot with a specialism in human resources had pointed out they could bin a few expensive senior officers on the way, most of whom were shitting themselves and checking their pensions. And, since his promotion to Chief Inspector, it had not escaped Daley's notice that now *he* was one of the senior ranks.

Not that he didn't welcome change was bad; it was the uncertainty it brought. The inevitable influx of people who assumed a degree in politics made them good coppers. And the staff movements, desk movements, and even bowel movements, a revised organisational chart brought with it. Everyone, including Daley, faced an uncomfortable level of scrutiny, and he was causing himself to question his abilities. On the upside, the trip to Hillingdon would halve his commute each morning - while they still employed him.

Most of Lambourne Road Nick was empty, abandoned in favour of shiny new offices and proper equipment in the new Hillingdon Command Centre. A small ops team remained on the ground floor, and the Murder Investigation Team on the fourth floor. The size of a tennis court, battleship grey carpets, battleship grey walls and battleship grey people, the team room bustled with activity as a phalanx of administration staff tried to corral the team's output into some kind of order. Of course, the mothballing of Lambourne Road was part of a grander plan of improvement. Nothing to do with the lucrative new shopping development earmarked for the area that would coin in a bob or two for the Met.

Being a weekend, the place hummed with a quiet industry as a skeleton staff wondered if they could slope off without being noticed. The team itself occupied six desks, dubbed the naughty corner, away from the dubious benefit of natural daylight, yet close to a supply of coffee. Detective Sergeant Dave Monaghan and Detective Constable Steve Taylor were already slouching at their desks. Constables Mike Corby and Jane Morris were chatting at the kitchenette counter. At the end of the block, Daley's old desk lay forlorn. Since his promotion, he had taken up residence in *Bilko Bob's* old haunt, a glass-walled office called the Goldfish Bowl, where he sat cradling a brew, summoning up the energy for the first team briefing into the explosion in Harrow. At the opposite end of the team room, in the claustrophobic briefing room, someone had cleaned the mammoth white Incident Board ready for anything Green Street might throw at them.

Everything pointed to an accident. A tart and her John, and an ill-timed gas leak, yet Daley was unconvinced. He had limited experience with prostitutes; once during his police training on a drunken night out, three of his mates copped off, while he sat shitting himself on the side of a bed as a lovely blonde girl, stuck her chewing gum onto the bedpost and draped her chest in his face. Her breath smelled of spearmint and he wondered what else she'd been chewing before his arrival. Needless to say, he could not go through with the transaction and ended up thirty quid out of pocket. Back then, the whole unsavoury incident was over in minutes, not hours. So why had the occupants of Number 5 Green Street not smelled gas and left the property?

***

'Right, guys,' Daley clapped his hands together, to instil enthusiasm into the team and himself. 'Gas explosion, Green Street Harrow. Two deaths and ten other casualties. What do we know about the deceased, Deb?'

Whetstone opened her notebook. 'Andrew Philip Mason from Ruislip. Though yet to be confirmed, neighbours identify the female as Sonia Judd, a sex worker, twenty-three years old, who lived in the upstairs flat. She had a few juveniles - possession, handling, and petty theft. More recently, she'd been cautioned for soliciting. She operated in Harrow town centre and online via several chat rooms and had a known heroin habit. The local force is speaking to the parents for a formal ID. The downstairs flat was vacant, apparently. We'll know for sure in a day or two.'

Daley nodded. The fire crews were still shifting the upstairs from the downstairs. 'And the neighbours, Mike?'

Corby shuffled himself upright. 'Everyone said a big bang around 1:00 am woke them. The neighbours at Numbers 3 and 7 are in intensive care - haven't spoken to them yet. Luckily, the rest received only cuts and bruises. The priest across the road at St Dunstan's was in the sacristy and heard the explosion. He went out to help and found Mr Mansell lying on the road. He saw no one else. Mrs Kelly at Number 1 came home from work at 6:30 pm. She saw a woman, whom she recognised as Sonia Judd, enter Number 5. Mrs Kelly says she was wearing a long black coat and a curly red wig she wore when she went out on the game. Mrs Livingstone at Number 9 smokes in the front garden. At around 7:30 pm, a woman, again identified as Sonia Judd, wearing the same coat and wig, left Number 5 and walked off towards town. Mrs Livingstone said hello but Judd ignored her. At 8:00 pm, Judd returned with a man and entered Number 5. Mrs Livingstone described him as tall, in his thirties or forties, medium height, stocky, dark hair, and wearing a dark leather jacket.'

'—which sounds like Andrew Mason.'

Corby nodded. 'Around 8:30 pm, Judd left and crossed over into the churchyard.'

'But not Mason?' Daley wondered why a prostitute would invite a client back and then leave him alone in her flat.

'No sir, but Mrs Livingstone took comfort breaks and might have missed him leaving. Later, around 10:45 pm, Mrs Kelly from Number 1 saw a couple walk across to the churchyard.'

'Male? Female?'

'She didn't get a good look. Medium height, hoods pulled down. The Frenchs at Number 3 reported a smell of gas at 11:30 pm and

An Invisible Murder

were told to turn off their stop-tap and wait for a visit. It wasn't their gas. They're in Harrow Central Hospital, not fit enough to be interviewed yet. Around 12:30 pm, Oliver Mansell walked his dog past on their way to the mini-mart, around the corner in Sefton Street. He walked back just as the explosion happened. The dog, Moxy, a small wire-haired terrier, is still unaccounted for.'

'Cheers Mike. Dave. What do we know about the house?'

Detective Sergeant Dave Monaghan was the father of the team. A confirmed backroom analyst, with the steady way about him of one who had seen everything. They said if a serial killer sliced him in two, he would have *Murder Investigation Team* running through his body. He clicked his keyboard, and in his steady Wicklow brogue, read from his screen.

'Mohammed Nazir, a private landlord, owns half the street. He had divided Number 5 into flats, one up, one down. All the relevant landlord's paperwork was up-to-date. The Fire Inspector will give his preliminary report tomorrow when they expect to sign the scene over to CSI.'

'Jane, you spoke to the landlord,' Daley asked. 'What did he have to say?'

DC Morris looked up, stifling a yawn. 'He only spoke Hindi, but his daughter translated and he confirmed Judd had lived there for around three years. He knew of her occupation and substance abuse, but she paid her rent on time and never gave him any grief, so he saw no reason to give her any. I showed him the photo of Andrew Mason, but he didn't recognise him. I also asked about insurance. Mr Nazir has a commercial policy which has been in force for many years.'

'Check with the company, Jane. See if he's upped the premium. And the downstairs flat?'

'Vacant, sir, for around three months while Mr Nazir's sons refurbished it. No new tenant as yet. The sons live in Wembley, within a few doors of each other. They were in all night.'

'What about the old guy who was passing?'

'Oliver Mansell, sir. Broken femur and concussion, but at his age...He said he saw someone under the lychgate in the churchyard just after the blast. A lean man was his description. He called out for help, but the person ignored him.'

'Thanks, Jane. As soon as he is fit to be interviewed, have another word. Dave? What do we know about Andrew Mason?'

'Lives in Saunters Green, Ruislip. Married to Hannah for fourteen years, with two children. No arrears or county court judgements. He lost his driving licence a decade ago but, other than that, nothing on PNC. He worked at Stratham Motors, Ruislip, as a car salesman.'

'I spoke to his boss,' added Corby. 'Mason had been overdoing the charm. A customer complained he'd touched her. One of the female staff also complained about him being a little forward. It got him a written warning.'

'A little over-friendly, visits to a sex worker. Follow it up, please, Mike.'

For Daley, it could be something or nothing. Some men believed they had a divine right and would not take no for an answer. Some women made more out of it than was necessary. It was a matter of intent. Was it an accident, over-friendliness, or even misguided flirtation? The law was there to protect everyone, but there was also a need for both sexes to exercise common sense. Yet, if many women lacked that ability, many men were also devious.

'Deb, what did Mason's wife say?'

'He left the house at 8:00 am. They didn't speak during the day, which was not unusual. Mason returned home between five and six, changed and went out for a drinks night with two mates, Jacob Foster and Willson Hughes. Hannah, his wife, took the kids to dance class between 4:45 pm and 7:00 pm, so didn't see him again. When he didn't return home, she assumed he'd had one too many and stayed over with friends, which he often did. The first she heard of his death was the next morning. She did not know why he would be in Harrow, rather than Pinner. I asked her if her husband seemed preoccupied in the days leading up to his death, but she said not especially. Sales were down at the showroom, but that's not unusual. I also asked if she knew anyone by the name of Sonia Judd - and she did. It's the name of the Masons' cleaner. She cleans for them between 1:30 am and 3:00 pm each Monday and Friday.'

Daley scratched his head. 'So, Andy started an affair with a sex worker and then offered her a job as his cleaner?'

'Yeah, I know,' said Whetstone. 'That's going to go down well with Hannah when she finds out.'

'Leave that to the FLO. So Judd was there last Friday afternoon?'

'Yep. I asked Hannah Mason why she thought her husband would be in Harrow with their cleaner. She refused to believe an affair or even just sex, preferring instead to believe it was a business thing - *buying a car and there was paperwork to sign, something like that. Perfectly innocent.* I think she knew. Whether she knew all the details, she knew he wasn't telling her the truth.'

'Enough to kill him?'

The cleaner, whom Mason invited into his home, was also the prostitute with whom he had sex. It was not unheard of for a working woman to moonlight as a prostitute, but Mason was shitting on his own doorstep, then asking her to clear it up - under the nose of his wife. Either Mason was brave or foolhardy.

When Daley's first marriage fell apart, things had not been right for months. Part of the problem was work. Crime didn't work to a timetable, so he was rarely there. When Lynne started playing around, she made sure Daley was on shift, and that she had an alibi. Eventually, he noticed. Chores she did were left undone. Chores *he* left undone were weaponised. In her defence, he was out so much she could have divorced him for desertion. And he could have handled the loss of their baby better.

With hindsight.

Daley scanned the incomplete Incident Board, the best they had this early in the investigation. Front and centre, the photos of Mason and Judd were probably closer than the pair were in real life.

They cut the picture of the widow, Hannah, from the same family snapshot used for Andrew Mason. Several centimetres apart were about right, too. Now, she and her husband were divided forever. On the right-hand side, Whetstone added names. Jacob Foster and Willson Hughes, the two Friday night drinking buddies. Mohammed Nazir, the owner of the destroyed properties, and his two sons. On the left-hand side, a question mark. Below it, a few keywords and aide-mémoire - *lean man in the churchyard, probs at work, an affair?* In the future, they would add anything relevant and any questions needing answers. It would plot the connections, register the disconnections, and hopefully show a pathway to the logical deduction that would solve the crime. Logic? When did that ever have a bearing on police work? Still, the emptiness of the board concerned Daley, as it did at the outset of every investigation.

'So, to recap. Andrew Mason was due in Pinner for a regular Friday night drink. Instead, he went to Harrow, presumably to pick up Sonia Judd for sex. Around one in the morning, they were involved in a gas explosion at Number 5 Green Street, where Judd, a known sex worker, rented a flat.

'Speak to the drinking mates. Find out why he cried off. And find Mason's car and mobile. We've circulated the index number. Dave and Steve, keep on top of that. Run a background check on the wife. Check out her movements and speak to their neighbours. Be insensitive and rattle some cages. See if there's any truth behind the suggestion he was playing away.

'Then there's the incident itself. We need to confirm whether the gas explosion was accidental or intentional. Request CCTV around the vicinity of Green Street and widen it out. We need to track Judd and Mason's movement up until the point of the incident. And the people the neighbours saw, not to mention the person watching Mr Mansell after the explosion - because if Mason died in the explosion, it certainly wasn't him.'

Men visit prostitutes for a short period with a defined purpose. Mason had travelled some way to meet Judd, perhaps to be discreet, but he arrived with Judd at 8:00 pm and died in the explosion five hours later. Why was he still there as the flat filled with gas? Based on that alone, Daley decided.

'I am treating the deaths of Sonia Judd and Andrew Mason as suspicious. I am initiating Operation Scion to cover the Investigation. I'll act as SIO, and Dave Monaghan will be the Single Point of Contact in to and out of this team. Anything and everything relevant goes through him. They appointed Judith Marner as the Family Liaison Officer. She is already at the Mason house with his widow Hannah.'

Chapter 6

It was past seven in the evening when Deborah Whetstone dropped the latch on her front door and let the silence envelop her.

Saturday had always been a lost day, when a work emergency was preferable to watching the clock, or the telly, or the raindrops running down the windowpane. Nothing else to do but clean or shop, and no enthusiasm for either. Sleep in late, go back to bed early and hope Monday comes quickly. Work was shit, but life was shitter; the lesser of two evils.

She shrugged off her coat, checked the kettle for water, and fed some bread to the toaster. Then she slumped into a chair and took a beat. Seventeen hours ago, she had just nodded off when Operations had called. Shouts like this convinced her she was getting old. Not in the age sense - she was only thirty-five, but in every other sense. Every muscle in her back ached. The house was becoming a morgue, and all she ever saw was the office. Work was too easy a diversion from real life. Her mother had been dead for six months, and Keith for four. She needed to move on. Her inspector's exam was behind her, and they were crying out for decent officers in the Met. Soon, her sister, Louise, would want to cash in her half of the house and, whether she liked it or not, everything would change. Maybe she should sell up, pay off Louise and rent for a while, flexibility while she waited. Her reclusive lifestyle meant she had saved a ton, enough for a deposit, even at London prices, or even further afield. Leave *The Smoke* altogether. She could buy a mansion up north.

A change is as good as a rest, but would she be swapping one empty house for another?

The toaster popped. The kettle clicked off. The bottle of supermarket Merlot alongside it required a lot less effort. Inside her, the guilt started early. Since her father's death, her mom, Maureen, had cared more for the bottle than the housework, or shopping, or her. She reached across and unscrewed the top and poured a large glassful, drinking it down. Then she poured out the rest. She felt a chill. Whether it was the cold of the house or the realisation she was becoming her mother, she wasn't sure. Too often, she'd finished the bottle.

Down the hall, the lights of a car passed the oval window in the front door, and her heart skipped a beat. She wondered if she had bolted the door. For a moment, the blue BMW was again in the street. For a moment, she was back in the alley watching Keith Parrish's head explode, and she was terrified. Saturday had always been a lost day, but these days she hoped it would pass quickly.

Her eyelids were drooping. She picked up the glass and drained it, aching with guilt as she realised she had not tasted a drop. Labouring up the stairs, cleaning her teeth, avoiding the creased face in the mirror, she got into bed and fired up a dating site on her tablet, examining the faces that filled her screen, swiping left more than right, wondering if the beaming, well-groomed photos were a lie, or something worse. Being a detective did that to you.

Her time with Keith *The Uniform* Parrish had been a train wreck but, for a while, she felt normal. No longer the sad single destined to be devoured by her cats, but a girlfriend, a partner, a significant other. She gained a sense of purpose outside of Lambourne Road and the Murder Investigation Team. She was punching above her weight; Keith was tall, handsome, sexy as fuck in his uniform, and great in bed, and whilst, in the back of her mind, there was always the inevitability it would end. She felt safe in the moment. But when the end came, it only amplified the isolation she felt without him.

Jane Morris's arrival only made matters worse. Aeons ago, before *The Hand in the Van* investigation, Jane and Keith had been together when Whetstone had poached him from her. Morris had ten years on Whetstone and far fewer pounds. She was ridiculously gorgeous and had all the men drooling over her. Even old married Dave Monaghan had taken a shine to her. But that wasn't the issue. The issue was Keith, and now, neither of them had him and each resented the other, and while they both remained single, the enmity would fester like a canker.

Sooner rather than later, there would need to be a resolution.

***

Operation Scion, the name for the investigation into the Green Street deaths, came from an algorithm. A random word conveying no meaning or emphasis. It was as good as any. It gave the detectives something tangible to refer to. Daley left the Fire Investigation and forensic teams to do their thing. His team concentrated on the reams of witness statements and background checks into the Masons and Sonia Judd. Notwithstanding, everyone they needed to speak to was off until Monday. Daley left his mobile on and ducked out of the office to devote himself to the joys of flat-pack furniture and wallpaper hanging.

Leslie Hacker, the new superintendent, never clocked off. She had called him, probably from the gym as she balanced her *Filofax* on the handlebars of an exercise bike, or the nail bar as her gel-coat set. She had demanded an update and urged him not to dally over his deliberations, suggesting it was probably accidental or misadventure. Daley doubted Judd or Mason would have remained in a room filling with gas, awaiting the inevitable. Her response was *some kind of suicide pact*, at which point Daley thanked her for her input and suggested they talk again during office hours. Then, with a crust forming on his wallpaper paste, she framed it in a departmental expenditure context for that quarter. She advised him against unnecessarily setting expensive hares running and gave him forty-eight hours to show some results. Given twenty-four of those were on a Sunday, Daley replied it was still early days, unwisely prefixing it *with all due respect*, which, of course, it wasn't. He rang off, leaving the crust to form a little longer while he fetched a beer. Few things were as important as the incumbent superintendent supposed they were - as *he* used to think they were.

Following his messy divorce and near-death under a Class 90 diesel locomotive, Daley's life had been spiralling. Now he had Theresa Somerville, the petite yet feisty Scottish inspector whom he had met in a car park and who had driven away with his heart. Less than a year, a wrecked Audi and a stratospheric mortgage later, they were expecting the arrival of Daley Junior in a couple of weeks. Which paradoxically meant bringing more work home, rereading statements whilst he feigned interest in the baby-related hogwash she watched on the TV, as they curled up on the sofa together.

Now though, it was 3:08 am on a Monday, and his mind was pinballing through all the dubious choices and poor decisions he'd made. It was never enough for him to believe he was competent and good at his job. He needed others to believe in him, too. If they did, they didn't show it, leaving him floundering in a mire of self-doubt. Of course, doubt can be a force for good. Not accepting anything at face value. The problem was as much as Daley's life was normalising, and his career was on the up, the imposter inside him always had a foot outstretched.

3:08, guys. Let me sleep, please?

He pushed his focus back to Operation Scion. Occam's Razor. The simplest solution is often the correct one. *Come on, Occam, earn your corn.*

Sonia Judd took Mason back to her flat for sex, but before that happened, she shot up and overdosed, hence the syringe in her arm. Or Mason could have injected her with the heroin. Then, having found her dead, or full of remorse for killing her, he set about taking his own life by turning on the gas, letting it build up, and then lighting a match. A *goodbye cruel world* gesture.

Nice try, Occam, but your theory has more holes than the back wall of Number 5 Green Street.

Mason was in a flat with a dead prostitute. Why not scarper, return to Pinner and join the lads for their drinks night? Why make things difficult? When Mason and Judd returned, if even a small quantity of gas had leaked out before they arrived, would they not smell it? Turning on a light could have ignited it, or Sonia's lighter as

An Invisible Murder

she liquified her fix. So, the gas must have started leaking *after* they arrived. Even so, Mason stayed there, with Judd dead and oblivious to the danger, for five hours until the gas ignited. Why? Unless he passed out first?

He got up to make a cup of cocoa. As the kettle boiled, he sat watching the timer on the cooker flash the seconds, ticking away the minutes. With twenty years on the force, he had seen many suicides. They had all been personal acts, selfish even. Many of them were unintentional. Cries for help that were not heeded or went too far. He couldn't recall a single instance of a suicide where the act destroyed half a street. Except for suicide bombers - but then, their intention was murder, the suicide a means to an end. Or a mass suicide, but then one could also consider that murder by coercion.

The clock on the cooker ticked over another minute. What wasn't he seeing?

He finished his cocoa and returned to bed, hoping the merry-go-round in his head would stop. Sophie Jennings, the Force's shrink, had taught him relaxation techniques, following the accident that nearly put him to sleep for good. He'd tried counting sheep, but the furry bastards wouldn't jump in an orderly fashion, taking the fence two, even three, at a time, leaving him struggling to keep count. So he'd tried tortoises, who sat at the base of the fence, lifting their tiny legs in vain, unable to find a way over.

Sleep, Scott, for god's sake.

One tip was to write the offending thought down, to consign it to paper and let it lie. So he sat up and penned a quick text to Harry Ramesh at Loughton Street Forensic Laboratory. *Harry, why did they stay in the flat as the gas built up? Why didn't they run out before the bang? Or switch off the gas?* There now, it was someone else's problem.

'Can't you sleep?'

Daley turned. Terri's silhouette was dark against the faint glow through the curtains. She smelled like everything good, buried in the warmest, most comfortable part of the bed. A hand moved across his chest.

'Ah, sorry. Did I wake you?'

'No, Junior is break-dancing on a nerve.' She was getting contractions - the doctor said *Braxton-Hicks, nothing to worry about*, which made Daley worry even more, and Terri take the piss out of him. The sooner this baby arrived, the better.

'What's up?' She rolled onto her back.

'Just a work thing.'

But it was more than a work thing. It was a career thing, even a confidence thing. With Judd and Mason, he hung two more images in the gallery of his mind, grotesque and other-worldly. Two more deaths laid on him to resolve. Two more families looking to him for justice.

'Would a cuddle help?' She pulled Daley's arm, and he inched across the plain of coldness to the pool of warmth.

He pecked the silhouette on the cheek. 'Always.'

Chapter 7

When Monday finally came, Daley had convinced himself he was up for it. Not that he had much choice. Astrophysics being what it was, the world would turn, regardless of his reticence to join in. So, still picking pale blue specks of paint from his hair, he kissed goodbye to Terri and joined the queue of other grumpy bastards for whom the weekend was already a memory.

The team room was lively, despite the hour. The Police Force bred insomniacs. Terri was always urging him to live in the moment, to enjoy each day as it came and for what it brought. The past is a closed book, the future is an undiscovered country, and all we can change is the present. Easy for her to say, perched in front of daytime telly nursing an imminent birth, while he flicked through a closed book of unimaginable horrors, and prowled the present for victims with the texture of crispy duck. Still, he imagined those poor sods who worked in a factory, or an office, pushing bits of paper around. And he had the joy of a double post-mortem straight after breakfast. Murder had its compensations.

Deb Whetstone was already in, leaning her elbows on her desk, holding a coffee like an umbrella in a thunderstorm. She, too, was an insomniac, trying to deal with everything that had happened to her in the past twelve months. Another book that refused to be closed. Still, it meant she preferred to be at work, which in turn meant she had already updated the Incident Board. Every cloud...

***

Long ago, Loughton Street Forensic Science Laboratories had been a teaching institution akin to a scene from an H.G. Wells novel.

Wood panelling, ornate ceiling mouldings, brass fittings, not to mention a decent restaurant on the second floor. Unfortunately, that day had been before two world wars, the National Health Service, and a torrent of cost-cutting governments. Only the grandiose Edwardian facade remained as a nod to better times, but as usual, it was closed up tighter than a swan's backside, so Daley and Whetstone used the service entrance behind the bins, and through a snake of drab grey basement corridors. The serious work happened upstairs. An examination room covered half of the first floor. Originally, it had been a theatre where gentlemen could watch the surgeon of the day disembowelling a convict who had been unfortunate enough to die. Now it was a clean, angular and functional space in a brighter, more utilitarian shade of silvery grey. Above, a gallery looked out over three stainless steel tables. Daley puffed as he noted the uneven linen sheets draped over them. These days, they were both mostly hardened to the sight of death, less so to the process of examination; sawing skulls and scooping out organs with a pop, like blancmange from a dish. As the swing doors creaked, Len Ganlow glanced up and waved them down.

'Be with you in a minute. Please feel free to browse.' Ganlow's shoulders twitched at his wit.

Daley followed Whetstone down the stairs to the main room, glad to have skipped breakfast given the pungent odour of cooked meat and disinfectant that met them. Presently, Ganlow stopped fiddling with the lab equipment and crossed over to the leftmost table.

'Shall we begin?' As if they had a choice. He drew back the sheet on a blackened crusty shape, only recognisable as a female by the build.

'An under-nourished female in her early twenties. Partial-thickness burns to most of the body. Multiple bone fractures, barotrauma to the lungs, brain and other organs - damage caused by a high-pressure wave. All consistent with close but not immediate proximity to the explosion and ejection from the building. All delivered post-mortem. There was no methane dissolved in her blood, or scorching to her trachea or lungs, no soot or ash, suggesting she did not breathe in the gas or the flames. I found signs of habitual intravenous drug use - older injection sites between her toes and on both forearms and, of course, the syringe still in her arm and a tourniquet burnt into her skin. Interestingly, I found a second puncture wound nearby in the same arm. More clumsy, tearing the skin and the vein.

'Her blood contained around thirty milligrams of unmetabolised heroin, a pretty normal dose for a user at her stage of addiction. It would render her unconscious, but not kill her. However, her system also contained enough fentanyl to floor a rhinoceros. On top of the heroin, this would have caused cardiac arrest within seconds. Lividity and rigor mortis suggest she died between three and six hours before the explosion.'

'Heroin and fentanyl? Were they both self-inflicted?' asked Whetstone.

'The syringe used for the heroin was still in her arm. We found one set of fingerprints on the barrel and plunger. Harry Ramesh will tell you more, but there was no fentanyl residue, suggesting the killer used a second syringe via the second, more amateurish puncture wound. This syringe is still missing. So, my conclusion is she died from cardiac arrest caused by a fatal dose of fentanyl administered on top of the heroin. Time of death between, say, 7:00 pm Friday and 1:00 am Saturday, when the explosion occurred. There were no signs of restraint or other assault, but given the state of her body, that would be easy to miss. I'll keep looking.'

'And Mason?' asked Daley.

Ganlow replaced the sheet and crossed to the next table.

'Less to go on here, literally.'

The body was arranged on the table, each piece in its place, like the glazed pictorial tile Daley remembered as a child from the wall in his local butchers. A transfer printed image of a cow with all the cuts of meat slightly separated, neatly arranged and labelled, except here there were no labels, they were human, scorched and undercooked, and the head resembled a pile of broken, charred earthenware, still containing the remnants of a stew. Daley, annealed to the sight of mutilated corpses, mouth-breathed. Whetstone held a handkerchief to her face. Daley could smell the menthol she had smeared on her upper lip.

'Similar soft tissue and internal damage, consistent with an explosion, but he was a lot closer. Full-thickness burns to the whole body except the anterior thorax. No evidence of rigor. Again, no signs of restraint or trauma inconsistent with the explosion and subsequent short flight from the building, although, given the state of the body, again they would be easy to miss.'

'Also, Mason's stomach contained around six units of whisky and a large quantity of an antidepressant, amitriptyline hydrochloride. My guess is he drank the whisky laced with the drug *after* he arrived. Before, he would have collapsed in the street. Within ten minutes, he was unconscious. His blood contained a substantial amount of dissolved methane, suggesting he was inhaling the gas as the room filled. So, Mr Mason entered the flat, passed out on whisky and amitriptyline, slowly asphyxiating as the room filled. He was dead by the time the explosion occurred. So, the cause of death is asphyxiation due to methane inhalation. I should have detailed toxicology in a couple of days.'

There were many ways to go, mused Daley. Quick and unexpected, as had happened to Roy Whetstone, Deb's father, hit by a car as he crossed the road. Hardly time to register. There were the slow deaths. Chronic illness and mortal injury, where one knew it was over and simply waited for the inevitable. Then there was what happened to Andrew Mason, drifting in and out of consciousness, until he finally succumbed to the methane.

'Had Mason and Judd had intercourse before they died?' Whetstone asked. It was why they were there in the first place.

'Ms Judd showed signs of recent sexual intercourse, and she had performed oral sex shortly before she died. I've sent off fluids for DNA matching, but preliminary results suggest none are a match for Mr Mason.'

An Invisible Murder

***

Harry Ramesh's office was across the corridor from the examination theatre, yet a world away. Glass-panelled offices, packed with high-tech gadgets, big screens, and weighty tomes. Light and airy, with no stench of death. Ramesh leant over his desk, staring at a screen of figures. To the unpracticed eye, he seemed to be enjoying it.

'It's like a morgue in here, Ramesh,' quipped Daley.

Ramesh stretched out the cramp. 'The Students are away seeing how clever people chop up bodies. All that blood and gore, not to mention the egg sandwiches. I'd be sick on the coach ride back.'

Professor Harbinder *Harry* Ramesh was a relative newcomer to Forensic Science. Qualified for five years, he still had a couple of decades to shake off the new boy tag. Short and stocky, with a quiff of jet-black hair, he wore a casual shirt and jeans beneath his pristine lab coat. He still looked like one of his students. Wide-eyed, as if he were about to burst out in a smile, which he did as soon as he spotted Deborah Whetstone loping through the door. Daley was sure he had a thing for her. After Keith's death, Harry had been a brick. He'd helped her through the trauma. And he expected nothing in return. Maybe that was the problem?

'So, Green Street, Harrow,' asked Daley. 'What do you know?'

'Forensically, a few things, although the blast destroyed much of the evidence. The landlord sent us a floor plan to work from.'

Ramesh swivelled his computer monitor around. Number 5 was a bay windowed terrace, divided into downstairs and upstairs flats. From the front door, stairs led to a landing, a cramped bathroom at the rear and a side door into a boxy windowless living area, from which an equally boxy kitchen looked out over the rear garden. A bedroom the width of the upstairs looked out over the street. All in all, hardly big enough to swing a cat without getting blood and brains on the walls. At least now it was airier.

Ramesh continued. 'The point of ignition was the combination boiler in the upstairs flat, mounted on the kitchen wall. They found Mr Mason in the rear garden. The damage to his body, along with scorch patterns on the top of the kitchen table, suggests he was seated at the table at the rear of the boiler, facing out towards the garden. He took the full force of the blast to his back, protecting the piece of tabletop he was leaning over, which in turn protected the front of his torso. Ms Judd was probably on the bed in the front bedroom, around ten metres away behind two stud walls. We found her vomit on the bed halfway across the street.'

'So, Judd was in the bedroom and Mason in the kitchen?' asked Daley. 'Prostitute and client. Seems a little odd.'

'Not something I have any experience of. Anyway, to matters I am more comfortable with - the evidence.' Ramesh reached for a box and removed a small evidence bag containing a smaller dusty baggie. 'This contained the fix Ms Judd injected. Only her fingerprints are on the bag and the syringe, so it's reasonable to assume she cooked and injected it herself. Mr Mason's wallet contained three credit cards, a fuel card, and pictures of his two young daughters. There were eighty pounds in cash, an ATM receipt for one hundred, and a receipt from a coffee shop for six pounds.'

Daley examined a photo of the wallet. Whilst fifty pounds remained neatly slotted into the wallet, the other thirty were creased and folded. 'Who carries their money like that?'

'Someone who has taken it out, then crammed it back in? Anyway, we also found this.' Ramesh brought up a photo of a single well-worn business card from Stratham Motors bearing Mason's name. 'Odd that he would have only this single dog-eared card in his wallet. As a salesman, surely Mr Mason would want to make a good first impression. More interesting is what is on the back.' He pulled up a second image, a string of characters written in biro:

AM - Dt 22:27

'Some kind of aide-mémoire? *AM* - Andrew Mason, an appointment at ten-twenty-seven with someone whose initials were *Dt*. Maybe someone wrote the message on the reverse and handed it back. Strange, they only capitalised the D.'

An Invisible Murder

'A bible reference, gov,' suggested Whetstone. 'Deuteronomy? Chapter 22, verse 27. Maybe a pithy quote he thought interesting?'

'Your catholic upbringing has a lot to answer for, Deb. Was Mason religious?'

She gave a disinterested shrug.

'On the other hand...' Ramesh turned his computer.

> "For he found her in the field,
> and the damsel cried,
> and there was none to save her."
> (Deuteronomy 22:27)

'That doesn't sound good,' remarked Daley. Perhaps a bible reference was nearer the mark. Was *he* Andrew Mason, the *damsel* Sonia Judd, *the field* representing her life in prostitution and drugs? Had Judd cried out and Mason heard? Offering her work as his cleaner, maybe an attempt to *save her*, to clean her up? *And there was none to save her.* Perhaps he had an ulterior motive. With a history of predation, had she needed saving from him? Or had Hannah Mason discovered the deceit, and Sonia needed saving from her? The more he thought, though, the more it seemed Sonia Judd was past redemption, and whoever tried to save her last Friday failed.

'I'm interviewing the priest at St Dunstan's later, so I'll have a word. What about prints on the card?'

'Two sets,' said Ramesh. 'Mr Mason's and another set, as yet unidentified. Interestingly, the cleaner's business card, provided by Mrs Mason, also had the same set of unidentified fingerprints, along with Hannah Mason's and Andrew Mason's.'

'But not Sonia Judd's?'

Ramesh shook his head. 'Both the cleaner's card and Mr Mason's business card carried the same set of unidentified prints. There is also this.' Ramesh held up a second evidence bag. 'A single artificial hair, coloured auburn or light brown. Possibly from a wig.'

'Where did you find it?'

'It was in the crook of Mason's right elbow, protected by his leather jacket. Of course, it could have originated elsewhere, and given Sonia Judd's profession, even a previous visitor to her flat. So far, we've found nothing like it in the ruins, but if it's there…'

Whetstone recalled witnesses reporting that Judd wore a red, curly wig as part of her uniform. She'd get him to check out the staff at Stratham Motors for women matching the description while he was about it. The sort who might wear a synthetic wig and hand out business cards.

'What about the fentanyl?' asked Whetstone.

Ramesh pursed his lips and shook his head. 'A puzzler. I agree with Len that the second, more agricultural injection was to administer the fentanyl. We haven't found a second syringe, suggesting the killer removed it afterwards.'

He gestured towards his screen, then set about pouring coffee. 'The Fire Investigators have emailed over their preliminary report.'

Over Scott Daley's shoulder, Whetstone skim-read the report. There was little Ramesh had not already told them. The investigation concluded that, in addition to an up-to-date safety certificate, the landlord had kept all appliances adequately serviced and in good working order. Except for one burner on the cooker.

'An elastic band?' Daley was rarely surprised at the level of human ingenuity when it came to destruction.

Ramesh cocked his head. 'I suppose it would work. Turn on the control knob, loop the elastic band around it, and over the pan support. The tension depresses the knob, allowing gas to escape. Without someone clicking the igniter button, the room just filled with gas. At 1:00 am, the central heating timer operated, the piezoelectric pilot light sparked, and the gas ignited.'

'And they know this how?'

Ramesh gave another smirk, this time more patronising. 'Elastic bands are not made from rubber, but from a polymer called EPDM. They found traces burnt onto the knob and hob pan support.'

'And once the gas started escaping, how long…?'

'Methane is heavier than air, so would collect on the floor, even given some seepage between floorboards or under doors, an hour, maybe two, for the gas to build up. Once the air had a saturation of around fifteen per cent methane, even a scuffed toecap could ignite it. The explosion would be swift and extremely violent.'

'So they just sat and waited? I get impatient waiting for the football results.' Daley pictured the pair sitting in the upstairs flat as the air turned toxic and the timer edged nearer to 1:00 am. He pictured himself in the small hours drinking cocoa, watching the cooker clock, and shuddered.

'Technically, the woman was past waiting, but the man, yes.'

'And there's no way this was an accident?' Whetstone asked.

'I doubt it. When I cook on the hob, I rarely use an elastic band and I always light the gas. And I never need the central heating at 1:00 am. Someone deliberately defeated the failsafe on the hob and set the timer, then left the flat to fill with gas.'

'Murder then, Ramesh?'

'I do the *what* and *how*, Deb. You do the *why*.'

'And the amitriptyline and whisky Mason took?'

'We have found no fragments of glass with whisky on them, nor any signs of amitriptyline outside of his body.'

'So,' reflected Daley, 'They enter the flat. Judd turns left into the bedroom and overdoses. Mason turns right into the kitchen, drinks whisky laced with amitriptyline, and passes out. Then, Judd receives a massive dose of fentanyl from a syringe that disappears, but Mason does not. Meanwhile, the flat slowly fills with gas, and at 1:00 am, it explodes. I just don't see it, Harry.'

'Well, that's a puzzle for you two to work out. It seems strange, but people do stupid things when stressed. Who knows what goes through their heads?'

'With these two, it was a microwave oven and a dozen bricks.'

'Sick, Scott, sick - but funny.'

Chapter 8

Andrew Mason's two drinking buddies, Jacob Foster and Will Hughes, both worked in Pinner, at a property development firm called Stanford Clarke-Mitchell. Whilst Jacob Foster was free to meet them, Will Hughes had cried off sick that morning, so they drew lots. Whetstone would visit Foster at work, and Daley would visit Hughes as he swung the lead a mile further north.

Stanford Clarke-Mitchell occupied an unassuming three-storey redbrick block, shoehorned onto a minute plot of brownfield near the railway station in Pinner. Whetstone announced herself to a curt voice on the intercom and waited an age as a flimsy white barrier jerked upwards. Nosing her Golf along the rows of expensive status symbols, she couldn't help thinking the other man's grass was greener than that of a lowly police sergeant.

Directed to the lift, a slim, elegant woman met her and made her feel dowdy in her jacket and slacks. She followed as the pretty young thing sashayed through an office of boxy acoustic partitions, where around thirty staff beavered away, invisible except for tufts of hair poking above the top. Whetstone quipped to the slim woman about a fairground game with moles and a hammer, but she just stared back and gestured to an anonymous glass-fronted meeting room. She assured Whetstone Mr Foster would be along soon, and sashayed back between the partitions, turned left and bobbed down.

The meeting room was just large enough for two tables and half a dozen chairs. Panelled on three sides in the same shade of dour blue-grey as the rest of the top floor. The walls sported photographs of buildings Whetstone assumed were just there for show, or an ego trip to impress visitors. Through the flimsy partition wall, muted voices were engaged in a heated discussion, just too muffled to provide any entertainment. She looked at her watch and huffed. Long ago, Whetstone resolved she could not work in an office because it would drive her insane. Then she mused, she did, and maybe it had.

Presently, the hubbub ceased, and a slamming door shook the stud wall. A woman around Whetstone's age, face set to stormy, strode past, clasping a leather daybook as if her life depended upon it. Across the outer office, heads bobbed up and bobbed down again. Glad someone else was getting a bollocking, not them. Then a figure walked up to the door, peered through the glass for a moment, and eased down the handle. Whetstone got the distinct feeling that, in half a second, he had appraised her, judged even. The man's expression changed as he crossed the threshold; flicking to a genial warmth, like someone tapping a sticky barometer.

'Hi. Jacob Foster. You must be Sergeant - Whetstone?' His grip was firm, sending a jolt through her knuckles, laying down a marker from the outset. She did the same.

'Yes, sir. Detective Sergeant Deborah Whetstone, North West London Homicide Unit. I'm here about Andrew Mason. I believe you knew him?'

Foster was power-dressed in a gunmetal suit, sharper than a honed rapier. Tall, cropped brown hair, tanned, just the right amount of stubble covering his angular chin. Behind the smile, his deep brown eyes scanned her, and she felt a frisson of arousal. She had to remind herself not to judge the book by its cover, even if the cover was this attractive. She had shelves of beautiful books only partly read. Some she'd resolved never to read again.

'Homicide? I thought—' The permasmile thawed a little.

'Standard procedure in an unexplained death. At the moment, we are keeping an open mind.'

'Ah, I see.' Foster nodded and gave her a look he probably gave his staff when they tried to bullshit him. He sat opposite Whetstone, pulled the chair in tight and leaned forward, elbows on the table.

'I only have a few minutes, Sergeant.' He nodded back through the stud wall. 'Somebody else's mess to clear up.'

Whetstone smiled. 'Me too, unfortunately, but that's police work when someone dies.'

'Yes, of course.' Foster gave a contrite glance out into the office. 'I heard about Andy on the news. What on earth was he doing in Harrow?' No *oh, dear, how sad*. Not *how terrible*.

'I was hoping you might help us with that, sir. How well did you know him?'

'He's part of our Friday night drinks group.'

'And what sort of person was he?'

'A family man, living the dream. Fantastic house, a splendid wife and two lovely kids. Not a lifestyle I aspire to, though, Sergeant. I prefer to leave my options open, so to speak.'

But enough about you. 'Were you aware of any problems in his life? Financial or with his marriage?'

Foster shook his head. 'Now and again, he'd avoid buying a round.' He bobbed a matey chuckle. 'But then, I wouldn't say we were close friends. Apart from Friday nights…'

In Whetstone's head, a cock crowed, Foster already distancing himself from his deceased friend. *Nothing to do with me, officer. I wouldn't say we were close friends.* There were four types of friends. Those who showed genuine compassion and concern for their friends, the close ones. And those who showed concern - a sympathetic word or encouraging smile; outside of that, they didn't care too much. Then, there were those to whom the description *friend* was loose. Where the association was more an onus, as for an elderly neighbour, who was lovely but oh-so needy. Finally, some would throw a friend under a bus at the slightest provocation. Those who treated a friend as a commodity and discarded them when they were no longer of value.

'So, last Friday. The night out?'

Foster picked a spot in the air over Whetstone's left shoulder for his mental autocue.

'Yes, a regular thing. In Pinner. Me, Andy and Will Hughes - he's one of my project team.' Foster cast a hand towards the plebeian ranks of boxy cubicles. 'A chance to moan about work. *Misery loves company* and all that. We met up around six-thirty in *The Queen's Head*, had a pint, and then went along to *Blenheim's*. Typical guys' night out.'

Whetstone raised her eyebrows. *Blenheim's* was frequented by adolescents who thought they were adults, and adults who wished they were still adolescents, and neither looked good on it come midnight. Desperate singles out on the pull and sad singles who wished they were. Aeons ago, she'd sat in a corner, unable to understand why it was fun. Her friends danced off, copped off, and pissed off. She sloped off to a sleepless night of ringing ears. What on earth would Andrew Mason, a married man with two daughters, want in a place like that?

'But of course, Andy wasn't there - again.' Foster huffed. 'He'd phoned at lunchtime, one-ish maybe, to cancel. He said to carry on without him as something had come up.'

Whetstone made a note. It didn't matter. Steve Taylor would access Mason's phone records and isolate the call if it was there.

'And when did you and Mr Hughes leave?'

Foster's brow furrowed, affronted at the need to explain himself.

'Just for the record.' She gave a disarming smile.

'I left Will drinking at the bar around nine-thirty. I met this girl, Yvette someone.' He grinned. 'And we left an hour or so later.'

'And Mr Hughes?'

'No idea after nine-thirty. He and Andy hung around chatting until eleven, maybe eleven-thirty, but with Andy not there…wife waiting at home and all that.' Foster's shoulders bobbed. Was the display of harmless chauvinism for Whetstone's benefit, or was he just a dick?

'Do you have a number for - Yvette?'

Foster pulled out his mobile and passed across the number.

'And the previous nights out? When Andy came along?'

'Same as. Will and Andy would perv at the women and wish they hadn't got themselves hitched. Then they'd go home, and I'd stay and *socialise* a little.'

Yep, a dick.

'Earlier, you said, "Andy wasn't there, again". Did Andy cry off often, or was this a one-off?'

Foster's eyes flicked back out to the spot of nothing. 'Maybe once or twice a month. Around payday. House, wife and kids to support, I suppose. The shackles of marriage.'

Definitely a dick.

Still, would not Mason bridge any financial shortfall with plastic to keep up appearances? Unless employing Judd as his cleaner and visiting her as a prostitute was leaving him short.

'The other victim of the explosion was a woman called Sonia Judd. She rented the top-floor flat.' Whetstone pulled out a copy of Judd's PNC mugshot. 'I'm sorry, it's not the best photo.'

Foster craned over, screwed up his nose, and then glanced back to his spot of nothing. 'No. I heard the name on the news but I don't recognise her.'

'Ms Judd was a prostitute,' said Whetstone, in her best matter-of-fact voice, irked when Foster remained unmoved. 'To your knowledge, did Andy have a history of frequenting sex workers?'

Foster puffed like a steam valve, labouring for a long, considered moment. 'No idea,' he grunted. 'We might have been old friends, but we weren't joined at the hip, and anyway, it's his business.'

In Whetstone's mind, the cock crowed a second time; *old friends, but we weren't joined at the hip*. More distance wedged between himself and Mason. That's what friends are for, she mused. To let you wade into deep shit, hold their noses and walk away as your boots fill.

'My God! Does Hannah know?' Foster's eyes widened in somewhat insincere horror.

'I'm afraid she does.' She let the silence settle like a blanket of slurry on a spring field. Foster scratched his head, crossed to a water cooler and poured a plastic cup, offering it to Whetstone, then poured one for himself. To lubricate the gears meshing in his mind. Or just another part of the performance she was being subjected to?

'Andy called and said something had come up, but he didn't elaborate. If I'd known he was playing away, I might have intervened. It could have been anything, even something perfectly innocent. Maybe she was in trouble and he gave her a lift home. Or it was something to do with a car she was buying.'

Whetstone underlined the words. *Perfectly innocent, a car she was buying.* Almost the same words Hannah Mason had used. The briefing had been thorough.

Foster stopped, as if a lightbulb had come on in his head.

'There was a problem with a customer at work some time ago, but I thought that had all blown over. I didn't want to get involved, to be honest.'

Whetstone's cockerel crowed a third betrayal, cementing her opinion of Foster. A prize-winning dickhead. Yet, as arrogant, chauvinistic, cock-sure and treacherous as he may be, only the facts mattered. There would be a record of Mason's call to Foster, and they could check his alibi, as well as Mr Hughes's. Foster himself would be on CCTV at *Blenheim's*. And if the lovely Yvette was as forthcoming with her corroboration as she was with her favours, he had an alibi after midnight too.

'Thanks for your time, Mr Foster. That's been helpful.'

The pain washed from Foster's face; the condemned man who had watched the trapdoor lever jam. Whetstone closed her notebook, slid the pen into the elastic strap, and dropped it into her bag. She reached out to shake Foster's hand, holding it for a long time. She had not finished with him just yet.

Before setting out, both she and Daley had agreed to hold a single question back until the end of the interview. They called it a

Columbo moment, like in the TV show where the detective floors the suspect with a question they were not expecting. Daley had a *Mars bar* riding on the answer.

'Mrs Mason said you and Andy were part of a poker school?'

Foster's eyes flicked left and right, momentarily lost, but then he rallied. 'Ah, yes. Just an occasional thing. Andy, Will and me. Seven-Card Stud with a pot limit.'

Whetstone nodded. 'How often would you play?'

'Oh, once, maybe twice a month, round my place. It's nothing. A few beers and a few rounds of cards. To be fair, Andy was crap. We needed a pot limit to save him from himself.'

'And when was the last time?'

Foster fidgeted, eager to escape, like a man with an urgent need to urinate. 'Maybe a month ago, I can't be sure. Look, I must be getting back. Fire fighting to do. Boss is always tetchy when she doesn't get her own way.'

***

Will Hughes's house in Pinner was a modest two-up, two-down, not unlike Number 5 Green Street, but there the similarity ended. Better maintained, hanging baskets round the door, better cars parked out front. Less tired, less decayed, and less seedy, and it still had all its walls and a roof. Scott Daley took a breath and raised a hand to the doorbell, jumping as the door opened, leaving his arm hanging, as a woman stepped back and smiled sympathetically.

'Oh, hello.' She was tugging a tan overcoat over a smart blouse and trousers. Dark hair cut short in a boyish style that didn't appeal to Daley. She lowered her head and examined him over her spectacles. 'Sorry, but we don't buy or sell anything, or discuss religion or politics on the doorstep, but thanks for calling.'

She made to close the door, but Daley thrust out a hand and flipped open his warrant card.

'Chief Inspector Scott Daley, Metropolitan Police, here to see Will Hughes?'

Caught off guard, the woman's mouth flapped, as her mind rattled through the list of minor misdemeanours for which the police would need to hunt her down. Warrant cards had that effect, but she regrouped.

'That was quick. He only reported it yesterday.'

Daley looked confused, the woman clarified. 'Someone nicked the bike, his silly moped thingy, last Friday.'

'No, ma'am. I'm from the North West London Homicide Unit.'

'Homicide?' The woman grimaced. 'Not about the bike, then - unless someone killed the angry wasp in the teeny-tiny engine?' She turned and called back down the hall. 'Will, put away the porn and do up your fly. The Feds are here. Come through.'

Daley followed her along a short, magnolia corridor and into an airy front room, modern, stark and bare. Wood-floored and empty of all but a pair of two-seater sofas, a standard lamp, a monumental TV set, and a two-metre-wide canvas of Manhattan. A millennial's wet dream. Except for Will Hughes himself, prostrate on the sofa, wallowing in a carpet of crumbs, holding a beer and watching football. Still, there were no mucky magazines, and he didn't appear to have been masturbating. In Daley's experience, Italian football can be quite sexy at times, but it had never driven him that far. Hughes hastily muted the TV and swung his legs onto the floor, brushing off debris, much to his partner's disgust.

'You'd better hoover that lot up before the nice police officer hauls you off to the nick, because I'm not. And ask him if he wants tea or coffee. Good manners might get you a shorter sentence. I'm off out now.' And then the front door rattled, and she was gone.

Daley cocked a sympathetic smile, recalling his first wife, relieved she was now history. 'Chief Inspector Scott Daley, North-West London Homicide. How are we feeling, sir? Nothing serious, I hope?' He gestured towards the empty sofa and, without waiting, dropped himself into it.

'No, just a jippy stomach. So, do you want tea or coffee?'

Hughes was short, wiry rather than athletic, shoulders stooped as if an invisible yoke carried the weight of the world. One-day-old stubble clouded his dark skin, merging into the tight cornrows across his scalp. Behind black-rimmed spectacles, tired brown eyes scanned Daley guiltily, as if he'd been caught out. Or maybe it was his default look. Like he was awaiting a diagnosis of the clap, or redundancy without severance. Or maybe worse.

Daley waved a hand. 'My bladder's not what it used to be, but don't let me stop you.'

'I've got a beer, thanks.'

So much for the jippy tummy. 'I'm investigating the incident in Green Street, Harrow. I believe you knew Andrew Mason?'

Hughes nodded and puffed his cheeks. 'Homicide? So, you think someone murdered Andy?'

Daley smiled. 'At this stage, we're treating it as a suspicious death, sir, to cover all bases.'

Hughes relaxed back and folded a leg under his lap. 'I only met Andy when I joined SCM three months ago. Jake - Jacob Foster, my boss - invited me out on a regular Friday drinks night. Male bonding, that sort of thing. Andy was there, maybe once a month.'

'Once a month? What he did the rest of the time?'

Hughes shook his head. 'He's in car sales. They have evening events at the showroom, so sometimes he works late. He also ran the kids to dancing or something.'

'So last Friday? What were your movements, just to eliminate you from our enquiries, you know...' Daley smiled. *Male bonding, that sort of thing.*

'I got home at five-thirty. Abi, my partner, was already in. We shared takeout, and I left at about six-thirty. I met Jake in *The Queen's Head* and he told me Andy had phoned him earlier in the day to say he couldn't come.'

Poor choice of words given who he was visiting when he died. 'Did Mr Foster say why?'

'No, Jake was a little annoyed, but we had another drink and that was it.' Hughes glanced at the TV, afraid of missing something, but Daley had seen the game and knew he wasn't.

'Okay, so you gave up on Andy. What then?'

'Around quarter-to-seven, we moved on to *Blenheim's*. We were just old guys, window-shopping in a bar full of half-cut women on a Friday. I know it's not PC, but it's what men do. At half-nine, Jake went off on the pull. If Andy was there, we would slope off when we got bored, back to *The Queen's Head* for a quick one before going home. Sometimes we bought a kebab or chips…but as Andy wasn't there, I just called a taxi. I was home by half-past nine.'

'And Jake?'

'Who knows? Monday morning, he was bragging about some girl he took home. Yvonne or someone.'

'Did you see Andy any other time, apart from Friday nights?'

'Not really. We chopped our old Fiat Panda in for the Passat we have now. Andy said he would find us a decent motor, and I reckon he swung us a good deal. High spec, low mileage.'

Once a salesman, always a salesman. Daley's ex-wife, Lynne, once met a chap in the newsagents and ended up with a £3,000 stainless steel vacuum cleaner. He sold her every attachment one could think of, a few one never would, and a couple Daley would have shoved up the salesman's backside. But enough of the chitchat and on to grittier matters. Daley pulled up Judd's mugshot on his phone and handed it across.

'The other victim, Sonia Judd. Do you know her?'

Hughes grimaced and shook his head. 'The prostitute? Her picture was on the local news, but I don't know her. I'm not into that sort of thing. Abi would have my balls for, er, she wouldn't approve.'

'And Andy? Did he ever give the impression he was interested in that sort of thing?'

Hughes pulled the face again. 'I got the impression he was happily married.'

'So why do you think he was in Harrow?' Daley made a bet with himself about what Hughes would say. He won.

'It was probably a work thing. He was always tying up deals, or maybe he was helping a friend.' Hughes took a drink of his beer and pointed the neck at Daley. 'There was this one time when Andy and I had gone back to *The Queen's Head*. He had his arse in his hands, so I asked him what was wrong. Some trouble at work, he said. He'd taken a woman out to test-drive a convertible. She bought the car but later she complained he'd touched her up while helping her on with the seatbelt. Work wasn't too happy about the allegations and he was thinking of quitting the job.'

'Did you believe him, Mr Hughes?'

'I don't know the full circumstances, so who am I to judge?'

Who indeed, thought Daley, but still we all do. Right now, he was judging Will Hughes, and his eyes and his demeanour suggested he was telling the truth - at least as he saw it. Some people have a flair for lying; so often it becomes second nature, weaving an alternate universe to house the lies, to construct an alternate truth. Hughes fell into the category of the rest, where lying created a house of cards which could tumble with the simplest of challenges. His eyes confirmed he was as transparent as his excuse for pulling a sickie.

'Do you think Andy envied Jake?' Daley asked. 'Single, not tied down. Do you think he missed the single life?'

'Don't we all occasionally and I'm not even married!'

Daley understood the instinctive pleasure derived from ogling women of any age, any background. Their shape, their clothes, faces, hair, their smiles. Non-threatening, non-sexual, just looking. Too often, it developed into something more. Fixation, obsession, possession. Was that what happened between Judd and Mason?

Daley put away his notebook and stretched out a hand. 'That's been helpful, Mr Hughes. I trust we can call on you again if we need to clarify anything?'

'I'm not sure what else I can…'

Daley smiled at the metaphorical step backwards. 'In my game, you never know,' he said. 'Just a courtesy, that's all.' Then he remembered his wager of a *Mars bar* with Whetstone.

'Just one more thing. Did you ever join in the poker school?' He watched as Hughes remembered the cover story.

Hughes's brow furrowed. 'Poker? Cards aren't for me.'

Daley could almost taste the caramel, toffee and thick, thick chocolate.

Chapter 9

The next morning, Jake Foster drew his car into his reserved spot outside Stanford Clarke-Mitchell. He sat for a moment to collect his thoughts, which, over ten hours of interrupted sleep, had been only about Andy Mason. Foster had expected the police to call. After all, Mason should have been out drinking with him and Will Hughes at the time. Yet nothing had prepared him for the full, lurid story of Green Street. He had never imagined his friend to be *that* kind of guy.

He left his car and winced as Will Hughes's Passat pulled up across the gates, and the cretin waved goodbye to his missus before strolling over.

'Ah, Will, fit and well, I see?' Foster could not hide his sarcasm.

'Well, you know.' Hughes was kicking the gravel as he tried to match Foster's large strides towards the front doors. 'What about Andy Mason, eh? The police came to see me yesterday. At home!'

'Me too, Will.' He swiped his keycard and held the door open as the shorter man skipped through beneath his arm.

'What the hell was he doing in Harrow? And in Green Street of all places. Just a row of brothels, isn't it?'

'Is it? You and I must move in very different circles.'

If Hughes had blushed, his dark complexion disguised it. Of course, it was common knowledge what went on in Green Street. Squalid terraces, easy women and seedy men. But Andy Mason? Respectable, a wife and kids, a sensible car, a good job and a house in the suburbs. Boring even, or at least that's the impression he gave. Maybe Hannah had withheld conjugals. Foster had heard that's what happened in marriages; they became stale and loveless, but then, marriage was not for him. Women came to him, and when they did, he always *sent* them away satisfied. *Treat 'em mean and keep 'em keen.*

'What a dark horse. Maybe neither of us knew him as well as we thought.' Hughes tapped the lift button and stared up at the illuminated number as if that would help the car descend faster. Once the lift doors sealed their confessional, he continued. 'So, last Friday, when he called to cry off, what did he say?'

'Oh, he explained it all. *Jake, can you cover for me? Love to join you lads, but I'm going to be balls deep in some tart before being blown to smithereens.*'

'Really?'

'Of course not. He said something had come up.'

'…too right it had.' Hughes raised his eyebrows. He was taking this all too frivolously. But then he hadn't known Mason as long as Foster had. There wasn't the shared experience, the shared history, shared secrets.

'He just asked me to cover for him. Look, Will, the lad's night is an informal arrangement. If any of us want to cry off - for whatever reason - we are not each other's keepers, and if anyone asks, that's what you say.'

'Yeah,' said Hughes, 'but aren't you just a *little* curious? A happily married man, found dead in a knocking shop? Well, in the backyard of one. The tabloids will have a field day. If Abi ever found out I was up to anything like that…'

'So don't tell her. When you get blown up, she'll know soon enough when some grubby-coated city hack turns up with a notebook and a Nikon.'

Still, Mason was not yet cold, and there was a definite smell of crap. The sort that rubbed off on other people. In Foster's view, doing someone a favour was like dropping your trousers and presenting your backside ready for a good kick. When Andy had phoned, asking for discretion, Foster had agreed, and not for the first time. In the space of two months, it seemed as if Andy had pressed the self-destruct button. Imaginary poker nights, fictitious football matches, even the Friday drinks nights he had skipped. There were more excuses than genuine attendances. But hookers? Hughes was right. Mason was a dark horse. Trotting out pre-prepared stories about work, or lads' nights and, all the time, playing away with a tart.

As the lift door opened onto the depressing field of tiny cubicles of woe, Foster glanced across at Sam Clarke-Mitchell's office in the far corner, and his heart sank further. The boss was in, and his misery was complete.

'Anyway, enough of this tittle-tattle, you idle bastard. Toddle off to your prison cell and sort me out an update on Bayhurst Grange. Ten o'clock, my office and bring coffee, the decent stuff, not the crap from the machine in the corridor.'

Foster's heart skipped a beat. Andy Mason, Green Street and Bayhurst Grange. It couldn't be a coincidence.

Stanford Clarke-Mitchell was a step up for Foster: a decent package, an executive car and a generous pension. The company was going places, and he would go with it, and, for a while, it lived up to the interview hype. Until Sam Clarke-Mitchell set her sights on Bayhurst Grange. It was the mast on which she had pinned her colours, her *cause célèbre*, her obsession. An innocuous Edwardian pile, nestled in the crook of the M25 and M40 motorways, a stone's throw from the hub of the UK film industry at Pinewood. Her dream was an upmarket senior citizen's complex. An idyllic later years retreat for those who wouldn't stray far enough from their gilded cages. And the real money spinners - the golf course, sports centre and private health clinic. If handled correctly, the rich old dears could fund the project, while the rest could bring in the real bucks if shielded from the aroma of lavender and urine.

Of all the properties she could have chosen, it had to be Bayhurst Grange. Of all people to die in suspicious circumstances, it had to be Andy Mason.

Closing his office blinds, he fired up his computer, reread the BBC London report and felt the same goosebumps.

House in Green Street, Harrow, destroyed in a suspected gas explosion. The two victims named as Sonia Judd, 23, who lived at the property, and Andrew Philip Mason, 34, a motor salesman from Ruislip. Police and fire officers are still trying to establish the cause of the tragedy...

Green Street. Of all places for Andy to die.

Hannah Mason had called around 6:30 am on Saturday, in hysterics, babbling about an accident. Andy had been killed. Foster had made all the right noises, asked about the kids, and promised he would help her. Then, at midday, less than twelve hours later, he received the text, and his blood ran cold.

Stop the Bayhurst Grange redevelopment or you will follow Andrew Mason.

An anonymous number, an anonymous sender. A burner phone, the American cop shows called them. Untraceable, bought for one purpose and dumped. Someone had linked Andrew Mason and Bayhurst Grange - and him.

But why now? It was so long ago, he'd forgotten - almost. Then, the sidebar on the web page in front of him drew his attention. A separate headline confirmed it was no coincidence.

Local anger as Bayhurst Woods Beast released.

For the first time since that September night, twenty years ago, Jake Foster felt the chill of utter helplessness. There was a perfect storm brewing, greater than the sum of its parts.

***

He looked up as the glass of the door rang and Will Hughes reversed through, coffee mugs in hand. He twitched his computer mouse to dismiss the web page and flicked to his calendar.

'So, Will, Bayhurst Grange. How's it going?'

Hughes placed the coffees down and sat. 'The preliminary surveys are good, the plans and initial costings are all in, and the proposal has received outline acceptance from the county council. We are ready to roll. We just need your go-ahead.'

'Okay, I'll look it over in the next couple of days.'

Will Hughes's jaw dropped. 'Days? You heard Sam yesterday. If we don't get this project moving, she'll tear someone a new one. Can't you look at it sooner?'

'I said, leave it with me. I'll speak to Sam. Now, what about the Eden Park housing development?'

As Hughes began speaking, Foster was not listening. The only project that interested him was Bayhurst Grange. Hughes was right. There was only so long he could hold Sam off, and soon, they would uncover *his* delaying tactics.

He'd told the police detective, Andy had called crying off the drinks night. No, he did not know why he was in a brothel. And his own movements? Yes, he had left Hughes at the bar and he had met Yvette, but he had spent very little of the night with her. So, he'd been economical with the truth; it didn't make him a murderer. Not on its own, anyway. What he had failed to tell her was he and Andy Mason went way back. Right back to school, in fact. Mason was the wimpy kid Foster had saved from a beating, and who clung to him like shit on a toilet bowl for the next nine years. But she was a *homicide* detective, and if she started delving into his alibi? If she started delving into his past...?

Mason was there twenty years ago. He saw it all. As someone once said, *three may keep a secret if two of them are dead.* Now one was. After twenty years of pushing the problem under the carpet, now he had run out of time. Bayhurst Grange was where the problem lay. They had earmarked every inch of the grounds for one development or another, and the outlying acres for a tournament-spec golf course and the amenities it deserved. But when the diggers broke ground, they might turn up more than they bargained for, leading them straight back to him, and a solid motive for Andy's murder.

Maybe it was time to deal with the problem once and for all.

Chapter 10

Tuesday was always the worst day of the week. Still reeling from the shell shock of Monday, with the balance of the week still ahead. In *Bilko Bob's* day, Scott Daley always tried to find an enquiry to keep him out of the Super's immediate eye line, or a field trip to harass a potential suspect. Superintendent Hacker, however, insisted on Tuesday to hold her catch-up. *Catch out*, more likely. A torturous couple of hours to highlight all his failings and side-step around any successes, pointing out that even those came at a painful cost to the departmental budget. She had booked today's debacle for 1:00 pm and Daley was eager to thwart her by demonstrating some progress on Operation Scion, but they had made none. Hannah Mason was still under investigation. A big house, a decent car, and money coming in. Maybe she was content to turn a blind eye until he brought it home with him. Sonia Judd, Mason's mistress, in Hannah's home, right under her nose. Daley found it hard to believe Friday, the day the affair ended abruptly, was the first time Hannah knew of it for certain. Yet there was still no evidence of her involvement in her husband's death.

With their accounts being strikingly similar, Hannah, Jacob Foster, and Willson Hughes had spoken before being interviewed. The nonsense about a sale, or helping a person in need. Maybe it was one of several prepared alibis when one of the lads needed to be elsewhere. Perhaps Hannah had repeated what Foster had said to her, but who was to know, right? Yet last Friday, a rapid expansion of natural gas had left Mason high and dry, and his friends with a problem, so they reeled off the story and clammed up. Nothing to do with us, officer, nothing to see here. The card school? Hogwash but, again, no evidence of their involvement.

So, what had happened?

Daley ran an eye along the timeline on the Incident Board, stretching from 7:00 pm on Friday to 2:00 am on Saturday. Judd returned home around 7:20 pm. Ten minutes later, she left, returning on foot with Mason at 8:00 pm. Another half hour and she left without him. Where did she go?

Despite the array of photos and scribbled annotations, there was still not enough; too many grey areas, but then, what was he expecting after three days?

Behind him, the blue swing doors squealed. Superintendent Leslie Hacker scanned the team room, purposefully turning her watch to check the date, the hour, and the millisecond with a tacit command for him to follow her into the Goldfish Bowl. As he latched the door and the hubbub of the team room gave way to an uneasy silence, she placed herself in Daley's chair, like someone trying to avoid patches of bird crap on a park bench.

'How's the Homicide in Domestic Violence report coming along?'

'On it, as we speak,' he lied. He had yet to write a single syllable. 'Our chief priority is Operation Scion.' Daley lowered himself into the Throne of Doom, dismayed to be back on that side of the desk, recalling how uncomfortable it was.

'About that,' she began. 'One of the tabloids has got wind that we are investigating it as a potential homicide. I need to give them something to stop them from making it up.' She reached down and played with the levers under Daley's chair, raising it to a position of superiority and destroying hours of effort from Daley. There were no similar levers on the Throne of Doom.

'Tell them, ma'am, the case is ongoing and we are following up several lines of inquiry.'

'I'm thinking of having that printed on your business card.'

'What, ma'am, no reference to a pithy bible quote?'

She stared blankly for a moment. Daley wondered whether she had read the briefing notes. Then she rallied.

An Invisible Murder

'Frankly, I am concerned about the lack of progress. *Ongoing* is not helpful when speaking to Assistant Chief Constable Fraser.'

The name dropped so heavily that Daley wriggled his toes to check for injury. After the previous ACC, Diane Browning had disgraced herself, Vic Fraser took the hospital pass of steadying the ship. A veritable sergeant-major of a man, they were all assured he would weed out troublemakers and jettison the dead wood. To date, he had weeded out new furniture for his office in Hillingdon and jettisoned some 1960s deal chairs.

'I am sure he understands the complexities, ma'am. As an experienced officer—'

'—Operation Scion,' she parried. 'Help *me* understand. A prostitute and a car salesman go into a house in Harrow, and the house explodes.' Daley stifled a snicker. It could still be a decent joke under different circumstances. 'What have the Gas Board said?'

'Nothing formal, ma'am. Their preliminary report shows nothing wrong with the supply. The Fire Investigation Team is confident the explosion happened house-side of the meter. Forensics suggest someone turned on a gas ring, allowing gas to build up and explode when the central heating pilot light ignited.'

'An accident?' Hacker sounded relieved. 'Or death by misadventure or sheer stupidity? Someone trying to be clever with the cooker?'

Daley shook his head. 'They defeated the cooker knob with an elastic band and set the timer to one in the morning. Few people set the timer to heat the house while they are asleep.'

Leslie Hacker, though, was not to be defeated. 'A sex worker, though? She must keep odd hours.' She was clutching at straws to preserve her budget. Still, the notion hadn't occurred to Daley. Never underestimate the power of guesswork. Even idiots get lucky sometimes.

'And,' he continued, 'I don't think Mason was a customer of Judd's. I think—'

'—Not a customer?' Hacker stared open-mouthed for a

moment of theatre. 'He picked her up in town and walked with her back to her *brothel.*'

Daley hoped she didn't use that kind of language in her tabloid briefings. 'It's not quite that simple, ma'am.' But, as far as the Press was concerned, it was. A prostitute and a car salesman go into a house in Harrow, and the house explodes. It sold copy.

'So, tell me how simple it is. What is *your* take?' Hacker lowered her glasses on her nose and settled back for the yarn.

'Murder, ma'am.'

'What? Both of them?' A few more zeros popped onto her bottom line.

'As well as heroin, Judd's bloodstream contained a lethal dose of fentanyl which we have yet to account for. Mason was rendered unconscious by amitriptyline hydrochloride, again unaccounted for. Admittedly, Mason could have taken his own life having murdered Judd, but what did he do with the syringe he used on her? And why rig the explosion to happen after both he and Judd were dead?'

Hacker leaned back, rested her chin on her steepled fingers, and rose to the challenge. 'Maybe he was covering his suicide? An insurance scam?'

Daley gave a cursory shake of the head. 'As soon as Ramesh found the drugs, that was out. Mason would have leapt off a bridge or stepped in front of a train, and nothing suggested he was suicidal.'

'Ah, I forgot, you have experience of being hit by trains. So you think they were *both* murdered? By whom?'

Daley could almost see a spreadsheet of numbers reeling across her eyeballs as the cost escalated from a fairly inexpensive accident to a stratospheric murder enquiry.

'Too early to say, ma'am. There are too many loose ends. We should have a clearer picture by the end of the day.'

'Well, I sincerely hope so, though I won't be holding my breath.'

More's the pity, thought Daley.

An Invisible Murder

***

After Hacker had ridden her broomstick back to Scotland Yard, Daley took a coffee to the Goldfish Bowl and closed the blinds. Down on Lambourne Road, rush hour was in full flow. Both *rush* and *flow* were ironic, as traffic was going nowhere. Across the road, a delivery van straddled the kerb outside the mini-mart, added to the gridlock. An athletic Asian man in a blue gilet hefted boxes onto a sack truck. If only police work was as simple as following a docket, loading boxes and pushing a truck, without the caustic breath of one's manager on one's neck, or the ever-present fear of failure.

He turned back to his portable whiteboard, purloined from the Drugs Team as they moved out. His musings looked like a map of the Underground before Harry Beck did his magic. He wished the great man were here now, to straighten the kinks and colour-code the pathways. Looking up as knuckles rapped almost apologetically on the glass door, he saw Jane Morris tentatively poking her head around the frame.

'You got a minute, sir?'

Daley waved her in and watched her lower herself gingerly into the Throne of Doom as if lowering herself into a bathtub full of thistles.

'How's it between you and Sergeant Whetstone today?'

Morris fidgeted and looked down. 'Alright, sir. I'm sorry.'

'These things happen in a charged environment like a Murder Team. What is important is how you move forward. Now, what can I do for you?'

'Oliver Mansell, the old man injured outside Number 5 Green Street? I've just visited him in the hospital. He has a fractured skull and a broken arm, and they are keeping him in to give him a new hip. They reckon he'll be in for another month or so, at least. He's missing his dog.'

Daley had forgotten about the dog. He wasn't a fan of pets himself; he preferred a house that didn't smell of canine body odour. His parents owned a dog when he was growing up. Walking the damn thing was one of his chores to earn his pocket money. At least in those days, you could leave the crap where the dog laid it. None of this messing about with an absurdly small plastic sack, walking down the street with a stinking trophy hanging off an extended finger.

'Did they ever find it?'

'Sir. Under the rubble. Anyway, I spoke to him about the incident. He had been to the mini-mart and was walking round the corner into Green Street when a couple passed him and crossed over towards the churchyard. He said hello, but they were in a hurry, heads down and ignored him.'

So many people had been about that night, Daley wondered if they'd added a new Tube stop to the Metropolitan line. 'Did he give a description?'

'The woman was of medium height, wearing a long coat and a curly red wig. He described the man as medium height with dark hair.'

Daley pondered for a moment. 'So, shortly before the explosion, Mansell saw a couple matching the description of Sonia Judd and Andy Mason, entering Green Street and crossing into the churchyard. Yet we know that moments later, they were inside the house when the explosion occurred. Could Mansell be mistaken? Head wound, concussion and all?'

'I suppose, sir, but we chatted about lots of other things. He seemed pretty lucid to me. He remembered the mini-mart; the shopkeeper spoils him with short-dated food to make sure he gets fed. He bought a paper. He remembered the headline and many other details. The perfume his wife used to wear - Yardley English Rose. He also said after the explosion he saw the same man under the lychgate in the churchyard, watching. He asked him for help but the man ignored him.'

Daley got up and crossed to the window. The delivery man was closing up the van, checking the traffic before returning to his cab. For the first time, Daley realised it was not the usual man. They all looked the same to Daley - not Asian men, but delivery drivers. We notice what attracts our attention and most of them pass by without a second glance. A notion occurred to him, and everything he'd thought about Operation Scion shifted sideways. He checked his watch. Time was marching on and the team would leave soon, unless he could persuade them to stay.

'This is good work, Jane. Give me half an hour to redraw this crap,' he cast a scornful hand at the portable whiteboard, 'then ask everyone to gather in the briefing area, will you?'

Chapter 11

'Sam, do you have a minute?'

Jake Foster snaked himself through the doorway as Sam Clarke-Mitchell looked up from her computer screen and sighed.

'Ah, Jake, I'm never going to get this bloody bid through. It's one thing after another with Bayhurst Grange, and Will Hughes has forgotten to print the contractor contingency plan again.'

'It's there somewhere because I saw it myself this morning.' Foster returned a reassuring smile, though he knew she wouldn't find it. He had removed it himself before distribution.

His eyes followed her as she walked over to a leather sofa, crossing her legs as she sat. She was undoubtedly attractive, with high cheekbones, feline eyes, and a narrow jaw and lips. White blouse, black jacket and knee-length skirt, parting to reveal endless legs honed on the cross-trainer. She was not Foster's type, though. Too headstrong, and when it came to empathy and compassion, the well was dry. Sam Clarke-Mitchell was as cold and self-centred as he was himself.

Five years ago, a colossal heart attack had felled Hugh Clarke-Mitchell, and Sam, his public-school-bred, socialite daughter, inherited the millstone that was Stanford Clarke-Mitchell. To her credit, she had reinvented the company, dragging it out of the Middle Ages. Foster admired her drive and her persistence, her imagination and, most of all, her bullishness. What she wanted, she got - and there lay the problem, as she wanted Bayhurst Grange, and who could blame her? Long derelict, the estate was a steal and a blank canvas on which to fulfil her dreams.

'I've told you, you're being overambitious.' SCM would carry the debt for at least a decade, even after the huge profits they would make, but that was all just business. The problem was Bayhurst Grange itself.

She widened her arms at the surrounding office. 'Do you think SCM would have survived this long if my father hadn't been ambitious?'

'Yes, but, Sam, the economic climate was very different, and you've invested everything and more into Bayhurst Grange. Remember Icarus and Daedalus, what happened when the son didn't heed the father's example?'

She stared open-mouthed. 'I bloody knew you'd say that - but honestly, quoting Greek myth?' She reached across and wrung the neck of a water bottle, snapping the seal on the screw top. As she poured two glasses, she paused.

'I want you to let Will Hughes go. Hardly a day goes by without something going tits-up, and it's usually down to him, so he has to go.'

Foster feigned concern. He had spent many hours digging traps for Hughes to fall into, and the fool had obliged each time. And now, at last, his efforts were paying off. The Bayhurst Grange bid would fail, and Hughes would take the fall. On the other hand, if Hughes went now, there was always the risk Sam might turn things around and his efforts would be wasted. Perhaps Foster should delay his removal for another few days, organise a few more traps, and guarantee the failure of the project.

'No, Sam, sacking him would put us back weeks. Just hold off until the bid is in delivery.' Then he added, 'I'll keep a personal eye on him, I promise.'

'Everyone wants to tell me how to run SCM. It's my fucking company, Jake, and I want Bayhurst Grange.' She bounced a fist off the desk. 'Success or failure, it's *my* problem, and if you're not fully on board, then maybe I should let you go too?'

For a long moment, he fixed his gaze on her. Below her left eye, a nerve ticked. He'd noticed it before; it was her tell, a sign of her weakness. An unconscious plea for him to step in and make it all go away.

'Come on, Sam. Sacking everyone will not bring you Bayhurst Grange, but I agree, Will Hughes has become a liability. I'll get rid of him and bring the project back on track. Just leave it with me for a few more days.'

Enough time to hide the secret of Bayhurst Grange forever.

***

When Foster peered over the acoustic screen, Will Hughes was in his cubicle, oblivious to the guano about to drop.

'Will, we need to talk. With me - now.'

He waited while Hughes sighed and stood up from his chair. They walked to a small booth office tucked in the corner, as far as possible from Sam's lair without falling out of a window. As the door wheezed shut and the automatic lights blinked into action, and without waiting for Hughes to get comfortable, he wielded the axe.

'I'm sorry to tell you, Will, but we have decided to terminate your contract with immediate effect. Today will be your last day.'

Hughes's brow furrowed as he processed the statement. 'I - I… Really? You must be joking.'

'If only. Sam and I spoke earlier. I tried to convince her it was a mistake, but the contractor contingency report was the last straw.'

Hughes shot upright. 'No, she's wrong! I distinctly remember putting it in.' His voice had raised a couple of octaves, like he'd caught his genitalia in his fly-zip. 'I made five copies and compiled the packs, and I had none left. It must have been there!' Hughes shot an angry finger across at the tinted windows of Sam's office. 'Ha! I notice she didn't deliver the bad news in person. I'm going to have this out with her right now. This is so grossly unfair.'

Foster grabbed Hughes's arm as he made for the door. 'Whoa, Will. You'll only make matters worse.'

Hughes shrugged Foster off and threw himself back in his

chair. 'If anything, it's your bloody fault. I've been telling you for weeks we needed to get the bid moving. So, just what didn't *I* do? Where did *I* foul up? Who was she ranting at in the meeting yesterday? You, Jake, so why isn't it you walking?'

'She's highly strung, Will, you know that—'

'She bloody well should be. Bitch!'

Foster sighed and looked theatrically at the ceiling. 'Go home and let me talk to her. I am sure we can resolve this.'

As Hughes stormed back to his desk, Foster felt a tinge of guilt, though only a tinge. Sam blew hot and cold. After a few days, the bid would recover, she would come around, and she would have forgotten Will Hughes's dismissal. He'd even throw in some comment about borrowing her copy of the contractor contingency report and forgetting to replace it. *Mea culpa*. Though perhaps not Latin. The Greek myth had gone down like Icarus into the Aegean.

Still, there was work to be done on Bayhurst Grange before any of that could happen.

Chapter 12

Too much caffeine was making Daley's forehead prickle, but at least the portable whiteboard looked less like an explosion in a knitwear factory. The team grabbed notepads and mugs and gathered around the Incident Board. Though he would never tell them to their faces, lest they become complacent, he admired their work ethic and determination to solve the case. It was a police thing; coppers never knew when they were beaten.

Taylor parked the portable board alongside its larger counterpart. It carried a rough drawing of Green Street, stretching from Mrs Kelly's at Number 1, where it joined Sefton Street, and past Number 9, where Mrs Livingstone enjoyed her smoke. Towards the bottom, a wire wool of blue pen denoted the boundary with St Dunstan's churchyard. As the hubbub died down, and the butterflies in his stomach began dancing, Daley took a breath.

'Let's go back to last Friday around 6:30 pm. Sonia Judd arrived home, wearing the long coat and red curly wig she wore when she was on the game, which is why the neighbours noticed.'

Daley drew dots, lines and times on his map.

'At 7:30 pm, she left the flat and walked into town to meet Andrew Mason, both returning at 8:00 pm, presumably for sex. Around 8:30 pm, Judd left the flat again and crossed into the churchyard alone. First, forensic evidence suggests Mason and Judd had not engaged in sexual intercourse. So what was he doing in her flat? Second, why would she leave him there and wander off through the churchyard? Then, at 10:45 pm, Judd and Mason crossed from Number 5 to the churchyard. How could that be? According to forensics, Judd was already dead and Mason was incapacitated. Finally, just before 1:00 am, Oliver Mansell saw Judd and Mason crossing into the churchyard, then after the explosion he saw Mason watching from the lychgate. Yet we know from forensic evidence Judd and Mason were inside the flat, either dead or comatose, or blown to pieces. So who were these people? Okay, Mansell may be mistaken. He's old and concussed. Mrs Livingstone or Mrs Kelly might also have got their facts a little muddled, but all three? They were all certain the people they saw were Judd and Mason, but what if they were *all* wrong? What if they saw Judd and Mason because that's what someone intended them to see? A man dressed in black and a woman wearing a long coat and curly red wig.'

Daley paused, expecting some fanfare of faint praise for his leap of deduction, but none came. At three in the afternoon, what could he expect? Instead, he grabbed a red marker and set about ruining his freshly drawn map.

'The only way any of this makes sense is if the two people we have been assuming are Judd and Mason are someone else. Judd wore her trademark coat and wig, but anyone could have worn those and been mistaken for her. And the man? As long as he can pass for Mason in the dark…so, here's a different take.

'Sonia arrives back at 6:30 pm. She goes upstairs with her fix and ODs. She never leaves the flat again under her own steam. Someone else is already in the flat. Let's call her *Female A*. She kills Judd with fentanyl, then dresses in the wig and coat, and goes to bring Mason back to the flat. The neighbours assume they see Sonia Judd. Once back in the flat, *Female A* takes Mason into the kitchen and laces his drink, hence the whisky and amitriptyline. Mason loses consciousness and remains in the flat until the explosion.'

'Sir?' Daley swivelled on his heel as Whetstone spoke. 'That would mean *Female A* knew both Judd and Mason, to enter Judd's flat, and to walk back arm in arm with Mason. The cleaner? If she called herself *Sonia Judd,* then she probably knew Judd.'

Daley nodded. He crossed to the Incident Board and linked the cleaner to Judd, adding the words *knew each other.*

'So,' he continued, 'Judd was dead and Mason unconscious in

the flat, where they stayed until the explosion. As yet, the gas wasn't yet on, which is why no one smelled it. *Female A* crossed to the churchyard and left by the back gate. My guess is she was creating an alibi.' He watched their eyes as he drew the new lines across his diagram.

'Sir. Why wait?' asked DC Taylor. 'If both Judd and Mason were incapacitated by 8:30 pm, why not set the explosion then and leave? Surely it wouldn't matter if the explosion took place at ten o'clock or one o'clock, and they were taking a massive risk by returning.'

Daley shrugged. 'I guess so early in the evening, someone might have noticed the gas escaping and prevented the explosion? So they waited until most people had gone to bed. Anyway, at 10:45, *Female A* returned, still dressed in the coat and wig, this time with a male accomplice - *Male B* - to rig the explosion before leaving. Mrs Kelly again mistakenly saw Judd and a punter. Around a quarter-to-eleven, Mrs Kelly saw the pair cross back through the churchyard.'

Daley added *Female A* and *Male B* to the Incident boards.

'Finally, at one in the morning, Mansell saw them as they returned to watch the fireworks. The old man later saw *Male B* under the lychgate at the church. His *lean man.*'

'Sir, what about the Masons' cleaner?' asked Morris.

Whetstone huffed. 'Jane, the cleaner is *Female A*. She was using Sonia Judd's name, that's all.'

Daley caught a sly look between the two women. He'd hoped they'd knocked their differences on the head. Maybe soon he would have to do it for them.

'As of now,' added Monaghan, 'we have been unable to trace the cleaner. None of the Masons' neighbours recall them ever having had one.'

'Hasn't it occurred to you, Jane, Hannah Mason could just as easily have made the whole cleaner thing up?' Whetstone's tone was condescending. '*She* could be *Female A*. Having sorted out the kids, she could have met up with her husband on the pretext of a date night or something.' Even to her, it sounded lame.

'Only Hannah Mason's fingerprints weren't on the business card we found, ma'am.' Equally condescending. Daley winced.

'Bu we don't know whose fingerprints they were yet, Jane.'

'So,' interrupted Daley, 'let's set about proving it. Deb, pin down Hannah's movements on the night in question. Then there's the amitriptyline. It's prescription only, so was she or her husband prescribed it?'

'Who's in the frame for *Male B*?' asked Monaghan. 'Jacob Foster and Willson Hughes both have equally shaky alibis. Either could have covered for the other. Foster only needed to be back at *Blenheim's* by 10:30 to meet his date. Then he could disappear again.'

This was not going quite to plan. Having resolved two perpetrators, *Female A* and *Male B*, the list was growing, and Whetstone and Morris were at each other's throats again.

'Okay, guys, let's rule some of these people in or out once and for all. Mike and Jane, find Foster and Hughes. Bring them in as a matter of priority. I think it's time those two gave us some straight answers, and, Mike, go along to *Blenheim's* again tonight. See if anyone remembers them, or even the girlfriend, Yvette. Deb, let's look more deeply at Hannah Mason and her cleaner. We need to know her exact movements during the day. And we need to know where the fentanyl and amitriptyline came from.'

***

As the team swivelled their chairs back to their desks, Daley invited Whetstone into the Goldfish Bowl.

'Whatever's going on between you and Jane, sort it out. Soon.'

'I just don't think she's ready for the team.'

'Bollocks. I may not be the sharpest knife in the box, but I am a bloody detective. This has nothing to do with her performance. It's between you and her.'

Whetstone huffed and looked away to the ceiling. She placed her palms on the arms of the chair and made to leave.

'You stay there - just for a minute.' *Dirty Harry* Callaghan in the film *Sudden Impact* stated that a man has to know his limitations. In one fell swoop, Daley had met his - women and team discipline. Whilst he had no prospect of conquering the former, he had to at least give the latter a go.

'Deb, I know things haven't been easy lately, but we still have to work as a team, and like it or not, Jane Morris is part of the team.'

'But even the simplest tasks seem either too much for her or bore her rigid. And she doesn't show the slightest bit of nous. I can't be micro-managing her all the time. She has to show initiative like I had to when I joined the team. It's sink or bloody swim.'

Daley was being drawn into places he did not want to go. He was ill-equipped to deal with the emotional stuff. He rested his elbows on Allenby's old desk, trying to draw some of his mentor's experience from the polished veneer.

'I remember you arrived to work amongst a team who knew their jobs so well they could communicate through telepathy. New rules, new etiquette, the tea round, and all the time trying to give a good impression and think for yourself. Oh, and now Jane's in civvies. Remember how you felt the first time you arrived at work without your uniform?'

'That's all very well but—'

'No buts. Cut her some slack and show her how it's done. Take her out with you more often. Get to know her a little better and maybe she'll get to know you too.'

'Scott, leave me to sort it out.' Whetstone gave a petulant drop of the shoulders.

'Just make sure you do. Jane is part of the team, and you need to work with her. If she screws up, tell her, but remember, you were once as green as she is. And, I'll let you into a secret, *Bilko* Bob had the same chat with me a few weeks after you joined, yet here we are. Anyway, sort it out before Hacker gets on my back because no one wants to experience that in the workplace.'

Whetstone gave a nod of appreciation, and Daley felt proud of himself. Maybe some of Terri's compassion had rubbed off.

'I want you to take the lead on Operation Scion. I'll remain SIO, but I want you to run the briefs and steer the investigation.'

She paused her fidgeting in the Throne of Doom and eyed him with suspicion. 'Is this about you and the Super? About taking a step back and putting a grunt in the firing line?'

Daley considered. 'I hadn't thought of it that way, but now you mention it…anyway, Hacker has warmed to you more than me.'

'As the iceberg warmed to the Titanic.'

'When Terri has the baby, I am going to need time off. You have a deep understanding of the case. At least I'll have someone at the helm I can trust.'

'As the White Star line said to Edward Smith when they made him captain.'

***

Whetstone left the Goldfish Bowl feeling a little bruised.

Operation Scion was about infidelity and revenge. Hannah Mason had met Andrew Mason herself in the town centre. She was Female A. And Male B? Foster or Hughes? But if Andy Mason was seeing Sonia Judd, he must have visited Green Street more than once. So, as he walked back that night with his wife, not Judd, why did he not suspect something was going on?

In her pocket, her phone buzzed.

'DS Whetstone?'

'Hi, it's Samantha Clarke-Mitchell. We met yesterday? It's about Jake Foster. It may not be strictly relevant to your enquiries, but there's something I feel you should know. Can we meet later?'

Part Two

Secrets and Lies

Chapter 13

Willson Hughes slumped down onto the sofa. It was the story of his life. Thirty-six years old, drifting from one job to the next. Was it him? Was there a neon sign hovering above him that yelled *loser* to the rest of the world? Or was he just incompatible with every organisation he joined? Other people always people shouted louder, seemed smarter and got heard, even when they had nothing to say. And now he was unemployed again, all because of Jake Foster. In hindsight, he should have twigged at the interview. Foster was personable, effusive, attentive, and eager to learn what Hughes offered; confident he would fit well into the team. Too good to be true, but again Hughes had been seduced. Decent offices, outstanding reviews, the company screamed success, yet he realised his mistake on his first day. Foster's interview facade fell like a magician's cape. Direct, self-obsessed, narcissistic. Still, Hughes settled in and got on with what they paid him for. He could tolerate Foster's egotism, even his petulant tantrums, confident the company would recognise his true worth. One had to grit one's teeth and rise above it, which he had done, yet still, they had sacked him.

Shit. What was Abi going to say?

He would probably get another ear bashing, another lecture over his laziness, over the rent and the bills. Same old, same old, yet they had managed before. They could scrape by on Abi's part-time wages, and another job would come up. She would understand the predicament Foster had placed him in?

He fired the remote at the TV and found a South American football championship. He needed to chill, then he would hit the job sites looking for something else. But, the pint or two, or three, to drown his sorrows had been a mistake and, despite his best endeavours, his eyelids grew heavier and his thoughts slid away.

***

'So what's all this?'

Hughes woke with a start. His tongue felt like a bar carpet. Across the room, the football had given way to half-time advertisements, and Abi was standing over him with her arms crossed, face like a bulldog chewing a wasp.

'Not much on. I came home early.' Feeble. If you're going to lie, at least invent a dead granny or a ram raid at the office.

'You were off yesterday.' Abi flounced out to the hall, and her bag and shoes clattered to the floor. She returned hopping on one foot as she tried to put the other in a slipper, admitting defeat and falling into a chair to have a better try.

'So what about the amazing project you were crowing about? The one they chose you for? It's been frantic for the last two weeks and now, all of a sudden, there's not much on?'

'You know projects. It's the work you put into the hours, not the hours you put into the work. Bayhurst Grange is a long-term thing. Prep's finished and now we are waiting for Jake to sign it off. Until he does, we're light on work.'

Office-speak cliches wouldn't satisfy her, but it was all he had. She paused a moment, deep in thought, then gave a vague nod.

'Fair enough. You can make tea while I skive in front of the TV for a change.' She switched over to soaps, leaving Hughes high and dry, at the scene of a fight that never happened.

Lately, they had argued a lot. About work, the house, where he dropped his dirty laundry. She would even argue about why he chose not to argue. The latent hostility had grown so large the elephant in the room had moved aside. It exhausted him. Even boiling pasta and opening cans was a drain when the unseen animus hovered just out of sight, waiting to take him unawares.

They had been together for five years, comfortable and safe.

An Invisible Murder

Maybe that was the problem? Too comfortable, too safe. Stagnation. Maybe every relationship needs a little danger to spice it up. To show how valuable comfort and safety were. They'd taken a trip to Spain, bought a new car, joined a gym, changed jobs, and even set up a new home in Pinner. But what had they got to cling to when the storms blew up? They were very different people. Maybe they were looking in different directions?

When Will took supper through, she was in the chair, legs up, scrolling on her phone while the TV showed some reality garbage. He made to say something, some pithy remark about missing the goals in the football game. Instead, he sat and ate in the suffocating silence. After a quarter of an hour, his mouth betrayed him.

'I'm quitting Stanford Clarke-Mitchell.'

Abi stopped eating and huffed. A single exhalation said it all.

'Less than six months? That must be a record even for you. The other day, you were saying how this new project was going to win you a big promotion. Now you want to quit?'

Her tone was matter-of-fact, as if she'd been expecting it. Maybe she had? The previous Christmas, he had lost his dream job in the City over a point of principle more important than the salary they paid him. Abi had found him the role at Stanford Clarke-Mitchell, threatening to walk out if he didn't apply. Lower salary, lower prospects, but it was a job.

'It's not like that, honestly.'

She clicked off the television. 'So what is it like, Will?'

'The job's fine. It's the Bayhurst Grange project. One minute, it's full steam ahead. I am busting my ass planning expenditure and construction phases, then Jake's slamming the brakes on. Everything grinds to a halt, and there's sod all I can do about it. And as usual, Jake dumps it all on me.'

'So stand up for yourself, for once in your life.' She'd stopped eating and was giving him the look. The one that froze the blood in his veins. That would send their children running to their bedrooms - if they had any children. But Abi couldn't, some medical issue.

Maybe that was part of the problem.

'It's not that simple, Abi.'

'What the hell is that supposed to mean?'

'They sacked me. I didn't resign. They sacked me, okay?'

'Bloody hell, Will.' She raised her arms, sending the tray spilling across the laminate flooring. 'What did you do this time? Open your bloody mouth again? A year ago, we were *that* far,' she measured a minuscule gap with her thumb and forefinger, 'from losing the house, and now, just as I'm getting everything straight, here we go again. I work my bloody arse off; two jobs to keep a roof over our heads so you can just swan around the house in your pyjamas, eating crisps. I can't go through it all again. I *won't*.'

'There will be another job, I'm sure.' He dropped to his knees and began scraping up the detritus of the spoiled meal. On his knees. How apt. How pathetic.

'With your CV, who's going to employ you now? You've worn underwear longer than you've held down a job.'

He knew work was a necessity, but they each expected different things from it. Abi enjoyed her administrative job, and she excelled at it. Will's job was more insular. He pushed numbers around a screen, wrote reams of meaningless prose, and created plans and projections that changed before the ink was dry. He dealt with people like Sam Clarke-Mitchell and Jake Foster. People whose self-serving opinions mattered more than his skills and experience.

She crouched down, so close he could smell her anger, see the fire in her eyes, as she corralled a slime of pasta with her unused serviette, and slopped it into the bowl.

'You listen to me, Will. Jake Foster is the bloody boss. When he says jump, you ask how high and collect the cheque. You don't go squealing like a stuck pig every time he asks you to do something you disagree with. Now, you get on your phone and you beg him to take you back, whatever it takes, or you and I are through.'

Chapter 14

The Goldfish Bowl was becoming claustrophobic by early evening and Daley had almost worn out Bilko Bob's square of carpet, so he decamped to the fire escape, where he could prop open the doors and enjoy some fresh air. The building site surrounding Lambourne Road Nick was a black scar, lit by bright pools of amber. Soon they would demolish the building beneath him. Change was inevitable, whether or not one wished for it. In the airtight über-modern box that was the West London Combined Homicide and Drugs Unit in Hillingdon, open fire escapes sounded an alarm in the extensive janitorial suite where they even kept the police under surveillance. He would soon need to find a different place to contemplate the world, and to make sense of it.

The Mason and Judd seen in Green Street were *not* Mason and Judd. Of course, they couldn't be dead or dying in the flat and walking about outside, but as to the identity of the imposters…? Monaghan was sure the cleaner was a fiction; there was still no evidence the Masons ever employed one. The phone number on her business card went to an unregistered unanswered prepaid device, switched off since the night of the explosion. If the cleaner were Judd herself, that would explain why. Or, if someone was masquerading as Judd or the cleaner, they had probably destroyed the phone already.

Whetstone suspected Hannah Mason herself was *Female A*. There were holes in her whereabouts during the evening, but she could have been at home watching television. Not that it mattered. Whoever *Female A* and *Male B* were, there would be a record of it somewhere. All they had to do was find it.

Below him, the fire door on the third floor squeaked open, and he heard the patter of size-nines up the concrete stairs.

'Hard day, Dave?'

'Don't Ask, Scott. Those arseholes at VERS are a pain in the bum. Anything you ask them to do…'

Detective Sergeant Dave Monaghan had promised his wife, Margaret, another two years on the force, at most. The *Big Six-Oh*, then he would hand in his cards, collect the pension and they could enjoy coach trips and foreign city breaks. Personally, Daley doubted he could take the excitement after over forty years on the force.

'Cut and thrust. You know you love it, so what's up?'

'You remember Father O'Donnell, at the church across from Judd's flat?' Monaghan sounded like a man who had found a pound coin down someone else's sofa. He pulled out a folded sheet of paper and handed it across.

'For real?' Daley stole Monaghan's tea, took a sip and scanned the page again. Entries from several databases which meant little in isolation, but together, less than ten words made Green Street the perfect location for the incident.

Monaghan gave a single self-satisfied nod.

'So not only did Father Joseph marry the Masons *at* St Dunstan's, on Green Street, but he was on the staff of the school Andrew Mason attended as a child. Kinda puts the kibosh on his claiming he didn't know the deceased.'

'For real,' remarked Monaghan, stealing back his cup. 'More blarney than a sackful of leprechauns.'

'Leave it with me, Dave. I'll have a little chat. Something like what the bible says about the truth. Hopefully, it will set him free.'

***

Whetstone could have expected the rush hour traffic between Ealing and Pinner if she had given it some thought. A little over eight miles turned into an hour, listening to her stomach rumble and bladder complaining about too much coffee. Buoyed by Daley's request she should lead the investigation, she had given him a night in with Terri, even though it was on his way home. After all, it was only she who had nothing better to do with her evenings.

The car park behind Stanford Clarke-Mitchell was an empty lake of evening amber, except for Clarke-Mitchell's Mercedes, silver turned orange as it waited for her to see sense and go home. Whetstone reversed her Golf into the space next to it, hoping the ten-year-old car didn't bring down the tone too much, and made her way over to the ground-floor reception, where a small man in a nondescript uniform glanced at the warrant card, gestured towards the lift and turned back to his portable television.

The team room at Lambourne Road was never quiet; there was never a time when everyone went home, but as the lift doors opened they revealed almost total darkness, a subdued emergency green with a solitary window lit in the far corner. A wake of automatic lights flashed and pinged behind her as she walked down the aisle of acoustic screens. *So much for the silent approach.*

Sam Clarke-Mitchell looked up from her desk, her eyes betraying her tiredness. 'Please come in, Sergeant and it down.' She directed Whetstone to a bank of sofas separated by a low table, buried under scattered papers, then followed her and sat opposite, hands clasped together and her lips tightly pursed.

'You told me on the phone there was something I needed to know about Mr Foster.'

'As I say, I don't know how relevant this will be to your enquiries, but I think something is going on behind my back and I am unsure what to do about it.'

'Go on.' At some point, every boss on the planet must suspect their workers of planning a lynching.

'Our largest project, Bayhurst Grange, is out near Iver. The company has an enormous amount of capital tied up in the project. I think Jake is sabotaging it. Every project hits snags, but this one has had the set. Hardly a day goes by without some delay or drama. Project files have gone missing from servers, deadlines missed, and just about every meeting cancelled or postponed. We are already late by almost a month, and there is a risk we will lose the bid altogether, which will be catastrophic for SCM.'

'I'm guessing there's some sort of bonus for Mr Foster, so it's in his best interests for it to succeed. What makes you think he is sabotaging it?' Whetstone's stomach rumbled. She wished Clarke-Mitchell would get to the point.

'Will Hughes, one of our project managers, joined us three months ago to handle several large projects. His performance has been faultless, except for the Bayhurst Grange project. He can't do a thing right. Time and time again. At first, he apologised, but he refused to accept the blame. In the end, I asked Jake, as Project Director, to step in, but to no avail. Everything about Will Hughes's work is exemplary, except for Bayhurst Grange. So I've spent the afternoon going over it all, and I noticed a pattern: Will screws up, Jake tears him off a strip and makes the problem go away. When you were last here, my copy of a report was missing. Will insisted he had included it. Jake lent me his. And it always seems to be my documentation that is incorrect. Surely he would learn to double-check. No one can be that stupid, can they? So I checked with Phil, our IT man, who found the printer log and, sure enough, Will had printed out the correct number of copies.'

'He still might have forgotten or compiled the copies incorrectly. Could it be this project is beyond his capabilities?' Industrial espionage was beyond Whetstone's scope.

'That was my first thought, only I found other anomalies, so I asked Phil to check the system audit trails, and it appears someone has tampered with Will's diary. They changed appointments in his diary compared to the rest of the team. They removed some altogether. The upshot is Will could have a point. Whilst he may be a fool, someone has been making him look more like one, especially on the Bayhurst Grange project. Phil told me the person making the changes used an administrator login, which only a few of us have.'

'Have MR Foster and Mr Hughes fallen out, do you know?'

Clarke-Mitchell stared at the ceiling, and let out a wearisome sigh. 'I think the problem is with the actual project. Apart from Will, he is the only person in a position to know everything about it. He can see all the project documentation and knows our external partners, and he has access to everyone's online diary. I believe he's been telling me Will has been holding things up when, in fact, he's to blame. He is out on site tomorrow trying to rectify the situation, but I suspect that may also be just another delaying tactic. Even now, it may be too late to save the project - if indeed he *is* trying to save it.'

'Why don't you have a word with Will Hughes? Clear the air. Maybe he can shed some light on it.'

'Not possible.' Clarke-Mitchell again gave a cursory shake of the head. 'This morning I had no option but to fire him.'

'How did he take that?'

'I don't know. It was Jake who did the actual firing.'

'I understand this is important to you and your company, but I am not sure what I can do. Even if Mr Foster is tampering with project documentation, or undermining his co-workers, it's an internal disciplinary issue. If you feel you have enough evidence, have it out with Mr Foster, even fire him instead.'

Clarke-Mitchell chuckled under her breath. 'Jake's clever. He knows with Will Hughes gone, he's all we have. Without Jake, Bayhurst Grange is dead in the water, along with SCM.'

Whetstone recalled the interview with Foster. Arrogant and self-centred, he had already thrown Andrew Mason under the bus. Was he now doing the same to Will Hughes? But why, and why this project? And strange it should crop up right now. Still, it was hardly a matter for a homicide detective.

Chapter 15

Jacob Foster had two key problems. First, Sam Clarke-Mitchell's insatiable desire for Bayhurst Grange meant the bid would progress. Come what may, the full site survey, along with a very costly set of penalties, would begin Monday. The bid would succeed and Foster would be powerless to stop it.

The other issue? How does one go about finding and disposing of a twenty-year-old corpse?

He opened his email, and penned a message:

Hi Sam,

I am going out tomorrow morning to sort out this thing at Bayhurst Grange once and for all.

J

On his desk, his mobile buzzed, a number he didn't recognise, so he cancelled the call, but it buzzed again, insistent and annoying. Reluctantly, he answered.

'Jake Foster? It's Abi, Will's partner. We've not met.'

'Hi. Look, I'm busy. What can I do for you?' It was typical of Hughes to go bleating to his wife, to let another poor bastard fight his battles for him. He pictured the wimp cowering behind her back.

'He says you've sacked him.'

'No, the CEO sacked him. I just delivered the bad news.'

'Semantics, Mr Foster. We both know he's your best project manager, so I want you to speak to Sam Clarke-Mitchell, petition the Pope, whatever it takes to get him his job back.' She sounded a little too earnest. What was her game?

'And why should I do that?'

'Because I am asking you to - no telling you to.'

'And that's supposed to make me change my mind?'

'No, but I wonder what the police would think if they knew the whole truth about you and Yvette outside *Blenheim's*, last Friday?'

The line went quiet for a while. If not for the ambient noise, Foster would have killed the call and assumed she'd gone, but he could hear her breathing.

'Eight tonight, Mr Foster. *The Crown and Sceptre* and bring your wallet, because since you sacked Will, the drinks are on you.'

***

The Crown and Sceptre was a short walk from Foster's apartment. The place was dead midweek. More life in a tramp's vest. He ordered a drink from a tattooed bar person with a face containing more rivets than the Forth Bridge, and sat at the quiet end, away from the TV. He wasn't one for tattoos and piercings, preferring his women *au naturel*.

After an age, the swing doors squealed and a woman's head edged around. Foster had forgotten how good she looked. Too good for the likes of Hughes. Cropped blonde hair, blue eyes, pale skin, shorter than his six-feet-two, not a stunner, but attractive in a way that crept up on men. A way that was creeping up on him. She removed the navy blue overcoat, revealing a pale blouse and tight-fit jeans. High-heeled boots. The chain of a pendant disappeared into the blouse, a matching bracelet around her wrist. God, he felt horny.

Remember, Jake, one hundred per cent charm offensive.

'Drink?' he asked.

'Why not, as you're paying. *G&T* - a humongous one. I need something to take my mind off Will.'

Foster inwardly sank at the mention of his name. 'I don't know what you see in an aimless wastrel like Will. You deserve better.'

Abi leaned back, folded her arms, and gave a derisive grunt.

'Like you, for instance? Seriously? With your track record? I bet your bedpost has so many notches, you think you've got woodworm. Let's stick to the agenda, shall we?'

'Which is?'

She made to speak, pausing as the drinks came. Foster offered across a crisp fifty-pound note, brought for effect, satisfied when Abi raised her eyebrows, abashed when the bar person said she had no change and refused it. He pulled out a gold Amex card instead, which was less impressive. She lifted her glass and took a sip, leaving a sheen on the muted red lipstick. Her eyes stared straight into his.

'I need you to get Will his job back. We cannot manage on my salary alone, and you know he is good at what he does. You and Sam Clarke-Mitchell need to sort out your issues and take him back.'

Foster felt a pang of envy. He wished he had someone who cared as much for him as she did for Will. 'And if I don't?'

She took another sip. 'Well, the police might just hear more about last Friday at *Blenheim's*. About Yvette and the ageing Lothario who chatted her up and with whom he claims he enjoyed a night of unbridled passion? I bet they'd be intrigued to discover that's not how it played out. That the lovely Yvette gave you the bum's rush, and you toddled out of *Blenheim's all alone*, tail between your legs? That the only thing she blew that night was your alibi.'

Foster held her gaze for a while. She was a hard woman to read, more so than his usual type, who were an open, rather predictable book. That night, at *Blenheim's*, he'd recognised Abi from some works thing, where she'd hung off Will's arm - *Beauty and the Beast*. She was standing on the far side of the dance floor, cradling a drink and staring indifferently at her half-cut friends cavorting like drunken fools. As Will Hughes brooded a hundred yards away, he'd corralled her outside where they talked for a while.

'So, we met up in *Blenheim's*. What about it? It doesn't alter the fact that I was nowhere near Harrow.'

'Still, you lied to the police, and when they track down Yvette - oh, but hang on, they won't, will they?'

'So I told the police a white lie.' Yvette was an alias agreed upon to spare Will's feelings. 'Neither of us wants him to discover you were hanging around *Blenheim's*, right under his nose. Least of all, with me.'

Will caught a taxi home, and Foster and Abi talked, but the subject naturally revolved around Will, the Bayhurst Grange project, and the challenges he faced at work. Whether Jake could ease the situation. After a few fruitless minutes, he had given up any idea of seduction.

'Will is a tame puppy,' she said. 'I can deal with him, but the police? It's not me they're interested in, is it Jake? Maybe I should tell them we met, that we talked, and you took me back to your place. I can tell them how good you were in the sack, about breakfast the next morning. Or I can tell them you lied. That by half-past eleven you had gone, and I don't know where you were when your friend was blown to pieces. Yvette? No, officer, I don't know an Yvette. *You know what it's like for a lone, vulnerable female, officer. So many evil men about.*'

He rested his elbows on the table and leaned in towards her. So close, he could smell the gin on her breath, that he could have kissed her full on the lips, but somehow, the desire had waned. Had he met his match in her? Frankly, he didn't care, but no woman, least of all Will's bitch, was going to get the better of him. He needed to press the point home.

'Say what you like, Abi. It's your word against mine. There is no evidence I lit the bomb under Andy Mason, so what's the worst that can happen? A rap on the knuckles for being economical with the truth?'

He reached under the table, feeling the roundness of her knee, moving up as she tensed her thigh muscles and her eyes widened. Then he squeezed until he felt the bones between his fingers, the sinews twisting and folding. Until the smile drained from her face. The corners of her eyes glistened, her jaw hardening against the pain.

'You think you can blackmail me? One word to the police and I will destroy you. I will make sure Will never works again and your little terrace? You be lucky to get a caravan on the Isle of Dogs.'

Her eyes still stared deep into his, but now they held only hatred and contempt. 'Get your filthy hand off my leg, or I will scream the place down. Remember what happened to Andy? It nearly destroyed him. Just think what it would do to you.'

Andy was a fool. Any brains he had were in his pants, but Abi's eyes told him she was serious, and he had enough to deal with already. He released the pressure on her knee.

'This is how it's going to be, Abi. You forget we ever met, that Yvette ever existed. You forget about me, and *Blenheim's*, about Andy Mason and Green Street. In return, I will square it with Sam Clarke-Mitchell and your husband will get his job back.' He tightened his grip once more and watched her lip tremble. 'But if anyone ever finds out about this conversation, you'll have me to answer to, and I won't be so forgiving next time. Now drink your drink and piss off.'

She stood abruptly, rattling the glasses on the table.

'Do you know Jake Foster? Will told me you were a bastard, but he doesn't know the half of it. And for your information, Will is not my husband. We're not married. Now, it's late. Will's due home from football soon and I don't want him to know I've been down in the sewer with you.'

Chapter 16

By chance, the FLO, Jane Marner, saw a wedding photo from the Masons' mantelpiece and recognised St Dunstan's church. Hannah and Andrew, bride and groom, outside twelve years ago, calling into question O'Donnell's claim he did not know Mason. A few lines on O'Donnell's CV had him as chaplain at Holy Mount Residential School in the 1990s, when Andrew Mason had been a pupil there. In the final analysis, Daley could forgive Father Joseph O'Donnell for not recognising him. He was one pupil among many at Holy Mount. Pupils come and go. Some stand out, others don't. Their appearances change as they grow, and twenty years is a long time. But, only six years later, Andrew Mason and his bride-to-be, Hannah, had sat with O'Donnell and discussed their nuptials. A few weeks on, O'Donnell had married Mason, even broaching the question in front of a packed congregation: *Do you, Andrew Mason, know of any lawful impediment...*so why had he not recognised him when Corby held up a mugshot? Daley decided on an early knock at the ungodly hour of 7:00 am, so he could ask him in person.

In Green Street, the crime scene tape was already sagging. A shell-shocked silence lay over it all. Even the birds in the churchyard were quiet, as if the street itself was mourning. But some things never stop, not even for death. Contractors had shuttered the windows and piled the rubble behind already graffitied hoardings. Vans and skips cluttered the road as work began to erase the tragedy. New windows, doors, and even a gardener or two to turn over the scattered human remains and plant new shrubs. Thank heavens for insurance, Daley thought. *It's an ill wind...*

Negotiating the slalom of white vans, he imagined Mason and

the auburn-haired woman rounding the corner and passing through the doorway into Number 5. Fast forward to 9:00 pm, the same woman left and crossed into the churchyard, all under the beady eye of Mrs Livingstone. Then what? A slow, insistent hiss of gas until the timer clicked over to 1:00 am and ruined everyone's sleep? Or were there other comings and goings? Green Street ran east to west. The rear gardens of the houses backed into an alley. One could enter Number 5 from the front or the back.

He crossed to St Dunstan's Roman Catholic Church, which cowered from an irreligious world behind a bay hedge, breached by the entrance to a car park, and the lychgate. The church looked mediaeval, squat and barn-shaped, its stonework soot-stained and algae-greened, topped by a mottled vaulted roof. A small bell turret jutted out from the side, like an architect's afterthought. A place from which to call the masses when the coffers ran low. High in the eaves, an arched stained-glass window gave the church the droopy, miserable appearance of *Eeyore* from the Disney films.

The church was locked up tighter than Sergeant Monaghan's wallet, so Daley crossed to the vicarage and tugged on an archaic bell pull. Out of the corner of his eye, a curtain twitched, then he heard muttering as footsteps creaked up the old floorboards and the latches went back with a deafening clunk.

Father O'Donnell was an elderly man, a thinning top of unkempt white hair over a sallow, stubbled, thread-veined face that had seen too much and understood too little, and been up all night fretting about both. He flashed a cardboard smile, creasing the worry lines that broke his pallid skin, but even that slipped when Daley opened his warrant card. Sighing his displeasure, he opened the door wider and ushered him out of the cold, down a gloomy, wood-panelled corridor and into a sitting room belonging to another century. One that smelled of nicotine, candle wax, body odour, and a faint undercurrent of anxiety, not to mention the designer poverty the church excelled at. O'Donnell gestured toward a pair of floral wingbacks, past their best, like most of the furniture in the room. An electric heater, set in a tiled fireplace, pumped three bars into a room that remained ill-lit and cold. The room seemed like a stage set, portraying a period drama with a wiry spinster who had a sharp mind and a talent for solving crimes. A room set up for business, taken straight from the pages of the Vatican's handbook. When he took off the dog collar, O'Donnell most likely relaxed in another room with a scotch and ginger and a huge plasma telly and binge-watched *Father Ted*.

'So, Chief Inspector, I only have a few minutes, I'm afraid. Parish business. I told your colleagues all I know.'

'Sometimes, after a day or two, other details spring to mind that might have been missed in the heat of the moment.' Daley inwardly cringed at his pun.

'Tea? I was just having one?' Father Joseph cocked his head in a direction Daley assumed to be the kitchen. A familiar attempt to delay the inevitable.

'Not for me, thanks, Father, but don't let me stop you.' Daley smiled as the priest covered his frustration with another cardboard smile. He sat and slapped his hands on his knees.

'So what is it you want to know?'

That was always a matter of perspective. He wanted to know who killed Judd and Mason, but no one was going to tell him. He just needed pointers in the right direction. The real conundrum was how to begin a conversation with a priest. To an extent, economies of truth were the church's stock-in-trade, and that made them adept at it. But maybe it was just Daley's scepticism. Virgin births and reincarnation might happen every day, just not in his small part of West London, and overlooked by a voracious media machine that would have broadcast them to the universe. So, Daley decided on the direct approach; simply the facts, please.

'Did you discover what happened last Friday?' O'Donnell asked.

'We believe a gas leak in the upstairs kitchen while they were - asleep.' With the Press already spreading rumours about the car salesman, the prostitute and the gas explosion, the less the priest knew the better. 'Sonia Judd, the woman who died. Did you know her?'

The priest pursed his lips. 'Yes, I did indeed. Despite her occupation and the drugs, she was a lovely girl. She took communion from time to time, but she was not a *regular*. I saw very little of her outside the church. I got the feeling she was seeking to change the destructive path she was on.'

'And Andrew Mason. The other person who died?' Daley pulled up the dead man's image on his phone and held it out to the priest. He studied it again, a furrowed brow, intense concentration, a brief shake of the head.

'I see many people, Chief Inspector.'

Daley showed him the photo the FLO had copied from the Masons' mantelpiece. 'This is Mr Mason and his wife Hannah at their wedding twelve years ago. Out the front of St Dunstan's. Do you remember him now?'

Father Joseph's jaw dropped. 'They married here? When was this?'

'June 2001. You were the priest here at the time, I believe?'

'Well, yes, but you can't expect me to remember everyone I marry. After a while, they merge into one.'

'Andrew Mason was also a pupil at Holy Mount whilst you were a priest there in the Eighties and Nineties. Do you recall him now?'

Father Joseph let out a helpless gasp. The pretence that Alzheimer's or dementia was preferable to deceit. He raised his head and looked around the room as if seeking a divine intervention that would rid him of this turbulent copper.

'It was a long time ago, Chief Inspector. People change. Faces change. They were children. They grow up.'

'Indeed.' Daley hoped his tone of voice showed the priest's argument did not sway him. He found the image of Mason's business card on his phone and held it out to O'Donnell. 'This was in Mr Mason's wallet. It could be an aide-mémoire or a brief note, but I wondered if it were a reference to a verse from the bible?'

O'Donnell sighed and leaned forward. He adjusted his spectacles and scrunched up his nose as he peered at the photo.

An Invisible Murder

Again, a curt shrug.

'Deuteronomy Chapter 22, verse 27.' The priest took a bible from the side table and leafed through it. '"*For he found her in the field, and the damsel cried, and there was none to save her.*" A reference to Sonia Judd, perhaps? Her profession. The hopelessness of her lifestyle. In the Lord's eyes, no one is ever beyond redemption, provided they repent of their sins. But in terms of context, isn't that a little unlikely?'

'How so?'

Father Joseph paused, his foot hovering over a trap.

'Oh, I just meant it is more likely a set of initials and a time. We clergy, seeing bible quotes where there are none.' He gave a nervous laugh. 'Still, perhaps it was not her business Mr Mason was after, but to help her from it and onto pastures new. Maybe she had reached out to him for help?'

'Possibly.' Daley moved on. 'Last Friday night. What were your movements before the explosion? Did you notice anything that struck you as odd?'

'I took a Latin Mass from 7:30 pm followed by a parish council meeting - the last Friday of the month. Afterwards, I must have nodded off in the sacristy because the sound of the explosion woke me around one. Naturally, I went to offer my help.' Father Joseph rested his chin on the points of his steepled fingers and Daley saw genuine pain in his eyes. 'I was in Enniskillen in 1987, the Remembrance Day bomb atrocity. I thought, please God, not again! Half the street was gone and there was a body on top of the rubble - I found out later it was Sonia. She was beyond help, so I read the sacraments and moved on to Mr Mansell, who was on the road, crying out for his dog. He had a broken leg, and I was fearful for him, his age and all. The emergency services arrived and, rather than being a nuisance, I said a quick prayer and opened up the church. We made tea and found biscuits, the British solution in any crisis.'

'One of the neighbours mentioned someone crossing into the churchyard around nine o'clock.' said Daley. 'Then before the explosion, someone standing under the lychgate, watching, waiting for the explosion. And afterwards, Mr Mansell described *a lean man* watching him from the lychgate. Maybe you saw him?'

'There is a shortcut through the churchyard, though very few people use it at night because of the residents in the graveyard.' He cracked a short dry smile, then glanced toward the window as if he were expecting a parcel or a visitor. Or something outside had spooked him.

'We now believe the explosion was intentional, Father. Mr Mason and Ms Judd entered the flat at Number 5 at seven-thirty last Friday evening and within a few hours, someone brutally murdered them both. Who knows, but for a few minutes for the gas to build up in the house, the explosion could have been far worse. Dozens of deaths, half the street in hospital, and even damage to your church. You must see how important it is we find whoever is responsible before they can kill again? So I ask again. The night of the explosion. The person standing under the lychgate?'

Daley sat for a moment, letting the silence suggest O'Donnell think about his previous answer. Experience showed that in a battle of wills, silence always wins out. It creates such a deep chasm that someone must fill it or it will consume them. After a long moment, O'Donnell puffed out a long breath.

'I saw no one by the lychgate, Chief Inspector.' Daley made to speak, but O'Donnell raised his hand. 'If they were there, I did not see them. My attentions were elsewhere, but I knew someone had been in the church whilst I was out tending to Mr Mansell. When I returned, the door from the sacristy into the nave was open. I was sure I'd closed it after the last of the ladies left. Come with me.'

Daley followed the priest out of the scant warmth of the vicarage, across ten yards of the windblown path and through into the echoing nave beyond. O'Donnell stopped in front of the altar. Above them, the Virgin Mary cradled the Christ child and gazed down onto a pristine white linen altar cloth embroidered in gold.

'He was standing there as if in judgement.' Father O'Donnell raised an arm towards a lectern draped in a similar cloth, a brass lamp and the bulk of a closed bible. 'His name is Raymond Asher.'

'How can you be so sure? The light would have been off.'

'You don't forget a face like that in a hurry. Not even after twenty years.'

Yet you seemed to have forgotten everything else until prompted. Given the events of last Friday, Daley could forgive O'Donnell for being upset, alarmed even, but, with Raymond Asher, his absent-mindedness had disappeared. God indeed moved in mysterious ways.

'Can you describe him? What he was wearing?'

O'Donnell huffed at the interrogation. 'Thin, stooped. He was wearing a hooded top. I told him he had no right to be here and threatened to call the police if he didn't leave. God knows there were enough of them outside. Then I turned and walked to the study room to fetch the blankets. When I returned, he was gone. He was here - in a house of *God*. After what he did!'

The priest spat the words with venom, taking Daley by surprise.

'Have you seen him at any other time?'

Father O'Donnell gestured for Daley to follow him through into the sacristy, thick with the odour of naphthalene and furniture polish. He crossed to the drawn curtains and hooked a finger into the folds, squinting into the brightness of the morning.

'It must have started three weeks ago. Since then, he's always here. Out among the gravestones in the churchyard or under the lychgate, twice, three times a week. Standing, watching, sometimes for hours at a time. I didn't see him last Friday, but I am not surprised if he was there.'

Daley peered out over the priest's shoulder. The small churchyard was shadowed by skeletal birch and oak, a frosted green carpet peppered with rusted leaf-fall and lichen-mottled gravestones, and small posies of flowers adding dotted pools of colour. No one was there now. But with Mason and Judd returning around 8:00 pm and the Latin Mass concluding around 8:30, the timings were not too far off. Enough time for this man to murder Sonia Judd and subdue Andrew Mason before returning to the churchyard. And if it took a few minutes for the congregation to disperse, then this could be the man Mrs Livingstone saw.'

'And you are sure it's Raymond Asher?'

'Most definitely. Mr Mansell was right. He saw Asher. He is your *lean man*, Chief Inspector.' O'Donnell lowered himself into his desk chair as if favouring a flareup of haemorrhoids and gestured towards another chair.

'So, tell me how you know him,' asked Daley. The truth was like a splinter, festering beneath the surface unseen, just an enduring pain, and he was the blunt needle fishing around until he could bring it to the surface. Eventually, he would gain purchase on a fragment and draw it out, painfully or otherwise.

'He was also a pupil at Holy Mount when Andrew Mason and I were there. Twenty years ago, he killed another pupil, Claire Dobson, and was sent to jail. Ray and Claire were the same age and had become close. A frequent occurrence amongst adolescents that would burn itself out, but this one didn't. One night, when they were both fourteen years old, they absconded from school. I sent out two of the older prefects - they knew the woods better than the staff. They searched half the night, but to no avail. I called the police, who instigated a separate search. They found a significant amount of Claire's blood out by the culverts, taking rainwater away from the motorways. Then, two days later, they apprehended Asher out on the far side of the woods. Asher later admitted to murdering her and burying the body. When I first saw him across the way, I made enquiries and was told he had served his sentence and been released.'

'And did he say why he killed her?'

O'Donnell shook his head. 'To this day, he has remained silent.'

'So, why is he here now?' As a juvenile, they would only release Asher when no longer deemed a threat. However, Daley couldn't understand why the parole board had sanctioned his release without the girl's body being found.

'Maybe he holds me responsible for her death. I was in charge of student welfare at Holy Mount. Maybe I should have nipped the relationship in the bud earlier and saved him from himself. As it was, I allowed the pair to abscond.'

'And could Asher also hold Andrew Mason responsible for Claire Dobson's death?'

'Andrew was one of the prefects I sent out, so yes. I thought, being similar in age, he might reason with them.'

'But standing around outside, even at the lectern. If he wants to talk, why hasn't he?'

The priest chuckled, a mirthless, dry laugh. 'The last thing he wants to do is to talk to me.' He crossed to a cupboard under the bookcases and withdrew a black refuse bag, tipping the contents onto the carpet and stretching it out. A similar altar cloth to the one in the church, except for the sequence of letters and numbers, sprayed in red across it.

JO - Dt 8:5

'It's from the King James Bible. Deuteronomy. Chapter 8, verse 5. "Thou shalt also consider in thine heart that, as a man chasteneth his son, so the Lord thy God chasteneth thee." That's how I knew the one you had was an Old Testament reference.'

'Yet you dismissed the idea out of hand!' Daley's patience was wearing thin. 'Okay, so why would Asher leave *you* this message?'

'Because, Chief Inspector, all those years ago, I failed him. No one escapes justice from the Lord. There will always be the Day of Judgement. He believes I am responsible for his predicament, but that is a long way from being responsible for him committing murder!'

***

Daley ordered O'Donnell to attend Lambourne Road and make a statement, sure eventually he would. So far, everyone they had asked to attend Lambourne Road had failed. Maybe Corby and Morris could drag him in kicking and screaming. They'd enjoy that. A chance to breathe in some fresh air and play with other children, rather than staying in and staring at those screens all day. Not that it mattered. He had more or less confirmed the account of a *lean man* watching from the lychgate, and he had marked O'Donnell's card.

He pulled his overcoat about his shoulders against a biting wind that swept across the car park at St Dunstan's. The churchyard was as silent as the graves it housed, except for the drone of a petrol lawnmower that, like so many aspects of this case, he knew was there but couldn't see.

For no apparent reason, an ancient gravestone caught his eye, stacked against the hedge after a storm, or the explosion, had made it fall. He bent over to read the worn, mottled inscription:

> In Loving Memory Of
> HAROLD STEVENSON
> Who Died March 23rd 1859
> Aged 63 Years
>
> Also Of BELINDA Beloved Wife Of HAROLD
> Who Died July 18th 1863
> Aged 53 Years
>
> Also Of BABY STEVENSON
> Who Died September 12th 1825

A single stone, perhaps the only remaining record of three lives lived, was now detached from the spot where their bones lay. The inscription saddened him. A child so young it had yet to be named, yet to live, invisible as if it had never existed. Perhaps he was the only person who had given any regard to the poor soul in two hundred years. Maybe the same was true of Claire Dobson, an orphan sent to a children's home. Who mourned her once she had died? Except perhaps Raymond Asher, alone in his cell.

Until now.

Chapter 17

'So where did you get to last night?'

Will watched as Abi slotted flaccid slices of white bread into the toaster. He had arrived home early from football practice to a dark house. She had left her work clothes strewn across the bed and the air smelled of the upmarket perfume he'd bought for her birthday.

'Just out. Met a mate for a drink.'

'Since when do you go out with a mate on a school night?'

She turned, hands on hips, and gave him a stare that made him question his very existence. 'Last week, the week before. You're just never here to notice, and anyway, I wasn't aware I needed your permission.'

He held up his hands in apology. 'I was just asking.'

These days, he was always treading on eggshells. Everything seemed to rile her, especially recently, and of course, it was always his fault. The bins, the washing up, not tidying away, tidying away wrongly, sometimes just being there. Perhaps that was the problem. She no longer wanted him there?

'No work today?' he asked. She was in jeans, a t-shirt and an old fleece hoodie, which she kept for running in the winter, not the navy jacket and skirt she usually wore for work.

She looked herself up and down. 'No, mufti. We're clearing out the stockrooms this morning, so I'm going to change later at the office.'

He had never thought himself good enough for her. His well-to-do middle-class background jarred with her working-class upbringing. His black African heritage with her white British ancestry. They held diametric views on just about everything. Even on the issue of his role at SCM, they could not agree. They say opposites attract, but they also repel.

Now Foster was sniffing around her. Early that morning, needing a pee, he had made a fatal error. He'd slid her phone from the bedside table, and found Jacob Foster's number in the call history. Last call 5:45 pm yesterday. So she met a mate for a drink? If ignorance was bliss, knowledge was torment. The nights out with her mates, the times she'd been an hour early leaving for work, or an hour later arriving home. Were they all just an excuse for her to walk less than half a mile and cosy up to Jake *bloody* Foster?

Okay, he saw her point. London was an expensive place to live, particularly in Pinner, and even two months without work could bring their house of cards tumbling down. With three different jobs, three different houses, countless credit cards, and debts piling up, he hadn't made her life easy over the last few years. And just as things straightened out, another problem at work, and the cycle repeated itself. No wonder she looked elsewhere for stability - but Jake Foster?

'I spoke to Jake last night.'

Will looked over as her toast popped up, inevitably underdone, and thrust back down. Had she read his thoughts?

'Oh yeah?' *On the phone, or while you bounced up and down on his dick.*

'I told him sacking you was grossly unfair, that he needed to get you your job back. I told him you'd be in the office later today to discuss it.'

'Yeah, right.' *And what price did you pay for that?*

'No, seriously, it's a lifeline, so take it and don't be such a drama queen about everything.' She grabbed her toast, dancing her fingers on the carbon-black surface like a lizard crawling about the desert, dropping it onto a plate and smothering it with butter.

'And what's in it for him?' The thought of *his* hands on her skin made Will want to vomit.

She paused with the knife and looked over. 'Don't be a wanker all your life, Will. Jacob Foster's a slimeball. A rich slimeball, but…'

Was he convinced? Foster was infinitely more successful and more attractive, and he had a gravity all of his own. There was simply no competition, and her denials just made him more certain. A lifeline? Jake had suggested he would have a word, but Hughes had never expected him to follow through. He never had before, so why would he now?

Maybe Abi was right. He should get a backbone, march into Sam Clarke-Mitchell's office, and lay it on the line. *You can't sack me because without me, the Bayhurst Grange bid would be a pile of poop and you all know it.* Then again, maybe he should just send them a *Dear John* email and hide under the duvet in the spare room until he decomposed into a thin film of self-pity.

Maybe he just had to come to terms with it.

Losing Abi was inevitable. If not now, then soon, so why not just let it happen? Leave her, forget SCM and move on, so she was free to do the same? The job market was buoyant. He could find a better role; one where he didn't feel so defeated all the time.

'Might be late tonight. I have some things to pick up on the way home. Remember what I said - and clear the kitchen up.' Abi took a bite of her toast and reached for her bag. The coffee he made for her left on the counter, as cold as he felt inside.

As the door shut behind her, Will let the tears flow, hoping for a catharsis that never came.

***

Jake Foster spent most of the night in the window of his apartment, trying to push Bayhurst Grange and Holy Mount from his mind. Twenty years ago, as a fifteen-year-old, Foster was feared by those who mattered and respected by those who did not. Raymond Asher, two years younger, was a scrawny, withdrawn kid, the weak, submissive type Foster preyed on and mistrusted in equal measure. Yet, in a single night, their lives became irrevocably linked. Father O'Donnell had sent him to bring back Asher and Dobson, but he failed. He had expected one day, the police would knock on his door, but it never happened. Asher went to prison and the whole affair slipped to the back of his mind. He left the school at sixteen, and shortly after, it was closed and Bayhurst Grange kept its secret safe.

When morning came, he had a full screen of voicemails from Sam Clarke-Mitchell. Abi O'Brien had not called.

He made breakfast, preoccupied with the image of Claire Dobson lying in the culvert as the torrent swept away her halo of blood. Now, her body waited for some hapless JCB driver to dig it up. He needed to find the body and move it. Then perhaps Bayhurst Grange would be less toxic and Sam less venomous.

He had only asked for a couple more days when the estate would be quiet, but, after twenty years, how much would remain? Dried flesh, rotted clothes, a grinning death's head, or just a pile of bones? He pushed away his breakfast, stemming the nausea. Could he even do such a grotesque thing?

Twenty years ago, they had scoured the estate and failed to find her. Yet, someone knew where she lay. The other person who was there that night, who heard their pleas for help, who hid Claire's body where even the police could not find it. It was time to pay them a visit.

Foster had been called many things in his time, many slanderous, most deserved, but never a grave robber.

Chapter 18

The traffic on the Greenford Road had snarled up, as usual. These days, Whetstone seemed to spend all her time staring at the grimy rump of the car in front, trying to make a face from the taillights and badge. Fortunately, Scott Daley was doing the driving, or lack of it. Capital FM was trying its damnedest not to provide a traffic report, instead concentrating on the so-called music that was more talking than singing - *rap with a capital C,* Daley called it, but then the shite he listened to was no better. All dogs dying, love betrayed and riding on boxcars.

The car in front inched forward; a distance so small she would need a micrometer to measure it. Daley ignored it. Life was one long wait. The wrong queue, never reaching the end. Five years as her mother slowly withered away. Decades of waiting for one human out of seven billion to kick-start her life, always in the slowest queue.

She thought about Samantha Clarke-Mitchell. Did she allow herself to drift on the wind, or had she long ago made a plan of action to navigate them? Single, loaded, in her early forties, she seemed sorted, even if she still had to deal with prats like Jacob Foster. Maybe that's what she needed? A plan, some goals. Something to take her mind off prats like Scott Daley?

But, as John Lennon said, *Life is what happens while you're busy making plans.*

Right now, she needed the queue of traffic to move. That and a pee. And as neither looked likely, she brought up her contacts and dialled DC Jane Morris.

'Jane. Have you been to see Oliver Mansell yet?'

'Yes, ma'am. Yesterday evening.' Morris's voice oozed boredom. In the background, the team room echoed with activity. 'Not much more than he told us at the scene, but he was in a lot of pain. He said he smelled perfume. It reminded him of his wife. He's a widower.'

'So, a woman wearing perfume, or a man - or any combination? Did it occur to you to ask what make?' A little brusque, maybe. Beside her, Daley gave her a look. She ignored it.

'He couldn't be sure but his wife—'

'And when were you going to share this information?'

'Sorry, ma'am.' Said with a hint of condescension. 'Only I thought—'

'You know what thought did?'

'Ma'am?'

'Nothing, he just thought he bloody did.' She sighed an explosive puff, probably more melodramatic than was necessary. 'Okay, check back through the statements. Speak to the neighbours again if necessary. The people coming out of the alley, crossing the street, standing in the churchyard. Was it the same couple each time, male or female? And Mansell, did he see two people, or was it the same one on each occasion? And get a name for the perfume. If it was his wife's favourite, he'd know.'

'Ma'am. He's got a severe concussion. The doctor said—'

'And what did you say? "Oh, okay. We can wait until they murder someone else. Thank you, doctor." Come on, Jane, this is a murder investigation. Start being proactive for a change.'

As she ended the call, Whetstone felt a tinge of guilt, but the girl had to learn.

Jane Morris was slim, blonde, beautiful, and newly arrived from Traffic, always immaculately made-up, in a smart two-piece black suit and a white blouse, hair tied up into a professional tight bun. The sort of woman men see. The sort that would have an easy ride. In contrast, Whetstone felt positively frumpy. Trousers and a plain blouse. Tired overcoat, hair short and expedient, blonde dye washed

An Invisible Murder

out to highlights and dark roots. Her response to Morris's arrival had been the same as her response when she had met Keith *The Uniform*. She had smartened herself up, dyed in the blonde, and bought new clothes, but that performance soon got tired. After all, shouldn't people take her as they find her, not as some catwalk caricature? But the world wasn't like that. She got it. Pop stars, TV presenters, and film stars. They only picked the attractive ones. No one listened to ugly people, however much they offered.

The traffic eased forward by a few car lengths. Daley filled the gap. Perhaps frumpy was her lot in life.

***

The third-floor video suite used to belong to the Drugs Unit. State-of-the-art a few years ago, they had spared no expense in the crusade against illegal drugs. The Homicide Unit, by contrast, squinted into small square monitors on their desks. But with the consolidation of services into the new headquarters, Superintendent Hacker had decided the *Narcos* needed an even more state-of-the-art set-up to go along with their new plush offices. After all, it was funded from a central budget rather than her own. The *VERS* - Visual Evidence Retrieval Service now formed the conduit, or barrier, between the new Combined Homicide and Drugs Unit and the various external agencies that controlled cameras across West London. More screens, better software, trained operatives, and one of those bubbly water dispensers in the corner. Sensing an opportunity, before the demolition crews descended on Lambourne Road, Scott Daley had petitioned Hacker to forget about the old suite, lamenting his team's lack of resources, and offering the carrot of improved performance and a reduced bottom line. If he recalled, Superintendent Hacker was, at the time, choosing wallpaper for her new Hillingdon office, so it was an easy sell.

Whetstone eased open the door and peered through. With subdued lighting and barely a whisper from the air conditioning, it felt like she was intruding on a wake. Monaghan and Taylor were kids in a sweetshop, commanding a control dashboard which reminded her of Colonel White's desk in the puppet series, *Captain*

Scarlet. Two mammoth screens, side-by-side, mirrored the computers on the desks, projecting staccato images of grainy Lowryesque figures strutting about, stopping, then taking a few juddering paces backwards before starting over. From the comfort of one of the Drugs Unit's ample chairs, one could crop and zoom, pan and scrub, and many other techie things she couldn't be bothered to learn.

'Deb. I was just about to organise a search party,' said Monaghan.

Whetstone frowned pointlessly from the shadows, cocked her wrist and checked her watch. It was too dark to see.

Detective Sergeant Monaghan was a wiry, dour Irishman with a quiet, unexcitable manner. The team's senior in age if not rank - at fifty-eight, he was some twenty years Whetstone's senior - methodical and rigorous, bringing the team's more fanciful speculations back down to earth. Dependable. Safe as houses. Perhaps more so given the recent explosion in Green Street. DC Taylor was cut from a similar cloth, albeit of a darker hue originally woven south of the Sahara. He was very different in appearance from Monaghan. Tall and slender, with a defined stoop and a more genuine smile, deeply hidden behind a facade of shyness. The pair made a good team if masses of data and hours of CCTV were the order of the day, which was good because DC Corby couldn't find his arsehole with a map.

'So what have you got? I hope it's enough to keep the DCI off my back.'

'Less of your perverted fantasies, Deborah. Take a gander at this. Traffic located Mason's Mercedes parked up in the Greenhill Way car park in Harrow. They also found another phone under the seat. A prepay as flat as a drunken folk singer, otherwise GPS would have located it sooner. We pumped some charge in and found an interesting text conversation.'

It was a cheap supermarket pay-as-you-go, probably kept by Mason for planning liaisons with tarts or cleaners. Calls and texts to and from a single number; the one from Sonia Judd's business card as a cleaner, going back around a month. The last text read, *"Need to talk. Usual place. 7:30."* Mason's curt reply was, *"Okay."*

'The other number is also an unregistered prepay,' added Monaghan. 'Cell site analysis will pinpoint where it was used, but that could take some time. In the meantime, we've traced Mason's car from Ruislip to Harrow last Friday. He left home at around 6:30 pm and drove directly to Harrow. Then he travelled on foot along Greenhill Way past the Royal Oak towards the Shopping Centre. He left his phone in his car.'

Taylor took over, changing to a different feed.

'CCTV shows him at the ATM withdrawing the cash, and in the centre entering Starbucks at around 7:30 pm, but cameras in the coffee shop were down, so Jane spoke to the staff. He met a woman who had arrived a few minutes earlier and bought two coffees, which tallied with the receipt we found. The barista's description was vague - slim, medium height, red-haired, long dark coat. They thought she was a tart. We checked the earlier CCTV but we couldn't see her arriving.'

The woman could not be Sonia; she was already dead on the bed at Number 5. Whetstone mused on the conversation with Hannah Mason. *Maybe this woman had a problem, and he stepped in or gave her a lift home. Helped her out - a kind act.* 'Maybe he didn't know the woman was a hooker, or they were meeting on other business?'

'Ah, you sweet, innocent girl, you,' mocked Monaghan.

'Anyway.' Taylor was slightly irked at the interruption. 'They left together. This is Greenhill Way on the far side of the shopping centre.'

The pair were facing away from the camera, waiting for the lights to change. The man in the video was patently Mason, and the woman had looped her arm through his. As the woman checked the oncoming traffic, Taylor froze the frame. Medium hair-dark blonde or even red, long dark overcoat, a large bag slung beneath her right shoulder. Frustratingly, the face was indistinct, an overexposed blur beneath the amber streetlights.

'After that, they crossed into the residential estate. There's a pole-mounted camera on the zebra crossing up by the school.' Taylor found the feed and scrubbed along to 8:00 pm. He froze the video with Mason and the woman still arm in arm.

'Which takes them along to Green Street?'

'Uh huh, past the all-night shop and around the corner.'

Whetstone stared at the frozen image, still indistinct, overexposed under the glare of the streetlights, caught mid-stride as they exited the frame. There was a familiarity with the way they walked, holding each other close. A couple rather than a tart and her John. She pulled across a chair next to Taylor.

'Steve, can we run it again from the lights on George Avenue? This time, start thirty seconds before Mason enters the frame and stop thirty seconds after he leaves.'

Monaghan turned in his seat. 'What is it?'

'I don't know, Dave. I've seen something out of the corner of my eye, and I'm not sure what it was.'

Taylor selected the track and reran it with different parameters. The grainy footage was in monochrome. Two lines of traffic on a juddering, slow-motion approach to the junction from the west along Pinner Road, one crossing the junction into Headstone Lane, one filtering right. Presently, Mason's Mercedes joined the filter, waited for the lights, then disappeared under the camera. After a couple more cars, the lights changed, and the traffic built up again.

Whetstone pointed to the screen. 'Can we get a registration for that car?'

It was a recent model white Mercedes A-class, three behind Mason's, frustrated by the lights and forced to wait as Mason motored off towards the town centre. Taylor edged the clip forwards and back, then enlarged the best frame until the registration plate almost filled the screen, blurry at first then sharpened by the software.

'I know that car.' Whetstone leant over to another computer and typed in the registration, a satisfied smile crossing her face as the details came up. 'Now show me the image of the zebra crossing by the school.'

Whetstone stepped up to the screen and examined the woman, the shape of her head, the contours of the trunk, and the relative proportions of the legs to the torso. Her height.

Another of Scott Daley's mantras was *Cherchez la femme*. A cheating husband, an aggrieved wife, the other woman. The unholy trinity of domestic crime. As boorish and misogynistic as he was, he was right more often than he was wrong.

Re-energised, they spent the next half an hour re-scanning the footage from start to finish. Mason's was not the only Mercedes travelling from Ruislip to Harrow that evening. The white A-class picked up his gunmetal grey model in Ruislip, two or three cars behind, and followed him into Harrow, parking up three rows behind in the Greenhill Way car park. As the driver purchased a ticket, there could be no doubt who it was.

'I'll get Jane to check her alibi for Friday evening. And she can speak to other stores in the centre. See if they had CCTV pointing out into the mall. Maybe we can get a better look at her. And send the best frame from the video to the FLO.'

They were no longer watching Andrew Mason. They were watching Hannah.

Chapter 19

After Raymond Asher completed the twenty-year sentence for Claire Dobson's murder, authorities transferred him to a parole hostel, the grandly misnamed Arthur Godwin House, which occupied a corner plot on a housing estate near Ruislip Common. Squat and solid, purpose-built (though for what, Daley wasn't sure), at odds with the genteel middle-classness around it. It had the air of an abandoned urban public house. Tired, unkempt and loosely held together by the pale cream render on the walls. The sort of place they sent the less dangerous psychopaths, like Raymond Asher, when the trick cyclists had cured them. A temporary stop-gap between incarceration and independence, or re-incarceration, whichever came first. At least, the local alarm companies and locksmiths did a roaring trade.

Daley saw little value in the rehabilitation of offenders. Plenty of criminals used prison to hone their skills or evade arrest when they re-offended. And those who saw the error of their ways rarely crossed his path again. It was not the concept of rehabilitation, but the notion that committing a serious crime irrevocably changed an offender. And that, given the right set of circumstances, an offender would always revert to type. Had Raymond Asher, convicted of murder at fourteen, fed into the sausage machine of British justice, been released better equipped to seek his revenge?

He pulled his Audi onto the pavement in front of a tired wooden door and dropped a Lambourne Road *With compliments* slip, bearing the words *On Call* in thick *Sharpie* black, onto the dash. He pressed a button and announced himself to the bored voice that came over the intercom. Presently, a shape filled the frosted glass and spent an age undoing the plethora of ironmongery that kept the neighbourhood safe. Then he flipped his warrant card at a bored middle-aged man in a tartan shirt and woollen tank top, who wasn't the slightest bit impressed.

'Peter Dennis?'

The man nodded for him to enter, and led the way to a cluttered shoebox office, little more than a series of half-glass partitions, fixed across an alcove, stale with cigarette smoke and neglect. Dennis gave the same nod towards a chair, then squirmed into a small space behind a wood and metal desk heaving under piles of paperwork, before twisting a knob and silencing a tinny transistor radio.

'I'm Asher's key worker,' he said, leaning forward onto the only space on the desk. 'but I told your officer earlier, he's at work until five, five-thirty. He sometimes goes for a pint with his mate.'

'His mate?' asked Daley.

'Danny Pearce. They were cellmates for a time. When they released Pearce about two years ago, we found him a job at the bowling alley. When Asher came out, they took him on as well.'

Asher's parole report mentioned Pearce. He had served a term for burglary and aggravated assault. 'And does Pearce stay here too?'

'I'm afraid not. He left twelve months ago. He has a place of his own in town.'

'Is it usual for offenders with such serious crimes behind them to be allowed to fraternise so closely?'

Dennis gave an irritated sigh and screwed up his face as if Daley was challenging his professional judgement.

'It was all ratified by their respective offender managers. Asher is a low risk. He committed his crime as a juvenile, and his prison record is clean. Pearce has been out for over two years without re-offending.'

'And how does Asher seem?'

'Quiet, a little withdrawn, but, after a long spell inside, it's still early days for him. It takes time to adjust to a less regimented way

An Invisible Murder

of life. Remember, Chief Inspector, Asher has spent his whole adult life in one institution or another. He has no experience of the outside world. Even travelling to work is a daunting experience. As his key worker, I went with him on the bus until he got the hang of it. But after six weeks, he is coping fine, thanks in part to Danny. He showed him how to handle money and do his shopping. How real life works. They have given Asher a programme of activities as part of his parole. He attends regularly and completes his diary as required. Truth be told, I wish all our residents were as fastidious.'

Daley didn't doubt it. Prison taught one how to behave when the screws were watching.

'I'm here in connection with an incident that occurred in Harrow, the explosion in Green Street. Someone matching Asher's description was seen nearby, so we are looking to confirm his whereabouts last Friday and Saturday, say, from six in the evening until two the next morning.'

Dennis again made the face. He made a play of searching the disorganised desk and landed on the file, right under his nose, he'd prepared earlier. 'Friday afternoon, Ray left around 2:30 pm for the bowling alley. His shift lasted until eleven o'clock, so he would be back here at midnight at the latest. Our curfew runs from eleven until six the next morning, so we had to get a dispensation from his offender manager for him to be on shift at that time. One of the staff would have let him in. It wasn't me, though. I don't live onsite.'

'So who was it?'

Dennis made the face again and craned around for a clipboard. Not that Daley blamed him. Arthur Godwin House accommodated fifteen scrotes at capacity. They all knew the rules and how they could be bent. On a good day, it would be like herding cats.

'Friday's clocking-in sheet. It says he signed himself back in at five past twelve on Saturday. Even if he hadn't, if he missed the night bus and had to walk, he'd be back by two.' Dennis beamed a self-satisfied grin. Pick the bones out of that one.

'Can I see his room?'

'Wouldn't help you much. All he has are a couple of changes of clothes, a few personal items, toiletries, and the holdall he carried them in. We have rules as to what a resident can keep in their room.'

'Even so.'

Again the face. Daley was concerned Dennis would stick like that if the wind changed. He grudgingly squeezed himself out from behind the desk; an effort which left him flushed. He rooted around in the top drawer of a filing cabinet and jangled a bunch of keys. They crossed a spartan hall and climbed a bland staircase to an empty corridor lined with identical doors. Dennis unlocked one and gestured Daley through. Inside was as depressing as the corridor; magnolia, a workaday console unit with a sink and a mirror, and a bed with a maroon bedspread. No posters or pictures. Apart from toiletries, a pair of trainers and a carrier bag containing dirty laundry, there was no sign anyone occupied the room. He wondered how much different this was from the prison cell Asher had left. Noticing his expression, Dennis smiled.

'Arthur Godwin House is a halfway house, Chief Inspector. If we make it too comfortable, they'll never leave.'

As they returned to the office, Daley peeked through a few doors; a TV room with ranks of leatherette chairs, a dining room that smelled of stew, and a recreation room with a pair of pool tables and a dartboard. A couple of the other residents eyed him suspiciously, so he nodded and left.

'This is what the prison forwarded to us.' Dennis passed across an anorexic manilla folder. The contents were the same as the ones Daley had read earlier.

'Does Asher get on with the other residents?'

'More than some, less than others. He reads a lot, but he's joining in more since he's realised they're not about to shank him with a sharpened toothbrush.'

'Just one last thing. Do you know if Asher had a lady friend - a girlfriend or sister who has visited him recently?'

Dennis chuckled wryly. 'Read the file. No siblings. Parents are dead. The nearest he gets to a woman is speaking to his psychologist. And I wouldn't know, anyway. We don't allow visitors into the hostel, but if he met someone outside, say on his lunch break or after work…It's not a monastery.'

Daley sensed there was little more to be had, that he had probably exchanged more words in his brief visit with Peter Dennis than Asher had in weeks of being a resident. Outside, the dull day seemed brighter, the air fresher, after the functional drabness of the hostel. He stretched out a hand and Peter Dennis gave it a feeble shake, like flicking off a drip of urine.

'Chief Inspector, you have a job to do but go easy on Ray. He's come a long way to where he is today. He's a clever lad, you know. While he was inside, he got a degree and studied several vocational courses. I got the feeling he wanted to make something of himself. I would hate to think of all that work going to waste.'

Daley winked. 'Alright, I'll break the habit of a lifetime and be sensitive. Just don't let him know I've been here, please, because even innocent people get the jitters.'

He'd seen both sides of the argument. Those who turned their lives around and those whose names graced the Operations feed with unerring regularity. It could be coincidental that Asher was loitering outside St Dunstan's, a church containing a former staff member at Holy Mount, as a house across the road exploded. A house containing a fellow pupil of the same school, who was present when Asher committed the most heinous of crimes.

But Daley wasn't a fan of coincidences.

***

The next stop was LA Bowl, one of a formulaic group of retail units on a park just outside Ruislip, the same eateries, amusements and cinema every town had, with parking for several thousand cars, albeit empty and rain-swept mid-morning on a weekday. Bowling wasn't Daley's thing; he couldn't hit a cow's backside with a banjo, so when the lads suggested a night out, he preferred a curry. Even then, he chose a korma.

Inside, an amusement arcade chimed to jingles competing for the attention of a handful of children and their grandparents' loose change. Twenty lanes echoed to the rumble of bowls, the wooden *pock* of tumbling pins, and modern muzak no one was listening to, accompanied by plasma screens no one was watching, and a sickly smell of popcorn and rancid polish. Daley, yet to master his thirties, wondered if it was this noisy in his day. He asked at the desk for Raymond Asher. The teenage attendant looked up from thumbing through stuff on her phone, as all teenagers seem to do, and pointed across to a tiny glass booth where the manager was also thumbing through stuff on his phone. When Daley asked again, he leant his head around the door and jerked a thumb.

'Door on the end marked *staff only*, mate.' Then, visibly huffing at the imposition, he added, 'Hang on, I better take you. Health and Safety…'

For a moment, the seven-year-old in Daley took over at the thought of what goes on behind a bowling alley, quickly growing up, when the glitz and glamour of LA fell away to the cinder blocks and stacked cardboard boxes of Ruislip, and a tight corridor that smelled of oil and dust. At the end, he followed the manager into a high narrow machine room where pulleys and wheels were picking up bowling pins and sending them off for another pounding. A stocky man in ear defenders leant against the back wall, scanning up and down, minding the machines. He looked over, hefted himself upright, and tried to look busy. Daley's warrant card stopped even that.

'Raymond Asher?' Daley shouted over the racket.

'Do what?' The stocky man removed an ear defender and replaced it with a cupped hand.

'*Raymond Asher?*' Daley enunciated the words like an idiot.

'No. Danny Pearce. Ray's on his break.' He nodded toward a door at the far end of the machine room. Then he glanced up at a red light over the machines, replaced his ear defenders and strolled off.

The door led to a small tired staffroom: a kitchen, a snack

machine, and a couple of scratched Formica tables surrounded by chrome and fabric chairs. A small screen played the same video as the ones outside, to a quieter soundtrack of the same music. There was a slight fug of weed, which the extractor was having trouble dispelling. A fire door hung ajar, bobbing in the breeze.

'Bollocks.'

Racing across the room, slamming through the door, Daley found himself in an enclosed yard with a couple of overflowing dumpsters, several chained-up push bikes, and a few parked cars. A girl of about twenty leaned on the wall, thumbing on her phone as a cigarette slowly burned in her left hand. She gave him a sadistic smile. Raymond Asher had gone.

Annoyed as he was, Daley didn't blame him. Fresh out of jail, an easy target for every misdemeanour on the patch. Of course, Dennis at the parole hostel had tipped him the wink. Or maybe tipped off Danny Pearce. Two people were dead, yet the police were still the bad guys. Meanwhile, some nutter was probably planning his next brutal murder. He messaged Dave Monaghan and asked him to put out the call. After all, no one runs without a reason.

Pearce was still in the machine room, a pair of legs disappearing into the mechanism, as he tried to remove an obstacle from the machinery. Daley gestured a thumb towards the staffroom and he reluctantly followed, the air of a naughty schoolboy with a textbook down his trousers. Pearce went straight on the offensive.

'Haven't you people got better things to do than harass me?'

'Not harassing you, Danny,' said Daley. 'Where's Ray Asher?'

'How should I know? I'm not his keeper.'

'Phone.' Daley flipped his fingers.

Pearce stood defiant. 'Don't you need a warrant or something?'

'Just hand the bloody thing over.'

Pearce puffed again, pulled out his mobile, tapped in a PIN code, and handed it over. The last call was from the parole hostel, which made Daley raise his eyebrows.

'Someone called for Ray,' explained Pearce. 'Could've been anyone. Like I say, I'm not his keeper.'

'We just need a word. Where's he gone, Danny?'

'Like I'm going to tell you, even if I knew. I'm not a grass.'

'Fair enough. Danny Pearce, I'm arresting you for obstructing a police officer—'

'Okay, okay.' Danny fell back in a chair and folded his arms.

Daley brought up the notes on his phone. 'You were sent down five years ago. Blackrose. Released in 2011. Is that where you and Raymond Asher met?'

'You know that already.' Pearce scowled as if Daley had mistaken him for an imbecile.

'After you came out, did you and Asher keep in touch?'

'Nah, I'd left all that behind. I got a flat, a job. Responsibilities.'

'So, how come you helped him when he was released? Surely, if you've left the past behind, he was someone else's problem?'

Pearce leaned forward, knees apart, elbows on his thighs, staring between his feet. 'We shared a cell for the last two years of my stretch and I thought he'd got a raw deal. Twenty years, man. Ex-cons don't get a lot of help, so I asked if there was a job here. You know, solidarity between former lags.'

Pearce was avoiding eye contact. Daley couldn't help smiling. Altruism, along with the tooth fairy and Santa Claus, was not something he believed in anymore.

'What did you and he talk about?'

'Lots of stuff. Life, the Universe and everything. Anything to take our minds off the food, the latrines, the psychos outside our cell, the four fucking brick walls.'

'Did he ever talk about Claire Dobson? The girl he murdered?'

'No. Never. I knew what he'd done, but he kept himself to himself. Most of the time it was as if it had never happened.'

'And Ray himself. What sort of person is he?' asked Daley.

'He's alright, I s'pose. Seriously clever, spent most of his time in the library when he wasn't banged up or working in the laundry. He got a degree in Religious Studies from the Open University. Fair play. But you know what? They sent him down when he was fourteen. He was a kid told to act like an adult. They showed him how to collect his benefits and go to the supermarket, those sorts of things, but apart from that. When he's not at work, he's in the hostel.'

The reports from the Youth Offenders Institute told of a solitary boy. Not sporty or adventurous, he excelled at classes, but little else. Adult jails were a more abstract, brutal world. If one didn't want to be eaten up by it, one kept to oneself, suffered selective deafness and watched one's back. If called upon to do so, one took the beatings and defilement. To do otherwise invited worse. The prison reports painted Asher as a quiet, self-contained individual, choosy about the company he kept.

'Is Ray in some sort of trouble?' Pearce leaned back, arms folded across his chest like a straitjacket. Careless talk costs livelihoods. Maybe he had already said too much.

'We just need a word. I need to check his whereabouts last weekend. Do you have any idea where he was?'

'Different shifts. Anyway, if he wasn't in the hostel by midnight, he'd turn into a pumpkin or something.' Pearce smirked and gave an involuntary bob of the shoulders.

'And where has Asher gone right now?' Daley nodded purposefully at the open fire door.

'No idea.'

'Andrew Mason, Sonia Judd, Jacob Foster. Do those names mean anything to you?'

Pearce pulled a face and shook his head.

Daley had had enough. This was getting nowhere. He pulled out a card and held it out between his forefinger and middle finger. 'If anything else occurs to you or Asher gets in touch, you call me, or the next time we meet, it'll be at *my* gaff, okay?'

Chapter 20

Father Joseph O'Donnell had watched the Chief Inspector through the window and prayed he would keep walking. He had held his breath as he dallied, relieved as he drove off. He was a bag of bloody nerves after the interview - no, interrogation. Forced to revisit events long forgotten, fearful his sins were catching up with him. How quick they found out about Holy Mount. After all, the whole sorry mess began and ended there. Twenty years ago, Claire's murder augured the death knell for the school, and he was sure Asher's release from prison was the catalyst for the trouble now. If he had not offered Asher to them, how long before they began delving into his part in the girl's death? He had to hope the police would run into the same cul-de-sac as they had back then. Maybe it would divert them from asking him too many questions.

On the side table, his bible was still open:
"Thou shalt also consider in thine heart,
that, as a man chasteneth his son,
so the Lord thy God chasteneth thee."
(Deuteronomy 8:5)

Mason's murder was a warning that O'Donnell's sins shall find him out on Earth before he was called to account before his maker. Death was coming, and it was already outside the gates.

Behind him, the whine of the vacuum faded away and Edith O'Hallorhan poked her head around the door.

'You have a visitor, Father.'

O'Donnell's heart skipped a beat. 'God bless you, Edith. Please leave that for now.'

He waved a hand at the vacuum cleaner and shooed her from the room. The dotty old bird had been prattling on forever as she cleaned the vicarage, but he was too preoccupied to listen, too polite to stop her. With her husband in the hands of the Lord, she had no one else to talk to, and her heart was in the right place; there were four Hobnobs on the tray, a treat for a busy morning's paperwork. As the vicarage doorbell rang again, he crossed to the window and peered around the curtain. He recognised the face from the past. Older, more lined, but equally challenging. A boulder formed in the pit of his stomach. What in heaven's name did *he* want?

'Jacob Foster!' His hands were shaking as he opened the door against the chain. 'I thought I'd made it quite clear I wanted nothing more to do with you.'

'That was then, and this is now. We need to talk.' No introduction, no pleasantries, as if even a hello was an imposition on his time. Some things never changed. O'Donnell tried to close the door, but Foster's foot prevented him.

'Let's not be stupid, Father.'

He unhooked the chain and stood back, awed by Foster's height. Back then, a whelp with no more on his mind than trouble, what trouble could he cause now he had grown? The priest led the way to the sitting room, sat and crossed his legs as Foster blocked the meagre winter light from the window.

'You are here, so say what you must, then leave.'

'Have the police spoken to you about Last Friday yet?'

'Yes, they have, just this morning and I told them the truth. I was busy with Latin Mass and meetings and saw nothing. With no help from me, they already knew Andrew attended Holy Mount, and that I was on the staff at the same time. And they already know it was not an accident.'

Foster was pacing the recess of the bay window like a caged animal. The cock-sure bravado O'Donnell remembered had deserted him. In his eyes, he saw the same terrified expression he had twenty years ago.

'Well, that's all they need to know. If they call again, act surprised, or have a bout of amnesia or dementia. After a while, they will move on, like last time. Just keep your mouth shut, for all our sakes. Is that clear?'

'All our sakes? Who do you think you are? I answer to a much higher authority than you ever will. And for God's sake, *sit down!*'

Foster threw his arms in the air, exhaled deeply and fell into the second wingback. O'Donnell's hand shook as he reached for his teacup and raised it to his lips. His heart was beating in his chest; a familiar frisson of fear that had always gripped him when he had spoken to Jacob Foster. Somehow, the nastiness leached out and tainted everyone in the room.

'For your information, Jacob, what happened across the road had nothing to do with me, so I have nothing to keep my mouth shut about.'

Foster leaned back, open-mouthed. 'Are you that naïve? This has everything to do with you. They let Raymond Asher out, and then someone murders Andy Mason, and you're gifting the police a link between the two. How long before they find out about Claire, about what we did?'

O'Donnell gave a dismissive grunt. 'What *we* did? What happened to Claire is solely down to you and Mason, and he can hardly corroborate your story. That night, I sent you to bring them back not to commit *murder*. If I am guilty of anything, it is of protecting you, so you did not go the way of Raymond Asher. An imprudent act of charity, nothing more.'

'And if Asher talks? All it takes is one stray word…'

'They convicted Raymond Asher of Claire's murder, so no one is going to listen to him now, Jacob. Just keep quiet and let the police speculate. Without evidence, they have nothing, and all that concerns them now is what happened to Andrew Mason last Friday.'

O'Donnell settled back in his chair, hoping he had said enough, because he needed no more trouble. At his age, he had scarcely the resources to deal with what he had. A familiar numbness in his elbow and forearm told him he was about to have more. But Foster had not finished.

'You haven't heard, have you, Father? Bayhurst Grange is being redeveloped, and one day, next week, next month, they are going to find Claire's body. Then the police will be forced to revisit her murder. Don't you remember? I wrapped her in *my* coat. Even after all this time, there will be something that links her to me.'

O'Donnell gave a wry chuckle. His heart was racing fit to burst, a band tightening around his chest. 'You are being paranoid, Jacob. All they will have is an old coat, and they cannot link that back to you because I checked the inside for name tags. And you? Do the police have your fingerprints, or your DNA?'

He pulled his GTN spray from his pocket and curled his tongue to the taste. As the tautness eased, he recalled the bible quotation. *...as a man chasteneth his son, so the Lord thy God chasteneth thee.*

'I can't take that chance, Father, so tell me where Claire Dobson is buried. If they don't find her body, they can't come after me.'

'What? You are going to *dispose of the evidence?* Same old Jacob Foster, riding in on your white steed and putting everything right. Well, not this time! Isn't it a coincidence all this blows up - ha! *Blows up* - the moment they released Raymond Asher? You know, he was here at the church last Friday, Jacob. He stood under the lychgate and watched as Andrew Mason died, and soon he will come for you too. Mark my words, body or no, he will come for you - and then he will come for me.'

He took a deep breath. This ordeal had to stop before the pain in his chest worsened. He cowered as Foster loomed over him and grabbed his lapels. He closed his eyes and braced for a blow that never came.

'You might be content to throw your shabby, worthless life away, Father, but I am not, so tell me, where did you bury Claire's body?'

O'Donnell made to speak, but his jaw was held in a vice. Pinpricks of red filled his vision. He felt the hands leave his jacket and his head hit the back of his chair. The pains in his arm and chest were almost unbearable, sending spasms through his neck, and it hurt to pump air in and out of his lungs.

'Where is Claire Dobson's body?'

A shadow swung above the priest. He felt the impact across his cheek and blinked away the pain. A metallic taste filled his mouth, and beside him, crockery clattered to the floor. He fumbled again for the GTN and took another dose, leaving him light-headed.

'And how will this help your cause?' he coughed. 'Go ahead. Beat me. Leave me lying in my own blood, like you did the girl.'

'Just tell me where the fucking body is.' Foster's eyes were wild. He was shaking. His hot breath moistened O'Donnell's face, and the priest felt a warmth spread over his crotch. It was as if his whole body was slowly being fed into a car crusher. The phone was a mere three feet away. He had to make this ordeal stop.

'Alright. I will tell you, for all the good it will do, but first, ring for an ambulance. I am having a heart attack. Please, Jacob.'

Through the spots in his eyes, he saw Foster lift the receiver.

'Where is the body, Father?' Low and controlled. The old menace was back.

'The furnace room, the old furnace room, and may god have mercy on your soul if you disturb the dead. Now ring for an ambulance, then leave me alone.'

O'Donnell leaned back, consumed by the pain tearing through his arm, chest, and neck. Somewhere, the phone clattered to the floor. He could hear a woman's voice - *Emergency, which service, please. Hello?* The front door slammed, and he was alone with the silence pressing the breath from his chest. A stray tear fell onto his cheek as he remembered Asher's message on the altar cloth:

> "Thou shalt also consider in thine heart,
> that, as a man chasteneth his son,
> so the Lord thy God chasteneth thee."
> (Deuteronomy 8:5)

Was it now he discovered the truth about his God?

Chapter 21

Will Hughes had lain awake most of the night, agonising over Abi. Since they had met five years ago, she had been his soulmate, the alpha and omega of everything right in his life. The only person he wanted to be with as he fell asleep each night and as he woke each morning.

Yet now Jake Foster was sniffing about her.

Conversely, Foster was the alpha and omega of everything wrong. *He* was the problem. A serial philanderer, an egotist, and a bully, Abi must know he was not a life choice. He went through women like Abi's knife through their low-fat plant-based spread at breakfast. One day, when it was too late, she would realise her mistake. Of course, he could not expect a guy like that to walk into Sam's office and demand she reinstate him. Right now, he was probably sitting behind his desk sharpening his knife for the *coup de grâce*.

In the end, it came down to common sense. With or without Abi, he needed a job, and he also needed to put Sam Clarke-Mitchell straight on a few things. If Sam threw him from her office window, at least Abi would see he had a backbone, even if it was broken and bent in the car park. And Foster? Will would deal with him in due course - when he had worked out how. As the lift rose to the top floor, a newfound sense of courage and purpose filled him.

On the other side of the main office, Jacob Foster's room was in darkness. Not even the dull, blue glow from his computer screen saver. Foster's time-keeping was meticulous. By 10:45 am, he was always in his office slaving away.

'Has anyone seen Jake this morning?' he asked.

As Lyall continued typing, craning over his keyboard, Carol looked up from her monitor, removed an earphone, and squinted at him. A mouse of a woman, surrounded by photos of children and small twee remembrances that cluttered her desk. She shrugged and nodded towards the empty office.

'Nothing in the diary.'

'Lyall?'

Lyall made a play of scanning around the room as if the mere act would conjure up Jake Foster. It was a mystery to Hughes how people like Carol and Lyall managed a piss without getting their fingers wet, or maybe they did. Carol always had a large box of Kleenex handy.

As the pair resumed the mindless tedium of their day, it struck Will as odd that Carol and Lyall had omitted to mention his dismissal. Neither one had seemed surprised to see him. Perhaps no one had told them, but then no one had confirmed it to him either, so did he have a job or didn't he?

In a flash of clarity, as bright as a million suns, it all suddenly became clear. This was not about him at all, but about Jake and Abi. About ruining Hughes's credibility over Bayhurst Grange, denigrating his abilities in front of Sam Clarke-Mitchell, and even suggesting his departure would get the project back on track. Jake had engineered the whole situation just to humiliate him in Abi's eyes, to turn her from him and leave Foster free to pick up the pieces.

Well, not on my watch, Jake.

Across the office, the impenetrable fortress that was Marilyn Tyler was at her desk outside Sam's office. Twenty years old, drop-dead gorgeous, dressed flawlessly in a pressed white blouse and black skirt. Far from the epitome of a bouncer, she was the last and arguably most formidable line of defence in a quest to speak to the CEO. As he approached, she stopped typing and gave him possibly the only smile he would get that day, even if it was just a professional courtesy.

'Marilyn, any idea where Jake Foster is?'

'No, but if *you* have, keep it to yourself. Sam wants to rip him a new one this morning.'

'Really?' Hughes feigned surprise, but his heart leapt at the image. 'What's the problem?'

'You need to speak to Sam.' Marilyn gave him the look his mother gave him when he was three and didn't use his spoon. 'She's off out in a few minutes. I'd leave it until tomorrow.'

'Don't worry. Let's surprise her, shall we?' With his heart in his mouth, and every sphincter clenched tight, Will Hughes pushed down the handle of Sam Clarke-Mitchell's door.

***

'What the—? Doesn't anyone knock anymore?' Sam Clarke-Mitchell cast down a pen and slouched back. 'You? What the hell do *you* want?'

'I want my job back, Sam. Please.' Manners cost nothing and were probably worth less. 'Jake sacked me. Remember?'

'Nobody's been sacked, Will. Just—'

'—with immediate effect, Jake said. Sounds pretty final.'

'Never say never. I've had a rethink. I was going to call you shortly to discuss. But first, where's Jake?'

Suddenly, Will's world flipped again, but he kept his cool. He gave an insouciant shrug and pulled out the chair. 'He said he was off to sort out Bayhurst Grange before the full survey.'

'He had things to sort out alright. Right now, he's probably cosying up to our competitors, cutting himself a lucrative deal while this place goes under. And how much do you get for screwing me over?'

Hughes grimaced rather uncharitably at the mental images she was conjuring up. 'I'm sacked, remember?'

'I'm willing to admit I was a little precipitous about that, particularly given your work on the project to date.'

'What? The work you have constantly rubbished over the past six weeks?' Self-preservation kicked in, and Will closed his mouth before his foot entered. 'Sorry, go on.'

'Do you know what I was doing yesterday? I'll tell you. I had to phone Bainhams and beg Geoff Bridger not to back out. Then, I had to sit in his pokey little bloody office with my legs crossed and my skirt split up to my snatch while he told me we had missed our window. It took me everything I had to get him to reconsider. *Everything.*'

'Bainhams? So, Jake signed off on the preliminary surveys?'

'No, *Will*, he bloody did not.'

Hughes took a deep, purging breath and exhaled slowly. 'Cut to the chase, Sam. What do you want?'

'Cards on the table, Will. Whatever Jake is up to, I need it to stop, and I need you to help me rescue the bid. It's the eleventh hour. If we don't do something today, we can kiss goodbye to our investment, forcing me to lay off half the people outside. We'll be in debt up to our eyeballs.'

She kept her eyes firmly on his. Will had witnessed the mesmeric stare before. He had seen many a grown man crumble to dust, faced with that stare, but he held fast.

'I'll help, yes. Give me half an hour and the paperwork will be on your desk, ready to sign. But first, what's in it for me?'

The stare softened much as a boxer's would after an impact under the chin.

'I've told you, you keep your job.'

'So you make millions and I keep my job. That doesn't sound entirely fair, given you've already sacked me at the drop of a hat. What's stopping you doing it again, once this is all over?'

Sam huffed. 'I will email HR before you leave this room. A minimum three-year contract. That's better security than even Jake has - much better right now. Thirty minutes, you keep your job. I can keep the promises I made to Bainhams, and Jake Foster will be completely out of the loop.'

Will was dumbfounded. Sam had cottoned on to Jake's deceit and realised Will's worth to the company. Hopefully, Foster would not set foot in her building again. If he played his cards right, his job was safe, Jake was out on his ear and he and Abi could start again. The secret was not to react. Not to seem too grateful. She had to know *he* was doing *her* a favour, not vice versa. He leaned forward and rested his elbows on the desk.

'I believe Jake *wants* the bid to fail. For over a month now, he has been playing you like a cheap fiddle and however much I tried to tell you, you wouldn't listen. Certainly not to me.'

'Like I say, I was a little precipitous, but I'm listening now.'

'There's something about Bayhurst Grange that, if it came to light, would finish him. Now I don't know what that secret of his is - yet, he's out there now trying to sort it out and if he does, you'll lose the bid and he'll get away Scot free. Give me half an hour on his computer. I bet I could find out what's going on. Then you and I will drive out to Bayhurst Grange and free this logjam once and for all.'

Across the desk, Sam resumed the stare and Hughes could feel his temples ache. Then she pressed the intercom button on her phone.

'Marilyn. Bring in two coffees - the decent stuff. Will and I have some things to discuss. Oh, and some biscuits.'

Chapter 22

'Dave, what do we know about Raymond Asher?'

Monaghan looked up as Scott Daley strode through the double door, almost tearing them off their hinges. He enjoyed these moments in the spotlight; a chance to show he did more each day than play Solitaire on his computer, at least since Daley had phoned in the name two hours earlier.

'Raymond Michael Asher, thirty-four years old, originally from Edgware. Sent to Holy Mount Residential School, aged eight. His mother died of an overdose. He never knew his father. In September 1993, Asher, aged fourteen, was convicted of the murder of fellow resident Claire Dobson, also fourteen. Forensics found two potential murder sites; one out by the floodwater culverts under the motorways, and a second in a derelict woodman's shed, where they found DNA belonging to both Asher and Dobson and a significant amount of Dobson's blood, which indicated a threat to life. The presumption was that after absconding, Asher and Dobson had argued, and Asher attacked Dobson. He took her back to the woodman's shed, where she died, then hid her body somewhere on the estate. A week later, they tracked Asher down to a hideout on the edge of the woods and arrested him. Dobson's blood was still all over his clothing. Despite an extensive search of the woods and lake around the school, they never found Dobson's body and, under the direction of the Coroner, Asher was charged and convicted of her murder. Because of his age, they sent him to a Young Offenders Institution in Lancashire. In 2000, when he turned 21, he was moved to HMP Blackrose and enrolled on an offender behaviour programme, where he shared the cell with Danny Pearce, and they released him on licence around a month ago. In prison, Asher trained as a plumber, so he would certainly have the knowledge to tamper with a cooker and set a central heating timer to explode at 1:00 am.'

'Can we place Asher at the crime scene, Steve?' asked Daley.

DC Taylor shook his head. 'CCTV does not cover the back gate into the churchyard. I've cast the net wider. Jane is having another word with Mrs O'Hallorhan, the church helper, to see if she can be any more certain it was him standing in the churchyard.'

'Keep looking. We need anything that places Asher anywhere other than his room at the hostel.'

***

In Deb Whetstone's mind, the Green Street incident became much clearer now they knew that Hannah Mason had followed her husband into Harrow. A woman betrayed. It would satisfy Superintendent Hacker's bean counters if they secured a speedy conviction without a lengthy investigation. She had fallen over herself to request ANPR data on Hannah's car to cover the period Asher had been out of prison.

Naturally, Scott Daley had his doubts. The school connection played on his mind like an aquarium full of red herrings. As a fan of Occam's Razor, he seemed to complicate issues, and it pissed him off Asher had given him the slip. Still, he would resurface eventually and in the meantime, they had bigger fish to fry in the form of Hannah Mason.

The tiny, airless interview room at Lambourne Road felt suffocatingly small. A table and four chairs sat against one wall, whilst a one-way mirror glass window filled the one opposite. The top half of the walls were a delicate shade of battleship grey. Underneath a panic strip dado rail, it was white and covered in scuff marks from furniture and shoes. The floor was a lake of ill-fitting puke-green carpet tiles. There was no natural light this low in the bowels of the building. A small wired glass window near the ceiling was wasting its time, deferring instead to a striplight that annoyed

An Invisible Murder

everyone with its intermittent burring and flickering. There was a trick - one needed to switch it on and off, then back on quickly. Something to do with transients, DC Taylor had said.

From the equally oppressive observation room, Whetstone studied Hannah Mason, sitting alongside FLO Judith Marner, every inch the grieving widow in a black dress and black woollen cardigan. Her hair was lank and greasy, tied back in a ponytail, and her face was without makeup. To Whetstone, it was the face of a woman lost in the void between a rock and a hard place. Hannah briefly glanced over as she entered the interview room, sighed deep and long, and then returned her eyes to the table.

Or it could all be a performance.

'Thanks for coming in, Hannah. Before we start, let me tell you that you're not under arrest, but we are recording this interview. Sergeant Marner is here, if you need any help. If you want, you can stop the interview and leave at any time. Is that clear?'

Hannah signalled she did.

'I'd like to go over last Friday again with you. You said Andy left the house at around 8:00 am, and that was the last time you saw him. Could you walk me through your day?'

'Like I said before, I ran the kids to school, did the weekly shop and was back home by around 11:30 for the cleaner.'

'You saw your cleaner Sonia Judd that morning?'

'Yes, she left at around three when I went to pick the girls up from school.'

'Did Andy call home during the day?' Whetstone asked.

'No. He never does.'

Hannah's tone hinted at resentment, reminiscent of the day after the explosion. *He kissed the girls, but he didn't kiss me. Never checked on me during the day. Ships in the night.* Maybe it summed up their relationship. One of convenience for the sake of the children.

'And Friday evening?' asked Whetstone.

'I took Keren to dance class for five, so we left at a quarter to.

Rhiannon stayed with her. She wants to enrol too but they only take them from eight years old. I was home by quarter past five.'

'And dance class finished when?'

'Around six-thirty. Their grandparents, my parents, picked them up for a trip to McDonald's and a sleepover.'

'We've spoken to Stratham Motors, Hannah. Andy left there at 5:30 pm and it's twenty minutes back home. So he arrived at 5:50 pm or thereabouts. If you arrived home at 5:15 pm, you and your husband were both at home until he left again at 6:30 - forty minutes, yet you didn't see him?'

'I wasn't looking at the clock. Maybe I got the times wrong.' In her lap, Hannah balled her fists, turning the knuckles white. Her brow furrowed. The annoyance Whetstone had seen at their first interview had returned, as if Andy Mason had died out of spite and there was nothing she could do about it.

'Okay. What about the rest of the evening?'

'I was in the house.' Hannah glanced at the ceiling, her reply soft under her breath, sure Whetstone would know she was lying. Whetstone laid down a photograph to remove all doubt.

'This is your husband's car. A gunmetal grey Mercedes, registration RU63SMC, waiting at the junction of Pinner Road and George Avenue. The timestamp on the photo is 6:47 pm. You can see Andy driving.'

Hannah glanced at the photo and swiftly looked away toward the window. Whetstone laid a similar picture beside it.

'And this car, a white Mercedes, three cars behind your husband's, caught by the same traffic camera at the same time - 6:47 pm. RU13MZH. That's your vehicle.'

Hannah looked away, refusing to acknowledge the image, so Whetstone pressed on.

'Both cars parked up in the car park on Greenhill Way in Harrow. You were several rows behind your husband's car. Here you are buying a ticket, and here on foot, following Andy into Harrow, on the night he died. Why was that?'

'No comment.' A response of no comment when faced with irrefutable evidence was like pissing into the wind. Whetstone pressed on.

'This is a list of APNR hits on Andy's car registration taken from cameras along the Pinner Road over the last three weeks, and this second sheet contains hits on your car registration on the same stretch of road, each within a minute of Andy passing the same point. Five times in the last three weeks, each time around 6:45 pm, behind Andy as he travelled into Harrow. I suggest you were well aware your husband was seeing another woman, and having cottoned on to his trips to Harrow, you followed him.'

'No comment.' Spat through gritted teeth. Judith Marner reached across and took Hannah's hand.

'The truth always comes out,' she said. 'Best it comes out now, and from you. The sooner we find out what happened, the better.'

Whetstone nodded, acknowledging Marner's help. FLO was a difficult role, dealing with people at their most fragile. It required patience, understanding and tact, qualities Whetstone herself lacked, as did Scott Daley. He was a fan of thumbscrews and waterboarding to extract a confession from a recalcitrant interviewee, but as the powers-that-be disapproved, they had to make do. She pulled another two pages from her file.

'Besides Andy's work phone and the one you gave us, we also recovered a third mobile from Andy's car. A prepay with only your cleaner's number in it. Phone records suggest they had met regularly for around three weeks, each coinciding with one of the journeys from Ruislip to Harrow. I simply cannot believe you have not picked up on your husband's behaviour.'

Across the table, Hannah was trembling. She was teetering on the edge of a collapse that hadn't yet happened. And she was trying to protect herself from a truth she did not want to believe, as her life slowly crumbled around her. After a while, she drew a deep breath.

'The first I noticed was about a month ago. He changed his hair and wore a different aftershave. Suddenly, they needed him to work longer hours. At first, I dismissed it as paranoia. You know, married with two children. But then he started coming home in a different shirt from the one he went out in. I rang his office and asked for him. He wasn't there, so I challenged him. He said it was a poker school. Something Jacob Foster had started. He hadn't told me because he knew how I felt about gambling. But I knew he was lying. I could smell her on him.'

'So, tell us about Friday.'

'We'd promised the children McDonald's after dance class. He was going to come with me to pick them up, and then afterwards, I'd drop him by *The Queen's Head* for his Friday night with the lads. But at lunchtime, he rang and said something had come up. A work thing, and could I order in takeaway instead? Well, I was just bloody incensed. Time after time, he makes these promises. Time after time, he disappoints them. The kids enjoy their time with their dad. When he came home from work, I had it out with him., but he just laughed and called me stupid. That it was just a work thing, but, after fourteen years, I should know when he's lying. He got dressed. Smart trousers, a smart shirt, smart trainers and his leather jacket, smelling like the perfume counter at Boots. A work thing, my foot! Even a drink with the lads has a sort of uniform, t-shirt and jeans, older trainers. More casual.'

'He left. What happened then?'

'I don't know. I was mad and ashamed for not being stronger., so I rang Mom and Dad and asked them to pick up the girls, take them to McDonald's, and keep them overnight. Then I followed him to Harrow. *She* was in Starbucks, sitting at the back. Sonia Judd, our *cleaner*. He walked over, she stood, and they embraced. I hid behind a stall in the mall. Andy bought coffee and sat next to her. Ten minutes later, they left. I don't think they even touched the coffee. They walked up towards Greenhill Way and over into the estate. I followed as far as Sefton Street, watched them turn the corner into Green Street and go into the house.'

'And what time was this?'

'Around 8:00 pm, I suppose. I wanted to march up to the front door and give that bitch what she deserved, but I couldn't. I had to think of the kids, you see. In the end, I turned around, went back to the car and drove home to Pinner. I knew I had to put a brave face on for the kids. Whatever he was doing - whoever he was doing - he was still their dad.'

'Can you describe the woman you saw?'

'My height, thin. Probably only ten stone wringing wet. Red hair, curly, probably permed, old-fashioned, and she was wearing a long black coat.'

'Is this her?' Whetstone laid out a picture of Sonia Judd from the PNC files. Hannah Mason leant over and studied it for a long moment, confused.

'No. She had a rounder face, but I can't say for certain. In Starbucks, she was too far away, then when they came out it was dark, so I didn't get a good look at the bitch.'

'—but this is the person who cleans for you?'

Hannah shook her head. 'No, who is she?'

'This is Sonia Judd. The woman killed in the same gas explosion in Green Street as Andy.'

'I don't understand.' She looked up at the ceiling, eyes flicking left and right. 'So, who was Sonia, our cleaner?'

Who, indeed, mused Whetstone. She decided on a perpendicular change of subject.

'Were you aware Andy had been in trouble recently at work? He received a verbal warning for over-familiarity with the female staff and customers around six months ago and a written warning two months ago.'

Hannah Mason scoffed. 'Andy was quite good at keeping secrets - obviously!'

He isn't the only one, thought Whetstone.

'You can understand it's important we find who he was calling and texting, if only to rule them out. At the moment, I do not believe the woman he met, with whom he went back to Green

Street, was Sonia Judd, so I have to tell you, Hannah, I am now treating Andy's death as murder.'

Hannah's already pallid complexion drained further, and her lips mouthed the word. *Murder*. Perhaps, for all its tragedy, she had seen her husband's death as a line drawn under the sordid business of their marriage. A death she could blame on someone else; murder was more expedient and face-saving than divorce. But now the inference was that she was involved, even if indirectly, that Mason's inappropriate behaviour was not because of his proclivities, but to her failings as a wife.

Or her success as a murderer.

'Okay, Hannah. I am not convinced you are being entirely truthful with me. We have evidence you followed your husband into Harrow in the weeks leading up to his death, and on the night of his murder, you cannot provide us with a sufficient alibi between 7:45 pm and 4:00 am the following morning. I am not charging you at present, so we will release you on police bail pending further investigations. Is that clear? One of my colleagues will be along shortly to take a full statement from you. I would urge you to tell him everything, the whole truth. If you need a solicitor, Judith can arrange for one to be present.'

Hannah Mason nodded almost imperceptibly. It bugged Whetstone that no one ever told the truth the first time around. How many hours of work had been wasted discovering that Hannah Mason had lied? How many more to prove her new story? As she tamped down her papers, she paused as Hannah took a breath.

'It was hard when I found out Andy was seeing someone else. I felt rejected, abused, inadequate even. But I lived with it. I loved him, you see, and we both love the children. I could bear the thought of him with another woman, as long as every day he came home to me.'

Whetstone thought back to when she discovered Keith Parrish had been cheating. Even in the face of overwhelming evidence, she refused to believe it. Maybe it was the fear of being alone, of being cut adrift, or simply the inadequacy. The knowledge she could not satisfy him. Naturally, it was never that straightforward. Even the very best, most loving, and most attentive partners get beaten and cheated on. If some women are guilty of being fools, some men are guilty of being bastards. Hannah Mason knew of her husband's betrayal and his infidelity. But would she seek revenge? Could she set the gas to explode? Could she source amitriptyline or fentanyl?

Or would she simply take scissors to his wardrobe?

***

She left Hannah Mason staring at a spot on the wall, stoic in the face of adversity, and returned to the observation room, where Scott Daley was finishing his coffee after watching the matinee.

'Steve Taylor tells me she's in line for a five hundred grand insurance payout plus his pension, around a million.'

Whetstone whistled dramatically. 'Yeah, but it's a colossal risk. If she's found guilty of involvement in his murder, the insurance won't pay out. Surely better to divorce the guy and rinse him dry - if only for the sake of the kids. We already know she lied about her whereabouts on the night of the explosion until we corrected her.'

'I just wonder if we are looking at this arse about face, Deb. After all, there is no evidence Hannah was involved in her husband's death, plus we know Judd was already dead when Hannah arrived in Green Street. All we have is CCTV showing she followed him back, but nothing points to her going in. She could be witnessing the crime rather than participating.'

'Or supervising it?' Whetstone would not be undermined.

'Where would she find amitriptyline and fentanyl? And according to her, Sonia Judd, the sex worker, was not the woman she believed was Sonia Judd, her cleaner.'

Whetstone hid her annoyance. She had found a way forward, yet Daley was having none of it. She caught a look she had seen many times before. As if something was so obvious, but she had not seen it.

'So you still believe it has something to do with Asher and a twenty-year-old murder?' she asked. 'Even if Hannah Mason knew what happened all that time ago, why would she wait for him to be released?'

'Is there any evidence she and Asher communicated?'

'Another burner we haven't located yet.' Whetstone felt they were veering away from Hannah Mason altogether.

'Look, Deb, we have to narrow down lines of enquiry. We need to identify the two people who entered the house and killed Mason and Judd. Find them and we will discover for certain whether Hannah Mason is involved.'

'And you think this Raymond Asher is the male perp?'

'He and Mason have history. The timing of his release is a tad coincidental, and witnesses saw him under the lychgate.'

'What about Foster and Hughes?'

Daley shook his head. 'Hughes would fold with guilt if he left the toilet seat up. Jacob Foster, maybe. He would sell his granny for a fiver. Ask Taylor to re-examine their alibis. See if he finds them making the trip. And on those nights Mason was unaccounted for, we need to know what he was doing, where he went, and who he saw, even if he was only playing piccolo in a Salvation Army band.'

'The Fire Investigators didn't find a piccolo in the rubble of Number 5.'

'No one likes a smart-arse, Deb, or so Superintendent Hacker keeps telling me. And we need to find the cleaner. Either she is Judd or she isn't, but either way, she's in this up to her curly red hair.'

Chapter 23

A familiar dread dragged at Foster's stomach as he turned between the two ivy-covered gateposts of Bayhurst Grange. It had been *his* home for nine years after the authorities sent him there. Or rather, Holy Mount Residential School had. He knew every room, corridor, and lock. But life was different. Sadistic and cruel, as only institutionalised adolescents could be. Joyless, never happy.

He recalled the old lodge a few metres inside the gate. Back then, it had been pristine, home to the live-in staff - Father O'Donnell, Sister Agnes and two teachers, and the pupils rarely ventured this far up the drive. Now it stood abandoned. He parked up on a rutted carpet of straw-coloured grass that used to be the well-manicured lawn. The Volvo he'd bought was old but sound, and anonymous, unlike his XKR which likely was already on bricks outside the motor dealers. He pushed back the car seat and struggled into a pair of overalls he'd bought, stretched on gloves, then exchanged his trainers for new Wellington boots.

A quarter mile further on, under a solemn, claustrophobic canopy of overhanging trees, the gravel drive turned into a deserted courtyard, utterly silent, except for the cawing of ravens and the restive patter of rain. The dour, imposing shape of Bayhurst Grange filched every scintilla of light from the leaden sky. The roof was skeletal, blackened, and broken, yet much of the building seemed to have escaped the flames. Behind an algae-greened cordon of mesh fences, the front doors thumped heavily on their hinges, a padlock clanking on the sagging chain. Foster felt a shiver; not the chill of the rain or the wind, but something more visceral, as if the building itself had recognised him. As if it knew what he had done.

The furnace room was in the warren of basement rooms in the old house. He hitched his holdall higher on his shoulder, and followed the barriers around, kicking away the brambles that tugged at his overalls. Twenty years ago, the back of the house surveyed a cloistered quadrangle, a playground and a lawn stretching to the boundary of the woods. Now, the cracked and uneven quad was heaving with tree roots and tufted with vegetation. The huge stone cross still dominated the quadrangle, mottled with moss and lichen. A symbol of the iron fist inside the velvet glove, the Lord's deputy on Earth dispensing praise and punishment in equal measure. For a moment, a wave of sadness overcame him. A perverted nostalgia. It had, after all, once been his home. But then he recalled the things he had seen in the name of God and shuddered.

The sooner he was away from this hell, the better.

At the rear of the house, a sweep of stone steps led up to a huge glass sunroom, which doubled as the dining room for the school. Sweltering in summer and arctic in winter. Now particle board covered it all. To the left of the steps, he found the basement entrance. He pulled a pry bar from his holdall, pushed it under the hasp of the lock and twisted, splintering the brittle wood. As the door swung free, he found his torch and headed down the low, dark passageway. Above him, asbestos-clad heating pipes descended from the house above into the bowels of the basement, where they would lead to the heating boiler in the furnace room.

After a while, the corridor ended in a fire door bearing a sign which warned *Danger of death* and *risk to life*. Above it, the pipework pierced the wall. There was a definite smell of burnt timber and the walls were black with mildew and fungus, where the damp from the water that extinguished the flames had permeated the brickwork. Luckily, the wood surrendered to the pry bar, and he was soon scanning his torch over a space around five meters square. The smell of old oil and rust tickled his nose. In the centre sat a monolithic central heating boiler, and the pumps distributing water into the pipes across the ceiling. Three sides of the unit were plain metal casing with only apertures for the piping. The fourth had a small control panel with grubby dials and switches.

The basement room had turned oppressive. Inside his overalls, he was already damp with sweat, and his mouth was as dry as the concrete floor. He pulled a bottle of water from his holdall and drained it. High in the wall, a small slit window filled with wired glass let in a feeble green glow through the weeds outside. He had located the furnace room, but had not found a corpse.

Where did he go from here?

***

The drive out to Bayhurst Grange was uncomfortably quiet. It didn't help that the stiff suspension of the Mercedes and the floral odour of Sam Clarke-Mitchell's scent made Will Hughes queasy. His only thought was for Abi. He had yet to tell her how things had gone. How he finally had the backbone she had nagged him so often to get. The security of a long contract would help smooth the troubled waters. The worm had finally turned. He had stood up for himself, so why did he feel he'd been duped? That everything he had gained could be swept away again just as quickly?

Could he trust someone as duplicitous as Jake Foster? After all, he had promised to sort out the whole job thing - and hadn't, but then, Sam was adamant he would no longer be welcome at SCM, and if Foster had to relocate for work, the problem would vanish completely. Every cloud…

Foster had also promised to stay away from Abi. Would he keep his word on that, too?

Finally, the claustrophobia of the drive gave way to an expanse of gravelled courtyard, bleak and weed-mottled.

'How depressingly gothic.' Sam peered through the windscreen, her nose wrinkled in disgust. 'Still, we're only going to tear the whole thing down.'

Will unbuckled his seatbelt and snaked himself out like an escapologist from a sack. He stretched out his arms and legs, feeling the blood surge back into his butt. It was silent, except for the ravens and the rain on the gravel. He could almost hear the place sucking the cash from Sam Clarke-Mitchell's bank account.

'I thought you said he was here?' she said.

Frustratingly, the place appeared deserted, but more annoying, Jake Foster's Jaguar was nowhere to be seen.

'Maybe he parked somewhere else and walked down?'

'We need to find him. Then you can hold him while I kick his arse.' She snaked out of the low-slung car and cursed as the moss under her feet made the ground spongy. 'Fetch me my boots and coat from the boot.'

In for a penny, Will trudged around behind the car and found a Burberry gabardine trench coat and matching rain boots in the car's boot. Sam was a country girl, even if she had not yet developed the flippers and gills to deal with the weather. The rain was already soaking through his inadequate jacket.

'Jake, it's Sam.' Will jumped as she shouted, but her only answer was a brief indignant silence from the ravens. 'So, Will, we're here, and I've paid your ransom. Now, are you going to tell me what is going on?'

Hughes rested his elbows on the soft top and leaned over. He set his voice low and conspiratorial, though there was no one but her and the ravens to hear him. It was his big moment.

'This morning, while I was in Jake's office sorting out the bid paperwork, I found a file of papers locked in his desk drawer—'

'—*locked* in his desk drawer? At last, you're finally showing some initiative—'

'—There were press cuttings relating to this place from when it was a school, Holy Mount. Someone committed a murder here in 1993, and they never found the body.'

'A body? What, a *dead* body?'

'No, Sam. This one was tap dancing on the hall floor. Anyway, one of the press cuttings mentioned they released the murderer a few weeks back. They called him *The Bayhurst Woods Beast*.'

'Whoa, spooky.' Sam widened her eyes and wiggled her fingers about. 'How does this interest Jake?'

An Invisible Murder

Will shrugged. 'I asked myself the same question, and all I could come up with was money. I reckon he has another interested party, one with deeper pockets, waiting in the wings. If that happens, you, me, and everyone else at SCM are expendable. All he needs is for our bid to fall through.'

'Bastard! And the body?'

Will shrugged. 'Who knows? Maybe the murder story is a smokescreen, something to reel out if the SCM bid went ahead. Anyway, even if they dug up a body, the police would be gone within a couple of days. The impact would be minimal. Jake would lose more in kickbacks than SCM would. If we were careful, we could spin it our way. *Local businesswoman brings closure to a grieving family* or something.'

He mimicked a ticker tape headline over his head. Sam stared into middle-distance and imagined the adulation.

'You're sure he's here?' she asked. Again, it troubled Will that Jake's car was nowhere to be seen.

Sam puffed out her frustration and looked up at the rain.

'Well, I'm going into the house. You can go search the woods and call me if he turns up.'

***

Jake Foster froze as the glass in the small slit window above him rattled in its frame. A car engine drummed through the brickwork. Someone else had turned up. That was all he needed.

He climbed up and looked, but the window glass was opaque. Outside, a car door slammed, two indistinct voices muttered. Maybe the surveyors from Bainhams had arrived early to scout the grounds, or curious passers-by? Whoever, they must not find him down here. Retracing his steps along the corridor, he found the outside door to the basement and closed it, removing the broken hasp and pushing the slide bolt home. Hopefully, that would fool a casual observer.

Then he returned to the task at hand. Where was Claire Dobson's body?

Apart from a few shelves and the boiler itself, there was nothing. A thick layer of dust suggested nobody had been there for a long while. There was no sign of a corpse, decayed to dust or otherwise. He flopped to the floor, defeated.

Only O'Donnell knew for certain about Claire's resting place, unless he had faked the heart attack. Spouting any bullshit to get Foster off his back. After all, duplicity was the church's stock-in-trade. But surely it was in the priest's interest for the body to disappear. This had to be the furnace room; there was a bloody boiler in the centre, for heaven's sake. If O'Donnell was telling the truth, Claire Dobson's body had to be here.

He scanned the torch over the boiler, pock-marked and water-stained, and across the control panel, searching for an answer. It came in a reflection from the commissioning plate. The date on it read 1987, yet the house dated back to the 1800s, when the boiler would have been bigger and less efficient. Massive heat exchangers and larger pumps, coal, wood, or oil-fired. In his experience, builders would incorporate units like that into the foundations, making them impossible to remove once they constructed the house. So where was it?

O'Donnell had said the old furnace room. He was in the *new* furnace room.

There must be another room.

***

As Will Hughes sulked off into the trees, Sam Clarke-Mitchell kicked through the swathes of fallen leaves up to the front steps. The once-majestic double doors hung ajar, creaking mournfully as he crouched beneath the padlock and chain and up into an echoing black void. As her eyes acclimatised, she switched on her torch and played the feeble beam out into the darkness. From the plans, she recalled an immense entrance hall, but with bare, blackened walls and fallen ceilings, any grandeur the place enjoyed had gone, replaced by the small circle of light in front of her. The smell of must and charred wood prickled her nose, and she felt grubby. The darkness raised goosebumps on her skin. Should she have taken the woods instead?

Still, she couldn't hear corpses tap dancing on the tiles.

She pointed the torch towards the floor and scraped her heel through the carpet of rubble; acres of black and white chequerboard tiles, just begging to be reclaimed and reused. Quality always sells.

'Jake, it's Sam.'

The blanket of damp air swallowed her voice. It clung to her clothes and wrapped itself around her, leaching the warmth from her body. This was a dire place to spend a Wednesday. Rats, spiders, creepy crawlies, and many unexplained sounds to set the heart racing. But no sign of the most troublesome rat of all, Jake *Bloody* Foster.

And now, Will Hughes was telling murder stories? What was it with men?

Above her, a thump echoed through the ceiling, like a suitcase falling over, followed by a scraping, dragging sound. A shiver ran down her spine. It was probably just a lump of plaster finally falling off the wall. She swept her torch about, picking out the shape of a staircase. Above it, dull patches of daylight filtered through the skeletal roof. Why the hell was he up there?

'For Christ's sake, Jake, stop messing about. I have a meeting at four.'

It was a lie, but she wanted to be away, and had no intention of heading upstairs, dirtying her coat and snagging her tights. She turned back to the hall, playing her torch into the darkness, through the floating motes of dust.

'This place is a dump. The sooner the wrecking ball arrives, the better.' One decent storm and Mother Nature would save the demolition crew a few weeks of work. Perhaps the hard hat had been a good idea after all.

'If you think I'm searching every bloody room of this mausoleum for you, Jake…'

No response, just the moan of the wind, the constant drip of rain, and the sound of her heartbeat thudding in her ears. She turned her wrist and checked the phosphor on her watch—a little after three. The morbid darkness of winter afternoons would soon descend. Despite her torch, she'd be virtually blind.

Another noise made her heart skip a beat. Scraping, like furniture being moved. That's when the penny dropped. There was no corpse, no lucrative other deal. Jake was stripping the place. He'd found something valuable and was having it away before the demolition teams could take it. No wonder they didn't see his Jaguar. He must have brought a bloody van around to the back of the house.

'The game's up, Jake. What's it worth? A thousand, two, ten even? I'll pay you twice that just to get this sodding deal done.'

She had the unsettling feeling, as her eyes looked out into the darkness. Someone, or something, was looking back. He was there somewhere waiting for her to call it a day and piss off. She wouldn't give him the satisfaction.

'Stop being a prat, Jake. If you think I am hanging about in this shit hole any longer, you have another thing coming.'

She gave an irritated huff and turned to look for the bright slit of light from the front doors, but it was gone. Had she closed them after snaking through? She had a serious attack of the willies, now.

Another sound made her turn. The scampering of feet, a fox perhaps or a - child? A child, that was it. There was a housing estate a mile away. The little bastards were playing a game.

'Well done, kids! You had me going for a moment.' Things that go bump in the dark are still just - things, yet every creak, rustle, or unexpected shadow amplified in her mind until they finally overwhelmed her. Swallowing back the fear, she turned towards where the door had been. Somewhere, a child was laughing.

'Who's there?' She sensed a shape cross her path. Feet were playing in the puddles. 'Seriously? Is this how it's going to be?'

Then, she caught sight of the sliver of light and hastened towards it. She had to get out. Her breath boomed in her ears.

An Invisible Murder

Above, rain fell through the open roof and ravens were circling in the grey clouds. She swung the torch beam in front of her. Two eyes stared back, and a breath breezed across her cheek.

***

Foster's blood turned to ice. Surely, that was a scream. He turned the torch towards the furnace room door, watching the shadows rear up on the wall outside. It had to be a scream. What else could it be? He wanted to switch off the torch, hide in the darkness, and wait for it to go away, but his terror of the dark outweighed his fear of the light. Slowly, he backed into the corner, reached for the pry bar, and listened.

Silence.

And then the window rattled again as the car engine outside revved, rutting gravel and racing back down the drive.

***

Will Hughes fell to his knees before his brain registered the sound. The screech of a fox, an owl, but weren't those nocturnal creatures? He was a city boy. What did he know about this wilderness?

Within twenty minutes, he had found himself lost and panic was setting in. He hated the countryside. Cold, wet, uncomfortable, and too many things that wanted to eat you. Little bitty crawly things that would take their sadistic time about doing it. And what the hell was that sound? The sooner he found Jake, the sooner they could piss off. Until then, there was no option but to press on. To earn his thirty pieces of silver.

Taking a breather, he sheltered beneath the scant cover of a meagre autumn canopy and brought up the map on his iPad. So many footpaths transected the estate. He had already taken several wrong turns. Finally, he found the clearing he was in, marked *woodshed*, rotating the tablet until the paths in and out of the clearing lined up with the image. He was two hundred yards north of where he should have been. The path that led toward the motorway.

According to the news reports in Jake's file, they murdered the girl there. Surely, if he was interested in the body, that's where Jake would go.

In the distance, the sound of a car engine broke the silence.

Shit! The bitch!

He began running, thrashing at the bushes and weeds, desperate to reach the road before the Mercedes sped past, but he was too late. All he caught was a flash of silver through the thinning leaves, the two bobbing heads through the window. They were heading for the gates.

As the note of the engine faded to nothing, he slowed to a halt and doubled up, his hands on his knees as he struggled to get his breath back. What an idiot he had been. She had set him up, used him to find Jake, then marooned him out here while she rescinded the job offer and sorted out the bid on her own. And the cock-and-bull story of the murdered schoolgirl? He had fallen for it hook, line and sinker. Meanwhile, Sam and Jake were inside her warm, cosy car laughing all the way home at the thought of him spending the night freezing in the middle of nowhere.

His only option was to find somewhere to shelter. To make the best of it until they all stopped laughing and sent help. But his heart sank further when the house emerged through the trees in front of him. Burnt and derelict, like something out of a horror movie, it gave him the creeps. Still, he could hunker down under the porch out of the weather, and if the night turned cold, he could find a corner inside to huddle into. A small room, a cupboard even. He had matches. If he could find enough dry kindling, maybe he could start a fire. He glanced up at the blackened brickwork. Perhaps that was not his best idea.

Climbing the steps, he noticed the marks. He noticed white scores through the dirt, as if someone had dragged something sharp out through the doors and down to the car. He switched on his torch, but the beam petered out in the darkness. It made the hairs on his neck stand on end. Whatever Jake had been playing at in there, he was welcome to it.

Will cleared the detritus and sat down on the top step, his back against the creaking door, feeling it bounce under his weight. Inside the house, the wind moaned in the rafters. The place seemed alive with clicks, plops, and bumps. It was as if it knew he was there and biding its time until nightfall. A breeze played across his face, sending a shudder down his spine. He thought he heard a child's voice, an echo in the darkness.

'Go now, while you can.'

It was as if the house could read his mind, and he wasn't about to disappoint it. Enough was enough. He pulled himself to his feet and hurried back down the steps. There had to be shelter somewhere on the estate that wasn't as creepy as here. He remembered the old lodge, up near the main gates. Then something occurred to him. If Jake had just left with Sam, his car would still be here somewhere. Maybe he had parked at the old lodge, and even left the keys? It was worth a shot.

Turned up his sodden collar against the persistent rain, he began the long, uncomfortable trudge back up the drive. He had never been afraid of the dark or one for ghost stories, but this house was weird. As if something preternatural stalked the grounds. No wonder Jake and Sam refused to hang about. The sooner the JCBs moved in, the better.

Chapter 24

Daley remained in the observation room after Hannah Mason had left with Judith Marner. Whetstone still believed Hannah Mason should be their focus, not a boarding school that closed sixteen years before. As for Raymond Asher, why, after twenty years in prison, would he want to buy a ticket back inside? In many ways, Daley agreed. The trouble might have its roots in Holy Mount, but it finished in Judd's flat. Maybe Hannah heard of his release and used it to her advantage.

Yet, the coincidences played on his mind. Green Street, St Dunstan's and Father O'Donnell. Mason, Foster and Asher, and Asher's timely release from prison after twenty years.

The observation room door wheezed open, and he turned, expecting to see Whetstone, only to be disappointed.

'Ma'am?'

Superintendent Hacker pressed the door shut and launched all her missiles at once.

'What the hell happened this morning at St Dunstan's? I've had ACC Fraser on the phone for half the morning. By all accounts, the priest phoned the dean, the dean phoned the bishop - *the Bishop of London, for heaven's sake!* Then the bloody bishop phoned Vic Fraser. Complaints of witness intimidation and police brutality. He's asked me to reassure the Bishop in person this was a one-off, a maverick Chief Inspector. This may have been okay in Bob Allenby's day, but not on my watch.'

Sensing a pause, Daley took his opportunity. 'Hang on, ma'am, with respect, what are you talking about?'

Admittedly, he could have been less direct or maybe said nothing. She was a slender woman. Eventually she would run out of stamina - not that it had happened before, but hope springs eternal. Instead, with the blue touch paper lit, he watched as all manner of pyrotechnics went off behind her eyes.

'Due respect? When have you shown any of that - for anyone? For Christ's sake, they're keeping him in hospital! You want to think yourself lucky the cleaner came back for her hat, otherwise you would have had his death on your bloody hands.'

She informed him he had gone too far this time and how she would not tolerate this kind of Nineteen-Seventies bully-boy policing in her force. Daley feigned listening while trying to piece together the facts of a conversation in which he featured but was not a part of. On the desk, his phone buzzed, and he turned it over. Ironically, it was Whetstone informing him of Hacker's imminent arrival, and that he should keep a low profile.

'Am I boring you, *Chief Inspector*? Is the life of a member of the public less important than your social media?'

Words formed on Daley's lips. He imagined the hand of Bob Allenby on his shoulder and let the words die. Hacker's otherwise wan complexion had taken on the hue of a ripened tomato, and for a moment he wondered if she too would need A&E before the haranguing petered out. With the room still ringing. He took a breath and spent a long moment, too long, formulating a response.

'What have you got to say for yourself?'

Priest, hospital, dean, bishop…click.

'Father O'Donnell is in hospital?' All those years as a detective had not been a waste. 'It's the first I've heard of it.'

Hacker rolled her eyes and made a noise like the air brakes on a bus. 'You're Senior Investigating Officer, Daley, for heaven's sake. He almost had a heart attack following your interrogation. You could have killed the man. If he brings a claim against the service…'

'A heart attack?'

'Damn near.'

An Invisible Murder

'So, he *didn't* have a heart attack?'

'I said almost. Look, I will not stand here bandying words with you, Chief Inspector…'

'Ma'am, I saw Father O'Donnell at eight and was gone by eight forty-five and he was fit and well then. Anything could have happened in the interim.'

'Yet it didn't, Chief Inspector. According to the cleaner, she left him in his study. But for her hat…'

True, O'Donnell seemed agitated, anxious even, but once he'd unburdened himself about Asher and the murder at the school, he seemed to rally; a problem shared, but a heart attack hours later? Daley recalled years before, paramedics struggling in vain to save his father on the living room carpet; it had all happened within an hour. The priest was a mess. He'd been drinking and looked like he hadn't slept, so maybe he was a ticking bomb, even without Daley's visit.

'When I left, ma'am, he was fine. If you need to check my whereabouts, by all means, please do so. I was at the LA Bowl in Ruislip, and the coffee shop across the car park from it. When I returned here, cameras watched me enter the car park. I used my door card to enter the building and signed into my computer; those will all be on record. I spent the rest of the day in my office, with the blinds open, so any of my team can attest to me being there. As for Father O'Donnell, I'm pretty sure the Catholic Church has yet to stump up for such a rigorous monitoring system.'

A little too cock-sure, maybe?

'Chief Inspector…' Then she hedged. Only for a millisecond, but it was long enough for Daley to notice. Dealing with management had never been his forte, especially those like Leslie Hacker, whose sense of entitlement led them to manage the person, not the role. The weight of Allenby's hand was still on his shoulder, but he shrugged it off. A line needed to be redrawn, one that had faded into the close-weaved carpet since Allenby retired. But if *Bilko* Bob taught him anything, it was the importance of keeping one's mouth shut and not insert one's foot into it. Eventually she would be hoist by her own petard, a day or two before she disappeared back up to Derbyshire to herd sheep through market towns, or whatever the police there did. So he steadied himself and spoke in a calm, low, hopefully not too threatening tone.

'Sit down, ma'am. Please.' He gestured to the small uncomfortable office chair and then performed his own sweep of the room, ensuring the microphones were off. She stood firm, back to the door, eyes blazing and arms folded so tight across her chest that Daley feared for the circulation in her legs.

'Please?'

She smoothed her skirt behind her knees and sat. He turned to the one-way mirror and stared for a second into the empty interview room before taking a breath and facing her.

'This has to stop, ma'am. This is my investigation and I will run it how I see fit. I am quite content to reporting our progress, or lack of it, and even debate any ideas you might have to help us along, but I will not have you second-guessing every operational move I make.'

She made to speak. Daley raised his hand.

'I know you don't like me and, at the moment, I don't particularly like you, but that's how it is when a new face appears, and I am happy to endure a period of adjustment while you get your feet under the table. Hopefully, you'll grant me the same courtesy, as I've only been in the post of Chief Inspector for four months myself. I can only imagine the pressures on you, managing the move to Hillingdon, and the assimilation of so many teams under one roof, and I am happy to offer any assistance you may request, though I am sure you're more than capable. Me, though? I'm a grassroots copper. I am not so good at handling the upper echelons of management, but my team? We understand each other, which is how it needs to be in a functioning Murder Investigation Team. Maybe I've risen to the level of my incompetence. I've yet to find out. Perhaps, in a few months, you'll have the pleasure of busting me back down, but until then, you and I need to work together without me feeling under the cosh. You need to step away from the coal face and let us do our job. So if that's all?'

An Invisible Murder

Hacker's face was still a fetching shade of puce, similar to the one Terri had decided against for their new dining room. She stared at him for a moment, formulating a response but letting it die on her lips. Instead, in a tone so low it left grooves in the carpet, she said,

'You are not to go near the priest again, is that clear?' A stake in the ground, fractionally beyond the newly drawn line.

'And if it becomes material to my investigations?'

Hacker glared at him as if he had smacked her across the face. He imagined it was how Vesuvius looked just before lunch on 24th August, 79 AD. 'Then you speak to me first.'

'So, I am supposed to consult with you every time I wish to interview a potential suspect?'

'Suspect? He was in the church across the road with a room full of old dears. How can he be a suspect? Stay away, Chief Inspector. That is an order.'

'Ma'am.' Daley let out a long, undiplomatic sigh. He could think of three or four Agatha Christie novels where one of a gaggle of *old dears* locked in a room had committed a murder somewhere else. Still, all this was getting him nowhere. He had a murderer to catch, and she had an office carpet to choose.

Hacker pulled open the door, leaning back through as she left. 'I'm seeing Vic Fraser in the morning at ten o'clock sharp. I'll speak to him. In the meantime, tell your team to pull their fingers out. It would help your cause if I could give him a progress update - with actual progress.'

***

Daley had bet Whetstone a posh coffee that Asher would abscond. Having fallen foul of his wiles before, she had declined. She believed not everyone was a total shit. However, anyone with twenty years at Her Majesty's pleasure was at least a partial one, so she would have lost the bet. Earlier, just after midnight, a mortified Peter Dennis called to report that Asher had failed to return to the hostel. Daley had used it as an excuse to voice his opinion of the parole system, then asked for anything they had on Asher. Dennis pitched in with some confidentiality bollocks, reminding him they didn't yet suspect Asher of anything. Then he tried the humanitarian route - the poor chap has been out of jail for five minutes and already you lot are hounding him. Finally, the defensive strategy - I can't be responsible for him twenty-four hours a day. I have other clients to manage. Daley, not known for his slow fuse or virtue of quiet patience, dropped the call before it got ugly. Instead, he arranged an appointment with Asher's psychologist and hoped he would get more sense out of them.

Ruislip Healthy Minds Centre, where Vanessa Morgan practised her trick cycling, was near the centre of Ruislip. Built like a Sixties technical college, with ranks of white metal-framed windows and plain red brick, it reminded Daley of Hendon, staring out of similar windows as a tutor droned on. He was not a fan of shrinks. Following his collision with a train a couple of years ago, they referred him to one. He always had the sneaking suspicion they would employ some verbal gymnastics to prove him a nut job. That a couple of big blokes in white coats would barrel in and throw him into a room with quilted walls. Hopefully, Asher's shrink would not ask questions about his relationship with his mother, or what he saw in a blot of ink.

The lobby of the clinic was a stark contrast to the grim exterior. Light and homely, filled with pot plants and leather sofas. Suspended ceilings, chequered blue carpet tiles, framed prints of nondescript bucolic scenes, and the strains of Vivaldi wafting down on the air conditioning. Perhaps that's how they caught you. A soothing environment, a false sense of security, so you dropped your guard. The trick was not to sit down, not to stand still and to avoid looking them straight in the eyes.

Opposite the door, behind a maple and glass reception desk, a woman smiled and raised her eyebrows at Daley.

'Oh, hello. Haven't we met before?' She scrunched up her eyes as if it would make his face clearer.

An Invisible Murder

'Detective Chief Inspector Scott Daley for Vanessa Morgan?' He flashed his warrant card and gazed down at her lapel badge. Embarrassed she might think he was studying her breasts, he added, 'Abi? Outside Willson Hughes's house?'

'Yes, I am his partner, for my sins,' she chuckled.

'Has the moped turned up?' he asked.

'What? Oh, no. Probably in bits by now, I shouldn't wonder. Please, could you sign in?'

She led him down the corridor and showed him into a compact, well-lit consulting room.

'Vanessa Morgan - Nessa.' A tall, auburn-haired woman rose from behind her desk and flattened her skirt. She extended a hand and smiled warmly.

'Detective Chief Inspector Daley - Scott.' He shook the hand like squeezing a warm, damp flannel. She gestured towards a pair of comfortable armchairs, separated by a demilitarised zone of maroon carpet. Next to one chair, a small table bore a file of papers and a prominent alarm button. Daley sat in the other. The room resembled a set in a furniture store. Nondescript ornaments and nicknacks, a better class of framed pictures, certificates and diplomas. In the corner, a large stuffed toy lolled on a beanbag.

'Coffee?' she asked, then turned to the receptionist. 'Abi? Would you rustle up a couple of coffees, please?' Nessa Morgan smiled fleetingly, waited for the receptionist to leave, and then got down to business.

'Now, Raymond Asher. How can I help you?'

'I understand you are his assigned psychologist since his release?'

'Longer than that. Our practice took him on when they sent him to the Youth Offender Institution. He was on my list when I joined in 2008.'

'What can you tell me about him?'

Morgan relaxed back in her chair, steepling her fingers under her chin, legs crossed, her long skirt splitting, accentuating the rake of her shins down to a pair of rather incongruous trainers. Her skin was pale, freckled pink, untouched by the sun, giving it an almost tender, painful appearance. For a moment, her deep brown eyes transfixed Daley. They made him feel vulnerable, as if he needed to corral all of his unsafe, uncomfortable thoughts and protect them. Or maybe she was wearing contacts, which he'd noticed widened the gaze of the wearer.

She looked up as the receptionist entered with coffee, then settled back into her chair.

'Raymond Asher had a tough childhood. Most of his early years he spent alone while his mother was stoned or drunk, or out on the game. He became insular and self-reliant. They took him into care aged eight, at which point it became clear he had been both physically and sexually abused.'

Daley had heard the story before. Broken homes, abusive relationships. One needs a license to hold a gun, to get married, even to go fishing, but as for having children…There were no theory tests, no certificates of competency, and often, little sex education. Invariably, the children suffered and perpetuated the pattern. Rules of behaviour deemed normal by parents and adopted by their offspring.

Nessa Morgan continued. 'After passing through a few local authority institutions, the local authority sent him to Holy Mount Residential School, a home for problem children out near Uxbridge. They described him as *feral*. Over the next six years, they gave him an education and moral guidance.'

Feral was a strong word. Animal, uncivilised. Brutal. Could they truly turn around someone like that, or would the animal hide deeper, remaining hidden until released back into society?

'Yet later he committed murder? What happened?'

'Claire Dobson and Raymond Asher arrived at Holy Mount around the same time in 1987. Same age and similar experiences, they formed an attachment, similar to the relationship between siblings - or twins. Over time, they separated from the other children, ate together, played together, and even developed a secret code to converse. Eventually, the staff intervened. The GP assigned to the school, Doctor Verma, suggested they discourage the relationship and encourage socialisation with a wider group within the home. The other children resented their exclusivity, particularly as they grew into adolescence. Claire was a good-looking girl amongst hot-blooded boys. By the time of the incident, there were fights and instances of bullying.'

Nessa Morgan paused and took a delicate sip of her coffee. She was too young to have worked at Holy Mount, so she was relating everything secondhand. The story was familiar. When the hormones raged, girls became women and boys became Neanderthals. Neither became adults for a long time.

'Bullying is one thing,' said Daley. 'Teenagers can be shits at the best of times. I know I was, but how did it develop into murder?'

'When the pair were fourteen, the staff decided to only allow them to socialise under supervision. That was August 1993 and, by then, it was clear Claire and Raymond's relationship had become a sexual one. Raymond became resentful and aggressive, so the staff felt it best to move Claire to a different home in the hopes he would settle down again. By September, Claire Dobson was dead.'

Morgan reached for the folder of notes and flicked through.

'On 28th September 1993, the staff discovered Claire and Raymond were missing. The police performed a search of the house and grounds and found a large amount of blood in a woodshed a few hundred yards into the woods. It was where the children went to smoke, to get some privacy and, yes, to be intimate. DNA testing proved it was Claire Dobson's blood, so the police mounted a manhunt for Raymond. Eventually, they found him hiding out in the woods around the home. He confessed to Claire's murder in a fit of rage over her flirting with the other boys at Holy Mount School. He claimed he had buried her in the woods beyond the motorways. Local police performed a search and found a shovel that staff identified as belonging to the school, yet they found nothing of Dobson. But it's a large area, budget cuts and so on. She was declared legally deceased in 2001. After his trial, they requested we conduct a psychiatric evaluation on Asher. He has remained with us ever since. We saw him grow into a normal, well-adjusted adult, albeit one inside for murder. He trained to be a plumber and took a degree in Religious Studies. Strangely, though, not once did he acknowledge his time in the home, or the reasons for his imprisonment. It was as if he had erased it from his mind, or locked it away and thrown away the key.'

'Was a psychiatric evaluation performed before his release?'

'Naturally. Let me see.' Nessa Morgan made the same face as Peter Dennis as if her professional judgement was being questioned. Daley sipped his coffee, uncomfortable in the silence, sure the stuffed toy was staring at him.

'As you know, parole is usually conditional upon an inmate accepting their crimes. Asher accepted he must have killed Claire, though he had dissociated from the event itself. Despite further psychiatric examination, nothing changed. Earlier this year, before his release, they took him out to Bayhurst Woods in the hopes he could tell them where he'd buried Claire Dobson's body, but he appeared not to even recognise the place.'

'Well, it had been twenty years.'

'In my experience, Chief Inspector, they never forget. It's a game they play. A battle of wills with the authorities. But with Asher, there was no game, no battle of wills. A barrage of tests and countless hours of psychological examination concluded he simply didn't know. He had wiped clean the mental slate. The parole board ordered his release under strict licence conditions.'

Had Raymond Asher somehow fooled a platoon of shrinks for nigh on two decades? Was it always on the cards he would revert to type and kill again?

'Is Asher particularly religious?' Daley asked. 'Only since his release, people have seen him hanging around outside a church in Harrow.'

Nessa Morgan raised her eyebrows. 'Well, Holy Mount was a

Roman Catholic institution, and, as I say, he had a degree in Religious Studies.'

'And did he - *believe*?' Daley had a low opinion of religion. Penance today for jam tomorrow. Salvation always seemed an aspiration rather than something one could genuinely achieve. Morgan seemed surprised by the question.

'He holds deep religious views, Chief Inspector, which is not the same as believing *per se*. He doesn't have faith, but a more academic curiosity, a need to understand why people believe. In the same way, crime writers rarely commit the crimes they write about, yet have an intimate knowledge of the subject. Or an entomologist might study insects without aspiring to be one.'

'When do you see him next?' asked Daley.

'Thursday afternoon - tomorrow. His parole officer attends as a chaperone. Tell me, Chief Inspector, is this to do with the gas explosion in Harrow? You said he was hanging around a church. Was it St Dunstan's, Father O'Donnell's church?'

Daley nodded.

'—and you believe Raymond Asher was responsible?'

'At this stage, he is a person of interest.'

'Did you know that Sonia Judd and Andrew Mason were also independently referred to this practice?'

So many worms were crawling out of the woodwork, mused Daley. Daley found it astonishing that London wasn't covered with a fine layer of sawdust.

'An outreach charity referred Sonia a year ago. WAVE - Women Against Violence and Exploitation. Her then-boyfriend-slash-pimp had beaten her within an inch of her life when her heroin addiction got in the way of her occupation. The police found her in a flat in Brixton, severely dehydrated. I took her onto my *pro bono* list. Andrew Mason was a self-referral, following some trouble he'd had at work.'

'The sexual misconduct allegations?' offered Daley.

Morgan raised her eyebrows, surprised at how well-informed he was. 'Yes. His employers gave him the benefit of the doubt, but as happens, the more one gets away with, the braver one becomes. After a second allegation, the police investigated but there was insufficient evidence; his word against hers. Still, his manager marked his card and suggested he seek help, so he self-referred to us. He had been with us for around three months.'

'Were you aware of a relationship between Judd and Mason? Did they ever meet here, or arrive and leave together?'

Morgan glanced across at the stuffed toy and then at the clock. A moment to vet what she was about to say.

'They would never have shared therapy sessions, but their appointment times would have coincided on occasions, so they may have talked in reception. Sonia saw my colleague, Peta, rather than myself. Abi may know. I can check appointment times?' Her look implied the weight of the imposition.

'That won't be necessary at the moment.'

Morgan gave a perfunctory smile. 'I don't know how much use that is but…'

'Me neither, Nessa, but you never can tell.' Daley took it as a cue his time was up, relieved he wasn't paying by the hour. He reached out a hand. 'Thanks for your time.'

'Abi made this copy of his notes for you.' She passed over the file, rose from her chair, and pressed a button on her desk phone. Presently, the receptionist knocked and entered.

Daley turned back to Morgan.

'Do you have any details for the school - Holy Mount?'

Morgan smiled and shook her head. 'Long gone now, Chief Inspector, sometime in the last century.'

Chapter 25

Daley had set a team briefing for five o'clock. He preferred them early morning, while the team was too tired, or hung over, to give him grief, but after four days, they had more leads than a closing-down sale at *Curry's*, none of which conclusively led anywhere. Not for the first time, he wondered if the promotion to Chief Inspector had been a wise move. In the old days, out in the naughty corner, he was just one of the lads, part of the team, with *Bilko* Bob Allenby as his backstop. Since Superintendent Leslie Hacker's appointment, the dynamic had changed. Without Allenby's wise ear and experienced counsel, the backstop had gone.

However, Monaghan had brought him some comfort. A different perspective away from the *what* and towards the *why*. The backstory of the Holy Mount School where Raymond Asher murdered Claire Dobson. Where Andrew Mason went to school and Father Joseph O'Donnell worked. In contrast, the investigations into Hannah Mason were slow going. CCTV and ANPR were all they had. The rest of her time she spent taking the kids to and from school or dance class, or inside the house in Saunter's Green.

As the team assembled, Daley took a deep breath, pushed away the imposter that always threatened to derail him, and strode forward to start the performance.

'It's Wednesday, 2nd October 20— at 17:01. Operation Scion Team Brief. Let's just plough on, shall we? Deb?'

Whetstone took her cue. 'There are currently two principal lines of enquiry. Hannah Mason and Raymond Asher. Let's look at Mason first. CCTV and ANPR show Hannah followed her husband to Judd's flat on six separate occasions, including the night he died.

We have CCTV showing Mason and a woman returning to the flat early Friday evening.' She tapped a photograph on the Incident Board. 'The long coat and curly red wig belonged to Judd. She wore them when she went out on the game, but forensics suggested Judd was already in a coma inside the flat when they returned. So who is the woman? Mike.'

Corby sat up straight and flicked open his pad.

'Jane and I did a round of the local hookers—' he paused for the suggestive whoops '—they all identified the woman as Judd, though usually, it was a percentage guess based on the quality of the image and the wig and coat. I showed them a picture of Hannah Mason. The same. I also had another word with Mrs Livingstone at Number 7. She confirmed the woman on the CCTV was the same person she saw crossing the road. Again, a percentage guess whether it was Judd or Mason.'

'And Jane, the parish ladies?'

'It was after ten when the parish meeting finished, although one lady, Mrs O'Hallorhan, saw the man standing under the lychgate. I showed her a photo of Asher, but she said it was too dark to be certain.'

Whetstone nodded. 'Okay, guys, keep at it. We need to establish links between Hannah Mason and a male accomplice, whether that's Raymond Asher or someone else. So, Dave, Holy Mount Residential School. What do we know?'

Monaghan pinned an image of the house onto the Incident Board.

'The property was originally a manor house and grounds near Iver. After the First World War, it became a boys' grammar school until the nineteen-fifties, when the local authority acquired it and set up a residential children's home. Eventually, in the nineteen-sixties, the Home Office rebranded it as Holy Mount, an approved school under the aegis of the Roman Catholic Church. The school finally closed in 1997. In 2004, a suspected arson attack partially destroyed the building, now known by its original name of Bayhurst Grange. Since then, it has been derelict.'

An Invisible Murder

'Bayhurst Grange?' Whetstone sat upright. 'That's the property Stanford Clarke-Mitchell is looking to redevelop. The company where Mason's drinking buddies, Foster and Hughes, work.'

Monaghan nodded. The link had not eluded him. 'The authorities were already considering the home's future, and the incident with Raymond Asher and Claire Dobson in 1993 was the final nail in the coffin. It closed in 1997. My contact wouldn't tell me any more, so, as a last resort, I called Tommy Sullivan.'

'Jeez,' Daley widened his eyes theatrically. 'Is he still alive?'

'Alive is a relative term, sir, but his memory is still okay.'

Sullivan was an ex-Evening Standard, world-weary, thread-veined old hack. His glory days long behind him, he eked out his pension with whatever he could sell to the locals. It astonished Daley that a man whose daily diet comprised junk food and alcohol could have persuaded his liver to keep functioning.

Monaghan continued. 'Sullivan sent me a copy of an article he wrote in 1993 regarding Dobson's murder, along with some of his notes. It mirrors what we already know. He also sent me this.'

He attached another old photograph to the Incident Board.

'A school photo of all the pupils at the school the summer before the murder, lined up and smiling their little heads off in the sunshine. Sullivan wrote the names of the pupils on the back. I've blown up those of interest to us.'

'Poor choice of words, Dave.'

Monaghan peered at Whetstone over his glasses and huffed.

'I've *enlarged* those of interest to us. Andrew Mason, Raymond Asher, and Claire Dobson. And Father Joseph O'Donnell is among the staff in the back row. But also this character - Jacob Foster, one of Mason's drinking buddies. Now, he didn't mention he was also a pupil at the school at the same time as the others, did he?'

Daley felt a thrill of excitement as Monaghan pinned the grainy images to the Incident board and gave them names. Another oversight by one of the key players.

'Dig deeper, Dave,' said Whetstone. 'We need to know everything about that murder, and let's do a background check on Father O'Donnell and Jacob Foster. Before, during and after their time at Holy Mount.'

'Bayhurst Grange.' Whetstone tapped the picture of the ruined manor house. 'Stanford Clarke-Mitchell, where Foster and Hughes work, is bidding to redevelop the estate. A residential home for the elderly, health clubs and a spa, not to mention an eighteen-hole golf course. With the film industry a couple of miles away, they're hoping for the big-bucks clientele. It isn't going too well. Delays and problems. They are on the brink of losing the bid.'

Daley sat up. 'House *and* grounds? So they believe Asher buried Dobson somewhere out on the estate, then when they release him from prison, someone murders a former pupil at the school. And Foster, another former pupil of the school, works for the developers, who might just dig her up, and the project is going badly. Seems to me like neither Asher nor Foster wants that body discovered.'

Whetstone cringed. Asher's release muddied the waters, sending them all running in different directions. What happened to Occam's Razor? The wife, the husband and his mistress? Daley's unholy trinity of domestic crime. Witnesses saw two people outside Number 5, as Mason and Judd lay dying inside. CCTV caught Hannah Mason at the scene before the explosion, and Father O'Donnell had identified Asher hanging around the church in the weeks leading up to it. A simple matter of adultery and retribution. Surely, it would be more beneficial to find a link between the two rather than heading off on a tangent? For all they knew, the school might still be the connection without being central to the murder.

'So, regardless of any circumstantial connection to the school, we keep on digging,' she said. 'We have *Female A and Male B* in Green Street. We need names - Hannah, Asher, whoever. And we have yet to trace the mysterious cleaner. I will follow up with Stanford Clarke-Mitchell. Find out more about the problems they are having. If Jacob Foster is sabotaging things, there has to be a reason. Jane, Mike, see if you can track down the other staff members and pupils in the school photograph. See what they remember. And speak to Jacob Foster and Willson Hughes. We need to firm up their alibis on the night of the explosion. As of now, Raymond Asher is our prime suspect for *Male B*. Eyewitnesses place him in Green Street around the time of the explosion, and he had the means and opportunity to effect it. He has a historical connection with Mason, Foster and Father O'Donnell, and to a serious crime at Holy Mount. Circulate his description. Let's bring him in.'

As the team dispersed, Whetstone's head was spinning. Instead of Hannah Mason being their primary focus, the investigation had taken a tangential turn, with Raymond Asher front and centre. And that damn school.

Chapter 26

Foster had lost track of the time. The light from the torch was dimming. He had to press on. He recalled a previous project, a house much the same size. The original boiler was massive. The room he was in was much too small to accommodate it. He recalled a pile of bricks stacked along the corridor and realised what had happened. Instead of removing the old boiler, they opted to leave it in place and wall it up in *the old furnace room.*

He sprang up and shone his torch into the corners, feeling for anomalies on the surface. On one wall, the brickwork was newer; the wall built from side to side to enclose a space behind it. He clasped the pry bar tight and slammed it into the wall. His heart leapt to the faint ring of an echo. With the torch off to preserve the battery, he chiselled at the mortar. He sensed movement in the bricks, starting small, increasing as chunks of mortar came loose. Finally, he could push a brick back into the hole and, heart in his mouth, he reached in and grabbed the back of the next brick, wrenching it forward and out. He raised the torch, coughing in the stale air, half expecting a grinning death's head, but all he saw were the pitted brown spines of the old boiler, filling the hidden room. Filled with renewed vigour, he set about the wall once more. The concrete dust was stinging his eyes; his overalls were now stiff and sweaty. His hands throbbed with pain and his fingers burned fiercely, but soon he had a hole large enough to step through.

The air inside was old. Brick dust, cobwebs and rats, the heavy metallic smell of the old boiler and the reek of oil. It stuck to his tongue, chilled the air and drew the sweat from his skin. Yet he sensed something else. Old books, the inside of suitcases, things locked away too long. Desiccated and brittle. Taking a deep breath, he stepped over into the new room, feeling his boots crunch through the decades-old detritus. Tentatively, he lifted the other leg and passed through. The darkness wrapped itself tight around him as if the light from the real world could not follow him. Almost pinned front and back by the huge fins of the cast iron boiler, a wave of claustrophobia hit him. His heart was pounding. The walls and ceiling pressed in, stealing his breath.

What was he doing? O'Donnell had entombed Claire Dobson's body two decades ago. What were the chances they could find viable DNA after all this time? But after four hours of spreading fresh DNA over the basement, what did it matter? He was at the point of no return. He closed his eyes and imagined himself somewhere else. Grass, sunshine, Abi O'Brien. He measured his breathing and soon it passed.

He snaked a hand into the pocket of his overalls, found the torch, and shone the weak beam around the boiler. The batteries were almost dead. He had to hurry. He crabbed sideways around the walls, past the side of the boiler, until the room opened out as he reached the angle of the back corner. Then the torch beam landed on a shape, indistinct at first, gaining form as he edged closer, yet still he couldn't make it out. He stemmed another wave of claustrophobia and swallowed back the bile. This was no time to pussy out. Just grab hold of the damn thing.

The torch finally died.

Consumed by the blackness, he panicked, as the monsters of the dark enveloped him. Disorientated, he pushed against the fins of the boiler, his feet scraped through the carpet of dust, scrabbling back around to the jagged gap in the wall. Then a light burned brighter than the sun through the hole. Blinking, shielding his eyes with his hands, he made out a shape, a face, and he gasped.

'So near yet so far, eh, Jacob?'

An arm swung, and he felt it thump against his neck, a scratch and a coldness spreading through his veins. Then his world folded inside out and exploded in a million biting, snarling teeth.

Chapter 27

As Lambourne Road turned in for the night, Whetstone wondered if she should too. These days, it was easier to lose herself in the investigation than drive two miles to a cold, empty house. The moment she had wrapped up the team brief, Daley had left, and Corby had gone off to play five-a-side or whatever he did in the evenings. Even Steve Taylor, whom many believed had been super-glued to his chair, had gone home. Morris was also conspicuous by her absence. Dave Monaghan remained, whistling softly as he tidied away his things.

'Dave. Holy Mount School. How did you find all that out?'

'If I told you, I'd have to kill you - and that wouldn't look good on my CV.'

'So it *was* you adjusting the heating timer earlier? Must make sure I'm out of here by 1:00 am.'

Monaghan smiled and sniffed the air. 'No, love, that's Mike Corby's new aftershave, but I won't light my ciggie until I'm outside, just to be sure.'

'Seriously though, do you think there's any mileage in it?'

'You never know til you know. Anyhow, Jane Morris helped too. She's a good wee girl, Deb. You need to ease up on her.'

Whetstone flounced down in her chair as an old record played again. 'For God's sake, not you as well. I've had Scott Daley giving me grief half the morning.'

'Then you'll know how Jane feels. Just give her a chance. You can tear her off a strip once she's put in the hard yards and still makes mistakes.'

Whetstone envied Monaghan. Married forever, rarely arriving home to a cold house. Coat off, slippers on, a plate of something warm on a tray in front of *The One Show*, and asleep in his chair before nine. That level of bliss seemed a long way off for her. Still, she'd promised Scott Daley she would look over his school stuff and another hour couldn't hurt. Holy Mount Residential School already had a separate folder brimming with documents, overwhelming the information on Hannah Mason and Raymond Asher. To her mind, Hacker was right. *Setting expensive hares running.* So Asher, Foster, Mason and O'Donnell knew each other in a former life, but what did it add to the inquiry into Mason's murder? One hour, then she'd head out.

With everyone else gone, she treated herself to tea and one of Dave Monaghan's biscuits from his secret tin on the top shelf of the cupboard. Stealing a second biscuit, she unclipped the school photo from the Incident Board and pulled a magnifier from Corby's desk drawer, turning the photo to her desk light for a better view. The school was only small, with thirty pupils tiered according to height, and a phalanx of ten teachers and assistants behind and on the ends. The resolution was poor, blown up and copied from the original. It could have been any photo from any school, with awkward hair and awkward clothes. But this was the summer before it all changed. The boys, Mason, Asher and Foster, were recognisable in the middle of the third row up, arms folded, squinting in the sunshine, impudence written across their faces as they fidgeted.

Along the back, staff members and teaching staff stood imperiously over the pupils. Father Joseph O'Donnell, slimmer with more hair, had a face like a smacked arse.

Claire Dobson stood behind the boys, unsmiling. Gangly as childhood turned to adolescence, her expression neutral, as she glowered at the camera through curtains of dark hair, she would have found embarrassing had she become a woman. Something about her intrigued Whetstone; a reflection of herself. She was never a pretty teenager, with hair she would prefer to forget, a constellation of acne spots, and boobs that failed to put in an appearance. Even the eager libidos of her male classmates overlooked her. But both she and Claire had been unaware their lives were about to change forever. At fourteen, Whetstone would lose her father, Claire Dobson would lose her life.

But there was something else. Amongst the array of sunlit faces, Claire Dobson and Joseph O'Donnell were the only two not smiling. Oddly, a hand rested on Claire's shoulder from behind - where Father Joseph stood. As if steadying her, controlling her. Could that be why Asher and Dobson had fled? Why Asher was now seeking O'Donnell following his release? She found her phone and dropped a text to Daley before it slipped away.

Need to check the School photo. Father O'Donnell and Claire Dobson.

Enough was enough for one day, so she downed her tea, ate Monaghan's biscuits and glanced at her watch - eight-thirty. Tomorrow, Jane could chase up the teachers and staff. Let her disappear down that rabbit hole. She grabbed her coat and waved to the night shift, then ventured out into the dark stairwell. In her pocket, her phone buzzed; a number she didn't recognise and, for a moment, she considered cancelling the call.

'Hi, who's this?'

'Hi, Deb. It's Harbinder. Harry Ramesh.'

'New phone, Harry? Number's different.'

'No, this is *my* phone. I left my work mobile in the office. You still at Lambourne Road?'

'Just leaving now. What can I do for you?'

'Er, just had some results back. Thought I'd share them.'

She glanced at the clock on her phone. 'It's eight-thirty. Couldn't it wait until tomorrow?'

'I suppose, if it's inconvenient…?'

Somewhere inside her head, a gear started in motion, like the machines that take a penny and emboss a pattern on it. 'Hang on, if your work phone's at work, how come these results came through to your personal mobile?'

A sigh rattled the earpiece, and the silence became uncomfortable.

'Ramesh. You still, there.'

'Don't take this the wrong way, but what are you doing this evening?'

'I'm knackered, so, probably a pizza and bed.'

'Oh…I just thought…'

Then the pattern became obvious, and the penny clattered into the little metal tray.

'Are you hitting on me, Ramesh?' she asked, amused.

This time the silence became palpable, as Whetstone pulled her foot from her mouth and cringed at her clumsiness.

'Oh, mate, that came so out badly. I can be such a cow sometimes.'

'No worries, Deb. Another time, maybe.'

Chapter 28

By morning, a few things were clearer in Daley's mind. For one, he would leave the investigation into Hannah Mason to Deb Whetstone. She had flown through the OSPRE and NPPF examinations for the rank of Inspector and they had even considered her for Daley's old post, following his promotion. But after the death of her mother and the business with Keith Parrish, her head wasn't straight. When the board asked his view, that was what he told them, but now things were different, and he felt she'd put those particular ghosts to rest. He felt bad about putting a stick into the spokes of her promotion, but he knew he had made the right call. The other decision he had made was to get Leslie Hacker onside. Murder investigations were difficult enough without worrying about one's senior officer at every turn. But he was also concerned about Terri and the baby. Pregnancy and homicide were uncomfortable bedfellows, and both were progressing apace. He needed to bring the case to a close before Junior put in an appearance. Terri and the baby deserved that much of him.

St Dunstan's was quiet as always when Daley parked next to Father O'Donnell's maroon Mazda. The morning was crisp, so he took a stroll out to the lychgate. Across the road, work was continuing apace. Only Numbers 3 to 7 remained untouched. The Fire Investigation team had yet to release the scene. He imagined Raymond Asher pulling his coat around him in the icy midnight air, watching and waiting. He felt the percussion blast, the plume of smoke and rubble, and saw Oliver Mansell lifted like a leaf on the breeze and dumped back down. Then the profound silence.

'Hello. You're the Inspector, from the police?'

Daley turned and smiled at an old lady, straight out of an Ealing comedy. 'Morning. Chief Inspector Daley, yes, and you are?'

'Mrs O'Hallorhan. Edith.'

'Ah, yes. I remember my constable mentioning your name. How is Father O'Donnell?'

'Would you like a cup of tea, Chief Inspector?' She gave a conspiratorial wink that he recalled his nan using. 'And I believe there are still some biscuits left.'

The vicarage was noticeably warmer; the electric fire standing down as the central heating took a turn. Mrs O'Hallorhan brought a tray of biscuits and tea, which made Daley feel all the warmer. He began by expressing his concern over Father O'Donnell's heart attack. She told him the hospital was fitting a stent and he would be in until the next week. He indulged the story of how her late husband had also had a stent. He indulged her with the biscuits; she reminded him of his nan, turning a blind eye as he stacked two together so it looked as if he only took one. Then he asked,

'So, Wednesday morning, what time did you arrive?'

'Around nine-thirty. Father Joseph was very upset. He said you'd been here, asking him all sorts of questions. I don't know what you said to him.'

'To be fair, not a lot. I asked about the explosion, about the people who died, and about his time at Holy Mount Residential School, and to be fair, he did most of the talking.'

She gave a brief, disinterested nod. 'And the other feller who arrived after you, was he one of yours?'

Daley stopped mid-bite. It was the first he'd heard of it. 'This other fellow, can you describe him?'

'Tall with short dark hair, rather handsome, very angry. I went down to the mini-mart for milk, and when I came back, he had gone and Father Joseph was on the floor.' She put her hands to her mouth, and a tear glinted in the corner of her eye. 'He had already called for an ambulance, but had not completed the call, and I thought I was too late.'

An Invisible Murder

'You needn't have worried. These days, they trace the location of the caller, so they would already have despatched an ambulance. Did you hear the man's name?'

Mrs O'Hallorhan straightened an ornament on the mantelpiece. 'Foster. Somebody Foster. He was here less than half an hour. Goodness knows what they talked about, but it nearly did for Father Joseph.'

'No, Edith, he wasn't one of ours.' Daley sat for a moment. The tea was a little insipid and made with sterilised milk; another reminder of his nan, but the biscuits were custard creams, so he overlooked it.

'You remember the night of the explosion across the road? Father O'Donnell mentioned someone standing by the church gate. Did you see them?'

Mrs O'Hallorhan shook her head. 'Not that night, no, but I saw him at other times. He just stood there. Gave me the creeps.'

Daley pulled up Raymond Asher's mugshot, taken upon his release. 'Is this the man?'

Edith O'Hallorhan nodded. 'Yes, he was here yesterday, too. When the ambulance came, he was standing in the car park, watching the shenanigans.'

Chapter 29

The sound of Deborah Whetstone's phone shocked her from sleep. Above, strings of dusty cobwebs scolded her from the unshaded bulb, lazily meandering in the breeze. Thin slivers of light edged around the drawn curtains, and for a moment, she was lost, but only for a moment, until the thrash metal started in her head. On a school night? What the hell had she been thinking?

Of course, she knew what she'd been thinking. Anything to dull the crippling embarrassment of having treated Harry Ramesh so badly. To take her mind off her low opinion of herself. How was she going to live that one down? Her mother, Maureen, had died in the spring, pining into a vodka glass, after years of meandering on the breeze, and Deb was thinking how, when left unchallenged, history repeated itself. Over the last six months, she could have been a clone of her mother, except for the vodka. She had replaced that with a supermarket plonk.

On the bedside table, her phone pinged again. She couldn't deal with Ramesh this early in the morning. Then she saw the time on the top right of the screen.

Oh, crap.

Swinging her legs from the bed, she found the bathroom and gulped down a glass of water and a couple of paracetamol, resisting the urge to throw up. Washing, dressing, and applying a skim of make-up, she grabbed a breakfast bar from the cupboard and headed out.

All too often these days, she was seeking solace in a bottle when life gave her none. Something would have to be done, but what? She lived her life in a tube with the house in Ealing at one end and

Lambourne Road at the other, and the inside of her Volkswagen Golf all that lay between the two. Parking the car, racing up the stairs to the fifth floor, she pushed through the double doors into the team room, as she had done every day for the past four years. Things had to change. *She* had to change. Not like last time - a new frock, blonde highlights, but a genuine change. New orbits, new opportunities, new friends. New hope.

***

'Ma'am. Ramesh called for you - twice.' Whetstone's stomach again folded with embarrassment, as Jane Morris ducked back down behind her monitor. He may have been hitting on her., but she could have handled it more delicately, more sympathetically even. She styled it out.

'Seven forty-five? He was eager. What did he want?'

Morris shrugged. 'Nine-fifteen now, ma'am. *Post-it Pam* took the message before I arrived at eight.'

Whetstone sighed at the string of small, square, yellow bucks being passed in a passive-aggressive cascade down her screen. A punch of stress before the day got into its stride. Across at the admin desks, *Post-it Pam's* shift had finished and now Becky kept the seat warm. Becky's forte was passive-aggressive emails.

'I'll call him. I need a brew first.' To be fair, she'd called straight back the previous evening. Out of spite, the damn thing went to voicemail. 'Where's Scott Daley?'

Morris grunted. 'Dunno, ma'am.' Being social secretary to the DCI was obviously a task too far.

'Have you got those statements from Foster and Hughes?'

'Not yet, ma'am.'

'Well, instead of sitting here not knowing stuff, don't you think you ought to?'

'Ma'am.' Morris muttered under her breath, flicked off her computer, collected her things, and flounced through the door.

Brew made, Whetstone settled back for another look at the

Holy Mount file. This was a domestic. The car salesman, his wife and the prostitute. Who cared what school he went to? Most of the teachers would have moved on, retired, or even died, and those that remained were likely senile. At least she could look, then tell Scott Daley to his face he was wasting his time.

The school housed around thirty pupils, aged eight to sixteen. Six classroom teachers worked across all subjects, aided by four support staff who all lived on the premises. The Department of Education records were brief and factual. The remaining detail was sparse; except for Tommy Sullivan's news articles, the Local Council had the rest in their archives.

In a rare moment of diligence, Morris had contacted the General Teaching Council, who required anyone working with children to be registered and undergo an annual check by the employing school. They confirmed that, of the six teachers at the time of the Dobson murder, three had left the profession and two had died, leaving a single individual, Miss Felicity McAllister, still registered as a teacher. She could not help smiling to herself. Maybe Scott Daley was barking up the wrong tree?

Then she turned to the Police National Computer.

***

The conversation with Edith O'Hallorhan had left Scott Daley incandescent. It was one thing to accept he may have pushed the priest's frail cardiovascular system over the edge. Quite another to learn that he had taken the fall for Jacob Foster doing so. With the traffic on Western Avenue still manic, he'd stopped at the Spitfire Cafe in Northolt. He felt he deserved a coffee after Mrs O'Hallorhan had given him absolution. Now, all he had to do was convince Hacker. As his coffee arrived, his phone pinged. Deb Whetstone suggesting a meeting about Holy Mount School. It was likely another rant about Occam's Razor and the unholy trinity of domestic violence. She'd been liberal with those, so he ignored it, at least until the pretty leaf pattern dissolved into his froth. Instead, he penned a quick text to Jane Morris:

Find Jacob Foster as a matter of urgency. He and I need a serious chat.

Still, O'Hallorhan had confirmed Raymond Asher had been loitering around the church as recently as the previous day, so perhaps he was a safe bet for *Male B*. Daley penned a second text to Deb Whetstone.

Get a patrol car to do a regular run down Green Street. Asher's been seen. We may get lucky.

Almost immediately, a text came back from Whetstone, which made him rush the coffee and burn his tongue.

Operation Scion. Holy Mount School. You need to see this.

***

When Daley arrived back, Whetstone was craning into her screen, deep in concentration.

'Okay, what have you got?' he asked, out of breath, following the dash up to the fourth floor. Perhaps a ground-floor billet at Hillingdon would be less risky, especially after hearing of Father O'Donnell's predicament.

'The school photo Sullivan gave us,' she began. 'We've run background checks and found nothing unexpected - Mason's caution, Asher's conviction for murder, and this.'

She touched her mouse. 'This is Sister Agnes McCarthy, matron at Holy Mount in 1993 when Raymond Asher murdered Claire Dobson.'

Daley took an inward pace back, as the hard, dour face of a woman in her fifties filled the screen, the scathing look challenging the photographer to click the shutter release.

'She's on the PNC? What, for nicking bibles?'

'Slightly more serious than that, and the case is still open.'

Daley reached over and scrolled the screen, scanning the notes beneath the mugshot.

'Right, gather everyone together around the Incident Board. We need a brief show and tell.'

Chapter 30

'Agnes McCarthy, born on 7th November 1947 in Balbriggan, near Dublin. At sixteen, she joined the Sisters of the Merciful Shepherd at Baile Fearainn Convent, Dublin, taking the name Sister Agnes. In 1983, the convent sent her to England to join the staff of St Bridget's in Reading, where she met Father Joseph O'Donnell in 1987. They both moved to Holy Mount in 1990, where they remained until 1997, when the school was closed. She left the order of the Sisters of the Merciful Shepherd in 1997, disappearing for around four years until she turned up in a housing association bungalow in Barnsley, South Yorkshire. According to the police report, she was living under her birth name, working as a care assistant in a home for the elderly. They found her murdered at her home on 28th September 2000.'

Monaghan pinned crime scene photos to the Incident Board. McCarthy lay on her back on the kitchen floor. Her arms and legs stretched out, like Da Vinci's *Vitruvian Man*, her greying hair a halo around her head. Below her, the balance of her blood pooled between her outstretched limbs to complete the tableau. A second photo showed a close-up shot of McCarthy's head and shoulders. The eyes stared, and the mouth gaped, caught in a gasp of terror. Below the open mouth, her throat had been torn open, and her larynx and part of her trachea pulled out over her upper chest.

'She'd worked at the care home for six months,' Whetstone continued. 'A hard worker, no reports of trouble with the police. The weapon used was a knife from McCarthy's kitchen, which was left at the scene, with no fingerprints. The investigating team put it down to a random violent attack. As yet unsolved.'

'But?' Whetstone's expression told Daley there was more.

'The killer had placed Sister Agnes's bible, from when she joined the sisterhood, on her chest after her death.' Monaghan pinned up a third photo of a small, well-thumbed bible, held open at the flyleaf by a thumb and forefinger in blue nitrile gloves. The surface bore an inscription written in florid handwriting. *Sister Agnes. The Sisters of the Merciful Shepherd. Baile Fearainn. 1963.* Someone had written something else in biro below it.

SA - Pr 19:9.

'The investigating team noted the inscription. They checked over her past in the convent and at Holy Mount, but found nothing of relevance. She renounced her holy orders in 1997 and had little to do with the church after that. Of course, we now know it *is* relevant, so I looked it up.'

"A false witness shall not be unpunished,
and he that speaketh lies shall perish."
(Proverbs 19:9)

Daley had assumed holy orders were a lifetime commitment. Yet, when the school closed, they turfed Sister Agnes out into the real world, just like the children. Education, indoctrination and rejection. Did she become disenchanted with the church, with The Almighty even, or did someone force her out?

'There's something else though, Scott,' added Monaghan. 'The Sisters of the Merciful Shepherd ran a Magdalene Laundry at Baile Fearainn. The Convent was closed in 1995 because of it.'

Daley took a deep breath and exhaled slowly. Of course, he'd heard the story of Magdalene Laundries. The scandal shook Ireland, and particularly the Roman Catholic church, in the latter half of the Twentieth Century. Over two hundred and fifty years, the detention of tens of thousands of girls and young women against their will because they had transgressed the church's strict rules on promiscuity. Hidden away, they were forced to work long hours under atrocious, oppressive conditions. Countless pregnant women had their babies forcibly removed and sent for adoption. Many suffered physical and mental punishment, and of those, a large

An Invisible Murder

number died, buried in unmarked graves within the convent walls. When the scandal finally broke, the state and church were slow to recognise their respective parts. The last laundry closed its doors in October 1996, Baile Fearainn Convent ceased its laundry a year before. The Sisters of the Merciful Shepherd, now disgraced, retreated to a more traditional, cloistered way of life.

Had Agnes McCarthy been forcibly detained when she joined the convent, or worse still, did she have her baby ripped from her arms? When Sister Agnes, aged forty, travelled to England to join the staff at Holy Mount, had twenty years of brutal indoctrination left their mark? For now, though, the Magdalene Laundry connection could be coincidental. After all, she left the convent when she moved to England. The focus had to be on the present.

'Whilst I agree the murder warrants further investigation, Dave, let's not disappear down a rabbit hole.'

Monaghan gave a diplomatic nod. 'There is something else, though, Scott. Deepak Verma, a GP in Iver Heath, provided healthcare to the school. In 2004, they found him lying across his desk with a knife from the nurse's treatment room in his back. He had a piece of paper under his hand placed there after his death. This time, the SIO understood the inscription as a bible quotation, but there was never any reason to link it back to Agnes McCarthy.'

DV - Jb 13:4

"But ye are forgers of lies,
ye are all physicians of no value."
(Job 13:4)

Now they had identified three victims, all connected to Holy Mount Residential School at the time of Dobson's murder, each later murdered, and with bible references linked to each murder. Daley's immediate thought had been Raymond Asher. He had taken a degree in Religious Studies while in prison, so he would know his way around the bible.

'Send copies of the bible references away for handwriting analysis. See if the same person wrote them. Have we traced anyone from the time of Dobson's murder who is still alive?' Daley asked.

'I spoke to Felicity McAllister,' said Morris. 'She was newly qualified when she joined the school and stayed at the lodge rather than the house. On the night of Dobson's murder, she awoke at 1:30 am, when Sister Agnes told her Asher and Dobson had absconded. She went up to the school, settled the remaining children in their dorms, and catnapped in the teacher's common room. When Foster and Mason returned at around 6:00 am, Father O'Donnell ushered them directly to the head's office. She knew something had happened that night but didn't know what until the police discovered evidence of Dobson's murder.'

Daley ran a hand through his hair, wondering how much he would have once this investigation was over. He felt they were so close to the truth. If only they could see a way through the veil of secrecy that O'Donnell had cast over the events of that night.

'What do you make of it, Dave?' he asked.

Monaghan took a deep breath.

'Three violent deaths and four bible references that refer to that night. I think the killer is playing with us, challenging everyone to decipher the clues. I'd start with the reference left with Mason. Initially, we assumed Sonia Judd was the damsel in the field, but I'd lay odds it refers to Claire Dobson. In the five hours between Mason leaving the school and returning, I believe he found Dobson, dying from her injuries, *in the field* and did nothing. Agness McCarthy, under orders to cover up what happened, literally had her voice, her larynx, ripped out - *he that speaketh lies shall perish*. And Verma, the doctor? *Forgers of lies, physicians of no value.* Whatever the lie was, he was complicit in it. Which leaves reference left on the altar cloth at St Dunstan's.'

> "Thou shalt also consider in thine heart, that,
> As a man chasteneth his son,
> so the Lord thy God chasteneth thee."
> (Deuteronomy 8:5)

'It is a prick at Joseph O'Donnell's conscience. He was the architect of the subterfuge. Soon, he will have to answer for it, on Earth and then before his maker.'

'Have another word with the SIOs on the respective investigations,' Daley suggested, 'and see what else they can tell you in light of recent events. Point out the link with Andrew Mason's death and see if they can shed any further light. And let them know there's another potential victim. Concentrate their minds a little. Deb? What do you think?'

Whetstone was quiet, taking in the information as Monaghan had transferred it to the Incident board.

'Until today, I believed this was a domestic, that the school angle was irrelevant, but two historic crimes with strong connections to Dobson's murder. Then Andrew Mason murdered just as they release Asher. And all three linked by the bible references. Unless it's all one hell of a coincidence, we can't ignore it. Everything suggests a link to a closed case that dates back to September 1993?'

'Looks like we have a religious nut on our hands,' added Monaghan dourly.

'But,' Daley pointed out, 'they locked Asher up in 1993 and didn't release him until six weeks ago. Whilst he may have researched the bible references, written them even, someone else murdered McCarthy and Verma while he was still inside.'

'—which means we have *two* religious nuts on our hands.'

***

Daley summoned Whetstone to the Goldfish Bowl after the Team Brief. She closed the door behind her, wondering which would be more uncomfortable - her lack of progress on Operation Scion, or the next forty minutes in the Throne of Doom. She watched him pace across to his favourite thinking spot by the window, though today there were no flashes of divine inspiration.

'Any sign of Asher?' asked Daley.

'Nothing. I reckon he's gone to ground, like before.'

'We need to chivvy up Traffic. Asher is out there somewhere. He's only been out of jail for a few weeks. There can't be many places he could hide.'

'I will, Scott, but unless he sticks his head up.' She fidgeted in the Throne of Doom, trying to edge it closer to the desk so she could put down her tea. 'You're certain he's our *Male B*?'

'Aren't you? Unless there's someone we've missed, we only have three candidates - Foster, Hughes and Asher. Have we confirmed their alibis?'

She huffed and rolled her eyes, rather too petulantly. 'I asked Jane Morris to do that. As usual—'

'Bloody hell, Deb, this is a murder enquiry and you two are still at each other's throats. I don't care who does it, just get it done.'

Whetstone turned away so Daley couldn't see her frustration. Because it's as simple as that, isn't it? *Sorry Jane, as a senior officer, I apologise for being a twat. Oh, no, it's not your fault…*

'Find someone in Foster's apartment block,' Daley continued. 'Someone who saw him coming home or heard his toilet flush, and check with Hughes's partner to find out when Hughes finally arrived home. Danny Pearce is the closest thing Asher has to a friend, so check on him, too. We need to know exactly where they all were when *Male B* was hanging around Green Street, so we can definitively rule them in or out.'

She made a mental note to look up the male equivalent of menopausal, and ways to insert a broom up her backside, so she could sweep the floor too.

Yet, Daley was right. Each scenario they came up with had a gaping hole. If they assumed Asher was conspiring with someone while in prison, then who? If Hannah Mason, how was she linked to the school? Jacob Foster? Whilst he had links to the school, nothing suggested they were anything but circumstantial. Willson Hughes? Despite the lack of a clear connection, it always came back to Holy Mount School and a series of historic murders.

'Okay, executive call,' sighed Daley. 'We concentrate on what we can substantiate. The deaths of Mason and Judd. Park motive and concentrate on means and opportunity. Our killer, or killers, engineered a situation that brought Mason to Green Street.'

An Invisible Murder

'Park the school angle?' Whetstone was dumbfounded. After almost two days of indulging Daley's fantastical notions that a closed case from decades ago could be behind the explosion in Green Street, he was shooting off in a perpendicular direction. She resisted the urge to remind him who was leading the investigation.

'Only until we have something concrete, Deb. I am certain Mason was the target and Sonia Judd was collateral damage. Mason may have been unaware she was even in the bedroom. I keep asking myself why now, and each time I come back to Asher's release from prison. Even before that happened, *Female A* had probably started a relationship with Mason, posing as Judd to prepare for it. Then six weeks ago, the Masons employed her as a cleaner. Next, they free Asher. O'Donnell sees someone under the lychgate, and Stanford Clarke-Mitchell actively begins the Bayhurst Grange bid.'

'Yes, and *Female A* is Hannah Mason,' insisted Whetstone. 'What other reason could there be for her to be in Green Street on the night?'

'*She followed her cheating husband, is all. What evidence* is there that Hannah Mason knew Raymond Asher, *let alone* conspired with him to commit murder? Phone calls, letters, emails while he was inside? Hannah was at school in Nottingham at the time of the incident at Holy Mount.'

'Her husband must have told her about it. When she hears about Asher's release, she sets about using him to get even with her love-rat husband.'

Daley huffed. 'Knowing the story is a long way from knowing Raymond Asher. There is no evidence they have ever met.'

'What about the cleaner? She called herself Sonia Judd, but when I showed Hannah a photo of Judd—'

'—Precisely. She didn't recognise Judd. The cleaner is a *Female A*. Part of the honey trap to entice Mason to Green Street. The neighbours haven't seen her, and the only physical evidence is a business card you could print from a machine in any shopping centre. Why would Hannah Mason go to the trouble of making her up?'

Whetstone reached over and grabbed her tea, now lukewarm, and resisted the temptation to throw it over Scott Daley, to wake him up. It was the same in every investigation. As the evidence came together, he would disappear off in flights of fancy that the Metropolitan Police Riot Squad could not hold back.

'It's not the wife, Deb. We need to focus on Andrew Mason. On his friends, associates, and customers. Anyone who entered his life six to eight weeks ago and struck up a relationship with him. Anyone with the potential to be *Female A* or *Male B*. And, if we are lucky, who also knew Raymond Asher well enough to know he was being released and persuade him to help.'

'What about Vanessa Morgan? She knew everything there was to know about Asher's plight. If she felt he'd had a raw deal, maybe she wanted to put things right? She's certainly the right build for *Female A*.'

Daley pulled a face and gave a perfunctory shake of the head. 'I don't see it, Deb.'

Whetstone rolled her eyes. 'What is it with men of a certain age? One flash of legs and they can get away with murder - literally. And you with a baby on the way.'

'You must be bloody joking. I've spent too much time with Sophie Jennings to fancy a psychiatrist. Any pillow talk would invariably involve discussions about my relationship with my mother. No thanks. Still, get someone to do a background on Morgan too, just to be sure.'

Whetstone was having sessions herself with Sophie Jennings, one of the Met's psychologists. It was her second time in therapy; the first followed her father's death, and she was much younger. Now she was older, scarred by Keith Parrish, scarred by the world, less trusting, less willing to trust. As a woman, she saw relationships differently. Women rarely thought with their genitalia. Unlike Andy Mason and Jacob Foster.

'Don't forget that Raymond Asher was at work from two in the afternoon. Someone would have noticed if he had skived off.'

'Speak to Danny Pearce, and there's a young girl, a blonde, who works there. If they covered for him, he only has to be back at the hostel by five past twelve to clock in, then immediately go back out, return to the churchyard and wait for the explosion - Oliver Mansell's *lean man*. It's a parole hostel full of jailbirds. If he can't find a way out of there…'

'What about Yvette, the girl Foster supposedly picked up at *Blenheim's*?'

'Get tech on it. See if they can trace the phone through the account, and ask Jane to press Foster, when she tracks him down. Send Mike along to *Blenheim's*. See if anyone who was there last Friday remembers Foster and Hughes, or even the girlfriend, Yvette. We need to rule these people in or out once and for all.'

***

As Whetstone left, Daley's phone pinged. Terri was reminding him of her maternity appointment at Harrow Central Hospital. The urgency to conclude Operation Scion was growing. The terse email from Leslie Hacker only intensified the situation. A less than veiled threat to hand the case on to a fresh pair of eyes at Hillingdon. To date, Whetstone had done little to convince him they were moving in any direction at all, let alone the right one, and now the number of suspects had increased.

Female A was still a complete mystery. She had appeared two months before to romance Mason into Number 5 Green Street. She had cleaned his house under the gaze of his wife, yet nobody could identify her. Then, she had met Mason in Starbucks, walked through the St Anne's Shopping Centre and back to Judd's flat, yet still no one could identify her. Even the combined espionage skills of Mrs Livingstone and Mrs Kelly had failed to pin down whether she was Hannah Mason, Sonia Judd, or someone else.

Nessa Morgan? He just could not see it. Or Yvette? Daley was certain she was a figment of Foster's libido.

At least they were on firmer ground with *Male B*.

Raymond Asher had yet to resurface. Innocent people rarely

run, guilty people make it their business not to get caught. Father O'Donnell, Mrs Livingstone, and Oliver Mansell all believed strongly that the lean man was Asher, but without him, it remained an assumption. Twenty minutes in an interview room under caution would likely clear the entire case up. As it would with Jacob Foster and Willson Hughes.

But if Asher was an irritation, Father O'Donnell was an annoyance. He knew something. Cowering in the sacristy, hiding out in the vicarage and now given sanctuary at the hospital, he was also beyond reach.

No firm identity for *Female A* or *Male B*. Half the persons of interest were missing. All in all, it was a complete shit shower.

***

'Any luck with Foster and Hughes, Jane?'

Morris felt Mike Corby's hand on the back of her chair. 'Both their mobiles are off. I rang Stanford Clarke-Mitchell directly but they are out on a project.'

'Out on a project? What the hell does that mean?'

*Here we go again…*Morris was through with the constant sniping.

'I don't know, Mike. That's why I am going to Stanford Clarke-Mitchell. We need to bring them in for questioning, so I'm trying to do that. Okay?'

Corby held up his hands in apology. 'Fair enough, Jane.'

Morris waited for another snipe from Whetstone. The cow raised her head, glanced around, and then ducked back down.

'Smoke?' She grabbed her coat and waited for Corby. Ironically, the fire escape was free of smoke detectors, so she drew a cigarette. It took a couple of flicks to ignite the flame and a couple of draws to burn the tobacco. A couple of lungfuls for the calm to come, as she knew it would.

'Penny for them?' Corby was staring out over the building site. He was a non-smoker. 'Back there. I only asked a question, and you bit my bloody head off. Is it Deb Whetstone?'

Morris huffed and took another deep drag of her cigarette, letting the smoke slip through her lips. 'From the moment I arrived, she's been on my bloody case, like I'm shit on her shoes. And she's watching me all the time, waiting for me to step out of line, so she can have another bloody go.'

'Dave Monaghan told me she's got a glass eye, that's why she looks at people that way. Squinting, trying to keep the thing in.'

Morris's mouth fell open. 'Really? I've never noticed—'

Corby cocked his head and winked. Jane Morris felt comfortable with Mike Corby. Tall, somewhat cuddly, with cheeks that blushed too readily, yet he was the only single guy in the place who had not tried it on with her. Which was good. He was more the dependable, older brother type.

'Have you ever thought it's her and not you?' he asked.

'I'm positive it's her, Mike. She's a first-class bitch. Everything I do, she just makes me feel stupid.'

'Scott Daley doesn't seem to think you're stupid.'

'He's a bloke. Blokes think with their dicks.'

'I don't think you're stupid, either.'

Morris stifled a guffaw. 'And that, Your Honour, is the case for the prosecution.'

Corby's cheeks flushed; it was his tell. She could see him considering a response, which he mercifully abandoned. 'This thing between you and Deb? Is it to do with Keith Parrish?'

Jane Morris and Keith *The Uniform* Parrish had been an item for almost a year. The twenty-nine-year-old stocky traffic cop and the young, shy constable, four years his junior. Everybody knew, and to be fair, the salacious gossip made her feel good. So what right had Deborah *Bloody* Whetstone to waltz in, pull rank and steal him away? What right had she got to all the pain, all the grief, and all the sympathy his death brought?

'For Christ's sake, Mike, she's old enough to be his mother.'

He did the mental maths. 'Thirty-five, so maybe his aunt—'

'And that makes it any better?'

'You haven't seen my aunts. Wouldn't touch them with someone else's. All I'm saying is give it time and it will blow over. Just remember, you have to work with her. Don't let her bring you down.'

Mike's gentle pragmatism was right. Very little seemed to fluster him. The only time she had ever heard him raise his voice had been in the pantomime of an interview room. Not that it made it any easier. Keith was gone, and she wanted to scream it from the top of Lambourne Road.

***

For much of Ireland, the Magdalene Laundries scandal was still an open sore and people preferred to accept it and move on rather than talk about it. Which made Monaghan's job more difficult. Eventually, he happened upon an organisation called MWRP - the *Magdalene Women Research Project*. Late the previous evening, he'd sent out several tentative enquiries, realising that he was asking a lot. Yet the MWRP came through. Along with a brief note - *thanks for your enquiry, hope the attached helps* - was a spreadsheet listing names and details dating back to 1823 when the Baile Fearainn Convent first opened.

The first sheet documented the nuns - the *religious sisters* - who lived at the convent or had connections to it. The second, much longer list detailed all the women and girls who had lived and died behind the convent walls. Children as young as fourteen and women well into their seventies. Each carried a name and surname, age and date of birth, and their religion, which invariably was Roman Catholic. Each had an occupation, listed as *Domestic* or *Laundress* or, more worryingly, as *Inmate*. In Ireland, such was the stigma of promiscuity, even the suspicion of it was regarded as a mental illness, and the shame locked away. Pregnant girls often delivered their own babies, alone and frightened, only to see the infant swiftly removed and sent away for adoption. Many babies died soon after birth.

Monaghan thought of his daughter and grandchildren. Not for the first time, he felt ashamed of the country of his birth.

He located Agnes McCarthy on the list of religious sisters. He found records for her induction as a postulant in 1963, through her noviciate until her holy vows in 1968. There were also records of her teaching assignment to Holy Mount Residential School from 1990 until 1996 when the convent closed, as well as *contemplative ministries*, periods of around a fortnight spent in contemplative prayer to support church work or causes elsewhere, starting shortly after she joined the school and continuing until she left the convent.

Sister Agnes disappeared back to Baile Fearainn Convent on six separate occasions between 1990 and 1996, including one between 29th September and 5th October 1993 - the six days following the murder of Claire Dobson by Raymond Asher.

***

Perhaps Daley had been a touch overbearing with Whetstone. After all, everything was still theoretical, so anything was possible. They had nothing concrete beyond what had happened the previous Friday. It was still as likely Hannah had conspired to murder her husband, as was any connection to the school. Everything was always so clear to him. Raymond Asher was *Male B*. He was the only logical fit across the board. The timing of his release, along with witness testimonies, made it a safe bet. And he could have slipped out of work, or Danny Pearce may have covered for him. Yet, until Asher showed up, everything was still theoretical.

But what of *Female A*? Hannah Mason, having learned of Asher's release, conspiring to off her deceitful husband. Or the untraceable cleaner with whom he was having an affair?

Female A need not even be a woman, nor *Male B* a man, for that matter. These were enlightened times when gender was disconcertingly fluid. They only had to be convincing in whichever role they played. Which then brought Foster, Hughes, Pearce, Uncle Tom Cobley and all back into the frame.

The drugs? Hannah had a prescription for amitriptyline in her bathroom cabinet. Asher could obtain fentanyl through connections in the parole hostel.

So, despite his dismissals earlier, it was perfectly possible Hannah and Asher drugged Mason, killed Judd and set the explosion, then watched the fireworks before they went their separate ways. But it all seemed too *theatrical* when a pair of scissors and a costly divorce would have delivered the same message with a lot less risk and greater reward. A car salesman in a house with a dead prostitute. Fentanyl, amitriptyline and whisky, a rigged gas explosion. When adding in the red wig, long coat and the bible quotes, it was worthy of P. G. Wodehouse. And all in Green Street - where Father Joseph O'Donnell, erstwhile chaplain at Raymond Asher's school, hawked his religion.

Which presented Daley with a problem, equally thorny but much more career-limiting. He needed to re-interview Father O'Donnell, to get to the truth of Holy Mount School, once and for all. The truth of the night of the murder, and Sister Agnes's contemplative ministries.

Not one to shy away from a challenge, he pulled up Leslie Hacker's email address and dropped her a message.

Ma'am. Significant fresh evidence has come to light. I need to re-interview Father Joseph and would welcome your presence and your input. Keep me on track. Pls could you book an interview room at Hillingdon? Let me know when and I will bring in O'Donnell and organise a doctor to attend.

Diplomatic enough? Who cared? He could buy her a bunch of carnations and she'd ask whose grave he'd pinched them off.

On the desk, his phone buzzed again. Terri again, reminding him of their appointment at Harrow Central Hospital later that day. Doctors were concerned her blood pressure was slightly high. It was the point of clinics to find an anomaly, however slight or innocuous, then worry the shit out of the patient. It had succeeded. A decade ago, Lynne had lost their baby. Not so much lost as never had. The doctor called it a blighted ovum. A little string of nothing in a black hole where a foetus should have been, followed by a string of recriminations where a marriage should have been, and five years in the house in Alperton, where a home should have been. Of course, Terri understood her body and could be much more rational about a slightly raised diastolic pressure, but the doctor had worried the shit out of Daley.

He returned Terri a *thumbs-up* emoticon, then reread his email to Hacker. The *Law of Sod* dictated everything clashed all the time, so he sent the Superintendent a second email.

If we can make it tomorrow or Monday, that would be good.

Even before the electronic ink on his email dried, his mobile began buzzing again.

'Ma'am?'

'O'Donnell's still in hospital. They are fitting a stent tomorrow afternoon, and will discharge him on Monday, and then a day or two to recover. Your interview will have to wait.'

And good afternoon to you, ma'am.

'I am not sure we can wait that long.'

'I don't care. You've rattled enough cages for now.'

'But we've uncovered more information about the school. Connections with the Magdalene Laundry scandal back in the Nineties.'

'*The Nineties?* What could that possibly have to do with what happened last Friday?'

'That's why I need to speak to Father Joseph, ma'am. We can link Sister Agnes to a convent at the centre of the scandal. Official records show she visited the convent on six separate occasions, whilst working as Matron at Holy Mount, including a visit in September 1993, just after Claire Dobson's murder. It cannot be a coincidence.'

'Convents? Magdalene *bloody* Laundries, for heaven's sake. Next, you'll find a connection with Roswell. *Little green men* everywhere. Even if there is some basis in truth to these *allegations*, how can it possibly have anything to do with Andrew Mason's murder twenty years later?'

Daley's patience was dangling by a thread again, a familiar feeling in his dealings with Leslie Hacker. Absolute exasperation when faced with tunnel logic, but with a team at Hillingdon poised to whip Operation Scion away from him, he needed to keep his head. He took a breath and spoke as calmly as he could.

'Is there any way we could interview him before the middle of next week? As I said in my email, I am happy to have a doctor in attendance and you could sit in…'

'My decision is final. Your reckless attitude towards the priest has already resulted in an avalanche of unfavourable press. I can't risk any more. I will speak to the bishop and hopefully, Father O'Donnell will be fit enough to interview next week.'

'And if the killer strikes again before then? Father Joseph has already received a coded death threat. The written bible reference on the altar cloth.'

Through the speaker, she grunted. 'A bible reference? I've had worse threats from the ACC before his first coffee. If you want my view, O'Donnell is in more danger from you and your steamroller approach than any killer. After all, he is in hospital!'

'And there's not a single case of anyone being killed whilst in hospital…?'

'That's enough, Chief Inspector!' Daley felt his eardrums ring. 'You will not approach Father O'Donnell or speak to him, *or* send any of your officers to do so. As and when he is fit to be interviewed, I will arrange it here at Hillingdon. Is that clear?'

'Ma'am.'

'In the meantime, organise a constable to stand outside his door. No uniform, keep it low key. I am sure it is a waste of resources, not to mention needlessly ruining an officer's weekend, but never let it be said I don't listen.'

'Ma'am.'

'And Daley? Bring me a coherent way forward by Monday, or I am moving the investigation across to Hillingdon.'

'Ma'am.'

Chapter 31

He was losing his patience with Leslie Hacker. Maybe the rural village where she cut her teeth had its resident idiot on whom they could pin every crime, but London was different. Operation Scion had mushroomed from a tragic accident into a meticulously planned execution by two people, least one of whom could be a serial killer. It wasn't sheep rustling, and Hacker needed to understand that. She needed to realise he knew his manor and the people in it, to trust his judgement and allow him rein to use it.

Edging out onto Lambourne Road, he brought up Terri's mobile on the dash screen and pressed *call*.

'And how's my knight in shining armour? Ready to carry me off to the fat lady clinic?'

There was something unfathomably reassuring about her voice, like arriving home after a long trip away, or his mother's smile after a hard shift, or his dad's broad grin as he carried his steak pie and *Coke* to their usual stand at Craven Cottage.

'Glad to be away, dodging the cones on Rayner's Lane. There in fifteen minutes. You ready?'

'Aye, I've been ready for weeks, but Junior is hanging on by his, or her, fingernails. Anything else?'

'No, I just needed to hear your voice.'

'Aw, you'll make me all teary. I already have hormones enough for that.'

Cancelling the call, he tried to push Operation Scion from his mind, at least for the next hour or two. To concentrate on Terri and the baby. With the due date looming, he was feeling the burden of expectation, not just as a prospective father, but as a senior in the team at Lambourne Road. A double murder, two suspicious historic deaths and a new baby. Daley had even scheduled his paternity leave, eschewing all requests for time off that might interfere with it. But now even that was in jeopardy.

Off the rat run, the traffic eased, giving him more headspace to fret about the investigation. As he drew up on the drive, Terri was already out of the front door. It was her thing. Being on time meant half an hour early.

'What's the matter, hon?' She gave him a sympathetic smile. For a moment, he couldn't remember. Then the day came back.

'Leslie *Fucking* Hacker, pardon my French.'

'Och, you take things too much to heart, Scott Daley. Her skin is thicker than a rhino's rump and, with all the shenanigans at the moment, she can ill afford to lose senior officers. What is it this time, Staples missing from the stationery cupboard?'

'She accused me of giving a priest a heart attack.'

Terri had picked an inopportune moment to drink from a water bottle and made a gurgling sound from her nose. 'You didn't, did you?'

'Of course not. When I left, he was fine.'

'Oh, well, you'll have to try harder next time.'

'That's what Hacker's afraid of. She's barred me from interviewing him, which I have to do. It's an ongoing major crime investigation and I am the senior officer.' He'd stood up for himself; that was a good thing. So why did it feel like he had slipped a noose around his neck and handed her the rope?

'Those two prefects. They were out in the woods all night? Fourteen-year-olds? Five hours in the dark in the woods? What were they doing for so long?'

Daley glanced over. Terri was massaging her side. An experienced inspector herself, she had taken her mind off the pregnancy by going through Operation Scion with him.

An Invisible Murder

He shrugged. 'I'll ask Morris to speak to Jacob Foster.' As a teenager growing up in Fulham, Daley was in a gang. Roll-ups, BMXs, girls, cars, and Fulham FC were everything.

'What happened at the school is ancient history by now, surely, though.' said Terri.

'That's what Deb thinks. She's convinced it's a domestic. She says I'm wasting my time chasing ghosts. But Mason was one of the prefects on the night Asher killed Dobson. Then, right after they release Asher, Mason employs a cleaner and gets murdered himself. Okay, a coincidence, but if you throw in the murder of Doctor Verma, the school GP, and Sister Agnes, the live-in matron, and all three were linked by references to the bible.'

'It could still be a domestic and the rest is noise?'

Daley frowned. Had Terri been speaking to Whetstone?

He pulled up in front of the Maternity Block, wondering why the car park was so far away, considering the number of sick and heavily pregnant patients they had. Still, maybe that's what happens when you leave clinicians to manage, and managers to argue policy. He unclipped her seatbelt, and she leaned over and kissed him on the cheek.

'I hope you're better at building flat-pack furniture than you are at investigating a double murder. We have a lorry load coming tomorrow and if you think Junior and I are crawling about on our hands, knees and bumps-a-daisy looking for screws…Just remember, Scott Daley, I am immensely proud of you, and I know you'll work it out.'

***

When Daley returned from parking the car, Terri had found a seat in the waiting room and was flicking idly through a dogeared copy of *Mother & Baby*.

'You booked in?' He sat down and took her hand.

'No, Scott. I just sat here hoping they'd notice me - the big fat whale that I am.'

'Don't be so hard on yourself. Fat maybe. Big? No! Five-foot squat isn't big.' He winced as the nails threatened to draw blood, swiftly adding, 'All good things come in small packages.'

'So does dynamite.'

His first wife, Lynne, had never wanted children, a blessing in itself as she was not the maternal type. Not the married type, as it turned out. An unexpected pregnancy and blighted ovum left an uncrossable divide between them. The problem being there was no baby to mourn. An empty gestational sac, a string of an umbilical cord tapering to nothing. A common thing, they were told; an inviable pregnancy. No pregnancy at all, just nature's way of preventing abnormal babies. Go try again.

He recalled the gravestone as he'd left St Dunstan's a couple of days before. Had Harold Stevenson and his wife Belinda spent a lifetime grieving the loss of their baby, gone so early they had not yet named it? Or had they tried again, to no avail?

After that, he had resigned himself to the single life once again, pushing all thoughts of children out of his mind. Until he'd met Terri, fallen in love and gazed at two lines appearing in a pregnancy test window.

Maybe now the time was right. Fate, karma, kismet, whatever. In three months, he would turn thirty-nine. A year on and the *Big Four-Oh*. By the time the child was twenty, he would be retired. At least he'd have someone to push his wheelchair and change his colostomy bag. Maybe his life would have been different had that first baby been born.

Maybe he should drink less coffee and chill the heck out.

Part Three

Bayhurst Grange

Chapter 32

After the team brief, Jane Morris continued her pursuit of Foster and Hughes by paying a visit to Stanford Clarke-Mitchell in person. She had already tried their respective mobiles, to no avail. But the trip was in vain. Not only were they not available, but neither was Samantha Clarke-Mitchell. Nobody seemed to know where they all were, except that they had intended to travel to the Bayhurst Grange Project in Iver. The atmosphere inside Stanford Clarke-Mitchell had been unmistakably tense. Everyone was in their separate little prison cells, each keeping their heads down. It left Morris with the impression the problems out at Bayhurst Grange were more serious than anyone had first thought. Which meant finding Foster and Hughes was more pressing. With both of them living less than a mile from Stanford Clarke-Mitchell, she had decided it wouldn't hurt to do a drive past before conceding defeat. But that had also yielded nothing. Her only other option was a trip out to Iver, to Bayhurst Grange itself, to see if they were there. The dash clock read quarter-past-five, and traffic out of the city would be at its worst, so she parked up at a coffee shop, grabbed a sandwich and a large flat white, then rang Steve Taylor.

'Hi Jane.'

'Steve, can you use your magic triangulation software and let me know the location of Jacob Foster's and Willson Hughes's phones?'

'Give me ten. I'll drop you a text.'

The problem with driving out to Iver was that Foster, Hughes and Clarke-Mitchell might well have packed up for the day, and she could pass one or more of them on the road. Instead, she waited for Steve Taylor to get back to her.

Eventually, her lap buzzed as Taylor's text arrived. *Foster's phone switched off. Last location his address Wednesday am. Checked Hughes also. Locates to around a mile and a half north of Iver Heath.*

Which left her in a quandary. She could travel out to Iver in the hopes they would still be there or call it a night and hope they all turned up the next day. After all, nobody had died. But what would Deb Whetstone say if she turned up empty-handed again? Another reason for the cow to have a go at her. The brittle situation with her sergeant was getting her down. Not for the first time, she wondered whether the move from Traffic had been a good one. She had to at least try to find Foster and Hughes, which left her no option but to at least try Bayhurst Grange.

***

By the time the baby quacks had finished with Terri, the scant winter sunlight had ceded to a leaden grey and points of sodium orange were popping up around the hospital. Daley gulped in the crisp chill air, refreshing after the institutionalised stuffiness of the waiting room.

'That was an hour wasted.'

'You only have yourself to blame,' she chided. 'If you hadn't wasted five minutes, eight-and-a-half months ago, we wouldn't be here now wasting an hour.'

Daley felt embarrassed. 'Five minutes? More like thirty.'

'Don't flatter yourself. You spent twenty-five of them getting your breath back.'

He left Terri on a bench and returned to the multi-storey, relieved it had been a wasted hour. A momentary fluctuation in Terri's blood pressure three weeks ago had set alarm bells ringing. His instinct for catastrophisation had feared the worst, life without the baby, the prospect of grieving again. Terri had passed it off as one of those things, but, in those moments when her eyes looked away to nowhere, he could tell she was as concerned as he was. Since then, her blood pressure readings were normal, and the quacks had assured them both that, in the third trimester, few pregnancies failed and that babies held onto their place in the womb for grim death. Daley had mused on the poor choice of words, but it reassured him. Now all he needed to do was wait - and finish building the wardrobes.

Maternity wards were awful places to be when the dreams turned to emptiness.

From nowhere, a thought occurred. Raymond Asher and Claire Dobson had absconded from Holy Mount School. The two prefects ran after them. Five hours later, Dobson was dead, Asher was missing, and the prefects came back empty-handed. Terri was right. Five hours was a long time. An hour chasing, and an hour back. So, what had happened in the intervening three hours? Until now, he had assumed the prefects had failed to find the pair, but what if they had found them? What if, in those three hours, something horrific happened to Claire Dobson, and Foster, Mason, and even Asher had kept it a secret for twenty years?

He pulled into the drop-off bay. Terri heaved herself up and waddled across the pavement. The birth of the baby could not come soon enough. The tiny parasite was indeed hanging on for grim death. As he trotted around to open her door for her, he noticed her hands cupped around the underside of her baby bulge, trying to ease the ache in her lower back, and he caught his breath. In the school photo, Claire Dobson stood awkwardly, her fingers linked. As if she was holding something, but her hands were empty.

***

On her first pass, Morris missed the entrance to Bayhurst Grange, the mouth of the driveway narrowed by hanging foliage. She pulled off the road and drove down to a galvanised barrier straddled the drive, a padlock and chain hanging loose. Stopping, pulling her jacket over her head against the rain, she raced over and shifted the barrier to one side. Hopefully, Foster or Hughes, maybe even Clarke-Mitchell, were still up at the main house, arguing over plans or budgets. With night falling fast, she needed to get a move on. What might pass as bucolic charm during the day was as scary as hell in the dark. She rummaged through her glove box and found her police-issue torch, scanning it around to find her bearings. The driveway ran off into the darkness beyond the range of the torch, but there were fresh tyre tracks in the gravel. A short way off, the beam alighted on a gatehouse or lodge behind an overgrown hedge. Several of the tyre tracks led through to an area of flattened grass and weeds behind it. Beyond the feeble torchlight, darkness enveloped everything, and she suddenly noticed the complete absence of sound.

Come on Jane, man up.

She pulled boots and a raincoat from the back of her Fiesta, then followed her torch beam through the cascade of glistening raindrops along the short, uneven pathway down to the dilapidated lodge. Boarded up and roofless, there was no sign of life. So much for the notion of Foster and Hughes, billeted for the night in the old lodge, toasting pikelets over a welcoming fire.

Finally, the siren call of a hot shower and a mammoth G&T became overwhelming. The trip out to the middle of nowhere had been a fool's errand. Rain was dripping off her nose and her feet were blocks of ice. Nobody said policing was glamorous, but this was just like being back on the beat. Her hunt for Foster and Hughes could wait until tomorrow, if she hadn't caught the flu - whatever Sergeant Whetstone thought of her.

A flash of orange through the hedge caught the beam of her torch. Intrigued, she took a few steps across the overgrown lawn. Angular. The top corner of a car where the roof joined the windscreen. Maybe the ground around the main house was waterlogged, so they found a hard standing behind the bushes and parked there? She swept her torch until she found a way through the hedge, and cautiously stepping through the blanket of weeds, walked towards it.

She stopped. How bloody stupid she was out here on her own? Back on the beat, she rarely went out alone for fear of being knifed or beaten up. The station sergeant would have had her guts for garters. Outside the narrow beam of the torch, the world was

An Invisible Murder

invisible. The night was so quiet that even the ravens had settled in, with only the sound of rain on the leaves. Nobody knew she was here, and if Whetstone found out, she would also have a field day. She turned the torch towards the shape once more, now nearer and much clearer. Undoubtedly, a car. She was here now, so with her heart pounding in her chest, she edged her way through.

It was an old Volvo estate, the colour of stale chocolate. The tailgate was open, the interior light casting an insipid yellow glow through the curtain of rain. No one was inside, but it couldn't have been there too long, otherwise the battery would have been flat. Behind it sat another car. Smaller, lower. A silver Mercedes sports car. The doors were closed; the interior shrouded in darkness. Strange. She recalled from the statements that Foster drove a company Jag and Hughes a silver Passat. On the beat, she would have radioed in the plates, but since joining Lambourne Road, they reserved radios for operations and she only had her mobile. Anyway, she wasn't supposed to be here. She patted her pockets and cursed. Her mobile was in the car. At last, her copper's instinct for self-preservation kicked in. Her teeth were chattering, the rain had seeped through to her bones. Time to call it a day.

The first she knew was the hand, cold and wet across her mouth, stifling her yelp. An arm pulled her in close and another grabbed tight about her midriff. Jane Morris's world went black as the torch fell with a plop into the sodden grass.

***

Harrow Central Hospital was five miles from Daley's new house, but for Terri, that was five miles of discomfort. Beside him, she was rolling her backside in the seat, desperate to find a position that stopped the gnawing sciatica Junior was causing. With the traffic, the baby, Superintendent Hacker, Operation Scion, and Holy Mount School, Daley felt helpless and overwhelmed, and he was in danger of drowning. Yet all he saw was the school photograph and Claire Dobson, arms hanging, linking her fingers, as if she were carrying something, but her hands were empty. Just as Terri had done outside the hospital.

Claire Dobson was pregnant with Ray Asher's child.

Twenty years ago, faced with the prospect of being separated, Raymond Asher and Claire Dobson absconded. However, if O'Donnell's solution for problem children involved separating them and sending them to different schools, it was already too late—the damage had already been done. Who would take a pregnant fourteen-year-old? How would that reflect upon a Roman Catholic Children's Home, on O'Donnell himself? With Sister Agnes taking her curious periods of leave, the contemplative ministries back to Baile Fearainn. Was there already a process in place to send the boy to another home and pack off the girl to the Magdalene Asylum?

Ray and Claire ran. Was that the backstory, a vain attempt to stay together?

Yet when dawn broke, Dobson was dead, and Asher was on the run. A fourteen-year-old, his girlfriend, maybe his only friend, lay dying in front of him. Had he tried to save her, to carry her back to the school, only for Claire to go into premature labour? Had her last act of charity been to give her life to save the baby?

Daley pulled up Dave Monaghan's number on the dash screen. Six-fifteen, he would be home and tucking into his tea.

'Monaghan?'

'Dave, those lists from the convent. Do they show adoptions?'

'No, Scott, nuns and inmates. Nothing regarding babies born there or passing through to be adopted. What are you thinking?'

'It's a long shot but, I think Claire Dobson was pregnant when she died and the baby survived. That's why Sister Agnes went to Baille Fearainn. To hand over the child.'

'Shit. I'll get on it in the morning. See what I can dig up. What are you going to do?'

'I am going to wreck Whetstone's evening. Speak in the morning.'

Cancelling the call, he dialled Whetstone. 'Deb, where are you?'

'Oh, Scott, I'm doing great. Thanks for asking. I was just about to call you. There's been a call from Thames Valley. An incident out at Bayhurst Grange. Potential fatality.'

'Okay, you head out there. I've just got to drop Terri off—'

'—Hi, Deb, how's it going?' Terri leaned into the screen. Daley tutted pointedly.

'Oh, hi Terri. Well, you know. We must go out for a drink and wet the baby's head.'

'If you two have finished... I'll meet you at Bayhurst Grange, but don't go in without backup. If I am right, that's where Raymond Asher has been holed up.'

Two things had been puzzling Daley for some time. Firstly, if Mason was one of the prefects sent out after Asher and Dobson, who was the second? Now he was certain it was Jacob Foster. The pair would invariably stick together, covering each other's backs, leaving Asher to carry the can. With Dobson dead, and the baby spirited away, Raymond Asher had lost the most important people in his life. Of course, he would want to seek revenge twenty years later. Mason was dead. Now he would be after Foster.

As for the baby, it could have died at birth, but Daley was convinced it had survived. Why else would Claire Dobson's body be so well hidden, if not to cover up her labour? And that led to another inescapable conclusion. Whatever became of Claire Dobson's body, Daley would bet his house Father O'Donnell knew. Without a body, neither he, Jacob Foster nor Andrew Mason could be charged with her murder.

The second puzzle was Yvette, the girl Foster had picked up in *Blenheim's*. Why had she not come forward? If Foster had made up the encounter, why mention it at all? It was an easy deception to see through. Foster was many things, but he was not stupid. So, Daley concluded Yvette existed, and if that was true, could Yvette, the Masons' cleaner, and the woman in the coffee shop, all be the same person - *Female A*?

If *Male B* was Raymond Asher, was *Female A* his grown-up daughter?

Chapter 33

Thames Valley had called at around 6:30 pm. Someone had asked for Scott Daley in person and an operator had relayed the message to Daley's old desk phone in the naughty corner. The message was confusing, but Mike Corby had understood the gist, which was that shit was going down at Bayhurst Grange. There has been at least one fatality and Thames Valley has dispatched a car to the scene. It was the turning point for Whetstone. She could no longer dismiss the school as noise. Old school friends often stay in contact; well, not hers, but there would always be exceptions. And Green Street, St Dunstan's, Father O'Donnell? More coincidences? If the explosion had occurred around the corner in Sefton Street, would they still be thinking the same? Now, though, it was a coincidence too far.

Bayhurst Grange was out in the sticks. She was a city girl, used to the bright orange nights and constant hubbub. Driving down unlit country roads unnerved her. The rain and the derisive scud of the wipers compounded the isolation. Was she the only person at Lambourne Road not to see the Bayhurst Grange link?

She used her crappy clip-on sat nav and was relieved to see the strobing blue lights ahead of her Golf on the roadside. She parked up beside the patrol car and reached into the back for the snazzy hi-vis police raincoat Keith The Uniform had purloined for her. A random act of kindness before things went wrong.

Scott Daley was leaning against a small Astra patrol car speaking to a short elderly officer with a greying beard and an excitable manner who had attended the call-out. John Stanton was having the time of his life, even if he was out of his depth. Uxbridge had also sent a detective inspector, a sergeant and a constable, and after a brief, rain-sodden period of negotiation, they were content to defer to Daley and his team. A wiry, dour-looking detective constable called Privan Satesh remained to assist - and wrest it back, if it turned out not to be part of Operation Scion.

'What the hell was she doing coming out here alone?' Whetstone spotted Jane Morris's Fiesta sat in forlorn darkness up the drive.

'Trying to impress you, probably,' remarked Daley.

'Cheers, Scott. Don't you think I feel bad enough already?'

Satesh led them a hundred yards, through a small river of rainwater to the lodge, a black scar haloed by the hastily erected floodlights. He gestured towards an opening across the sodden grass, a tree-framed silhouette of blinding white, cut and shaped by shadows crisscrossing the beams. Daley showed his card to the constable on the perimeter and lifted the tape for Whetstone. The two cars, an ancient brown Volvo estate and a silver Mercedes sports car, were under three gazebo tents erected alongside each other. Whetstone's stomach knotted as she read the registration.

'That's Sam Clarke-Mitchell's car - the CEO of the place where Hughes and Foster work.'

'Bit late for a site visit.' mused Daley, pulling on the oversuit and bootees.

Around the far side two figures, swathed head to foot in white, were leaning into the door of the Mercedes.

'Len?' Whetstone took a gamble and was relieved when at least one of the white-suited figures looked up.

'Deb, Scott. Female around forty years old with blunt-force trauma to the head. Based on core temperature, she's been dead for over twenty-four hours, but I'll need to get her back to the lab to be more precise. What I can say is that the murder took place somewhere else because there's not enough blood on the inside of the car, and it would be difficult to wield a weapon with enough force. Blood in the car boot suggests they transported the body here before placing it in the driver's seat.'

An Invisible Murder

Sam Clarke-Mitchell was hanging through the open door, with her head canted at an angle on the wet ground, and her left arm stretched across her face, as if shielding her eyes from the bright floodlights. Rivulets of rain had leached away some of the blood that turned her high-end gabardine raincoat scarlet.

'Murder weapon?'

The white shoulders shrugged. 'Who knows? Baseball bat, chair leg, metal pipe. I will know more when I examine the wounds more closely for fragments, but with the rain…'

'And the Volvo?'

'Empty. When we arrived, the tailgate was open. There are a few tools in the back under a tarpaulin.'

'Tools? What sort of tools?' asked Daley.

'Rope, a garden fork and spade and a change of clothes. I'll get them sent to Ramesh for analysis. However, this is quite interesting.' Ganlow pointed to the windscreen. Through the drops of rainwater, they could see words or graffiti.

'Someone wrote "Stay away" on the inside of the glass using a thick red marker pen. We'll take samples.'

Daley puffed. 'What the hell do they mean by that?'

Ganlow stood upright, stretching out an ache in his back. 'I dunno, but there are tyre tracks which suggest the Mercedes was driven off the drive, through a gap in the hedges, and parked up here. Though less distinct, similar tire tracks show that the same thing happened to the estate car.' Ganlow pointed to deep ruts behind the Volvo's rear wheels and explained that someone had attempted to move it, causing the car to sink in the mud. 'Oh, and there are also signs of a motorbike or motor scooter driving around here, too.'

Daley knew the tyre marks were significant, but wasn't sure why. He let it go as Simon, Ganlow's assistant, rose from the Mercedes and held a plastic evidence bag aloft.

'This was on the dashboard. It's one of Ms Clarke-Mitchell's business cards. Look at the back.'

SCM - TIM 6:9

'Google tells me it's Timothy, Chapter 6, verse 9,'

"But they that will be rich fall into temptation and a snare,
and into many foolish and hurtful lusts,
which drown men in destruction and perdition."
(Timothy 6:9)

***

Satesh walked them back to an ambulance parked near the gates. As if on cue, a uniformed officer arrived with hot drinks. One could say many things about the police service, but they could always conjure up a brew in a crisis - as long as they could also find a Portaloo. Jane Morris sat in the back of the ambulance, wrapped in a warm blanket. Her makeup resembled a late Picasso study in grey, and her beautiful blonde hair hung in rat's tails around her face. Beside her, Willson Hughes shivered as he leaned despondent against the window.

'Sir, ma'am. I'm sorry. I should have called for backup but—'

Whetstone held up a finger and nodded at Hughes. 'Later, Jane, when we're in the warm. I'm just relieved you're safe.' She turned to Hughes. 'So, Mr Hughes. Tell me what happened. Start from the beginning. You went to Stanford Clarke-Mitchell yesterday morning.'

Hughes squinted off into the dark, past the painful memories. 'I went to see Sam. She believed Jake was trying to sabotage the Bayhurst Grange bid, and I agreed to help Sam discover what he was up to. We knew he had come out here, but when we arrived we couldn't find him, so we split up.'

Whetstone recalled Clarke-Mitchell telling of her suspicions a few evenings ago. Documents going astray, meetings being derailed.

'Sam searched the house - in the dry,' continued Hughes. 'She sent me out into the woods. Jake had been researching an old murder that happened here, out near the motorways, so I wondered if he had gone out there.'

An Invisible Murder

Daley shared a look with Whetstone. 'A murder?'

'I found a file in Jake's office. He'd been looking into the history of Bayhurst Grange. It used to be a school, and according to the file, a pupil was murdered back in the Nineties. They never found the body. I think Jake was searching for it.'

Daley remembered the tools in the back of the Volvo. 'Why would he be doing that?'

Hughes shrugged. 'Maybe finding the body now would delay the project. Anyway, I walked into the woods, towards the motorway where the murder was supposed to have happened, but I got lost. I was checking the map when I heard the engine of Sam's car and figured she was abandoning me here, so I legged it back. Through the trees, I glimpsed the car as it drove off, two people inside. I thought Sam and Jake were having a laugh at my expense, so I went back to the house. I figured I could wait there until they returned, but I was mistaken. There is something bad about that place. Odd.'

'Odd, how?'

'It sounds weird, but I heard voices, kids' voices, whispering, laughing, like children playing tricks. In the end, I decided the house was too scary, so I walked up the drive to the lodge. Then the next thing I knew, I was waking up in the front seat of the Volvo. I looked at my watch and I realised I'd been out for ages. Almost twenty-four hours. How could that be?'

Whetstone watched as Hughes massaged the top of his arm. She felt sure the medical officer could tell him how.

'So the Volvo. Do you know whose car it is?'

Hughes shook his head. 'I've never seen it before.'

'And the message on the windscreen?'

'When I saw it, I freaked out. The keys were in the ignition, so I tried to drive off, but the wheels got stuck. That's when I saw Sam's car. She was just sitting there, her head against the side window. All that blood. She must have been there all the time.'

Hughes squinted his eyes to banish the image and began crying. Morris passed a tissue and placed an arm around him. 'You're doing great, Will. What happened then?'

'I ran to the lodge, but found it locked, and it occurred to me that maybe there were ghosts in the lodge too, so I ran and hid in the bushes at the edge of the clearing. I don't know how long I was there, but I just kept hoping Jake would return and we could get out of this place. As it got dark, I heard a car coming up the driveway. I watched it park up and Constable Morris shining her torch about. I was sure they would get her too, so I pulled her into the bushes and told her to keep quiet. Sorry.'

'What do you think is going on here, Mr Hughes?' asked Daley.

Hughes took a deep breath and pulled the blanket tighter. 'It sounds absurd, but it's as if the children are still in there. As if they don't want us to take away their school. Maybe that's why Jake was trying to stop the redevelopment. To save the school for the children. Maybe he knew something.'

Daley leaned back and sipped his coffee. He was no connoisseur, but even to his palate, it resembled the mud running down the driveway outside. Will Hughes had endured a harrowing ordeal and, in extremis, imaginations go wild. In the absence of a rational explanation, they create one. He had heard something, but spirit children? Voices? If not ghosts, what had he heard?

'Okay, Mr Hughes. We'll take you back to Ealing and get you checked out by a medic. Constable Morris will follow on and take a statement from you. Then we'll drive you home.'

Will Hughes's eyes widened. 'What? I'm being arrested?'

Daley smiled and shook his head. 'Not at this stage. You're just helping us with our inquiries. Is there anyone you'd like us to call?'

'My partner. She'll be worried.'

Daley nodded. 'Jane, can you handle that?'

At that moment, the rear doors of the ambulance cracked open and Constable Satesh poked his head inside.

'Sir, Ma'am. Can you come up to the main house, please? There's something you need to see.'

Chapter 34

With the rain showing little sign of abating, Daley persuaded Satesh to taxi them to the main house, embarrassed at the amount of mud left on the seats. At the end of the quarter-mile of rutted gravel, the hall was a smudge in the blackness of the moonless night, broken only by the piercing beams of the headlights, as Satesh turned his car around in front of the building.

'Mr Ganlow has left the other team to finish up at the lodge and come down here already, sir, and I've taken steps to preserve the scene.' He nodded to the far side of the courtyard, where a platoon of uniforms had spread out around the perimeter of the house. A smaller platoon of crime scene officers was disgorging from a van and erecting portable tents and lights.

They followed the fence around the building to a small parapet wall topped with rusted railings and down a short flight of steps. A portable generator thrummed away to itself as it held open an old wooden door. Under orders from a CSO, and to avoid cross-contamination, the trio swapped out their nitrile gloves, white overalls and plastic protective bootees. Then they followed a snake of heavy-duty cabling down under the building. Daley had always been unnerved by tight spaces, and now the hairs on his neck stood on end. The reek of must and mould made his nostrils twitch. If it got onto his chest, he'd be hacking for weeks. Hanging cobwebs and the stringent smell of rodent urine suggested no one on two legs had been down here in a long while. But there was something else. Something more poignant. Here and there, the lime-stained brickwork carried the rough inscriptions left by former occupants, stealing an illicit few minutes away from the regime above. Initials, love hearts pierced with an arrow, the odd cock and balls. It reminded him of the old air raid shelter in the playground of his school in Fulham. Some marks looked fresh. Maybe Hughes was right and children were still in here?

Eventually, the labyrinth opened up into a space cluttered with stacks of chairs and tables. Through a doorway, floodlights silhouetted the cobwebs that shimmered from the ceiling. Inside, an old heating boiler dominated the centre of the room, radiating pipes like the legs of a giant inverted spider hanging from the ceiling. The air was stale and heavy to breathe, laden with floating motes of dust and debris, thick with the funk of decay.

'Someone's been busy,' remarked Whetstone. A fresh layer of brick debris carpeted the floor, and a rough-hewn hole pierced the far wall, the bricks stacked against the side. Len Ganlow stood astride the hole that separated the boiler room from the darkness of a further space. Whetstone noticed Satesh had not followed them. Maybe he knew what they were about to find. Sensible chap.

'Len?' she called. 'We must stop meeting like this. People will talk.'

'Let them talk, sweetheart. We have tonight. Is that not enough?' Ganlow let out a grunt of ironic amusement. 'Come in, and keep to the chequer plate.' A figure lay sprawled over the jagged bricks, caked in dust and grime. Only the head and torso were visible. At the feet lay a pry bar, a mallet, and a torch.

'A well-nourished male, mid-thirties or early forties. There are signs of a brief struggle, but no evidence of significant physical injury, though it's hard to tell with him covered in all this dirt. Currently, no obvious cause of death, but I'd wager my modest civil service pension whatever was in this thing did the trick.' Above the collar, a large syringe protruded from the left side of the neck, the plunger pushed in all the way. Ganlow reached a hand down to either side of the head and, as delicately in death as in life, turned it so they could get a look at the face. Whetstone took a sharp breath.

'That's Jacob Foster, Scott. From Stanford Clarke-Mitchell.'

Daley closed his eyes tight. When they had connected Foster to the school, he should have acted with greater urgency, put a man outside his door, or even found Foster himself and dragged him back to Lambourne Road. While Asher was on the loose, no one would be safe. These were the ones that lay heavy on Scott Daley, the ones that kept him awake at night. They were the faces he saw when he closed his eyes and the fingers that pointed at him.

But now, the pieces were falling into place. They sent two prefects to bring back a boy and his pregnant sweetheart. Three missing hours and a night spent by the priest covering the truth, ensuring it stayed buried for twenty years. Now, the prefects were both dead, and the priest was on borrowed time.

'I found this stuffed into his right hand. Similar to the last.' Ganlow held up a ziplock bag containing a sheet of crumpled notepaper torn from a pad.

JF - Dt 32:35

"To me belongeth vengeance and recompense;
their foot shall slide in due time:
for the day of their calamity is at hand,
and the things that shall come upon them make haste."
(Deuteronomy 32:35)

Daley gazed down at the corpse and sighed.

'Foster realised that upon his release, Raymond Asher would seek *vengeance and recompense*, and knew he would eventually he would come for him. With *the day of his calamity at hand*, he came out to the school to find Claire Dobson before Asher could, and to remove any evidence of his involvement, but *the things that shall come upon him made haste*. Asher found him first. Foster's *foot slid*.'

'What's in there?' Daley could see nothing but a vast rusted upturned cauldron pockmarked and brown with rust.

'The original heating boiler,' replied Ganlow, 'left in place when they upgraded to the new one.'

From the darkness of the room, a white overall peered out from behind the massive rusted boiler.

'Len. Over here.'

'The perfect place,' said Daley, wryly. 'Knock out a few bricks, slide the body in, and put them back. Rub a bit of dust into the cement, and Bob's your uncle.'

'We think it's Claire Dobson,' suggested Whetstone. 'The girl who died here in 1993.'

'No, ma'am,' replied the forensic officer, stepping out of the room. 'Not a body, something else. Someone else has been in here recently, and left footprints in the layer of dust. Distinct prints, no protective bootees, so not one of us.'

Ganlow squeezed around behind the boiler until all that was visible was his shadow dancing in the lamplight across the walls.

'There is a uniform layer of dust over the entire floor that does not appear to have been disturbed until today. There are two sets of distinct footprints. Scott, compare them to the shoes our victim is wearing, will you?'

After a few brief bursts of light, a phone appeared around the boiler. Daley crouched down. The first matched the boots Foster was wearing, but the pattern on the second was noticeably different and of a smaller size. Raymond Asher or Will Hughes, maybe? He fired off a text to Jane Morris, asking her to take a photo of the soles of Will Hughes's shoes and send it over.

Ganlow reappeared from behind the boiler. 'I believe whoever left those prints has removed something. There is an indentation, as if an object, around twenty centimetres in diameter, has rested there, like a box or a tin. The edge has left a ring of rust.'

It took a moment for it to make sense to Daley, for the last piece of the puzzle to fall into place and confirm to him what happened twenty years ago. It told him why McCarthy and Verma, Mason and Foster, and soon Joseph O'Donnell, all had to die.

'Deb, we've been looking at this from the wrong angle. We need to wake Leslie Hacker. She and I need a serious talk.'

Whetstone huffed. 'Suicide Scott Daley is back. Might make inspector this year, after all.'

Chapter 35

Thames Valley had checked the lodge and found evidence that Asher had made it his bolthole since leaving the hostel. They offered to watch the lodge in case he returned, but, in Daley's view, that bird had flown, most likely on the missing Honda motor scooter. Whetstone offered to remain on scene until operations at the grange had concluded.

How could they have got it so wrong?

Investigating Hannah Mason was a valid line of inquiry that would usually be rewarded. Had they spent too long on it? Back at the police college in Hendon, he'd been told the story of Flight 19, five Avenger Torpedo bombers lost in the Bermuda Triangle in 1945. Theories abounded, everything from giant squids to freak air currents. It is now accepted that the pilots believed their compasses were malfunctioning. They flew out into the Atlantic, then one by one, dropped into the sea. One mechanical compass may lie, but five? Occam's Razor. The compasses were right. The pilots were mistaken, yet they spent so long building a case against their equipment they were doomed.

Who could predict a killer would seek revenge after twenty years? The clues had been there. The bible references suggested more than domestic infidelity. Even when they connected O'Donnell and Andrew Mason, they preferred to chase the wife, yet Daley was certain they had been barking up the wrong tree, in the wrong wood, in a different county.

But who killed McCarthy and Verma? Asher was in prison, so who was his accomplice? Who was *Female A*? Asher had no family. A stranger, then - a prison visitor, a guard, or Claire's baby? Yet, in

2000 when McCarthy was murdered, she would have only been seven years old, and in 2004 when Verma was killed, she would have been eleven.

The rain had stopped several hours ago, but Daley's feet were still wet and his trouser legs clammy against his skin. Apart from a few biscuits, he'd eaten nothing for twelve hours. He brought out his phone and found Terri's number. It took all his strength not to press the button just to hear her voice, to know some things in the world were alright. That not everything was as screwed up as Operation Scion. At 2:26 am, though? There would probably be another murder.

Instead, he broke out the emergency crisps from the glove box and drove the empty streets back to the real world. Everything would look better in the morning.

***

But morning came too soon for Scott Daley. He couldn't get Foster and Clarke-Mitchell out of his mind, even in the few meagre hours of sleep exhaustion had gifted him. As usual, Terri had hauled herself, Junior and her sciatic nerve out of bed early, and he had lain awake beating himself up. Could he have done anything more to protect Foster and Clarke-Mitchell?

Yesterday, he had believed Claire Dobson's murder was the catalyst, the precursor of everything that had happened since. Agnes McCarthy in her tiny house in Barnsley. Deepak Verma in his Iver Heath consulting room. Then, an almost unimaginable nine-year gap before Mason and Judd. And Foster and Clarke-Mitchell? They were a knee-jerk. When Foster had decided he had to move Claire's body, the killer knew they had to act.

He firmly believed that they were not dealing with a serial killer, but with someone whose need for vengeance was so strong that it smouldered for decades, patiently waiting for the perfect moment to strike. And that made them less predictable.

Chapter 36

Lambourne Road was buzzing when Whetstone arrived. Besides the small phalanx of early shift administrative staff, Monaghan, Taylor and Corby had all turned in, energised at the prospect of a juicy double murder to get their teeth into. Jane Morris was noticeably absent, probably keeping her head down, having behaved like an absolute twat the previous day.

Whetstone had babysat the activities at Bayhurst Grange until five-thirty in the morning. It had given her plenty of time to think. Operation Scion had exploded exponentially, well beyond the front door of Number 5 Green Street and the probability of a woman scorned. Unfortunately, it meant she would have to suspend the investigations into Hannah Mason unless they found a smoking gun. Reluctantly, she had to accept the school was front and centre.

Daley had exiled himself to the Goldfish Bowl, giving himself a hard time over Foster and Clarke-Mitchell. When she poked her head around the door and asked Daley if he wanted a brew, he was scrawling on the small portable whiteboard. Gone was the spider's web of disconnected thoughts, replaced by an orderly list of things too small for her to see. She had noticed before that the size of Daley's writing diminished in line with his confidence. He turned and raised a red pen.

'Felicity McAllister, the teacher. We need to bring her in.'

'She's in Manchester, Scott, so it might take a day or two.'

Daley stopped writing and looked askance. 'Whatever. Weren't you making a brew?'

She wrangled the cups, looping her finger through the handles.

If you made a brew for yourself, it was expected that you made one for everyone. How would that work out at Hillingdon when their small team would be subsumed in an ocean of bodies? The fifth floor of Lambourne Road was tired and oppressive, and some days were like walking into a mental asylum with the guards on holiday, but she had become accustomed to it. It was more of a home than the terrace in Ealing she went back to most nights, and the team was the only family she had.

When she returned to the Goldfish Bowl, Daley was leaning back in his chair, squeaking it back and forth, staring at the whiteboard. He looked tired, old beyond his years, just as she had looked when she caught her reflection in the hall mirror earlier. Murder Investigation did that to you. The carnage just kept on coming. Each case ate away at your soul, and each new victim pinned an image in the gallery of your mind. Of course, you wanted to catch the perpetrator, to bring closure to the victim's loved ones, but also to bring closure for yourself, to justify your own abilities to solve the worst of all crimes.

'O'Donnell's my immediate concern,' Daley remarked. 'A murder on his watch at Holy Mount School. He is the only person left who knows what happened, and he has still not told me everything he knows. And the bible reference meant for him on the altar cloth. I reckon that puts him at the top of the list. Hacker has asked for a constable to sit outside his room, but I'm not sure I trust her to boil water without burning it.'

'And Superintendent Hacker? What does she think?' Whetstone emphasised the rank.

Daley drew in a breath. 'I rang her last night, er, early this morning. She was a little tetchy—'

Whetstone raised her eyebrows. 'Maybe she had someone staying over?'

Daley shuddered. 'That's a sobering thought, unless she has a bank of freezers in her basement, and thaws one out whenever she feels frisky. Anyway, after she'd finished attacking my competence with a sledgehammer, she agreed to come in. She should be here—'

Daley twisted his wrist despite the clock on the wall, '—around now, so better make another brew. Get the maid to use the best china and posh biscuits.'

And, mused Whetstone, plenty of sugar to keep her sweet.

'What are we going to tell her?' It was the $64,000 question. Two more deaths linked to Holy Mount, whilst O'Donnell was safely tucked up in hospital. Whetstone could hear Hacker's voice already. Theories and suppositions, Daley. Unless you can bring me facts…

'I don't know, Deb. I know O'Donnell is the key, but the problem is, so does the killer.'

Daley's body language betrayed his frustration. He and Whetstone had always debated, even argued, their differences. But Leslie Hacker had not budged so much as a millimetre. Was Daley on a hiding to nothing? Behind her, predictably early, the swing doors creaked. Superintendent Hacker stood for a moment, a meerkat scouting for predators, or maybe an eagle for prey. Then she turned and pushed through the Goldfish Bowl doors. Seizing her opportunity, Whetstone made a break for the kettle.

***

'Can we make this quick? I have squash at one over in Hammersmith.' She wore a blue tracksuit top over black leggings with the whitest designer trainers Daley had ever seen. He waited as she squeezed herself into the Throne of Doom, relishing her discomfort, fearing it would soon be his.

'Ma'am, it is imperative I speak with Father O'Donnell.'

'Have I not already made myself quite clear on this? Father O'Donnell is too poorly to be interviewed. What are you trying to do, finish him off?'

'With all due respect, ma'am, the heart attack is sod-all to do with me. I've spoken to Mrs O'Hallorhan, the cleaner at the vicarage. She told me Jacob Foster arrived shortly after I left, that he and O'Donnell had a blazing row, and it was that which caused

O'Donnell's heart attack. There was no way I could have predicted it or intervened to stop it.'

Hacker feigned an expression of surprise. 'So now, we take the word of a church cleaner over that of an experienced senior police officer?' She raised her eyes to the ceiling and huffed.

'No, but if he and Foster argued—'

'There is still no proof it caused his heart attack, and now you're telling me Jacob Foster has also been murdered, so he can hardly refute your allegations.'

'Being dead would be at the top of his priorities right now, ma'am?'

'Don't be bloody facetious, Daley. Now let me think.'

If only we had that long, mused Daley. He leaned back in his chair, contemplating other careers. Eventually, she finished pontificating. She stopped for a moment and stared hard at Daley.

'Okay, I accept perhaps we should have questioned O'Donnell, but it doesn't alter the fact he is in a hospital in a serious condition. I cannot allow you to make that any worse. There must be another way to proceed with your investigation.'

Daley considered drawing a donkey on the whiteboard, blindfolding the team, and giving them a tail and a pin.

'There is no other way. He is keeping something from us, and it has already cost two more lives. We are lucky it wasn't more. I believe this all stems from that night twenty years ago. Thanks to our inaction, everybody else that was there on the night is dead, except O'Donnell. We must speak to him as a matter of urgency.'

'What about the murderer, Asher?'

'We can't question him if we don't know where he is.' It was like banging his head on a brick wall.

'Are you intent on arguing with every point I make, Chief Inspector?'

Daley threw his hands in the air. How much clearer could he make it? Asher was out to eradicate everyone who was involved that

An Invisible Murder

night. Sister McCarthy, Dr Verma, Andrew Mason, Jacob Foster, and anyone else who got in his way. O'Donnell was next on the list. Even an imbecile could understand he needed to speak to O'Donnell before Asher did.

'Ma'am, this is a major crime investigation. I need to speak to Father O'Donnell—,' then Daley's mouth overtook his brain in the race to end his career. '—and I am going to do it with or without your blessing.'

'Chief Inspector! I'm sick to death of this insubordination. I am not Bob Allenby and I will not argue with you. Stay away from O'Donnell - and that's an order. If you set one foot in the hospital, you'll have Vic Fraser to answer to. Is that understood?'

***

Outside the office, Whetstone struggled to hear the ruckus above the sound of the kettle, despite moving to a corner of the Goldfish Bowl where she would be obscured by blinds. She remembered Stanford Clarke-Mitchell. Jacob Foster and Sam Clarke-Mitchell arguing next door, and now both were dead. For a moment, she considered walking in, diverting Hacker's fire, but then, this was Suicide Scott Daley, and it wasn't her problem. Yet.

'Deb, over here.' Dave Monaghan was leaning over Steve Taylor's shoulder, watching rows of numbers scroll up his computer monitor. 'Go get Scott, before he commits hari-kari.'

'What is it, lads?'

'The cleaner's phone has just been reactivated. Mast triangulation puts it in North Pinner.'

Before the explosion, the cleaner used the phone to speak to Mason, then it went silent. Either it died when Mason did, or someone took out the battery. Now they knew. Monaghan fired up a program to track activity on the phone as a call was initiated.

'It's another unregistered mobile, somewhere in East Harrow.'

Whetstone's heart missed a beat. Her eyes flicked between the maps side-by-side on Taylor's screen. Both dots were stationary.

One near Pinner. One in Harrow, south of the railway line.

Then, both dots disappeared.

Taking a breath, she pushed through the Goldfish Bowl door. Daley and Hacker were facing off across the desk. They both paused mid-breath and stared at her, the Superintendent's face a picture of displeasure at being interrupted, Daley's one of relief.

'Sergeant?'

'Sorry, Ma'am. Sir. *Female A* has switched on her phone and called *Male B* at Harrow Central Hospital.'

Daley spun on his heel. 'We have to get over there, Deb. Call the hospital. Make sure the man on the priest's door is awake.'

'Chief Inspector!' Hacker's voice had raised an octave. 'I have made myself quite clear. You are under no circumstances to go near Father Joseph.'

'Quite clear, ma'am, but with all due respect, this is an operational decision and I am making it. You might be content with another death on your conscience, but I am not.'

'Based on a *phone call?*'

Daley lifted his coat from the stand in the corner.

'The choice is yours, ma'am. Either you come with us over to Harrow Central, where you can make sure I don't give the priest another heart attack, or you can ring ACC Fraser and have me arrested - he is #3 on speed dial, but right now, I believe two killers are homing in on the last remaining person who knows what happened at Holy Mount twenty years ago. We have an urgent situation in progress. This is the Met, Superintendent, not some hick command in Derbyshire.'

Whetstone had to stifle a chuckle as Hacker's face turned more shades of red than a chameleon in a paint factory. Her lips flapped as she looked between Daley and the phone. For the first time in Whetstone's memory, she was at a loss.

'Well?'

'Okay, Chief Inspector, let's go, but on your head be it.'

Part Four

The Sins of the Father

Chapter 37

There were three routes north to Harrow Central Hospital, each taking twenty minutes on a good day. Today was not a good day. The Uxbridge Road was rammed, so Daley turned on the blues and twos for the first time since he'd had them fitted to his new Audi. The effect was disappointing. People were annealed to police sirens on the streets of the Capital. As they crossed the railway bridge, he headed for Hanger Lane, then through Alperton and Wembley. Busy but with wider roads, maybe the traffic would move over. To his utter satisfaction, in the rear-view mirror, Leslie Hacker was ashen as she slewed across in the back seats. Whetstone contacted the hospital and spoke to Constable Dan Hodgkins, the man on O'Donnell's door, and everything was quiet. With Asher's photo distributed to hospital security, unfortunately, it was a waiting game.

Twenty-five agonising minutes later, Daley flashed his warrant card at a security officer at the hospital gate and followed a waved finger towards a parking area near the main entrance. Whilst not the largest hospital in London, it was still huge and complex., with many departments, thousands of rooms, corridors and cupboards. It was Daley's worst nightmare, a dense haystack of people milling around as Raymond Asher, the needle, used them all for cover.

The main entrance dog-legged through a busy foyer, past a coffee shop and restaurant, and down a glass-walled corridor towards the ward block, a massive concrete structure at the heart of the site. Three separate wings and ten floors of corridors and rooms, offices and closets for Asher to hunker down in. They couldn't hope to search them all, but once up on the ninth floor, the only access to the Coronary Care Unit was a single set of squeaky swing doors, and the only access to O'Donnell was through Constable Dan Hodgkins.

Behind a curved desk, a group of nurses chattered amongst themselves. Daley asked for the ward sister, and a small woman, around his age, stretched herself out of a chair.

'Hello, I'm Sister Johns. Father O'Donnell's room is over there.' She pointed toward the thickset man, who looked up from his broadsheet. 'Since your sergeant called, we've all been keeping an eye out and supplying your officer with tea.'

'Not a wise move. I told him not to leave his post for anything.'

'And he hasn't, bless him. We have Urology on standby, not to mention a cleanup team. Eventually, something's got to give.'

She smiled, and her eyes smiled too. Daley had had a thing for nurses, more so since his stay in hospital following the incident with the train. In an induced coma for what seemed like years, but was a matter of days, a young nurse called Siobhan had sat with him, read to him and scolded him when his vital signs changed on the monitor. Her voice kept him sane while monsters roamed around the darkness.

'Were you able to get the things I requested?' asked Daley.

The ward sister reached behind the counter. 'Yes. It took a little *persuasion*. A white coat, a stethoscope and clipboard for you, Chief Inspector, and this is for you?'

Whetstone took the package. 'Scrubs? Seriously?'

'You know what they say about women in uniform, Deb. Anyway, the less we look like coppers, the better.' Daley pulled on the coat, loosened his tie, and hung the stethoscope around his neck. He rubbed a hand wearily over his stubble. 'Next patient, please nurse.'

As Whetstone sulked off to change, Daley showed his warrant card to the constable, peered through the window in the door, and then crossed back to the nurse's station.

'How's it been?' he asked. 'Anyone acting strangely?'

An Invisible Murder

The ward sister raised her eyebrows. 'Mr Colson in bed 5 is a little free with his hands, but apart from that. We are keeping this low-key, and I would ask you to do the same. It is, after all, a coronary care ward. Father O'Donnell's procedure is at three. He should be back from the theatre within an hour and a half. Just in time for tea.'

Leslie Hacker was standing behind Daley like a spare hand in a brothel. He recognised her difficult situation, but there could only be one incident manager, and Daley was determined it was him, so he gave her a straightforward job to keep her happy.

'Ma'am, could you manage the situation up here? Dan Hodgkins will stay on after George Brennan arrives to relieve him. No one, except clinical staff, into Father O'Donnell's room, and then only with Sister Johns's express authority. And keep me in the loop.'

Hacker nodded. Now, all he had to hope was that Asher showed up, or he would be the one they banished to a hick command in Derbyshire.

'Sister, business as usual. If our man appears, leave it to us.'

The ward sister threw him a stern schoolmarm frown. 'As long as you remember, this is still a hospital.'

Daley nodded. It was as far as the clash of wills went.

'I've spoken to Dave Monaghan, Scott.' Whetstone was fidgeting in the scrubs. They felt insubstantial in the face of a prolific killer, but at least she wouldn't get blood on her own clothes. 'The two burners are still off. They're monitoring them.'

Daley crossed to the window and stared out, in the vain hope that Raymond Asher would come sauntering along the service road, nine floors below. He was rewarded, though not with Asher. He pulled out his phone and asked Monaghan to text him Will Hughes's number, calling it as soon as it came through. Hughes picked up after a couple of rings.

'Hi, Mr Hughes, it's Scott Daley, Metropolitan Police. How are you feeling today?' In the background, a game was on the television; he guessed Hughes wasn't too traumatised.

'Just tired. I can't believe what happened yesterday. I keep thinking I will wake up and it's last Thursday.'

'Indeed. Did you ever find your motorbike?'

'No, not yet. Probably stripped for bits by now.'

'Well, at least you have insurance. Was it expensive?'

'Not really. Just a runabout. Why?'

'Blue Honda SH 125, registration RD11 ASD, right?'

'Er, yes.' Daley sensed bemusement in Hughes's voice.

'I think I've just found it.'

Asher's hostel was in Ruislip, yet he had been seen outside St Dunstan's in Harrow and likely dossed down at Bayhurst Grange before murdering Foster and Clarke-Mitchell. And now he had to be at Harrow Central Hospital. He needed transport to do that and Will Hughes's small blue motorbike, stolen before the explosion, was simple to ride. It explained the motorbike tracks on the muddy lawn behind the *lodge*.

But, of all the bikes in London, why Will Hughes's? If, of course, anyone had indeed stolen the motorbike.

Closing the call, Daley dropped a text to Steve Taylor, asking him to locate the phone Hughes had just used. Then he pulled Whetstone and Hacker together.

'Will Hughes's stolen motorbike is down in the yard between the buildings. Ma'am, please keep Hodgkins and Brennan on their toes. Deb, meet me in the newsagent's outlet downstairs in fifteen minutes - and let's keep our radios on.'

***

Leslie Hacker lolled in a chair, crossed her ankles and puffed her cheeks. What the hell was she doing, taking orders from a *Chief Inspector*, especially one with Scott Daley's questionable record? There was always something dangerously dramatic about how he solved his cases, and she was at the sharp end. Still, if things turned ugly, she was in the right place. However, she would much prefer to

An Invisible Murder

be pummelling a small ball against a wall in Hammersmith, pretending it was Daley's head, rather than chasing down a quadruple murderer who might never turn up.

Daley and his team were a poor fit for her nascent West London Combined Homicide and Drugs Unit. Policing had changed. It had become more accountable - *she* had become more accountable - yet Lambourne Road had not. She couldn't risk the WLCHDU descending to the lowest common denominator. Bob Allenby had been popular, one of the Old Guard, and none of her peers could see her problem. Even Bilko Bob's oh-so-sad departure had not altered their perspective, and as a relative newcomer, still to establish herself, she was in no position to influence them. But desperate times called for desperate measures. Yet, not too desperate. Daley was a maverick. He bent the rules so often, they'd given him a copy made from latex rubber. One day he would inevitably fall foul of them. The problem was that Hacker was not good at waiting. Dally about in a rank too long and one becomes part of the furniture, overlooked when the glass ceiling opens for a few precious days. No, she had to take any opportunity to show his incompetence. That he was not suitable for the WLCHDU. Mercifully, Daley was going all out to show it himself.

From the outset, she had kept ACC Vic Fraser apprised of the situation, of Daley's incompetence and his inability to see past that bloody school. The situation with Father O'Donnell was a gift, and she had been quick to point that out to Fraser, too. Of course, it didn't matter if Daley spoke to O'Donnell or not. The padre was in the right place should his ticker throw a wobbler again. A few six-hundred-joule shocks and he would be as right as rain. No, it was the principle that mattered. She had given Daley an order, and he was intentionally defying her. Tolerate insubordination in the ranks and there would be anarchy. It didn't help that ACC Fraser had been the one to ask Daley to step up in the wake of Allenby's departure, but Scott Daley was a clone of his erstwhile mentor, and if nothing changes, you just get more of the same.

Down in the yard, the Chief Inspector was poking around behind a dumpster, chatting on his radio. Even Sergeant Whetstone had wandered off. Maybe, when she dealt with Daley, she would deal with her too. Find them both a post in the Outer Hebrides, where they could sit and drink coffee and ponder the murder rate amongst a thousand sheep and a couple of crofters.

She checked her watch, desperate for a coffee, desperate for a pee, and desperate for this to be over. There was no way she'd make the booking for the squash court, and ACC Fraser had already asked for an update, probably from the tenth green whilst tipping his hip flask against the cold. At least, when it had all gone tits up, she could lay it squarely at Daley's feet. Setting expensive hares running on a hunch, disrupting the important work of a major hospital for a gut feeling, and risking the life of an elderly member of the clergy. She had already informed the ACC of the situation and that Daley was attempting to manage it, despite her offer of help. The way she saw it, there was every chance the Chief Inspector would take enough rope to hang himself.

With Constable Brennan arriving to relieve Constable Hodgkins, and the call of nature becoming ever more urgent, she decided they could cope without her. And maybe she could find coffee on the way.

***

Asher was nowhere to be seen. The engine of the Honda was as cold as the air on Daley's neck. He guessed he had arrived the previous night, after murdering Foster and Clarke-Mitchell, then had been hanging around since, somewhere in the building, but why had he not gone straight up to the ward? The hospital was a lot quieter at night. Maybe he and *Female A* hunted as a pair and he was waiting for her to arrive. According to DC Taylor, Hughes's phone was at least half an hour away in Pinner somewhere near, if not in, his home. He would need to get a wiggle on to reach Harrow Central in time to witness Father O'Donnell's demise. Though Daley somehow doubted he was *Female A*, as there was no direct connection between O'Donnell and Willson Hughes.

The fire door behind Daley had slammed shut. It bore a sign -

An Invisible Murder

Keep out - Danger of Death. With Asher on the loose, it was very appropriate. Daley had no option but to find an alternative route back via the main entrance. It took ten precious minutes, and only then because he flashed his warrant card and pleaded with a passing member of staff to swipe him in. The main corridor was a long tube of glass, coloured yellow and blue, and raised on stilts. A busy, moving chicane of collateral damage. Deb Whetstone was leaning against the window opposite the newsagents, swiping her finger on her phone, trying to blend in. The crackle of her police radio was doing its best not to.

'Anything, nurse?'

Whetstone tutted and shook her head. 'Are you sure he will turn up today?' she asked.

Daley puffed. It was all so clear in his head. It always was.

'I am sure he's already here. He arrived on the motorbike last night, waiting for the go-ahead. When the burners came alive, that was his instruction that today was the day. So far, except for the explosion, which was meticulously planned, they've been making this up as they went along. Once we discovered the bodies at Bayhurst Grange, they were forced to accelerate their plans. Now Father O'Donnell has been admitted, so it has to be today - or tomorrow. At least before they discharge him.'

'Today or tomorrow.' Whetstone squirmed in her ill-fitting tunic. 'You're the one making it up as you go along. He could be anywhere in all this. Can't tell the staff from the patients.'

Which gave Daley an idea. 'Just hold the fort. I'll meet you back on the ward in forty minutes.'

'Forty minutes? What am I supposed to say to Hacker?'

'Tell her I'm having a confab with Security or something.'

***

When Daley peered around the door of Father O'Donnell's side room, the priest was sitting up in bed, watching *Celebrity Catchphrase* and ignoring the irritating yet steady beep from the machine beside him. However, his heart rate climbed a little when he recognised the tall doctor was a Chief Inspector.

'Father Joseph. Good to see you looking so well. Mrs O'Hallorhan was very upset when I spoke to her yesterday.'

O'Donnell groaned himself up higher onto his pillows and made himself comfortable. 'She's a good woman, if a little verbose. Sure, she could talk the hind legs off a donkey and then persuade the creature to walk.'

A phrase involving pots and kettles sprung to Daley's mind. 'Still, she almost certainly saved your life.'

'So what can I do for you on this fine morning - as if I could not guess?'

Daley stole a glance at the heart monitor and took a breath. 'I have to inform you we found Jacob Foster murdered yesterday morning, out at Bayhurst Grange near Iver. He was in the building's basement. We believe the person who murdered Andrew Mason and Sonia Judd also murdered him. You must understand you are also in danger.'

O'Donnell raised a hand to his mouth and let out a minute whimper. The numbers on the monitor rose by a couple of points and then rallied, so Daley continued, but not before checking the location of the emergency alarm button.

'The last time we met, we spoke about the murder of Claire Dobson. How, on that night in September 1993, you sent Andrew Mason and another prefect into Bayhurst Woods to bring back Asher and Dobson. Was the other prefect Jacob Foster?'

O'Donnell nodded sombrely. 'Jacob was the head boy. He and Andrew knew the woods better than anyone there. It made sense.'

Daley pulled the school photo from his pocket. He had one final issue to address. 'Claire Dobson.' Daley tapped her face. 'It struck me as odd that she's the only child not smiling. Your hand is on her shoulder. Her hands are linked in front of her.' He passed it to Father O'Donnell, who smiled sadly.

'You have worked it out, Chief Inspector.' O'Donnell fumbled for a glass of cordial and took a drink. The heart monitor was holding steady. Daley hoped whatever was being fed to him through the IV drip was keeping it that way.

'Maybe you can tell me in your own words. And this time, Father,' he glanced sideways as the machine beeped slightly faster, 'the truth, and leave nothing out.'

***

Leslie Hacker leaned against the window in the main corridor, her phone wedged between her shoulder and her ear, and pulled a face as she sipped her coffee. She was no connoisseur, but it tasted more like used motor oil.

'I'm telling you, Vic, this is a fiasco. Daley's a bloody embarrassment. We are all traipsing around this hospital, hoping his killer turns up, and based on what? A phone call between two unidentified phones and a stolen motor scooter. It's all I can do to stop him barging in on Father O'Donnell and giving him another heart attack. I gave him a direct order, but he ignored it. In my view, he can't take orders from a woman. I thought we had weeded out all the misogynistic, sexist dinosaurs a decade ago.'

'So what's the current situation, Leslie?' ACC Fraser's voice epitomised frustration. The golf club served an excellent Friday lunch, and she was making herself a nuisance. But people remember calls that interrupt lunch, especially *why* they were interrupted.

'I have two officers guarding the priest, while Daley and Whetstone are strolling about buying coffees, treating it like a jolly. I can understand he wants to be seen taking action after his incompetence led to two more deaths, but how could anyone anticipate the priest was going to be admitted? And, anyway, what evidence is there Father O'Donnell is in any danger from this man, Asher? It's all just a sorry string of ifs, buts and maybes. A complete waste of time and resources, if you ask me.'

The handset rattled as ACC Fraser sighed. 'Daley is an experienced officer, Leslie. A *senior* officer who is used to making tactical decisions every day. If he has a reason to be in the hospital, then it's his choice to make. We can't go around second-guessing a senior officer because we disagree with him.' Another long sigh rattled the handset, drowning out the sound of clinking cutlery and clubhouse bonhomie. 'So what do *you* think he should do?'

Damn Vic Fraser, always the politician, with shoulders slopier than a black diamond ski run.

'Call it off, sir. I'll leave a man on the door; it's the wise thing to do, but it's a thankless task. And God alone knows the overtime bill.'

'It's eleven fifteen. If Daley's man is a no-show by three, suggest he call it off, but it's his inquiry, his call. Anyway, the starters have arrived. Keep me posted and I want a full report on Monday.'

Hacker huffed as her phone screen faded. That had not gone as planned. Was Vic Fraser also part of the problem rather than the solution? Another of the *Old Guard*, safe and conservative, wary of making any rash moves. Yet, he had promoted Scott Daley to the level of his incompetence. It was infuriating. Hacker had herself already made radical strides in weeding out the dead wood. Maybe she should also turn her sights on Fraser himself.

Conscious she'd been absent for some time, she joined the swollen lunchtime throng down to the wards. Something caught her eye, and she turned towards the restaurant. Wiry and stooped, hood up as he sat at a table, ladling soup into his mouth, holding his spoon like he was grabbing a puppy's tail. Raymond Asher.

Bollocks!

Why couldn't he have appeared *before* she played her hand to the Assistant Chief Constable? Now it seemed fortune would prove both him and Daley right, although nothing yet indicated Asher was heading to the Coronary Care ward. He *was* a suspected murderer, though, so maybe she could still spin this to her advantage. She strolled over to the sandwich bar, and pretending to be interested in the triangular boxes of unappetising fare, she kept an eye on the table ten yards away, before circling back to the door and leaving again. Unshaven, haggard, but yes, it was Raymond Asher. Think Leslie, there had to be a Plan B.

Eventually Asher would leave. When he did, she would call Security to detain him. Daley, Brennan and Hodgkins would all be caught with their thumbs up their arses and she would be the hero, quick to point out that all the fuss Daley was making on the ward could have been avoided.

***

Thankfully, Daley's visit to O'Donnell had passed without incident and he'd made it back to the reception without anyone suspecting. Whetstone was behind the nurse's station, reading a magazine. He checked his watch. 'Where's Hacker?'

Whetstone shrugged. 'Loo, I suppose. She wasn't here when I got back.'

'You don't think she's fallen down the hole?'

'We can but hope,' smiled Whetstone. 'I reckon she's in the canteen.'

Daley hissed a curse. 'Divide and bloody rule.'

They turned toward the main door as an orderly wrangled a trolley around the corner, heralding the start of lunchtime. A bell echoed in the ward, Brennan and Hodgkins squeaked in their chrome-framed chairs and peered over their broadsheets. Nurses emerged from behind the desk, shared a conversation with the orderly, and checked the list. The somnolent reception area quickly became busy. Diversions, distractions. The ideal time for Asher to strike. Daley crossed to the trolley.

'I'd like the ward sister to take Father O'Donnell his lunch, if that's okay. What's he having?'

The nurse returned an affronted smile. 'A light lunch before his procedure. Soup and bread, a pot of fruit, and a yoghurt. And tea.'

'Is there a spare meal we could swap with Father O'Donnell's?'

The nurse tutted and reached for a tray on a lower shelf. 'Fortunately, he's not on a diet regimen. Do you want to taste it? Make sure we're not poisoning him?'

***

Just how long can a bowl of bloody soup last?

Hacker was running out of ways to make herself look inconspicuous. There were only so many leaflets to read, sham phone calls to make, and windows to stare out of. In the restaurant, a chair scraped and at last Asher rose. She pressed herself to the wall, improvising a conversation about her car on her mobile, and followed his reflection in the window glass, then pocketed her phone and turned after him. Lunchtime was now in full swing, and she found it difficult to keep track of the bobbing head in the black hoodie. In her pocket, the police radio weighed heavy and, for a moment, she considered calling Daley, but that would only hand the initiative back to him.

Then Asher was gone.

Blast! How could she lose him in a straight corridor? A seed of panic formed in her stomach. What if someone learnt she'd found him only to lose him again? What if it got back to ACC Fraser?

Just then, a nurse appeared from a corridor to Hacker's right, tray in hand, moving expediently. Hacker dug in her handbag and produced her warrant card.

'Did you see a man pass by here - just a moment ago?'

Taken aback, the nurse stopped and took a breath, glancing down at the warrant card, around at the multitude, and then up at Hacker. 'What? No, I just work here. I was in the nurse's station…'

'Thin, stooped, wearing a black hoodie,' Hacker urged. 'Just a second ago.' What was it with people? Walking around with their eyes shut.

The nurse turned her head and pointed with her free hand down the short corridor, toward the hospital chapel. 'I think I saw…'

Without stopping to thank her, Hacker raced down and through the door. Small, bland-painted brick and huge vertical windows, a sea of pews washing up to a raised altar. Pop-art posters proclaiming messages of worship. Modern, utilitarian, non-denominational. Not her idea of religion, but then this was a hospital. It served a need, though right now the place was empty. She took an echoing step away from the door, wondering how the hell he could have evaded her with such ease. It was as if he'd vanished, but then he was a religious nut. Maybe he had divine assistance.

The flash of red took her by surprise, pushing all the air from her body, and she fell back as her ribs exploded. A fire extinguisher clattered to the floor, and she heard footsteps racing back out into the hospital. With spots in front of her eyes, she lay there, fighting for breath, feeling her ribs grate. She reached inside her pocket, fumbled for her radio, and held down the button.

'This is Hacker. Asher is in the main corridor. He is on his way up to the ward.' Then she fell back and closed her eyes.

So much for Plan B.

***

As Hacker's call came through, Whetstone requested a couple of traffic units to attend, while Daley informed hospital security that Asher was on site. The priority remained to intercept him as he reached O'Donnell's room and, now they had rumbled him, there was every chance he could bail altogether, keeping his powder dry for another day. Daley gestured to Constable Brennan.

'Move to the ward entrance, George. Anyone in or out, give them the once over.'

'Sir.' Brennan nodded to Hodgkins and wandered off towards the double doors. Daley contemplated moving Hodgkins to the emergency stairwell at the rear, but that would leave the single point of access - the door to Father O'Donnell's side room - exposed. So he took the stairwell himself.

Whetstone closed the call and sighed apologetically. 'Ten minutes for reinforcements, maybe fifteen. I'm going down the main stairs.'

'Keep out of sight and don't spook him, at least not until the cavalry arrives. Let him think we haven't noticed. Ideally, I want him up on the ward.'

Some hope, thought Whetstone. Hacker was to covert ops what Liberace was to the Society of Introverts. At the top of the stairs, she peered down between the snake of bannisters before taking each floor. But there was no sign of Asher. She was losing hope. Three different stairwells, seven floors above, two below, and an infinite number of routes he could take to reach the Coronary Care Unit. In his situation, what would she do?

In cop shows, everyone ran up to the inevitability of capture or a plunge to the ground. Asher would know they would cover the stairs, but if he descended to the lower service floors, he could hide in the warren of passageways while the police scoured the floors above. Once they passed him on the service floors, he could head back up. And if she was mistaken, Brennan and Hodgkins were still on hand to apprehend him.

In her tunic pocket, her radio handset chirruped.

'Any sign, Deb?'

'No, Scott. He's lying low until the fuss dies down.'

'Copy. Security is sending some people over for a systematic search of each floor from the ground up. Remain at the entrance to the ward block until they arrive. If you see him, just monitor him. Don't engage.'

'Sir.' And of course, that's what *Suicide Scott Daley* would do, she mused. And who says copy on a radio any more?

Chapter 38

Through the slit of the open door, Raymond Asher saw the nurse take the radio from her pocket. A copper. He had seen her before, in Green Street, which meant the tall copper was around too. And her in the chapel. They must know that the medical staff didn't carry Motorola Airwave handsets. Dead fucking giveaway. He watched her grow impatient. He understood the feeling. Time was not on his side, either.

With Mason and Foster dead, only Father O'Donnell remained. Like it or not, he'd be back in the slammer, and the sooner the better. He was tired of running, sleeping rough, scrounging food, of riding around trying to make that sodding moped work. For twenty years he'd imagined life on the outside, but not this. He'd had spent most of his life running and hiding. Now he was running and hiding again. Was that all normal people did? The irony was prison was the only place he had ever felt safe.

In the main corridor, a percussion of heavy footsteps heralded the arrival of Security. Four of them, barely enough to search an empty room, let alone a hospital this size. Still, it would be fun watching them. Now, though, they were panting, hands on hips, as the nurse-cum-policewoman gave them the gen. With so many places to hide, it was a fruitless exercise.

He waited another five, then slipped out of the cupboard and closed the door. In prison, where everyone is on high alert and even a scuffed shoe can get you shanked, invisibility is a skill, moving around without attracting attention. On the outside, you could dress as a clown and no one would notice. All on their mobiles. Taking the north wing, he passed the nurse's station and headed towards the rear stairwell. He heard mumbled voices below. Security people or hospital staff skiving. He didn't care. They were down. He was heading up to the eighth floor, then he could cross back out into the central stairwell. He'd walked the route the previous night. Piece of piss. No one gave a toss. The ward clock read 12:30 pm. Another quarter hour and it would all be over.

O'Donnell was one storey up. Twenty-six steps, two doors. About a hundred yards and twenty years. Mind, his legs ached. Fitness was also not on the curriculum at Blackrose. He peered through the rear doors into the ward. The lanky copper was strutting about, chatting up the nurses and waving a clipboard around like he was swatting flies. He had a stethoscope hung around his neck like it would fool anybody. That's where taxpayer's money went. Not that Asher was a taxpayer, but the principle remained.

He eased open the door with the palm of his hand, wincing as the hinge whined. Across the corridor, the tall copper swung round and their eyes met. For a moment, the copper looked confused, but they'd been that way since the explosion. Then he cottoned on and set off across the floor, like a baby giraffe on ice. Asher turned and bounded down the stairs, taking each flight in two strides, grabbing the bannisters and swinging around the corners. Above him, the tall copper was panting like a twenty-a-dayer, falling behind, as his shoes tip-tapped on the steps.

Asher heard a shout and leapt into the face of a surprised security officer, who barrelled backwards into the wall. He scarcely broke his stride, hitting the concrete of the ground floor and taking off into the maze of service corridors. Behind him, the chase was on, but he was well ahead, reaching a steel exit door, leaning on the horizontal bar and blinking in the harsh light. There was a shout. Hands and arms came from all sides, sending him onto the rough tarmac. A knee pressed into his back. Knowing the score, he fell limp as the cold cuffs pinched his wrists.

The tall copper tumbled from the door behind him. His cheeks were cherries, and he was wheezing like bellows. With what seemed like an immense amount of effort, the copper began.

An Invisible Murder

'Raymond Asher. I am arresting you for the murder of Andrew Philip Mason and Sonia Marie Judd on 28th September at Number 5 Green Street, Harrow. You do not have to say anything, but it may harm your defence if you do not mention, when questioned, something which you later rely on in court. Anything you do say may be given in evidence.'

'Shit. That was easier than I thought.' Asher beamed a self-satisfied smile. 'She said it would be easy, but you guys? Running around like blue-arsed flies.'

The tall copper's brow furrowed. Then, with a look of realisation, he reached for his radio.

'Deb. we have Asher under arrest, but he's a bloody decoy. You need to get back up to the ward as soon as possible.'

***

Whetstone hammered her finger on the lift button, as the two red numbers ticked down, waiting for an age for a car to arrive, another for the door to open and again for them to close. As it finally lurched into motion, her radio crackled.

'On my way, Scott.'

***

Constable George Brennan heard the noise and gave it little thought, but it persisted. The ping of a bell and a swoosh click, another swoosh, then round again. He could ignore it no longer. He pushed off the wall and strode around to the lifts, gasping as he turned the corner. Sergeant Whetstone was lying on her face, half out of the lift. A young nurse stood over her, shaking.

'What's happened, nurse?'

'I don't know. The lift wasn't working, so came up the stairs, and she was just lying there. I think she's still breathing.'

Brennan knelt by Whetstone. Her pulse was weak and her breathing shallow. Her eyes had rolled back. Brennan was out of his depth.

'Get help.' He pulled Whetstone free of the lift and turned her over. Then he felt a scratch on his neck, and for a second, his head filled with a million buzzing bees before the world swirled away.

***

The young nurse returned the syringe to her kidney tray, walked around to the ward, and called to the thickset man across the reception area.

'I need help out by the lifts.'

'I'll get the ward sister. Go back and see what you can do.' The man heaved himself to his feet and made for the main ward.

The young nurse placed her tray on the reception desk. It had been a mistake to only bring a single syringe of fentanyl. She should have learned that when she dealt with Sonia Judd before Andrew Mason. Then she'd filled the tart so full of fent, she'd had to improvise the amitriptyline. A whole syringe was enough to stop a horse, so today she only shot half into the policewoman. Plenty left for the priest. But then the constable had turned up, and she had no choice but to give him the rest. Spur of the moment, but she was adaptable. Air was as effective if administered correctly into the bloodstream, pulmonary embolism, cardiac arrest, and death. Who needs fentanyl?

She walked across to the side room, measuring her breathing, measuring her steps. Nothing too *expedient*, just a nurse in a hospital. The occupant was lying asleep under the bedclothes as the TV played to no one. A saline IV drip hung above him, the slender tube snaking beneath the sheets.

'Hey you can't go in there…' Out in the ward, the thickset man had turned.

Idiot! You had one job.

She reached for the transparent IV tube and located the secondary port, fitting in the syringe, and depressing the plunger, watching the slug of air worm its way down the tube.

He wouldn't know what hit him.

An Invisible Murder

In front of her, the bedclothes exploded, and a woman dived towards her, sending her groaning to the floor. She felt herself pinned to the ground, as two hands clasped around her wrist, squeezing until her fingers went numb. But still she kicked out, hearing the cries of pain, turning the other woman, raining blows into her chest and face. Then someone reached down and dragged her arms behind her back and she felt the cuffs clip tight.

***

Something had to be wrong. Where the hell was Brennan?

Daley raced from the ward, catching his breath at the scene around the lifts. Brennan and Whetstone lay side by side on their backs, respirators over their faces, surrounded by medics. The ward sister was on her knees, pressing buttons on a small box which whined into life. She placed paddles on Whetstone's chest, the shout of *clear,* and Daley watched her body leap off the carpet. He remembered his father, slack-jawed, eyes wide, as a paramedic pummelled at his chest and counted. Back then, there were no defibrillators available to restart a damaged heart. This was Deb Whetstone. He prayed today it would be enough.

Drained of every ounce of energy, utterly helpless, he slumped down the wall and buried his head in his hands. Why had he followed Asher down the stairs? Surely, the plan was to remain on the ward, let *Female A* and *Male B come* to them. They needed to catch them red-handed, but he'd insisted on playing *Bodie and bloody Doyle*. He wanted to scream and shout. *Do something. You must help her,* but they were doing everything. He knew they were, but would everything be enough? And what if it wasn't enough? She couldn't die here, could she?

He sat, the voices shouted, the machines whirred, and Whetstone's body jumped. Again and again…and again.

He didn't know how long he'd been sitting there, eyes screwed tight, but Daley felt that if he stayed there, on that small square of carpet and let the world revolve, he would snap out of the dream and it would all be right again. He felt a hand on his shoulder and looked up into the troubled eyes of the ward sister. The corridor was littered with medical bags and discarded equipment. A few yards away, gurneys had arrived, and the two were being taken away.

'Chief Inspector. We've got her back, but she's in a critical condition. The next twenty-four hours will be crucial. Luckily, she didn't receive the whole syringe. It was a good call of yours - asking us to bring naloxone up from the pharmacy.'

'Just a hunch, sister. What about George?'

The tear in the corner of her eye spoke volumes.

Chapter 39

When the two burner phones started communicating, and they had figured out Asher was heading for Harrow Central, Daley's gut told him time was running out for the killer. So, as a precaution, they moved Father O'Donnell to a different ward, leaving Hodgkins and Brennan to guard Jane Morris, who had spent the morning watching game shows on the promise of a free packed lunch. As for Leslie Hacker, Daley had kept her in the dark; she would only have kicked up a fuss, anyway. Once she regained consciousness, she would probably still do so.

Daley's sole concern had been for O'Donnell and the public, so he and Whetstone needed *Female A* and *Male B* to make their move up on the ward, with the least risk to anyone else. But Hacker's unwarranted interference had alerted Asher. Only when Daley apprehended him did he realise he had been duped. All along, *Male B* was the decoy, leading the eye away from *Female A*. While the police were chasing him, they were paying scant regard to her. *Find the Lady* with real people.

Asher was no more a killer than he was. He never had been, but Daley would leave recriminations to the inevitable enquiry.

Daley had reached the ward as the nurse prepared her syringe at the nurse's station, and everything had fallen into place. But a primed syringe was not enough. *Female A* must enter the side room, so when she appeared, Hodgkins left his post, as Daley had instructed him to. Then, he followed her into the side room and, along with DC Morris, made the arrest. In only a dozen minutes of excitement, the serene normality of the ward block resumed. Except out at the lifts. It took another two hours to clear the scene there, much to the disgust of Sister Johns, who appreciated everyone had a job to do but felt they needed to do it somewhere else. The appearance of Len Ganlow didn't help, nor the SOCOs he brought with him. O'Donnell, none the wiser, was then moved back from the private suite, to recover from his stent procedure amongst the hoi polloi, with an officer outside his door until he was despatched back to the vicarage.

After a bastard of a day, all Daley wanted was his front room, an obscenely large scotch, and his arms around Terri. In moments like this, he missed her the most. Times when, however successful he was, the cost was always too high. He had solved the case, yet the victory was hollow.

Trapped in a lift with a killer, Deborah Whetstone had not seen the syringe coming. The fentanyl had caused pulmonary arrest and stopped her heart. But for the quick intervention of the ward's team, and the naloxone, she would have stood no chance. Now she was in a high-dependency ward, and doctors were hopeful she would be okay. A couple of cracked ribs from the defibrillator, or rather her muscular reaction to it. She'd be sore for a few weeks, but she would be alive.

As for Leslie Hacker, she had several completely broken ribs and, in Daley's view, deserved it for wandering off-piste. Even in Derbyshire, they would send two uniforms to round up a stray sheep. So what was she thinking tackling Asher alone? Fortunately for Whetstone, she was in a different ward, far away from the Sergeant.

George Brennan, though, was on a slab in Loughton Street. He had received the lion's share of the fentanyl, and even modern science could not restart his heart.

They took *Female A* to the custody suite at Hillingdon. She would wait until tomorrow when Daley had the strength of character to deal with her without ripping her head off. The Traffic officers had taken Asher, *Male A* to Ealing. Mike Corby could deal with him.

An Invisible Murder

***

Before he left Harrow Central, Daley called ACC Vic Fraser, who listened to his case and understood the need to process evidence from the Bayhurst Grange and Harrow Central scenes before further questioning. They had already charged Raymond Asher, so his accommodation was secure. Fraser granted a thirty-six-hour extension of custody on *Female A*, after which time she must be charged or released. He suggested she remain in the Hillingdon custody suite so Daley's team could concentrate on making the case against her.

He did not comment on Superintendent Leslie Hacker.

As usual, Daley spent the night dwelling on it all. He could not sleep, nor did he want to. He wanted to suffer for the pain Whetstone went through. For the pain George Brennan's family would go through. Terri had helped, framing the incident in her usual optimistic way. After all, Deb was alive thanks to his hunch with the naloxone. Little could be said about George Brennan. Daley would ask the manager at Fulham FC if he could get a tribute read out, and he'd place a pint of stout and a pie on his empty seat for the next home match.

The truth was the evidence against *Female A* was overwhelming.

If only they could find it.

Chapter 40

Saturday was football. Not that Daley played much these days on account of his knees. The 2013-14 season marked Fulham Football Club's thirteenth in the Premiership. Unlucky for some, they were having their worst season start he could remember, and for *The Whites* that was saying something. After five winless matches, the home tie against Stoke City promised much. *The Potters* were having an equally lacklustre start, despite surprise wins against Liverpool and Crystal Palace. It was the second home game in a row he would miss. His first in five years without George Brennan. Today, though, football took second place.

Today, he would nail the nurse's arse to the wall.

He owed Whetstone a visit, so he took a detour on the way into Hillingdon. He'd even bought grapes. Propped up on her pillows, her eyes closed and her hands by her side. A transparent pipe attached to an oxygen supply had brought the colour back to her cheeks. Daley left her to sleep, aware she was there because he sent her back up to the ward.

'How is Ms Whetstone, Sister?'

'Are you a relative, sir?'

'A colleague.' Daley flipped open his warrant card. Whetstone's sister, Louise, was training it down from Sheffield later.

'Her breathing is troublesome and her ribs are uncomfortable, but she managed breakfast. Give it a day or two.' The nurse smiled and held out her hands for the grapes. Daley had forgotten he was holding them.

'Got to go.' No one needed to see a policeman cry.

***

The young nurse sat in Interview Room 5 at Hillingdon, staring at her hands in her lap, picking at a hangnail. She nodded as the duty solicitor, Deirdre Brown, a rather stiff-arsed witch, dispensed words of advice. They had taken her scrubs for forensic examination, replacing them with a drab sweatshirt and tracksuit bottoms. Her pallid, drawn face suggested she had not slept a wink. The air conditioning in the Hillingdon cell block hummed, more of a hiss, like a gas valve leaking. Given events in Green Street a week ago, it bordered on torture and Daley expected grief in due course from her solicitor. He had slept little himself, but for entirely different reasons.

Behind him, Jane Morris poked her head through the observation room door. 'Ready when you are, sir.'

He heaved himself up and followed her through into the interview room. As the door whumped shut and a uniformed constable took station beside it, the nurse raised her head, then dropped it back down. Jane Morris started the recording tapes, introduced the room, and reminded her of the reasons for her arrest and that she was still under police caution.

'Can you tell me why you were at Harrow Central Hospital today?' Daley asked.

She furrowed her brow and looked puzzled. 'I am a part-time agency nurse. I was on shift.'

Daley checked the document in front of him. 'You're not due in until today, Saturday, according to the schedule Sister Johns gave me.'

'I can't be responsible for admin cock-ups. No one checks anyway. I just submit the timesheets and get paid.'

'And Father O'Donnell, the patient in the side room? How do you know him?'

She glanced at Deirdre Brown, who shrugged. 'I don't. He's a name on the whiteboard. He has a treatment plan.'

'According to Sister Johns, his pre-op procedure was being carried out by another nurse. It wasn't due for another hour after we apprehended you.'

'No comment.' Said with more than a hint of indignation. Daley needed to put down a marker, lest she take him for a fool, as everyone else had this past week. He leaned forward, forearms on the table.

'I believe you knew Father O'Donnell was in the side room, and your sole intention was to murder him.'

Deirdre Brown gave him a scathing look. But she'd been in the business long enough to ignore the rhetoric. The woman remained silent.

'Friday, 28th September. What were your movements from around five in the evening?'

She looked to the ceiling, as if the mental effort was overwhelming, then shrugged. 'I was at home, alone, watching TV all night.'

'Can anyone vouch for you?'

Deirdre Brown peered at him over her glasses. 'My client has stated she was alone, Chief Inspector.'

Daley smiled his thanks for her contribution and produced two photographs from his pack.

'This is from CCTV on the traffic lights outside the cinema, Greenhill Way, Harrow, around 7:45 pm. The man is Andrew Mason. The woman wearing the wig and long black overcoat, I believe, is you. And this is from the CCTV outside *Blenheim's* nightclub in Pinner on the same evening, around 9:50 pm.' Daley tapped the shapely legs of a woman with cropped blonde hair and wearing a short dress, in conversation with Jacob Foster. 'This woman called herself Yvette. Do you accept this is also you?'

A huff of insincere annoyance and a curt *no comment*. Deirdre Brown glanced at the image and spoke for her.

'So, my client was in Pinner and Harrow on the same night?'

Daley indicated the timestamps. 'Harrow at 7:45 pm, Pinner at 9:50 pm. Plenty of time to travel between the two.' He laid down a mugshot.

'And this person? Sonia Judd. I believe the wig and long coat you were wearing belonged to her.'

The woman leaned over and scanned the photo.

'No comment.'

'What about this one? Raymond Asher. Do you know him?'

She rolled her eyes as if he'd asked her to solve a simultaneous equation, then again said, 'No comment.'

Deirdre Brown leaned forward. 'What does any of this have to do with my client, Chief Inspector? You arrested her for incidents that took place at the hospital, not in Pinner or Harrow town centre.' Teatime was approaching, and Daley had heard her stomach rumble.

'Hopefully, that should become clearer in a few moments. Ms Brown.'

'Well, make it quick. I am sure we all have places to be.'

He flicked a businesslike smile. Rome wasn't built in a day, but it fell swiftly. He swapped the photos for a few typed pages and studied them for a minute. They were working on his time, not Brown's metabolic clock.

'Have you heard of Bayhurst Grange? It's an old estate out at Iver. In the late Eighties, until 1997 in fact, Bayhurst Grange was a residential school - Holy Mount?'

She cocked her head as if to emphasise the whiplash as the direction of the conversation changed.

'The point, Chief Inspector?' Brown was glaring over her spectacles again.

'The point, Ms Brown.' He arranged the pictures in a line across the table and moved his finger along as he spoke. 'Last Saturday morning, Andrew Mason, with whom your client was seen arm in arm, was murdered in Green Street Harrow, along with Sonia Judd.

An Invisible Murder

Then last Thursday night, Jacob Foster, with whom your client spoke in *Blenheim's*, was murdered at Bayhurst Grange. In the Eighties and Nineties, when it was Holy Mount School, Andrew Mason and Jacob Foster were pupils there, and the patient in the room your client entered, Father Joseph O'Donnell was on the staff at the school. We believe the deaths of Mr Mason and Mr Foster, along with the attempted murder of Father O'Donnell, are all connected to the school.'

The woman puffed and leaned back in mock astonishment. 'Except, I have never heard of this place.' Brown rested a hand on her arm and again glared at Daley, who laboured over his papers for another moment.

'Okay, we've danced around our handbags long enough. Ms Brown's getting hungry and, to be honest, I am just bored with all the lies. We caught you entering Father O'Donnell's room with a syringe filled with air. You had connected it to the drip and injected air into the IV line. We have your fingerprints on the syringe. None of that is up for debate.'

'I was drawing a sample *out* of the tube. I turned my back and this cow here tried to kill him.' She cocked her head at Jane Morris, who gave a faint smile. 'I was trying to stop her from depressing the plunger. It's *her* you should be questioning.'

Morris made to speak. Daley shuffled a shoe and tapped her foot to stop her from inserting it into her mouth. This was a game he knew well. Cat and mouse. With no one else present apart from the nurse and Morris, either course of events could be true.

'Only Father O'Donnell was not in the room, was he?'

'How was I to know? The bedclothes were up over the patient.'

'Wouldn't it have been wise to check before fiddling with the equipment?'

'I wasn't to know *she* was going to jump me.'

'And my officers in the corridor? Did you stab them with a syringe to take a sample, too?'

'—Chief Inspector, what evidence do you have my client

assaulted your officers? Do you have the syringe? Did anyone see her use it? My client has already told you she used the stairs because the lift was broken, and that she found them lying there.'

Daley ignored the interruption. Ms Brown frequently displayed her righteous indignation when the tapes were rolling.

'So,' he continued, 'last Wednesday, the third of October, I believe you were out at Bayhurst Grange. I believe you murdered Sam Clarke-Mitchell. And later, around 8:00 pm, I believe you were back there to murder Jacob Foster.'

'—Chief Inspector!' Brown threw down her pen, aghast, as if someone had urinated in her coffee cup, but Daley held up a hand.

'Ms Brown, just give me five minutes to put my case to your client. Just let me have my say for now, then she, or you, can shout at me all you want.'

'My client has the right to representation, Chief Inspector—'

'—She also has the right to remain silent and seems to manage that well enough on her own. May I continue?'

Brown harrumphed and settled back. 'Don't push your luck, Chief Inspector.'

The woman had watched the exchange, arms folded across her chest, gaining in confidence. She knew it was all circumstantial. The syringe was the key, as was a similar one used in Green Street. Fingerprints on it and the composition of the drug inside were absolute proof. Unfortunately, they had yet to recover either.

'Okay,' Daley began again, 'here's another name. Sister Agnes McCarthy? On 28th September 2000, in Barnsley, South Yorkshire, she too was murdered. She, too, was on the staff at Holy Mount when Asher, Mason, Foster, and O'Donnell were there. The case is still open. Then, on 28th September 2004, Dr Deepak Verma, a GP in Iver Heath who covered the school, was stabbed to death. Another open case. Did you murder Agnes McCarthy and Dr Verma too?'

The woman remained impassive. Deirdre Brown frantically scribbled.

An Invisible Murder

'Inside Agnes McCarthy's bible, police found a reference to a bible quotation. The GP, Dr Verma, had a *Post-It* note under his hand, bearing a reference to a different bible quotation. Jake Foster, a bible reference on a scrap of notepaper in his pocket. Even Andrew Mason, a reference to a bible quotation in his wallet as he was being blown to pieces.'

The woman fixed her stare on him, yet her eyes flickered as he mentioned Mason. A brief gaze upward. Had she expected the explosion to destroy the wallet?

'O'Donnell, McCarthy, Verma, Mason, and Foster, all connected to Holy Mount School in the early 1990s. One school, four deaths, four bible quotes. Five, if you count the one on the altar cloth of Father O'Donnell's church. I believe you killed McCarthy and Verma and, more recently, colluded with Raymond Asher to kill Mason and Foster and, but for us, Father Joseph O'Donnell. I believe you are also responsible for the murders of Sonia Judd, Samantha Clarke-Mitchell and Constable George Brennan, and the attempted murder of Detective Sergeant Deborah Whetstone, all of whom, simply got in your way.'

Brown threw down her pen, unable to stay in her box any longer.

'Hah! So, historic murders, then three more murders this week? Boarding schools in the early 1990s? Bible quotations? You've been reading too much Enid Blyton, Chief Inspector. You'll be accusing my client of abducting Shergar next.'

Daley smiled, more condescendingly than was necessary, given he wanted to drill the harridan a new one with his ballpoint pen. 'I suspect she would have been a little young back then.'

'What evidence do you have that my client was involved in the deaths of all these people?'

'Okay, Ms Brown. Let's spell it out.' Daley cleared the table and laid out several computer-printed sheets side by side. He fixed his stare on the woman.

'*Historical* crime number one. A print of your left forefinger found in Agnes McCarthy's bible, next to the quotation. *Historical* murder number two, your right thumbprint on the handle of the knife found in Dr Verma's back. Current murders? Your right thumb and forefinger are on a business card in Andrew Mason's wallet, and again on the card on Ms Clarke-Mitchell's dashboard. Now what are the odds that you just happened upon all these people, that you left your prints in passing? We have evidence that places you at the scene of each one of these murders, and once the SOCOs have finished, probably at the scene of Mr Foster's death. And I suspect when the graphologists examine the bible references, those will be in your handwriting too.' Daley slammed his hand on the table, making them all jump. 'This was all meticulously planned and executed, even down to the dates, each on 28th September. You hunted down these people one by one and murdered them.'

The woman leaned back in her chair. For the first time, she rose to the challenge.

'I don't know how my fingerprints got on that bible, but unless you can prove I put it there when I murdered her…Same with the doctor. I do not know whether I ever met him, but the agency has sent me to Iver Heath occasionally. You already know Mr Mason sold me my current car. He handed out business cards. I gave mine back because my partner already had one. Same with Ms Clarke-Mitchell. We met in the summer when her company had a do. I can't remember, but she may have given me a card.'

'And you expect a jury to believe that?'

'Juries aren't all twisted, suspicious bastards like you, Mr Daley.'

Brown laid a hand on the woman's arm. 'Enough, Chief Inspector. I need to speak to my client now.'

Daley's temper teetered on the edge and it took him a supreme effort to drag it back. Paradoxically, the woman was still calm, tears glistening in her eyes as her performance turned to pathos.

'So, I was on shift when I shouldn't have been. Suddenly, rather than doing my job, I am *Public Enemy Number One*. How should I know where I was on specific days, decades ago? And—and just because I wanted a new car, I'm guilty of killing the salesman? And last Friday? You even have a picture of me chatting up Jacob *Bloody* Foster, yet you still won't believe me. What have I done to deserve all of this? Tell me that.'

'Chief Inspector. We need a break. Now.'

The truth was, she was correct. She had done nothing to deserve all this. He glanced across at Jane Morris, who had been taking everything in, and nodded for her to conclude the interview, at least for now. By the evening, everything would be resolved.

***

Mike Corby felt as if his right arm had been severed as he entered the interview room at Lambourne Road. Steve Taylor was alright but interviewing was not his forte. They had agreed beforehand that he should sit silently and take notes. Still, Corby wished Deb Whetstone was there, and he was the one sitting silently. He had blanched when he'd heard what had happened to her. But for an accident of rotas, it could have been him.

An accident of rotas. That was what the nurse had claimed, like anyone would turn up for work when they weren't on shift. Except for him, today, but this was different.

Daley's email had told him very little. The nurse's word against theirs. Corby had resolved not to debate with Raymond Asher, but to ask him questions and get answers. One of Bilko Bob's well-used aphorisms sprung to mind. *Lies are like shoe laces. No matter how tight the knot is, eventually they'll trip you up.* If the scrawny scrote tripped himself up, then maybe he would press him further.

When they entered the room, Asher was in police-issue clobber - and, to Corby's dismay, he was wearing slip-on shoes. Steve Taylor loaded the tapes, introduced the room, and reminded Asher of the charges. Arms folded, Asher gave a snotty sniff to imply he understood. With Deirdre Brown over at Hillingdon, Asher had the company of Duty Solicitor John Brakespeare, an altogether more amenable proposition.

'So, Ray - can I call you Ray? What were you doing at Harrow Central yesterday?'

'No crime being at a hospital, is it?'

'Well, it is when you're on parole and the hostel hasn't seen you for days. Where have you been since Wednesday?'

'No comment.'

'If it's not a crime, why did you run when Chief Inspector Daley clocked you?'

'He was poking around the bike I nicked.'

Beside him, Brakespeare drew in a sharp breath. 'I would advise caution, Mr Asher.'

Asher's dabs were all over the bike, so Corby moved on. 'Last weekend, the gas explosion in Harrow. Where were you, say five on Friday evening until eight the following morning?'

'Work and then bed.'

'We have witnesses who put you in Green Street around the time of the explosion. You qualified as a plumber while inside. You'd know how to mess with the cooker and set the timer.'

'I must have a twin because it wasn't me. I bet half of London knows how to do that.' Asher gave a smug grin. He was lapping up the attention. 'Look, I admit I've been to St Dunstan's in Green Street a few times since I've been out. I found out Father O'Donnell was the priest there and, well, old times…'

'—Yet you didn't go in, or speak to him?'

'It's been a while. I was waiting for the right moment.'

'Defacing the altar, the bible reference, was that you?'

Asher shook his head piously. 'It's a church, for heaven's sake.'

'What about Andrew Mason and Jacob Foster? You remember them from Holy Mount? Of course, it's now Bayhurst Grange.'

Another emphatic shake of the head. 'I can't even remember where the place is anymore, let alone anyone there.'

'You remembered Father O'Donnell.'

'Hardly likely to forget him after what happened.'

'Yet, last Wednesday, we found fresh tyre tracks there matching the motorbike you stole. How do you explain that?'

'No comment.'

Corby sighed to himself. The first *no comment* of many. Not that it implied guilt or innocence, just reluctance. 'Ah, come on! It's a simple enough question. What were you doing out at Bayhurst Grange last Wednesday night?'

'No comment.'

'Did you murder Andrew Mason and Jacob Foster, Ray?'

'No comment.'

'I believe you killed them. You stood in the churchyard as a gas explosion you had rigged blew Mason to pieces. Afterwards, you absconded from the hostel and waited at Bayhurst Grange for Foster to turn up, then you murdered him.'

'I never. I never murdered anyone.'

'You expect me to believe that? Sent down for killing your girlfriend, and as soon as you're out, two of your old classmates are murdered? We have witnesses that put you in Green Street on the night Andrew Mason died, and forensic evidence that links you to Bayhurst Grange on the night Foster died.'

'Look, I hold my hands up. They saw me in the churchyard, but I was never anywhere near that house, I swear. And out at the school, when the police came to the bowling alley, I was spooked. I went there on the motorbike and dossed down in the lodge by the gate, but I never went in, I promise.'

'You remember where Bayhurst Grange is, then?'

'I know where Tower Bridge is, but it doesn't mean I murdered the bridge keeper.'

Brakespeare laid a hand on Asher's arm. 'Constable, could I have a few minutes with my client?'

***

After the interviews, Daley and Corby agreed to postpone follow-ups until the morning. They had fired the first salvos and the return of fire had been much as expected. Claim, counterclaim and flat-out denial. The problem was evidence. Everything so far was circumstantial.

The woman had dodged and weaved. She was an agency nurse, and she had worked at Harrow Central before, so she could have muddled her dates. As for being present in the side-ward, she claimed she was there to sample the IV, rather than murder a cleric. As for the fingerprint evidence, her defence had been stalwart. She might have come into contact with all the murdered parties at one time or another. Holding a business card, scanning it and handing it back did not a murderer make. It was not enough on its own. Reasonable doubt. A decent barrister would rip their case to shreds.

And Ray Asher? He was under no obligation to say anything, let alone incriminate himself. He had admitted assaulting a police officer, stealing a motorbike and absconding from the parole hostel, all of which breached his parole conditions. Once this was over, he'd be back in Blackrose without leaving skid marks on the lino. And he had admitted bunking off work to stalk Father O'Donnell in Green Street, which was a smart move because it negated much of the witness evidence relating to the lean man.

It meant that between the two, neither the nurse nor Asher had admitted to knowing each other, or to conspiring to murder anyone. There was every possibility that, as Asher stood in Green Street watching the pyrotechnics, the woman could have been in Pinner. *Female A* and *Male B* could still be different people.

But Daley didn't believe so.

They were lacking the slam dunk. The smoking gun. Something connecting Asher and the woman on or around Asher's release from prison and afterwards. Even then, it was not enough to link them. He had to prove they were there together when the explosion happened.

He had to prove conspiracy to murder *and* murder.

For the rest of the morning, he and Morris commandeered desks in the CID suite. To be fair, though enormous, the room was light and airy and a far cry from the dated despondency of

Lambourne Road. Maybe it would not be such a wrench to move here, as long as he could bring Allenby's old chair. He had mastered the levers. The chairs at Hillingdon came with more features, and Daley had enough to think about. Daley also took time with Deirdre Brown on items of disclosure, in the hopes she would interrupt him less when he was in full flow, and in the knowledge she would apprise her client beforehand. He also coached Corby on an approach that might pay dividends with Ray Asher.

In the afternoon, he, Morris, and Corby travelled to Loughton Street, where Ramesh and Ganlow would give them an update. Hopefully, the one key piece of evidence would appear before then otherwise, he'd be bluffing it when they all reconvened in the morning.

Chapter 41

Daley had endured another sleepless night, filled with thoughts of George Brennan, his wide eyes staring at the ceiling, a scum of froth around his mouth. And of Whetstone, a mass of tubes and machines as she fought for life. When one removed all the politics and the management game-playing, he could not imagine a job better than the one he had, but always, lurking in the background, was the ever-present threat that one day he wouldn't come home.

Was it fair to inflict that on Terri and the new baby? How would they have managed, if he were in a hospital corridor, staring at the ceiling? The Police Force looked after its own; they would not want for anything, except the one person they could never have again. But one could not think like that. One could only believe that when the moment came, one would be ready. Otherwise, what else was there? Paralysis, powerlessness and, ultimately, failure.

Still, no matter. Once they finished this, they would have a real train wreck of a night out. Except for Daley. He'd had enough of trains to last him a lifetime.

***

At eleven-thirty the next morning, he and Morris filed back into the interview room, and Morris once again ran through the preliminaries. The situation had progressed swiftly overnight. They had carried out searches across several properties and recovered several items of interest. Ramesh and his team had then put in a sterling shift at Loughton Street. All they could hope now was that they had uncovered enough to put this thing to bed.

'So,' began Daley, 'Elizabeth Abigail O'Brien, born in Dublin, on 12th November 1979. You moved across to England in—' he flipped over a page, '—2000. That's when you began working for the Healthy Minds Centre. You moved to Pinner in 2008 when you and Mr Hughes moved in together.'

O'Brien gave a deep, forlorn sigh but said nothing. Deirdre Brown remained silent.

'I'm assuming Sam Clarke-Mitchell was in the wrong place at the wrong time, collateral damage, but why did you murder Andrew Mason and Jacob Foster?'

'No comment.'

O'Brien was refusing to be drawn. Daley had booked Monday off to spend some quality time with Terri. This would all be over by then. Come what may.

'So, Abi,' continued Daley, 'was it the redevelopment of Bayhurst Grange that started all this? Something had to be done or the secret it held - your secret - would be lost forever. And when they released Raymond Asher, that was the catalyst, as if the planets had aligned. So, did you contact Asher? After all, locked away for twenty years, it couldn't have been easy to convince him to risk the rest of his life. Or did he contact you?'

'No comment.'

'I'm guessing you already had Foster on the radar, with Will working alongside him at Stanford Clarke-Mitchell. You were waiting for the right moment. You found Mason when you and Will bought the car. At first, I was confused. If you and Andy both attended Holy Mount, why didn't he recognise you? But then I remembered something Father O'Donnell had said: *People change. Faces change. They were children. They grow up*, and even *he* didn't recognise Andrew at the Mason's wedding.

'You engineered a plan to lure Mason to the house and sedate him with amitriptyline and whisky, fill the house with gas and set the central heating timer. Again, I'm guessing Sonia Judd was collateral damage. You needed somewhere for Mason to sit and contemplate his demise, and she should have been out on the game for the night.

An Invisible Murder

But she wasn't. Where did you get the fentanyl, Abi?'

O'Brien glanced up. 'No comment. Either charge me with something or let me leave.' She returned her eyes to her lap.

***

Corby arranged his papers and regarded Asher for a moment. After a night in the cells, he seemed more relaxed than he had the right to, which was more than Corby could say for himself. He expected Asher to clam up, to rely on the indiscretions they had already put to him and say no more. It could be a long morning.

'Ray, tell me what happened at Holy Mount twenty years ago?'

'No comment.'

Corby laid down the school photo. 'You must've loved her. Twenty years is a long time, and all the while, O'Donnell, Mason and Foster living the high life and you're banged up.'

'I deserved it.'

'You took the fall for Mason and Foster.'

Asher's expression hardened. 'What would you know?'

'So tell me.'

Asher shuffled in his seat and shared a glance with his duty solicitor, John Brakespeare.

'Mr Asher, since you have served a life tariff, you cannot face charges again for the same crime, but exercise caution.'

'I remember looking down on her. I couldn't leave her there, so I carried her to the woodshed, out of the rain, and when Father O'Donnell came, he shone his torch in and saw Claire. There was so much blood. He was raving at me, asking how I could have done such a wicked thing, threatening me with hell and damnation. I was fourteen fucking years old. He was telling me she was bleeding out, that I'd killed her. He told me to run, that he would sort it out. When they found me by the lake, they said I'd murdered her. What could I say? I told them about the woodshed, about the blood. I believed I had killed her.'

***

'Then, everything became more urgent,' continued Daley. 'Will told you Jake was delaying the project, and while he did that, the secret was safe and you had time to plan your next move. But, with Mason dead, we investigated. Foster started getting antsy. If the secret came out, it would be the end of everything for him, so he set about finding it to dispose of the body for good. And he almost succeeded. Only you murdered him before he could, didn't you?'

O'Brien raised her head. 'No *fucking* comment.'

'Well, here's the thing, Ms O'Brien. I don't need your comments. I don't need lies or prevarication because I have proof.'

Brown huffed. 'Chief Inspector, if I had wanted theatrics, I would have booked a ticket to the West End.'

She was right. It was time for facts. 'DC Morris?'

Jane Morris placed the school photo in front of O'Brien.

'This was taken in 1993 at Bayhurst Grange when it was known as Holy Mount Residential School. Jacob Foster, Raymond Asher, Andrew Mason, and this is Claire Dobson, standing in front of the chaplain, Father Joseph O'Donnell. Shortly after the photo was taken, on 28th September 1993, Claire and Ray absconded from the school into the woods. Foster and Mason ran after them to bring them back, but returned empty-handed. They told Father O'Donnell they had found Ray and Claire out by the motorway culvert, that a fight broke out and Claire died.'

'Only she wasn't, was she, Abi?' added Daley. 'All along, I was convinced this was about the death of Claire Dobson,' he repositioned the school photo, and tapped a finger on the girl, 'but it's not. Look at how she's standing. My partner and I are expecting a baby soon and I saw a roomful of women standing that same way. Arms hanging, fingers interlinked, as if they were about to give someone a boost up over a wall. That's why the school was seeking to separate them, and that's why they needed to run before it happened. Claire Dobson was pregnant.'

***

'Did she tell you about the baby, Ray?' asked Corby.

Asher was shaking and the corners of his eyes were wet. 'We could have made a go of it. I know we could. All those years, I thought Claire and the baby were dead. What did it matter?'

***

O'Brien had started to sob, puffing angrily into her lap, but Deirdre Brown had had enough.

'Okay, Chief Inspector, I've indulged the fairy story long enough. Can we have some facts, please?'

Daley found a page of numbers Ramesh had provided earlier.

'Back in 1993, when the police searched for Claire's body, they took samples of the blood found in the woodshed. It never occurred to them to look for uterine or even foetal blood. I asked the lab to retest those samples, and they found hCG and hPL, hormones only present in the blood of pregnant women.'

He pulled out another couple of sheets.

'This is the birth certificate for Abigail Elizabeth O'Brien, dated 12th March 1979. Your partner Will gave it to us yesterday. But it's not yours, is it? Records taken from Baile Fearainn reveal that Abigail Elizabeth O'Brien died aged six months old. They also show that, on 29th September 1993, one day after Claire's murder, Sister Agnes arrived for a brief stay at the convent, bringing with her Abigail Elizabeth O'Brien, aged fourteen.'

He collected the papers and closed his folder.

'Ray carried Claire back to the old woodshed. She suffered serious complications from the fall, but she didn't die. O'Donnell and Dr Verma did what they could, but she was miscarrying the baby. Yet they saved Claire's life. Within a week, Sister Agnes abandoned Claire at Baile Fearainn Convent, in the Magdalene Asylum run by the Sisters of the Merciful Shepherd. I'm guessing the accident left her concussed or with temporary amnesia, and by the time she reached Dublin, it was too late. They gave her the identity of Abigail O'Brien and languished there until 1997, when the laundry was closed. Who would know, and as her memory returned, who would believe her anyway?'

***

'When did you find out Claire had survived, Ray?' asked Corby.

'About six months ago. I got a prison visit request from my cousin, only I haven't got a cousin, but I went along with it. As soon as she walked in, I knew it was her. She'd changed her hair and everything, but you just know. When my parole came up, we met up on the outside and she told me about the convent, and how she'd lost her memory, then become trapped there. She said she'd found Jake and Andy, and Father O'Donnell.'

'Was it her idea, Ray, or yours? Revenge, retribution. I mean twenty years is a long time if you're innocent, and after all, Mason and Foster had got you into this mess, Father O'Donnell had done nothing to help. Who decided they had to pay?'

'No, man. It wasn't like that. All that time in jail, I just accepted I'd done it. Now I was out, I just wanted to move on. We are different people from back then. It was a different time.'

***

'But then, if it was Claire sent to the Magdalene Laundry, what happened to the baby?'

Morris squared a photo in front of Abi O'Brien. The sweet tin was old, cylindrical, still bearing traces of the product name.

'We found this in your house in Pinner, Abi. You took it from Bayhurst Grange when you murdered Jacob Foster.'

O'Brien stared at the tin, her lips trembling and her cheeks streaked with tears.

'Did you open it?' she asked.

'We did. We had to, I'm sorry.'

Chapter 42

Mike Corby had decided on a break. Ray Asher had been holding it together, but inside Corby could tell he was raging. Whether it was the loss of Claire, the baby, or twenty years of brutal incarceration didn't matter. He held no sympathy for Asher. The events out in Bayhurst Woods were heinous and wrong, but did they justify what had happened since?

He waited as Taylor restarted the tape and announced the resumption of the interview.

'Why were you on Green Street on Friday 28th September?'

'I told you, I went to speak to Father O'Donnell. I needed to clear my head. There was so much buzzing around. Claire, the baby, and what happened that night. All those years believing it was me, I was the murderer. How can that be right? How could he let me fester there all those years without saying something?'

'And Claire Dobson - Abi O'Brien?'

'We met up a few times. It wasn't the same, though. We'd both changed. She said she wanted to get back at them for what they'd done, but I told her to drop it. What could it achieve now?'

'That Friday, you met in Harrow?'

'No. If she was there, I didn't see her. I haven't seen her for over three weeks.'

'Walk me through that evening.'

'I clocked on at work as normal, then around seven, I asked someone to cover for me, and bunked off. I went to St Dunstan's and stood by the gate, afraid to go in, hoping Father O'Donnell would come out and decide for me, but he didn't. I must have stood there all night because the next thing I knew, the house across the road went up, so I scarpered.'

'What about the old guy in the street?'

'What old guy?'

Beside Corby, Steve Taylor passed a note across. The two shared a glance. Not that Taylor did expressions, but still he showed the briefest glimmer of satisfaction.

'Something you said earlier. You told us you were in Green Street on Friday 28th September, that you were outside St Dunstan's but never went in.'

'I never. I just bottled it.'

'To confirm, you didn't enter the house across the road, or meet Andrew Mason that night?'

'No.'

'And you don't wish to change your account?'

'No. I went to St Dunstan's but didn't have the nerve to go in.'

Corby leaned in over the table. 'I need you to think very hard, Ray. This is important. Are you sure you didn't meet Andrew Mason at any time on the night of Friday 28th September?'

'No, I'm positive.'

'Constable?' asked John Brakespeare. 'What are you getting at?'

'Well, Mr Brakespeare, on his way to Number 5 Green Street, Andrew Mason stopped at an ATM just outside Harrow town centre and drew out cash. Ten £10 notes, presumably to pay Sonia Judd her fee.' Corby placed an evidence bag containing the ATM receipt on the table. 'A few minutes later, he went for a coffee in the Shopping Centre with the woman calling herself Sonia Judd, and paid with one note, leaving nine.' Corby brought out a second evidence bag containing the till receipt. 'When we recovered his body after the explosion, we found eight and change, which left one ten-pound note unaccounted for.' He turned to Asher. 'Do you have any idea where that note went, Ray?'

Asher grunted. 'Maybe that tart snorted coke through it.'

An Invisible Murder

Corby placed an email sent over from Ramesh on the table.

'This ten-pound note was in the back pocket of your jeans. On it were Mason's fingerprints and yours. If you had not met Mason that night, how could you have a ten-pound note bearing his fingerprints? A note that he had just taken from a cash dispenser in Harrow? We also have a witness who followed Mason from his car, via the cashpoint and coffee shop, and is certain he met no one other than the woman on the way.'

'What it means,' added Steve Taylor, 'is that you must have taken, or someone must have given you, that ten-pound note in the flat at Number 5 Green Street after Mason entered.'

'Can you explain that, Ray?'

***

'I'd like to talk again about 28th September, Ms O'Brien. Why did you travel to Harrow? To Green Street?' Daley placed the CCTV picture in front of her.

'I didn't. This woman is not me.'

'It certainly looks like you.'

O'Brien craned over and squinted. 'No, it's blurred. It could be anyone. They are wearing a wig and a long coat, and at that angle, you can't tell how tall or short they are.'

'Okay, let's cut to the chase. What you've told me is a pack of lies. When Will left, you travelled over to Green Street, Harrow, and entered Sonia Judd's flat. You found her on the bed, off her face, and you finished her with fentanyl.'

'I was nowhere near Harrow—'

'—Then you went into the town centre to the coffee shop where you met Mason and you both walked back to Green Street.'

'I didn't go to Harrow!'

'Of course, you went to Harrow. There are witnesses who saw you arrive. You took Mason upstairs. You killed Judd and drugged Mason. Then you went back home and glammed up for *Blenheim's* in

Pinner to establish your alibi. Afterwards, witnesses saw you return with Asher to turn on the gas and set the timer.'

'Your witnesses are mistaken. I was not there. I don't know where Raymond Asher was, but he wasn't with me.'

Daley glanced at Deirdre Brown, who scribbled but did not interrupt. He'd already told her his rant would soon make sense.

'Asher has admitted to being in Green Street that night. Please look at this.' Daley placed a photo on the table. 'It took time to find it, but this is the syringe you used on Detective Sergeant Whetstone and Constable Brennan. The only fingerprints on it are yours, Ms O'Brien. We found it on the fourth floor after you dropped it down between the lift car and the shaft, and the fentanyl residue it contains is an exact match for that used on Sonia Judd, even if it was from a different syringe.'

'How does that prove my client was in the flat?'

'On its own, Ms Brown, maybe it does not, but, Ms O'Brien, answer me this. Mason's wallet contained eight ten-pound notes from ten, which he took out of an ATM before meeting you at Starbucks. He spent one on the coffee, leaving nine. It seemed odd to me that, while he had neatly slotted in five of the notes, he'd jammed the other three in haphazardly. When we examined those three notes, we found your fingerprints, Ms O'Brien. You must have handled three of the notes after the coffee shop. And the last note? We found that in Ray Asher's trouser pocket. If Asher was not in that flat with you, how could he have on his person, the tenth note? One note, out of ten withdrawn that night, that bore the fingerprints of Andy Mason, Raymond Asher and you.'

'I told him not to pick up the bloody money—'

'But he did. The only way all three prints could be on that one note is if you were all in that flat together.'

'Chief Inspector, I think it's time I spoke with my client.'

'Yes, Ms Brown, I think that would be wise.'

Chapter 43

'I'd been in the convent for around three weeks before I realised something was wrong. I started getting flashbacks. Other children's faces. A life before, but it was just disjointed memories. Then, there were the periods, or lack of them. I was almost fifteen yet to start. I'd noticed the scar on my abdomen but hadn't yet put it all together. Sister Bernadette told me to forget it all, that it was stuff and nonsense, evil thoughts placed there by the devil himself, and in time, that's what I did. What else could I do? Baile Fearainn was my world, for better or worse. More of my memory came back as time went on. Raymond Asher, Holy Mount, the baby. Those fearful nights waiting for Sister Agnes to come with a knitting needle and *sort me out*. But there was always a gap, a missing piece of the jigsaw. Where was Holy Mount, and how had I arrived at the convent?'

'Eventually, the convent closed.'

'It happened so quickly. The women and girls either left or took holy orders. I took a job in the convent offices, where I discovered the records relating to my induction, that this girl, Claire Dobson, was me. It wasn't long before found out about Holy Grange and the murder of Claire Dobson, that Raymond Asher had confessed to Claire's murder and was in prison for it. I also found out about the baby.'

'Is that when you decided they must pay?'

She took a breath and stared at the ceiling for a long moment. She was in another place, on another plane.

'I'd learned that Holy Mount had also closed, that Sister Agnes had moved to Barnsley and Father O'Donnell was now a priest in Harrow. When I was eighteen, I left the convent and moved over to

Pinner. I took a train up to Barnsley and knocked on that bitch's door, but she couldn't have cared less. I was a dirty slut who had debased herself for a man and didn't deserve to be a mother. It was a blessing my baby had died, that Father O'Donnell had got rid of the bastard.'

'So you killed her?'

'She killed herself, Chief Inspector. That night she took me to that *place*.'

'What about Deepak Verma, the doctor?'

'Like I said, I did agency work, and he was at one of the GP practices I worked in. He took away my baby, he just left it to die in that filthy woodshed, and then he took away my chance for any more children. I took away his children's father. An eye for an eye.'

'Then what? You waited?'

'No, I got on with my life, and I thought no more about it until Will wanted a new car and we stumbled on Andy Mason. He didn't recognise me, but why should he? Claire Dobson was dead long ago. Like you said, the planets aligned and Ray Asher came up for parole. We planned it together. The *affair* with Mason - I nearly vomited every time I saw him - Sonia Judd, the junkie whore with a quiet top-floor flat. Ray thought of the gas. Boom.' Her eyes widened as mimicked a mushroom cloud.

'Then you went after Jacob Foster.'

'You made me do that, to be honest. You spoke to Will about Bayhurst Grange. I knew he'd speak to Jake, and I'd have to do something. I waited for him to go to the house, then watched and waited for him to discover the furnace room. The world's better without him, don't you think?'

'And Father O'Donnell?'

'I wasn't interested in him. Like the bible reference said *as a man chasteneth his son, so the Lord thy God chasteneth thee*. He knew what he'd done and that his god would never forgive him.'

'Why the hospital? If you were not interested in him, why seek him out and attempt to murder him?'

She chuckled and shook her head. 'You again, I am sorry, but if you stick your size nines in, you must expect consequences. With Sister Agnes, Doctor Verma, Andy and Jake all gone, eventually, the Father would say something. Especially if, as you did, you worked out about the baby. He just had to go.'

Daley could feel the contempt building inside, but he refused to give in. There was nothing else to say, and honestly, Daley was done with talking. He had always understood the denials, that someone, when faced with the truth of their crimes, would either lie or vehemently refute the allegations against them. It served as a defence mechanism.

He never understood the rational ones. Those who, when presented with the opportunity to wield power over another's life, could justify removing that life. They were the ones that disturbed him the most.

'Just one thing that bothers me, Abi. The Bible quotes.'

'Oh, them? It was an in-joke between Ray and me, back in Holy Mount. When something happened, we found a quote from the bible to cover it. I just did the same. Why, did you think they were something more?'

Chapter 44

Daley took the rest of Sunday off. On Monday, he and Terri tackled the nursery. Well, Terri sat crossed-legged in the tub chair, shouting orders and eating Doritos. By the end of the afternoon, Daley had a wardrobe, a changing table, a cot and two blood blisters. The back garden was an adventure playground of boxes and polystyrene, yet they had finally finished the nursery.

So he took Tuesday off too. Just to be with her.

The interview with Abi O'Brien gave him renewed vigour. She emphasised how important every life was, even the shortest, most fragile of existences. It revealed to him that, however much he tried to deny it, he felt excited about becoming a father, nurturing a new life, and shaping it. As he'd hammered his thumbs and searched for the right washer, he had given the prospect of fatherhood a lot of thought. Terri understood his reticence, given what happened to Lynne, even to Claire Dobson. She couldn't empathise with their loss, but she understood the importance of keeping a low-key, realistic, even pessimistic approach in case it happened again. But it wouldn't. Fifty per cent of early pregnancies ended in miscarriage, many without the mum knowing, but less than two per cent of late ones. Daley Junior was coming, and he'd better get used to it. Of course, George Brennan's bequest was a seat in the Hammersmith end, so he or she had better like football.

The previous day, they had returned Abi O'Brien to the cells. Daley arranged for the door of the cell to be left open and a female uniformed officer to sit outside. Despite it all, despite the ruthlessness of her vengeance, he understood her loss.

Over the next few days, Corby and Morris found anomalies in

the drug register of the pharmacy connected to the Ruislip Healthy Minds Clinic. The fentanyl in stock matched that given to Judd, Foster, Whetstone and Brennan. Although Nessa Morgan had signed off on the entries in the Drug Register, they had cleared her of any wrongdoing. It seemed Abi O'Brien was also an adept forger.

They also found the burner phones, dumped in the skip behind the ward block. Though the call histories and been wiped, nothing is ever lost and Steve Taylor retrieved them, showing the phones had been in operation for around two months, and only spoke to each other. They found Asher's fingerprints on one phone, and Abi O'Brien's on the other.

So, O'Brien or Dobson - he'd let the smart people sort that one out - had coughed to the murders of McCarthy, Verma, Mason, Judd, Foster, Clarke-Mitchell and George Brennan, and the attempted murders of Father O'Donnell and Deb Whetstone.

Asher's part was, as Daley had suspected, one of interference. Appearing in Green Street, under the lychgate, running from LA Bowl, leaving tyre tracks at Bayhurst Grange, distracting them all at Harrow Central. He would still go down for the assault on Leslie Hacker and maybe conspiracy to murder. After a life in institutions, maybe he would be happier back inside.

As for Father O'Donnell, he had concealed a crime and a body and was complicit in the kidnapping of Claire Dobson. He was also old and frail. Whilst the Bishop would be told, O'Donnell was unlikely to face a court. Instead, his peers would find him a place to while away his retirement and ponder on his sins.

Claire's baby almost went unnoticed. An invisible murder. Like Baby Stevenson in St Dunstan's graveyard, an adjunct to history.

***

Whetstone didn't return to work for four weeks. By that time, she was going stir-crazy in the house in Ealing. She still had a cough, but her ribs hurt less. During that time, she attended sessions with Sophie Jennings, the Force's shrink, to process the attack. The paradox was that there was nothing to analyse, as she had not seen it coming. The problem with death is we approach it from the point of view of the living. We see the loss, the void when, in fact, there is nothing because no one ever feels loss after they die; that is the curse of those left behind. No one ever returns to express the terrible emptiness they experienced. Death is a closure. An end. Jennings had joked what doesn't kill you makes you stronger and then asked for help to move the consulting room bookcase, which Whetstone had refused on account of her ribs, but she took Jennings's point.

Her sister had also visited, dropping the bombshell that she was moving in with her boyfriend, so would need her half of the equity in the house. Perhaps not now, but once Deb was better. In the end, she decided she would take out a mortgage and buy her sister out. Property prices were exploding. She thought of Number 5 Green Street and felt her ribs rubbing as she chuckled to herself. The problem with her terrace in Ealing was there were just too many ghosts floating around to move anywhere else. At least for a while. Until she had some living, breathing company to talk to.

As for Ramesh himself, the situation remained uncomfortable. Because of her callousness, something had changed between them. She felt bad she hadn't given him a chance and wondered if she would get an opportunity in the future. Wondered if he could ever accept her as a friend again, rather than just a colleague.

***

Oliver Mansell remained in the hospital for almost six months. They'd replaced his hip with a space-aged version, but the council had taken back his flat and thrown all his stuff into storage, so he had nowhere to use it. But as usual, he kept chipper. They fed him three times a day, and loads of interesting people had passed through the ward. Plenty were worse off than him.

But today was the day. Sick of his bed-blocking, they were turfing him out. Ground-floor flat in a nice block in North Harrow. Warden controlled no less. Make a change from the four walls of Hampton Ward, that's for sure.

As the ambulance drew up outside Harrow Central, he wondered if he was too old for all this change. He missed the old days. His old place. He missed Cheryl. But life goes on until it doesn't. Then it's some bugger else's problem. No sense harping on about the past. That's what makes them old 'uns as old as they are; always looking back, wishing they were there, back in the past, but with rickets and the rationing, polio, diphtheria and those bloody doodlebugs, was it so good?

The ambulance took him a short way, to a brand new block not so far from his old place. They wheeled the chair off the back of the ambulance and chucked him out in front of this brand-new building, far posher than the place he had in Sefton Street. More modern. It would take a bit of getting used to. Maybe, once he got his legs working, he could visit Mr Mohammed in his shop. Check he was okay. It'd be great to see the old fella again. He'd missed him. Always had a friendly smile, and he was so generous. That wasn't the only reason for visiting, though. Ashad Mohammed took people for who they were. No Darkies or Arabs or Indians. Not pensioners or old 'uns, but just people. We are all just who we are.

'Hello, Oliver. How are you doing today?'

Mansell beamed up at the young police officer. 'Hello, Jane. I'm just chipper, and today I am going to make you and your brother a cup of tea. With my own bloody kettle, for a change.'

He smiled at the boy on Jane Morris's arm. Mongols, they used to call 'em on account of their eyes, but David was no Mongol. Down's syndrome. An accident of genetics. He was clever, but you'd never know it to look at him. Just try beating him at chess. Never judge a book…

Jane Morris knelt in front of the wheelchair Oliver Mansell didn't need. 'As you're in your new home, Oliver, David wanted you the have a friend, so you wouldn't be lonely.'

Jane Morris walked back to her car, opened the rear door, and pulled out a tiny Jack Russell puppy.

'This is Ozzie. He's only a baby, but me and David think you two are going to be very happy together.'

Author's Note

Thanks for taking the time to read AN INVISIBLE MURDER I hope you enjoyed it. If you did and would like to help, then maybe you could leave a review on my Amazon page. This QR Code takes you straight there.

If you would like to find out more about my other books then please read on, or visit my website for full details.

The most important part of how well a book sells is how many positive reviews it has. Some of the best books never see the light of day; some of the worst are bought in their millions. So, if you leave a review, you are directly helping me continue this journey as a full-time writer.

Thanks. It means a lot.
Ryan Stark

The Daley and Whetstone Crime Stories

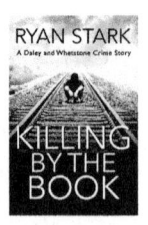

Four years ago, a young woman was murdered. The Murder Book is open. First, there were eight. Now there are six.

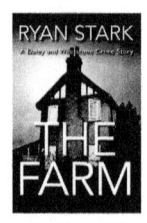

As the Zone 6 Snatcher terrorises North West London, a young nurse tries her hand at blackmail. Now she has vanished.

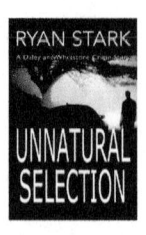

As a devastating Organised Crime war breaks out, an elusive European overlord is muscling in, orchestrating the violence and fuelling the bitter feud. Then Daley and Whetstone become his next target.

The Aidan Beckett Thrillers

Luciano Moretti is selling Amber Rock's secrets to the highest bidder. When Beckett is sent to stop him, he finds Moretti and his minder dead. The only trouble is, he should have fired the gun. Now he is out on his own. Can he protect the woman wrongly framed for Moretti's killing, before the assassin stops them all for good?

What is Amber Rock? What dark secret has it protected for thirty years? And what makes Max Anderson so dangerous?

Under the constant scrutiny of Amber Rock, Beckett searches for Max Anderson. Soon, he is trapped at the epicenter of the mystery. Meanwhile, after learning everything he understood is a lie, he questions his own loyalties, even his own identity. Can he expose Amber Rock's dark secret before they bury it forever? Before they finally get to him?

Printed in Great Britain
by Amazon